FALLEN SHROUD

TWISTED CURSE BOOK ONE

D. J. DALTON

WEEPING SPIDER
PUBLISHING

WEEPING SPIDER PUBLISHING

ISBN-13: 978-1-7368219-1-6

FALLEN SHROUD

Visit **https://www.djdalton.com** to subscribe to D. J. Dalton's newsletter and receive updates on new releases as well as other freebies. As a subscriber, you'll receive access to a free download of the novella *The Dragon War*, prequel to the *Twisted Curse Series*.

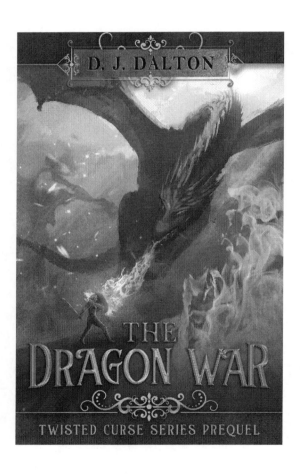

CONTENTS

CHAPTER ONE

KEREN

It wasn't uncommon for kids to have an imaginary friend. Keren lucked out. She had four of them. However, the fact she was twenty-one and still interacting with her imaginary friends proved problematic. Employers frowned on having conversations with yourself or staring into what they saw as empty space.

She focused on the hulking mist creature standing before her. The scent of pine filled the living room. Its bear stature towered over her. A feline head crowned with a golden mane brought the creature to its ten-foot height. Its name was Three.

"Let's see what you've got." Keren darted left, hopping on the arm of a beige sectional couch. She launched herself at Three's head. At the last minute, Three ducked. Keren sailed over its head. Landing in a tuck and roll, she sprung to her feet.

At an early age, Keren made up this game of tag with her imaginary friends. It taught her speed and agility, which came in handy in school defending her shifter friends from bullies, seeing as shifters didn't come into their magical powers until they were teenagers. As she got older, the game grew more extreme.

She charged at Three's midsection. With uncanny speed, it shifted to the side. Keren twisted, reaching out to grab the branches and vines that hung over Three's dark green fur. Her hands missed the target.

She landed hard on the wooden coffee table. It groaned and cracked under her weight. The legs gave out, dropping Keren to the floor. She grunted, then looked at Three.

"Mom's not going to like this."

Three wrinkled its brow and shrugged. The adorable gesture contradicted the ferocity of the oversized canine teeth.

She kipped up from the floor. Picking up a coffee table leg, she inched closer to Three. Feigning right, she waited for it to pull left. She thrust the table leg into Three's belly.

"Ha, got you."

Three lowered its head, letting out a heavy sigh.

She pulled her hand back, tossing the wooden leg on the floor. "Don't be sad, Three. We'll play again tomorrow."

Three nodded, the mist dissipating into the air.

"Alright One, you're next." Keren walked to the kitchen. Taking a deep breath, the crisp air reminded her of the wet earth smell after a thunderstorm.

She stared at the mist creature hovering near the ceiling. Bat wings supported a lizard body. Its wide mouth displayed needle-sharp teeth. Two horns extended backwards from its head.

"Let's see what you've got." She lowered her stance.

Bead-like ruby eyes stared at her. One's long, thin tail swung a sharp-tipped end over its head. Keren leaned right, shifting her weight at the last minute to hop left. One followed her movement, avoiding the feint.

Her cell phone rang, the caller ID showing Mom's Work. Mom taught psychology and linguistics at UCF. Her award-winning dissertation about analyzing documents of cultural heritage won her a research grant last year.

It was almost 5 pm, past Mom's normal quitting time. Frowning, Keren hoped nothing was wrong. She answered the call. "Hi, Mom."

One swung its tail at Keren's head. She ducked, lunging for its foot. It moved just out of reach by flipping over. One seemed pleased with itself. It enjoyed winning the game.

"Hey, good news." Mom sounded excited. "The head of the linguistics department at Berkeley is visiting. He wants to view my presentation on *Linguistic Topology of Sampling Strategies Bias*."

"Wow, Mom, that's great." One righted itself, and Keren prepared for its attack. It dove, reaching out with its taloned feet. She hopped back, knocking over a cup on the counter, causing it to crash to the floor.

"Thanks, honey." The *mom* voice kicked in. "Is everything alright?"

"Yeah, clumsy me. I knocked over a cup."

"Be careful not to cut yourself cleaning it up." Mom's voice relaxed. "I'm calling because I've scheduled Azalea to come by this evening and strengthen the protection spells in the house. I canceled last week."

"I can take care of it." Keren inched her way closer to the broom in the corner as One's eyes tracked her every move.

"Are you sure? Remember to point out all the problem links. And you also-"

She peered at the shattered cup on the floor. The appointment would give her extra time to clean up the mess before Mom got home. "Mom, I've seen you manage re-protect visits a thousand times. I got this."

"Thank you. I love you. Gotta run." Mom hung up.

Keren lunged for the broom, brandishing it like a sword. She took wide, wild swings at One. It swooped and dodged around the attacks. A loud *crash* startled them, and One dissipated into the air.

Keren's chest heaved from the combat. White-knuckled hands maintained a firm grip on the broom. She took a large breath, then exhaled. Something crunched under her foot. She saw the coffee maker in pieces. "Are you kidding?" She searched around, but One was nowhere in sight. "We're not done yet," she shouted into the air.

The phone rang again. This time, it was Nadria, her best real-life friend since nursery school. She was an assistant manager at the Kitty Café. Somehow, Nadria convinced the café owner to overlook Keren's poor excuse for a resume and month-long stretch of unemployment. He agreed to give her a shot at a job as a Cat Concierge. She loved that title.

Her first and only day so far had been last Tuesday. Nadria told her she would start part-time, but if she proved herself to be an exemplary employee, it could turn into full-time.

Setting the broom down, she answered the phone. "Hey, Nadria."

"Hey, girl. I need a favor," she shouted over the crowd noises in the background. "Molly called out sick, and we booked the cattery solid until close. I know it's late notice, but I could use a hand here."

"I can come in." She wished Nadria had called earlier before she agreed to cover the re-protect appointment.

Would skipping the appointment be that big a problem? Mom's obsession with protecting the house baffled her, but she just accepted it as one of her quirks. She canceled an appointment herself last week. What difference would a few more days make? Mom would be in her presentation now, so she couldn't ask her. Besides, she could use the hours. "I can catch the 6 pm bus."

"Thanks, you're a lifesaver. See you soon." Nadria hung up.

The clock display on her phone screamed at her to hurry. With less than half an hour to change and get to the bus stop, adrenaline raced through her body.

She sprinted upstairs to her room, storming into the closet. Clothes flew in a chaotic flurry as she rummaged for her good pair of jeans and a white

button-down shirt. After changing, she froze. The sweet smell of burning
wood caught her attention.

She turned around, seeing Two blocking her way. Its misty wolf's body
filled the entire width of the bedroom doorway and half its height. Orange
and crimson flames swirled around oversized, curled ram horns. Its head
tipped, aiming the horns at her.

Where One played games, Two got right to the point. It charged.
Keren grabbed the closet door frame, swinging her knees to her chin. She
launched over Two. The mist dissipated upon impact with the closet wall.

Not missing a beat, she snatched her backpack, racing to the bathroom.
After twisting her chestnut hair up in a messy bun, she snatched her tea
container off the counter. The antique art deco tin box had an ornate
design in gold, blue, and coral with white mandala flowers. It was her
sixteenth birthday gift from Mom.

It had depressed Keren that her imaginary friend's interference caused
her to fail four driving tests. If she had failed a fifth time, she would have
had to reapply for her permit. The tea contained a special blend of herbs,
reducing how often she saw them. After drinking it, she had passed her
driving test.

She turned the box over in her hand. Mom always said antiques hold the
secrets to our souls.

She chose not to drink the tea since losing her restaurant job last
month because she enjoyed interacting with her imaginary friends. But she

couldn't afford to lose her new job at the café. She was broke and now needed extra money to buy a new coffee table, cup, and coffee pot. Nadria would brew her a cup. She stuffed the container into her backpack and ran downstairs.

She felt bad about ditching Ms. Oakdove. Truthfully, her harsh personality made Keren feel uneasy. Not being here when she arrived was the best solution.

Glancing at her phone, she felt confident she had enough time to catch the bus. She ran out the door, colliding with Azalea Oakdove.

Upon impact, Keren rebounded, grunting as her backside slammed to the ground. Seeing Ms. Oakdove, her heart sank. The lightweight fairy, only half Keren's height, lay on the porch, sprawled on her back. Her potion bottles were scattered around her.

Keren had known Ms. Oakdove all her life. She did all the house protection spells and any one-off work Mom needed. How old was she? Small wrinkles lined the outside of her eyes. But fairies aged slower than humans. If she were injured, Keren would never forgive herself. She reached down to help her up.

"I'm so sorry. Are you alright? I didn't see you."

Slapping her hand away, Ms. Oakdove forced Keren to stand there and watch her struggle to stand up in her tailored navy-blue pencil skirt and blazer. After regaining her feet, she glowered at her.

"You should be more careful, child." She brushed dirt off her blazer, then gathered her potion bottles. "I have an appointment with your mother."

"I'm sorry, we'll have to reschedule." Keren closed the door and scooted around her. "I'm late for work, and Mom's not home."

Ms. Oakdove put the last potion bottle in her bag. "No, the house is due for re-protection."

Keren swallowed against the lump in her throat. Re-protecting the house took at least an hour. Given Ms. Oakdove's sour mood, she'd probably take longer.

"I could let you in and you can do the job while we're out."

"No, I need a person who lives in the house to be present when casting the spell."

Keren let out a sigh. She could call Nadria back and tell her she couldn't come in after all. But that not only left Nadria shorthanded, it would make her look bad for pushing the owner to give Keren a chance at the job. Or worse, she could even lose her job over this. She had already committed.

While gathering her courage, she pushed her shoulders back. "We have to reschedule."

Ms. Oakdove fluttered her iridescent butterfly-like wings. They were as wide as she was tall. Sparkling fairy dust lined the outer edges. She rose, her Christian Louboutin red soul pumps lifted off the ground until she looked down her nose at Keren.

"The house is due."

Keren's courage melted. Her voice peeped out, "I've got to go." She took a few steps backwards.

Before she could leave, Ms. Oakdove grabbed her arm. "I'll return tomorrow, at the same time." She glanced up at the house. A worried look showed on her face.

"Thank you." Keren wondered if Ms. Oakdove caused Mom's paranoia about the house. That was one way to drum up business.

Looking at the time, Keren's chest tightened. If she ran, she could make the 6 pm bus. She caught the scent of burning wood. Two's misty body appeared behind Ms. Oakdove.

Keren smiled. Two lowered its head and charged. She turned, running at top speed to the bus stop with Two close behind.

CHAPTER TWO

BRIGGS

B riggs parked his Land Rover a block away from the crime scene. He had received the dispatch call while he was driving home. After a grueling twelve-hour workday, he looked forward to a drink and some sleep. But the Dark Guild's arcanum had other plans for him.

These past few months, his inquisitor squad's jurisdiction had been plagued with unspeakable violence against shifters. Evidence showed at least some attackers were sorcerers, humans who could wield magic spells.

The arcanum had ravaged businesses and homes. Shifters had been brutally beaten, some murdered, and others had gone missing. So far, his squad had received nothing but dead-end leads and they were no closer to solving the crimes.

The Chief Inquisitor had put pressure on him to make arrests. Apparently, the chief had the judicial system on deck to expedite a trial and imprisonment of the magic criminals. With elections coming up, these crimes tarnished the chief's otherwise exemplary persona.

After arriving at the crime scene, Briggs skirted around the outside of the crowd, who pressed against the crime scene tape. Reporters from every channel in Orlando, as well as major broadcast networks, pushed microphones and video cameras into the faces of anyone they thought might be coerced into talking about the crime.

"There's an inquisitor," called a voice within the crowd.

Heads turned in unison, as if by some magnetic force, in his direction. A young reporter, who smiled like he just won the lotto, trotted toward him.

Briggs had no patience to deal with reporters. He let out a rumbling growl.

The reporter skidded to a halt, swallowing hard as he looked up into Briggs' bloodshot eyes. Briggs, being a bear shifter, stood six-and-one-half feet tall, towering over the reporter by nearly two feet. The reporter's eyes drifted across his burly chest, then down to his clenched fists. He turned around, pushing his way back into the crowd.

Briggs slipped under the crime scene tape. The gated chain-link fence of the Green Thumb Gardener's Supply lay on the ground, or at least what was left of it. Something melted most of the metal into a charred, smoking lump. Next to it, etched into the ground, was the all too familiar circle with two lightning bolts crossing over one another. The arcanum's symbol for the Dark Guild.

After crossing the entrance, Briggs examined the devastation. Forensic scene tripods with lights set up around the property replaced what normally would have been a gorgeous display of trees and plants. Nearly everything had been reduced to piles of dirt and rubble.

He'd been a frequent customer of the garden center last year when he had landscaped his yard. Mr. Hadley, the bear shifter owner, passed on earth magic tips to him so he could keep his Oakleaf Hydrangeas at their peak foliage.

Off to the side, the pergola covering a picnic area where he had frequently shared coffee and cookies with Mrs. Hadley and her two young sons appeared partially intact. The hair stood up on the back of his neck. What kind of evil would attack a decent family like the Hadley's?

"Captain Wilson," a uniformed officer called out. Briggs recognized him as Officer Jordon, a two-year veteran on his squad.

Tramping through the debris, being careful to avoid any area marked for evidence, Briggs approached the officer.

"Officer Jordon," Briggs said. He noticed the fox shifter's drawn face and the dark circles rimming his eyes. Briggs had been pushing his squad hard. But he knew it wasn't only the long hours that wore on them. The attacks were pinpointed at shifters, some well-known citizens of the community. This took a heavy emotional toll. "What's the update? Do we have any witnesses?"

"No witnesses, sir. Same MO, quick attack, substantial property destruction, and..." He paused, nodding his head toward a white tent leaning precariously to the right at the back of the property.

Briggs clenched his jaw. He knew what horrors he faced inside that tent. While clapping his hand on Officer Jordon's shoulder he said, "You lead the investigation out here."

"Yes, sir." The officer's body relaxed. "Thank you."

With a heavy sigh, Briggs forced his feet to carry him to the tent. When he pushed the tent flap aside, his heart sank. Two bodies lay on the far side of the tent. A medical examiner knelt on the ground, gathering evidence.

"This was vicious." Tabitha's raspy voice sounded both harsh and exhausted.

Tabitha, a bear shifter, led the warrior pack, who were the organized army of the magical races. They had worked on every Dark Guild case with Briggs. Her team contacted the shifters and fae that lived in the Magic Underground. Did they know of any recent issues with sorcerers that may have started this crime spree? Have they heard anything that could give them a clue to who these arcanum were or where they could be found? So far, she hadn't come with any significant leads.

It frustrated Briggs when shifters and fae felt forced to withdraw from the world and live a life of seclusion in the underground. But given the current state of open discrimination and antagonism humans had toward the magical races, he respected their choices. He hoped one day things would change.

"Are they the Hadley's?" Briggs asked. His eyes remained on the two bodies.

"We won't know until we run a DNA test."

That meant their bodies were too mutilated to visually identify.

"Did you know them?"

"Yeah, nice folks." Briggs scrubbed his hand over his mouth, then looked over at Tabitha. The sides of her head were shaved close while her blonde crown hair, which was normally tucked into a tight bun, fell loosely over one shoulder. A tank top showed off her muscular arms. She must have been off duty when she got the dispatch call.

"What about the boys?" asked Briggs.

She pulled out a notebook and pen. Her shoulders sagged and her voice saddened.

"No sign of children. Do you know their names?"

"Johnny is eight and Peter is twelve." Briggs clenched his fists as he swallowed the lump in his throat. "I'll put out an APB."

Tabitha sighed. "Right, I'll check the underground." She put her hand on Briggs' arm. "I'm sorry for your loss."

He nodded. "Thank you. Are you taking care of the arrangements with their family?"

"Yes. Faraday should be here anytime."

"Let me know about the service. I'd like to attend."

"Of course."

"Can you meet me in my office first thing tomorrow?" There had to be something they were overlooking. His head throbbed as his mind went over the memorized cases.

"I'll be there, first thing." She patted his back. "Now, go home and get some rest."

After stepping out of the tent, Briggs saw Faraday striding toward him. The wolf shifter carried his wiry frame with confidence. In his brief career with the warriors, he had received a commendation award and two promotions. He ranked just below Tabitha. Two more wolf shifters followed behind.

Faraday stopped in front of Briggs, motioning for the other two to go into the tent. It was rare a wolf shifter was tall enough to meet Briggs eye-to-eye.

"Another tragedy." The scar running down the right side of Faraday's face looked gray in the artificial lighting. "Are we any closer to finding the sorcerers who are killing our kind?" His lip curled in a snarl.

"We're working on it." Briggs met his sharp, icy eyes. Faraday always seemed on the brink of losing control. "Keep your eyes and ears open for a couple of kids. Tabitha has the details."

Faraday nodded as his nostril flared. Then he moved around Briggs to enter the tent.

While walking past Officer Jordon, Briggs raised a hand. "I'll see you in the office tomorrow."

Officer Jordon looked up from his work long enough to give Briggs a return gesture.

"Yes, sir. Have a good night."

Briggs avoided the reporters on the way back to his Land Rover. As he unlocked the car, another dispatch call came over the line. His stomach dropped. Two calls in one night. He answered the call.

"Captain Wilson."

The dispatcher confirmed another magic attack report. When they told him the address, a chill ran down his spine.

"Repeat the address." His heart raced.

After the dispatcher repeated the information, his mouth went dry. He tore the Land Rover door open, started the car, and slammed on the gas before the door was closed. Smoke came from his tires as he raced out of the parking lot.

CHAPTER THREE

KEREN

When Keren opened the door, a nutty, rich smell poured from the Kitty Café. Customers chatted and laughed, enjoying their precious brews. Some had pastries, handmade by the owner's wife, sitting on china plates. No plastic or paper here, only the best for the customers.

She spotted Ordell, focused on his laptop, sitting at his usual high-top table tucked in the back corner. The owner installed a higher footrest on the stool so his feet would reach. Jet black hair fell over one eye while his horse ears relaxed toward the sides. Even though he was just a sophomore at UCF, he made the Dean's List every semester. He won last year's Knight Hacks Hackathon and planned to run a workshop during this year's event.

Keren made her way over to him. "Hey, Ordell. How's it going?"

He looked up. His warm smile reached all the way to his emerald-green eyes. "Hey, Keren." He turned his laptop so she could see the screen. "Wanna see something exciting?"

She leaned closer. "Sure. What am I looking at?"

"This is the website I created for Magical Race Equality."

Keren knew this was a passion project Ordell and Nadria started two years ago. Since then, the organization had grown into a respectable non-profit, bringing awareness of unequal treatment to those of a magical race.

"I created a web page for the demonstration." He clicked a link. "The page connects all the volunteers to a master database to be more efficient with campaigning. I also wrote a process allowing the volunteers to select an option on their profile that sends a Facebook friend request to people they recruited."

A pie chart showed on the screen.

"We reached over fifty percent more people during this campaign than the last one. Look how the chart is interactive." When clicked, the pie pieces moved and showed detail behind the statistics.

She nudged him. "Careful, your geek is showing."

"Come on, the volunteers loved it." He nudged her back. "They had name cards and pamphlets with QR codes. People used their phones to get on the mailing list or sign up as a volunteer right there on the spot."

"Nice, you've done a great job."

"Wait, there's something I want to get your opinion on." He turned the laptop back toward himself and tapped a few keys.

"Volunteers found most humans they talked to knew very little about the magical races. Or they had misinformation. So, I'm working on a page to summarize it for them."

"OK, what do you have?"

"For shifters, I list the three types and their elemental power. Bears are earth magic, wolves are fire magic, and foxes are water magic."

"Are you going into details on any of the spells they can do?"

"No, every shifter is different depending on the strength of their magic."

"That makes sense. What else have you got?"

"Even though *shifter* should be enough to figure this out, I do mention they can change into their animal forms. Should I take that out?"

Keren shook her head. "No, it's a fact about the race. I don't see why you shouldn't keep it."

"OK. That's what I thought, too. But I wanted another opinion." He nodded in agreement.

"Shouldn't there be an air elemental race?"

Ordell looked up with a scowl on his face. "Didn't you pay attention in history class? The dragons were air elementals, but they were killed off in The Dragon War."

Keren hung her head. "Sorry. History was never my best subject."

Ordell turned back to his screen. "Anyway, for fae, I listed the fairies. They can cast protection and location spells, set wards, imbue artifacts with power, and create potions."

"Do fairies create the artifacts?"

"No. See, that's another misconception. The elves, another fae race, disappeared after The Dragon War. They had the power to create artifacts capable of holding fairy magic. But they couldn't imbue the artifact with magic themselves."

"Are there many artifacts?"

"No one knows how many are left. According to history, they were split among the fairies once the elves disappeared. Should I add elves to the page?"

She frowned. "It might help explain artifacts. But if elves disappeared, I don't think you need to add them. Although the artifact information is interesting."

"OK, I'll leave them off for now. If questions come up about artifacts, I can add the elves later." He typed for a few moments before continuing, "Then, of course, there's pucas." His ears pricked forward. "We don't have magic, but we can change into other animal forms. That's confusing for most people. They tend to group us with shifters."

"That's understandable. Did you list the animals you can change into?"

"I did. First is the horse."

Keren poked his side. "That's your favorite, isn't it?" She remembered him cheating during a race and changing into his horse form. The sleek ebony body and flowing midnight-black mane were an impressive sight.

"It is." Ordell's face blushed. "The other animals are mouse, rabbit, raven, dog, and cat."

"You've mentioned there were more." Keren smiled at him. "Spill."

Ordell shifted in his seat, his face full-on red. "No, those are the main ones." He quickly changed the subject. "And I have a section on sorcerers."

Keren's smile faded. Stories related to the Dark Guild's arcanum attacking shifters filled the news. According to the inquisitors, one or more of the arcanum had to be a sorcerer. She wondered if mentioning them on the website was a good idea.

"What do you say about them?"

"Just they're humans with magic. And they need to use their hands to cast spells. That's all I really know."

"That's enough." Not including the sorcerers might be seen as a slant toward them. It seemed safer to include them. She pushed the dark thoughts of arcanum out of her mind.

"It's very impressive." She ruffled Ordell's hair. "Hey, I'm working in the cattery tonight. Will the cat-form you come over and help me figure out the cats' personalities? I'd like to get the award for most forever-home placements this month. Being part-time makes it tough."

"Isn't that cheating? I mean, shouldn't you get to know the cats on your own?"

"I want to make a good impression." She put her palms together, touching her fingertips to her chin. "Please. It's how I'll get to full-time."

With a sigh, Ordell shook his head. "Sure, give me a few minutes."

She clapped her hands. "Thanks, see you later."

After weaving her way through the crowd, she slipped behind the front counter.

"Oh, good, you're here." Nadria's snow-white hair was pulled back into a neat bun. Her warm skin tone seemed to shimmer with her movement. Intense pale blue eyes pulled up at the outer edges. She filled the expresso machine and squirted syrup into a large cup. "It's crazy busy tonight." She handed the drink over to a barista to finish and turned to Keren.

Nadria had received the best qualities from her fairy mother and fox shifter father. Unfortunately, mix-raced children faced discrimination from both humans and magical races. Her painful experiences were what drove Nadria's enthusiasm to bring awareness to the public and end intolerant, biased views.

"I see that. Thanks for getting me the extra hours." Keren pulled the tea container from her backpack. "I know you're busy, but can you squeeze in a cup of tea for me?"

"Everything alright?" Nadria's eyes scanned her from head to toe.

"Nothing a cup of tea won't fix." Wanting to change the subject, Keren pointed to a pin on Nadria's shirt. "So, how did the demonstration go?"

Her face lit up. "Fantastic. We handed out fliers on magical racial equality to hundreds of people."

She took a latte from the barista and waved her hand over the cup. Tiny dots of light danced on her forearm as a perfect picture of a cat formed in the foam. Nadria enjoyed adding her special touch to orders. The customer laughed when the foam cat meowed.

"I met this interesting group of fairies. They specialize in Herbology and invited me to join their group." She took another order from the cashier and started up the expresso machine. "Did you know in ancient Greece they rubbed mint on tables to welcome visitors? Weird, huh? I can't wait for the next meeting. You should come, too."

Before Keren could answer, Nadria frowned. Her forearms sparkled. "Are you going to pay for that?" She turned her head.

Keren turned in the same direction, seeing a middle school boy standing at the counter. His palm lay flat on the countertop. He pulled and tugged, but his hand refused to move. He clutched a bag of almonds in his other hand.

"What did you do to me?" His face reddened. "Let me go." He pulled harder, but his hand didn't budge.

Nadria put her hands on her hips. "Pay for those almonds or put them back."

The boy scowled, tossing the almonds back in the display. "There, now let me go."

The sparkle left her forearms. The boy tumbled back, landing square on his rear. He sprung up, bolting out of the café.

Keren remembered herself at that age during her rocky middle school years. How Mom survived it, she would never know. She refused to wear anything but jeans and T-shirts labeled with heavy metal band names. Not too much different from today, just without the heavy metal bands.

Her spree of stealing candy bars from the corner gas station ended when Mom found her stash under the bed. For a week, between school letting out and dinner, Keren swept the gas station's floor and cleaned the bathrooms.

"Does that happen often?"

"More than you'd think. But my sticky fingers spell reduces the losses."

"Sticky fingers. That's new, isn't it?" Keren straightened the almond display.

Nadria started making hot chocolate. "It is. Everyone has at least a bit of sweat on their palms. I use that for the spell." She gave the hot chocolate to a customer. "Anyway, what do you think about the Herbology?"

"Sounds fun, let me know when you're going, and I'll tag along." Keren put on an apron and pinned on her nametag.

"I will." She nodded toward the cattery. "You better hurry. I asked John to fill in until you got here."

Keren rolled her eyes, and they both laughed. "Is that guy ever in a good mood?"

CHAPTER FOUR

QUINLIN

Quinlin drummed his fingers on the desk while watching his drone circle over the city. The Eye of Discovery, which he had strapped to the bottom of the drone, emitted a pale blue light. Although that proved it had detected his father's *Book of Shadows*, it couldn't pinpoint the exact location.

He had repeatedly flown over this fifty square miles of Orlando. What kept the artifact from exposing the book baffled him. He knew leaving this flight radius caused the Eye to turn black. So that meant the book resided somewhere in this area.

In Father's foresight and wisdom, he requested a fairy empower the Eye of Discovery with magic to emit a deep green color when homed in on his *Book of Shadows*. The fairy also imbued the book with protection spells, preventing its destruction. Father knew the great value of his book and expected, one day, someone might try to steal or destroy it.

"Any progress?" asked Dan.

When he turned, Quinlin saw Dan relaxing on the office's supple leather sofa, a magazine balanced across his leg.

"No." Quinlin balled his hand into a fist, letting his fingernails bite into his palm. "Don't you have work to do?"

Dan shot up from his seat, the magazine falling to the floor. "Right. Yes, Mr. Turner." He raised his eyebrows, forcing acne scars to collide on his forehead wrinkles. "I should see to securing the two young shifters from the last job." He remained frozen in place.

"Well, Mr. Mann, are you going or not?" Quinlin believed Dan was a lazy good-for-nothing. But his spell casting strength impelled Quinlin, against his better judgment, to allow his recruitment into the Dark Guild. In order to keep close tabs on him, he had appointed him as his lieutenant.

Without another word, Dan bolted from the room.

While pushing away from the desk, Quinlin let out a long exhale. Something hid the book from the Eye. For a moment, he thought of resorting to a house-to-house search. But that approach might make the book thief run, leaving him back at square one. No, he had to wait it out. The thief would eventually make a mistake.

He stood, stretching out stiff muscles. After four hours of sitting, he deserved a break. The camera on the drone would trigger an audible alert should the Eye's color change, so he put the drone on autopilot, then walked to the window. Palm fronds swayed in the breeze, beseeching him to come out and enjoy the beautiful evening. If he fell prey to this lie, the oppressive heat would snare him, suffocating him with sticky, humid air. He brushed at the lapel of his Givenchy suit, opting to remain indoors.

After strolling to the bookcase, he pulled out his father's *grimoire*. He had committed the entire book to memory by the age of ten, but drew comfort reading from its pages. It contained years of detailed, resolute research. He turned to the section describing shifters.

'Today, the human population far outnumbers the magical races. But only a small percentage are elevated by bloodline to sorcerers. Dirty shifters are feral, vile creatures looking to tear out humankind's throat, sending us back into a time of fear and darkness. They are beyond redemption and undeserving of their magical gifts. Regrettably, they cannot be eliminated before sorcerers harness the power of elemental magic. We cannot risk the world losing this vital resource.'

After flipping a few pages, he read further.

'We are seeing success with curses drawing elemental magic into creatures of the Earth. Unfortunately, the creatures cannot maintain life for very long. It is my belief an amplifier to strengthen the curse would help. The following pages contain detailed experiments I performed to determine how the foul beasts survive with elemental magic. I'm close to a breakthrough'

Unfortunately, Father died before realizing his dream. He closed the book, thoughtfully placing it back on the shelf. All his life, Quinlin had prepared to fulfill his destiny of finishing his father's work and avenging his death. With notes and experiments of his own, he believed he had the solution to his father's enigma. He ran his hand through his hair, pacing back to the window.

Last year, he had stolen the Amplification Disk from a sorcerer faction in Las Vegas. Elves had forged the unique artifact during The Dragon War using a secret alloy. To this day, the metal's origin remained unknown, making the artifact irreplaceable and nonreproducible.

The Las Vegas faction's inferior security made it effortless to replace the artifact with an inert replica. As far as he knew, the sorcerers still hadn't realized it had been stolen.

The four-inch diameter, washer-shaped disk had a thin, claspless chain running through its center, which allowed him to wear it safely around his neck while he had traveled home to Orlando.

He had refrained from using the Amplification Disk since historical reference books state its magic was restricted to one-time use. After a sorcerer used the artifact for a spell, they could never use it again. However, the spell's effect would last as long as the artifact existed, or the sorcerer ended the spell. If a sorcerer cast a spell upon a stone, making it hover in the air. The sorcerer could walk away from the stone, and it would remain in the air.

Quinlin had formulated a theory it would work the same way for curses. Only he couldn't test his theory until he had his father's *Book of Shadows*.

A *beep* drew his attention to the computer. The Eye of Discovery glowed a dark green color.

"Finally," he said, snatching his car keys off the desk and sprinting to his car.

Quinlin parked across the street from a small, two-story house. The boring gray exterior with white trim looked similar to the neighbors' houses. While looking around, he spotted a human couple walking hand-in-hand several yards down the street. Otherwise, the road was empty.

He picked up the drone remote controller. After working the levers, he made the drone hover just above the house. The Eye's green glow intensified. Finally, he had found his father's *Book of Shadows*. He took a full-faced mask from the glove box. For now, the Dark Guild's success hinged on anonymity, at least until he completed the curses. He pulled the mask over his face.

As he got out of the car, a station wagon pulled into the driveway. A woman stepped out, balancing several books in her arms as she struggled to close the car door.

While trotting across the street, he formulated a plan to get inside the woman's house. His heart beat faster as he considered she could be his father's murderer.

She fumbled with her keys but finally slipped one into the lock. Once the door opened, Quinlin rushed into the house, knocking her forward. After closing the door, he pulled off his mask, tossing it on the floor.

She yelled, rolling over to face him. Blood dripped from a cut on her forehead. After looking at his face, her eyes widened.

"Marcus?"

At the mention of his father's name, Quinlin hesitated.

While taking advantage of the moment, she jumped to her feet, racing across the living room. Quinlin chased after her.

She skidded into another room. Once inside, she tried slamming the door in his face. Quinlin threw his full weight against the door, causing her to crash onto the floor. *No more games,* he thought as he raised his palms toward her.

"*Postestatenum,*" he shouted.

An energy blast struck the woman's side. She screamed, but somehow crawled on her hands and knees to a filing cabinet. Smoke came from where the blast struck her. She sat, pressing herself into the cabinet while extending her hands.

"*Protegioum.*"

A protection shield surrounded the woman and the cabinet. That must be where she hid the book. This shield shouldn't be a challenge for him. He held out his hands.

"*Potestatenum.*"

Quinlin's energy blast struck her shield. Her arms flexed, absorbing the hit. But she extended them again, sustaining the shield. She snarled at him while her shaking hands held the shield in place. Twice more he struck her shield.

"*Potestatenum. Potestatenum.*"

As the woman screamed, black specs appeared on her palms. She scooted away from the cabinet but held the shield over herself. Now free from the shield, Quinlin focused on the cabinet.

"*Concitatusiumus.*"

The cabinet flew across the room, striking the wall. Its contents spilled onto the floor upon impact. He rushed over, digging through papers until his fingers brushed against leather. He caught his breath. Could this be it? Had he found his father's *Book of Shadows?*

After pulling the book from the heap, he held it up, admiring the gold-leaf lettering. He ran his fingers over the name Marcus Turner.

Remembering where he was, he turned back to the woman, but she was gone. His heart pounded as he ran out of the room. While looking around, he couldn't find her anywhere, but then he noticed the front door stood ajar. After snatching the mask from the floor and tugging it on, he dashed outside. He saw her staggering down the street, clutching at her side. Only one more shot needed to finish her.

"*Potestatenum.*"

At the last minute, the woman turned, holding up her hands. He couldn't hear her, but he saw his attack strike her shield just before she collapsed on the street.

Another woman's scream drew his attention. The couple he saw earlier stood across the street, staring in terror. Several other people, after hearing the commotion outside, walked into their yards, gaping at the spectacle.

Quinlin ran to his car, jumped in, then threw it into drive. While stomping on the gas, the BMW responded with a burst of speed. He looked in the rear-view mirror. A crowd had gathered around the woman. The strength it took to hold those shields would have killed the average sorcerer. He scowled. She must have been Father's murderer. Why else would she be protecting the book? He'd check the news stories tomorrow to verify he had finished the job.

While pulling back to a normal speed, he realized he clutched the *Book of Shadows* to his chest. After releasing his hold, he set the book on the passenger's seat. Once again, he ran his fingers over his father's name while ignoring the pain radiating through his black-stained hands.

"I've avenged your death, Father. Now, I will complete your work."

CHAPTER FIVE

KEREN

The cattery housed twenty-five cats. A cat concierge kept the cats and the cattery clean. They watched the guests' interactions, ensuring everyone, both human and furry friends, stayed respectful. The goal was to place cats in their forever homes. But customers just wanting to enjoy time with the cats kept the room booked.

"Thank goodness you're here," said John. A sour expression crossed his face. "It's all yours. I'm heading back to the café." He marched out of the room. Keren watched him retreat, focusing on his backside, which was by far his best quality.

After making the rounds and answering a couple of customers' questions, Keren sat at the concierge's desk. She pulled out her sketchbook and some colored pencils from her backpack.

One day, she planned to enroll in animation college. She dreamed of getting a job at Disney Studios, earning money, doing something she loved.

But animation college was expensive. Working at the Kitty Café wasn't getting her any closer to that dream.

Sighing, she started a new drawing. Mom encouraged her from a young age to draw her imaginary friends. She wanted to see everything Keren saw. So that's what she did, day after day. She drew all the creatures. How they moved and how they pretended to interact with the actual world. Drawing became a part of her. She couldn't imagine life without a sketchbook.

It was Mom's idea to name her imaginary friends, make them less mysterious. The most inventive names she could come up with as a small child was numbering them in the order she first saw them.

"What's that?" A young girl pointed at Keren's drawing.

"It's those cats in the corner." She motioned with her pencil to three cats sitting in a circle.

"But what's that?" The girl's pudgy finger pointed to Four.

The creature's white upper body resembled a fox. Royal blue covered the tips of its ears, around its eyes, and the underbelly. It tapered down to an elongated, narrow body. Like an eel, the lower body had no scales. The navy blue faded to light blue as color cascaded down the tail. She glanced over at Four. It hovered over the cats, seeming to entertain them by spinning in a circle, causing a corkscrew effect with its tail.

"It's a bird." Keren slid the sketchbook under the desk. She wished Nadria would hurry with her tea. This was the first time she'd seen her imaginary friends at the Kitty Café, and she didn't want them to interfere with her job.

"I like to pretend I know what they're staring at." Keren walked around the desk, squatting next to the girl. "It looks like Ginger likes you."

A fat orange tabby rubbed against the girl's legs. The girl bent down, fawning over the cat. Maybe Ginger will get a forever home today. She'd give the girl a few minutes to bond with the cat, then have a chat with her parents.

She felt a paw touch her knee. Looking down, she saw a black cat with emerald-green eyes. "Hi, Ordell." He purred and kneaded his front paws as she scratched his head. She picked him up, putting him on the desk. To her, it seemed a strange coincidence the cats stared at the same place she saw Four.

"Do me a favor." She pointed at the cats in the corner looking at Four. "Can you tell me what those cats are looking at?"

Ordell's eyes trailed from the cats up to Four. While arching his back, he hissed, jumping behind the desk, and changing into his human form. Eyes wide and dilated, he motioned for her to join him.

Sitting on the floor next to him, she rubbed his back. "What's wrong?"

He peeked over her shoulder at the cats. "There's a monster hovering in the corner of the room." He stood, pulling her up with him. "I've never seen anything like it before."

She turned, staring at Four. "Do you still see it?"

"No, only when I was in my cat form."

"What does it look like?"

"It's like a fox with a snake or eel's tail."

Her body shivered. How could that be? Four was just her imagination. Ordell had to be playing a trick on her. He had seen several of her imaginary friend drawings.

"Keren." Nadria's voice drew her attention. "Keren, come over here."

She turned toward Nadria's voice, thinking she had her tea ready. Instead, she saw Briggs in his inquisitor's uniform, standing next to her.

When she met Briggs in sixth grade, they immediately clicked and had been close friends ever since. As a bear shifter, middle school kids stayed away from him, intimidated by his size. But everything changed in high school.

The football team begged him to join. Girls pretended to be Keren's friend to get close to him. She couldn't blame them. His chiseled jaw and fire red hair showed off his lavender eyes. But Briggs preferred a quiet life with a small circle of friends. She felt honored to be in that circle.

Nadria motioned with her hand for Keren to come over.

While holding up a finger to let Nadria know she saw her, she turned to Ordell.

"We're not done with this conversation." She wanted to know exactly what Ordell saw in the cattery. Keren made her way over to Nadria and Briggs.

"Hey, Briggs. What brings you here?"

His thick arms crushed her in a hug, squeezing so tight she could hardly breathe.

"Air," she grunted, tapping his back.

He released her, letting her gasp in a breath of air.

His eyebrows knitted together as he opened his mouth to speak, but he closed it again as if collecting his thoughts.

This can't be good. Did Ms. Oakdove report her for knocking her to the ground?

Briggs put his burly hand on her shoulder. "Can we step outside?"

She fought to swallow the lump in her throat. "Am I in trouble?"

He scrubbed his fingers through his hair. "Can we step outside, please?"

"Sure, this way." Nadria led them out the back door. "I'll leave you alone." She turned to go.

"No," Keren reached out for Nadria's hand, "please, stay." She looked at Briggs. "Can she stay?"

"Yes, of course."

Nadria took her hand. The warmth comforted her nerves.

"Your mom," his voice cracked, "someone attacked her."

Nadria's grip tightened on Keren's hand. "Oh, no."

Keren's muscles went numb, and she struggled to breathe. "Is she alright? Where was she attacked?" Could this have something to do with the re-protect spell? She should have stayed home and let Ms. Oakdove finish her work.

"It happened at your house. They transported her to Orlando Regional." He rubbed the back of his neck. "She's in critical condition."

She struggling to focus. The thought of losing Mom ripped her apart. After Dad, Grandma, and Grandpa died in the car accident, Mom was all she had.

"I can drive you to the hospital." Briggs glanced at Nadria. "Can you follow behind? I'm on duty and I won't be able to stay with her."

"Of course. Let me tell my manager there's an emergency and we have to leave." Nadria wrapped her arms around Keren, giving her a tight squeeze.

"Thanks. I'll pull my car around." He disappeared around the corner.

"I'm right here for you." Nadria released Keren, then lifted her chin. "Look at me."

Keren locked onto Nadria's pale blue eyes, using them like an anchor, keeping her grounded and able to function.

"I'm here for you, whatever you need. Your mom will pull through this, she's strong." Nadria used her apron to dry Keren's face. She hadn't realized she was crying. "I'll meet you at the hospital." Nadria gave her one last squeeze before Briggs pulled up.

After hopping out, he hurried around to open the passenger door. Keren got in, twisting her body to face Briggs. One's misty image appeared in the backseat.

CHAPTER SIX

QUINLIN

Quinlin turned down International Drive, becoming ensnared in the usual traffic nightmare. I-drive's variety of restaurants and entertainment drew massive crowds of tourists searching for an amusing evening after their 'magical' day with the mouse. On any other day, watching the horde move through their rituals of social normalcy entertained Quinlin. But tonight, he concentrated on getting to the lab. He used the car's Bluetooth connection to call Dan.

"Hello?" Dan shouted into the phone. The bar noise in the background made it difficult to hear him.

"Dan, I need you and the elites to meet me in the lab." Quinlin had hand-picked twenty arcanum who showed the most promise in spell casting. He called them the elites, and they were being trained for his mission. They drilled and studied eight to ten hours a day, honing their spell casting skills and growing stronger each day.

"Tonight? It's kinda late."

Quinlin clenched his teeth, letting out a long breath. "Yes, tonight. I'll be there in a few minutes. Make sure you're there when I arrive." When he ended the call, he let out a series of swear words, wondering how that simpleton survived.

After waiting through a third light rotation on the same signal, he laid on his horn, speeding through the intersection. A shifter jumped to the side to avoid being run down in the street. Quinlin smirked. He might have escaped his fate today, but soon all shifters would be wiped from the face of the Earth.

The BMW's tires screeched as he turned into ICON Park.

With the *Book of Shadows* held close to his chest, he walked into Madam Murphy's Wax Museum.

Quinlin had chosen the wax museum as his base of operations because of its proximity to Sunset Suites, a hotel owned by the Dark Guild. Years ago, Uncle Rob had invested Dark Guild funds in hotels around Florida, including Orlando, Daytona, and Tampa. Gambling the coveted *Book of Shadows* remained somewhere in the state. Once the Eye of Discovery confirmed Uncle Rob's gamble had paid off, Quinlin wasted no time setting up the lab and moving the elites into the Sunset Suites hotel, all expenses paid.

The museum's owner fully cooperated with stepping down and allowing the arcanum to run the business. He preferred his wife and children alive. The first order of business had been shipping the stored wax figures to a nearby climate-controlled warehouse, leaving the warehouse space for the lab.

"Good evening, Mr. Turner," said the young arcanum receptionist at the counter.

"Good evening." Quinlin rushed behind the counter, brushing past the receptionist to enter the back office. He made a mental note to discuss proper makeup application with her. Those over-rouged cheeks and black-lined eyes nauseated him.

Once he closed the office door, he moved to the bookshelf, pulling out his father's *grimoire*. After setting both books on the desk, he crossed his arms, staring at the leather binding and gold-leaf lettering. He'd dreamed of this moment all his life.

"This is for you Father."

With reverence, he opened the *Book of Shadows*. Memorized words from the *grimoire* guided him to the pages, documenting the curses, one to draw elemental magic into an animal, and one to siphon the life force from a shifter. After he located the curses, he read them repeatedly, committing each one to memory.

Once satisfied, he gathered the books, then took a deep breath as he walked out of the office, preparing to make history.

As Quinlin entered the lab, goosebumps popped up on his skin. He couldn't tell if it was cold air or from the anticipation of finally completing his father's work.

"Dan!" shouted Quinlin, then he mumbled, "That buffoon had better be here."

"Mr. Turner." Dan trotted in from the back entrance, the elite arcanum scrambling after him. "What's the emergency?"

Quinlin could smell the alcohol on Dan's breath and his bloodshot eyes made Quinlin wonder how long he'd been at the bar. While glancing at the wide-eyed, eager elites, a grin spread across Quinlin's face.

"I have the *Book of Shadows*."

Energetic whispers rolled through the group. A young woman, Shela, clapped her hands as she bounced on her toes.

"You," Quinlin pointed at Shela, "run through an equipment review." Over the years, Quinlin had made tweets and additions to the equipment used in his father's experiments.

Without hesitation, she bolted to a large wooden platform taking up one corner of the room. A table, draped in a banner displaying a black-rimmed circle containing a two lightning bolts crossing over one another, sat at the back of the platform. A gold vessel and the Amplification Disk both rested on the table.

On the far side of the platform were two metal cages. One was large enough to hold an adult man if he were on his hands and knees, while the other stood taller and wider. A thick gold rod connected each cage to the gold vessel on the table.

While laying her hand on the smaller cage, the young elite spoke in a clear, confident voice. "The shifter cage, made of reinforced steel, is locked with a hardened steel padlock." She touched the larger cage. "The animal cage is also made of reinforced steel. Not only is it secured with a built-in mechanical lock but with a spell that conceals the keyhole as well as the door seams."

Quinlin joined her on the platform. "Very good, continue."

She beamed at him. "The gold rod inside the shifter cage will conduct life force from the shifter to the gold vessel when casting the siphoning curse."

She pointed to the other cage. "The gold rod inside the animal cage will conduct life force from the vessel to the animal in the cage when casting the elemental magic curse. Transferring the life force must happen quickly because the vessel's limitation for retaining the shifter's life force is thirty seconds."

With a gleam in his eye, Quinlin prodded her on. "And the last item?"

"Yes," she said, hovering her hand over the artifact. "We'll use the Amplification Disk to magnify the elemental magic curse. Which will allow the animals to animate and respond to our control."

By this time, the elites had gathered around the platform. Dan sulked near the back, standing with his arms crossed while he glowered at the young elite standing next to Quinlin.

"Very good. As a reward, you'll take part in the first experiment."

The elite's eyes sparkled as she covered her mouth with her hands. Quinlin looked at the remaining elites. He pointed to the two men on the end.

"You two, come up here."

The men scramble up on the platform, standing next to Shela.

"Dan, you and the rest of the elites load the cages."

Dan jumped as if jabbed by a hot poker.

"Let's go." He motioned to the elites to follow him. They ran across the room, where three rows of ten shifter cages were stacked along the wall. Each cage held a shifter who had been kidnapped during a raid. A few moved lethargically, fighting the drugs in their systems. But most of them remained motionless.

After pulling a key from his pocket, Dan unlocked a cage.

"This one won't make it much longer. We'll use her."

The elites pulled the wolf shifter out of the cage, dragging her across the floor to the platform. Blood matted hair and a broken nose showed the torture she had endured during her captivity. The three elites on the platform secured her in the shifter cage.

"The dogs are in the storage room." Dan's lip curled as he looked over at the wall of cages. "We don't want them around the dirty shifters." He left for a moment, then returned with an adult Siberian Husky. After walking the dog onto the platform, he secured it in the animal cage.

"Come here," said Quinlin, motioning to Shela. As she approached, he picked up the Amplification Disk. "Hold up your hands."

She lifted her arms, extending her palms toward Quinlin. He wrapped the artifact's chain around her hands in such a way that the disk hung at the center of one of her palms.

"Go stand by the animal cage."

She stepped away, holding her hands as if the disk would shatter at any moment.

"You two, stand by the sifter cage." Quinlin set both books on the table. Then he opened the *Book of Shadows* to the siphoning curse. After turning the book so both elites could read it, he shouted, "Let this historical event be forever seen as the moment humankind was saved from the savage shifters!" He closed his eyes for a moment, taking a deep breath to calm his pounding heart. Then he looked at the elite men. "Begin."

They held their palms toward the shifter, reciting the siphoning curse. The gold rod in the shifter cage rattled, then glowed. After lowering their hands, the elite men stared at the gold rod.

"Again," shouted Quinlin. "Recite the curse again. Don't stop until I tell you to stop."

Their hands flew back up, and they restarted casting the curse. The gold rod rattled, its glow growing brighter. Suddenly, a bolt of electricity flew from the end of the rod to the wolf shifter. A chilling shriek echoed through the room as her back arched and her body spasmed. Her skin grayed then contracted around her bones, leaving bulging, oversized eyes staring out in an unanswered cry for help.

One of the elite men vomited on the stage while the other jumped off, distancing himself from the horror. Shela screamed but held her place, holding her trembling hands and the artifact toward the husky.

Quinlin looked at the shimmering liquid substance swirling in the vessel. A malicious grin appeared on his face as he moved close to Shela. He flipped the page in the *Book of Shadows*, holding it up for her to read.

"Now you. Keep repeating the curse until I tell you to stop."

While blinking tears out of her eyes, she focused on the book, casting the curse at the husky. Sweat dripped from her face as she recited the curse again and again. After her voice raised an octave, the smell of burning flesh filled the room, and smoke came from her palm.

Quinlin looked at her hands. The artifact was burning itself into her skin. The gold rod in the animal cage jerked.

"Keep going!" He demanded.

Shela dropped to her knees. Her solid black fingers cracked while tiny chips flaked off, falling to the ground. Black tendrils traveled up her forearms. Then a bolt of electricity shot from the gold rod to the husky. The dog let out a tormented yelp while the snapping of bones emanated from the cage as the dog's body contorted, reshaping itself. Shela fell over. Her arms, neck, and jaw were solid black. The dog let out a final yelp, then collapsed in a heap.

"No," growled Quinlin. He stepped over Shela's dead body, then knelt next to the husky. The smell of burnt fur filled his nostrils. It was dead. He rubbed his forehead with his fingers. What could have gone wrong?

He mentally paged through his father's *grimoire*. The answer had to be there. Father said the elemental magic curse needed an amplifier. Maybe the Amplification Disk had killed the elite before the curse could finish. With this thought, he decided to use two elites when casting the elemental magic curse. One with the artifact and one without.

After peeling the artifact from Shela's scorched hand, he pushed her body aside. While turning the artifact over in his hands, he contemplated the historical reference book's referral to 'one-time use'. He'd have to keep that in mind when researching other artifacts. He then walked to the front of the platform, his eyes scanning the remaining elite.

"I need four elites."

When none of them moved, Dan stepped forward, grabbing two by the arm and pushing another with his foot. He herded them onto the platform.

Quinlin looked into Dan's bloodshot eyes, seeing, for the first time, a positive attribute of loyalty. While giving him a respectful nod, Quinlin spouted orders.

"These two will cast the siphoning curse. You," he pointed at Dan, "and the other elite will cast the elemental magic curse." Quinlin held the artifact up in front of Dan, waiting for his reaction. Without hesitation, he placed his open hand underneath, his eyes never leaving Quinlin's.

"Wrap this around his hands." Quinlin motioned toward the elite standing next to Dan, dropping the Amplification Disk into his palm. Then Quinlin raised his voice, "Bring another shifter and dog."

When, again, none of the elites moved, Dan stomped across the platform. "You heard Mr. Turner," he growled. The elites jumped, then ran back to the cages.

Once the shifter and Siberian Husky were prepped for the next experiment, Quinlin reiterated the process. This time, the shifter's body repeatedly thrashed itself against the cage bars before the curse finally drew its life force away. A flesh-covered, skeleton-like hand reached out from between the bars before the shifter shrieked out its last breath.

The book trembled as Quinlin held it out for the casting of the elemental magic curse. "Begin!"

He licked his lips as his eyes darted from the sorcerers to the husky. This had to work. He imagined himself controlling a fire elemental creature, incinerating dirty shifters on his mission to free humankind from the ruthlessness of the wretched beasts.

After noticing the elite's hands lowering, Quinlin pressed a palm to his head.

"Die with honor or die a coward," he said through gritted teeth.

The elite's eyes glazed over. He lifted his arms, resigning himself to his fate. The spoken curse reverberated through the room with Dan's boisterous voice and the ever-weakening voice of the elite. When the elite collapsed, his charred arms fell across Quinlin's feet. While kicking him aside, Quinlin stepped up to Dan.

Sweat and snot flew from Dan's lips as he repeated the curse again. His saturated clothes and hair were plastered to his skin. Suddenly, a bolt of electricity shot from the gold rod to the husky. The dog flew back against the bars, letting out a ghoulish sound. The snapping of bones overpowered Dan's voice as the dog's body contorted, reshaping itself into a larger animal. Only the reshaping put the husky's limbs in unnatural positions. Most of its fur fell away, leaving small, mangled patches across its skin.

The bolt of energy disappeared.

"Stop!" ordered Quinlin.

Dan lowered his hands, staggering back to lean on the wall. When he wiped his face with his arm, he noticed his black hands and minuscule tendrils running up his forearms. While lifting his trembling palms to his face, he cried out.

Quinlin turned his concentration to the creature in the cage. Its head swung back and forth as drool dripped from its snout. After stepping into the cage, he fell to his knees next to the creature, unable to contain the grin on his face. His father's lifelong goal had come to fruition. While running his fingers across the creature's head, he wondered what to call it. Dog seemed mediocre, but wolf sounded dignified and powerful.

He stood, then threw his head back, shouting at the top of his lungs, "The cursed wolf initiative is complete." With a laugh, he secured the husky in the cage.

While Quinlin headed off the platform, he said, "Dan, follow me. We have control spells to create."

"Mr. Turner?"

At the sound of Dan's pitiful voice, Quinlin turned, observing Dan's damaged hands. He held up his own blackened hand.

"Those will heal in a few days. Once we have the control spells written, I want you to schedule an initiative update meeting with all the arcanum. This will be a celebration of our victory." He headed toward his office with a spring in his step.

CHAPTER SEVEN

KEREN

Once they were on I-4, Briggs started talking. "I'm not sure how to say this other than straightforward. They charged your mom with using magic as a weapon."

Keren didn't believe her ears. Mom was human. "Did you say using magic as a weapon?" Out of the corner of her eye, she noticed One fidgeting.

"There are witnesses who saw her fighting with her assailant. She's suspected of being a member of the Dark Guild." He paused. When Keren didn't respond, he continued, "Right now it's assumed she had a falling out with the guild, which instigated the attack."

Keren ran her hands through her hair. "Are you kidding? Mom teaches linguistics at UCF. You grew up around her." She folded her arms over her stomach. "She's not a member of the Dark Guild, and she can't use magic." Keren's voice got louder as she spoke. "My mom is in the hospital, a VICTIM of an attack, and she's under arrest?"

"I know. It sounds crazy. But like I said, we have witnesses." He took a deep breath, scrubbing his face with his hand. "And there's other evidence."

"Who are these witnesses, and what evidence could they possibly have?" Keren put her hand on his arm. His bicep flexed under her touch. She softened her tone. "I need to know."

"That's all I can tell you." He glanced over at her, a pained look in his eyes. While rubbing the top of his head, he messed up his red hair. "If they find out I gave you inside information, I could lose my job."

Wiping her eyes with her apron, she realized Briggs was taking an enormous risk. He always had her back, ever since they met. He took the blame for filling Ms. Henderson's desk drawer with shaving cream in the eighth grade. And he saved her life, catching her when she climbed too high in the old oak tree at the park and the branch broke under her weight.

She never worried about getting home safely from high school parties because he always took the role of designated driver.

"I won't say anything. I'm just upset and confused."

Briggs bit his lip, clutching the steering wheel and shifting in his seat.

She took a ragged breath. "Is there something else?"

"You're under suspicion of being a Dark Guild member. Sorcerers' magic is hereditary."

Keren's eyes widened. "Me? I can't even hold down a job. Why would they suspect me?" Her heart raced. She shuddered from the chill running down her spine. This can't be happening. It felt like the oxygen was sucked out of the car.

"Keren, there's more." His face paled.

Mom lay in a hospital bed, possibly dying, charged with a magic crime. She herself was under investigation.

"What more could there be, Briggs?" Tears streamed down her face. Pulling her knees up to her chest, she wrapped her arms around her legs.

"They've seized your property, citing it as a Dark Guild hideout. Also, they froze your mom's bank accounts. Her trial starts next week." He reached out, putting his hand on her shoulder. "You can stay with my mom. I'm sure she won't mind."

Her head spun. This moment felt surreal. She hadn't thought about a trial. How could it be so soon? A trial meant lawyers, and lawyers meant money. How could she hire a lawyer with her salary at the Kitty Café?

Magic crimes had a mandatory sentence of life in prison. Thinking about Mom behind bars triggered a fresh wave of tears. If she didn't die from the magic attack, she'd die in prison.

Briggs' voice jerked her back to reality. "We're here."

CHAPTER EIGHT

QUINLIN

Quinlin couldn't believe he hadn't killed that woman in last night's attack. He studied his swollen hands. The black tips of his fingers throbbed. It might take days for them to recover. He'd take care of this problem quickly, then get back to the lab.

He slipped into the hospital employees' locker room. Thank goodness he didn't need magic to steal Paul Jacobson's access badge. He proved to be an easy target. The hungover look in Paul's eyes gave him away.

While checking the lockers, he found one used but unlocked. People were too trusting. He reached into the locker, pulling out a pair of scrubs. As he held them just below his nose, Quinlin sniffed a couple of times - detergent and a hint of bleach. At least they were clean. The thought of wearing used clothing made his blood run cold.

After changing into the scrubs, he pinned the access badge on backwards just in case he ran into someone who knew Paul. He snatched a clipboard from the locker, attaching a map of the hospital he brought with him.

Time for sweet revenge. The potassium chloride syringe in his pocket should finish the job.

While walking down the corridor, he gave courtesy nods to other employees in passing, trying to blend in. After checking the map, he took the elevator to the fourteenth floor. Upon exiting the elevator, he saw the next corridor led to the Restricted Ward.

After turning the corner, he stopped. The number of inquisitors around the door surprised him. A fairy stood with them.

Another elevator bank sat between Quinlin and the Restricted Ward doors. He walked to the elevator doors, turning his back on the inquisitors as he pretended to read from the clipboard.

"Here are the magic analysis results."

Quinlin guessed that was the fairy.

"Thank you. We'll call if we need further services," a flat, unfriendly female voice made it clear the fairy's business had ended and he should leave.

Two sets of footsteps came toward him. The fairy had an escort.

"Let's test your security status, Paul," Quinlin mumbled as he slipped the access badge into the elevator's reader. The light stayed red.

While cursing under his breath, he flexed his hand. He'd need magic to gain access to the elevator.

"*Parioida fulmenten.*"

A sharp pain jolted up his arm. He groaned. His arm felt like it was on fire.

"This is a restricted area. What are you doing here?" the unfriendly female voice asked from directly behind him.

"I'm going to maintenance." Quinlin reinserted the badge with his other hand. "But my badge isn't working." He turned around to face his accuser.

"Like I said, you're in a restricted area." She pointed away from the Restricted Ward. "Turn left at the end of this corridor. You'll find accessible elevators a few yards down." She waited for Quinlin to move.

"Thank you." He walked away. In case the inquisitor was watching, he turned left at the end of the corridor as instructed.

A woman and a burly inquisitor approached. Her chestnut hair covered half her face. The inquisitor's eyes shifted his direction. Quinlin nodded but got no reaction from him.

"Sir, excuse me," a woman shouted.

While clenching his teeth, Quinlin turned. A middle-aged fox shifter rushed toward him.

"Me?" He raised his eyebrows, pointing to himself.

She stopped a few feet away. "Yes, I'm Nurse Bradshaw. I run the adult volunteer program. Are you new?"

His mind spun with potential answers. The lie needed to be believable. "I'm a new nurse's assistant." He glanced at the clipboard. "I seem to have gotten turned around." He gave her his best smile.

"Oh," she frowned, "I didn't realize we were hiring."

He flexed his aching hand. Just a tiny jolt to knock her unconscious would do the trick. He would call for help, then slip away among the chaos. His arm jerked, reminding him of his last magic attempt at the elevator. No, he would do this without magic.

"Welcome to Orlando Regional." She extended her hand. "We can't have enough assistants. Like I said, I'm Nurse Bradshaw."

While staring at her extended hand, his nose wrinkled. The thought of touching a shifter turned his stomach. With no other choices, he took her hand, his face giving no indication of the excruciating pain shooting up his arm. "I'm Quinlin Turner, nice to meet you."

"Come with me. We'll review your schedule in my office."

Quinlin fell in step with Nurse Bradshaw. As she babbled on about various topics, he nodded and threw in some 'uh-huhs' to feign interest. With inquisitors guarding the doors, the Restricted Ward proved harder to penetrate than he had planned. He needed an alternative plan to get through the heightened security.

She stopped at an office door with Adult Volunteer Coordinator stenciled on the window. "Here we are, Quinlin. I'll log into Human Resources and pull up your schedule."

He followed her into the office. As the door closed, he pulled the syringe from his pocket, jamming it into her neck.

While she let out a scream, he jerked her around, covering her mouth with his hand. More contact with a shifter. It made his skin crawl.

"Now, this will only take a minute." He smiled, watching her go into cardiac arrest. Her body shook, and her eyes widened with fear. Once her eyes closed and her body went limp, Quinlin let her drop to the floor.

"Dirty shifter."

Quinlin left Nurse Bradshaw's office, circling around to the employees' locker room, where he changed out of the scrubs. The dirty shifter had given him an idea.

CHAPTER NINE

KEREN

Keren followed Briggs into the hospital. The bitter antiseptic smell with undertones of soaps and cleaners attacked her senses. One hovered over their heads.

"They aren't letting visitors in. She's under protective custody." Briggs smoothed his hair.

"But I'm her daughter. Shouldn't they let family in?"

Briggs faced her. "Keren, you're suspected of being a Dark Guild member. You're lucky you're not in jail."

She noticed the dark circles under his eyes. This was taking a toll on him, too. "Please, Briggs. I need to see her."

He looked both ways down the corridor, then let out a low growl. "Alright. Follow behind me. Cover your face with your hair. I'll do my best to get you in to see your mom."

She reached up to his shoulder. While standing on her tiptoes, she pulled him down and kissed his cheek. He reminded her of the forest after a spring rain shower.

"Thanks, I appreciate what you're doing."

They navigated their way through the corridors and elevators, arriving on the fourteenth floor. Turning a corner, her eyes locked on the large Restricted Ward sign. She fought her impulse to run to the door, smash it open, and demand to see Mom.

A woman guard stopped them at the door. "Can I help you?"

Briggs towered over the woman. He pulled out his badge. "Yes, I'm Captain Wilson, and I'm here to see Captain Holloway."

She took the badge, then nodded toward Keren. "And the young woman?"

"Captain Holloway asked to speak with her." His authoritative tone impressed Keren.

The woman handed back his badge. "Wait one moment." She turned to a control panel. It scanned her retina, and the door slid open. "Have a nice day, Captain Wilson." The woman gave him a wink.

Keren pursed her lips, scowling at the woman. Briggs didn't realize the power he had over women. Every inch of him was muscle. His chest strained against the starched blue uniform shirt. She shot the woman a nasty look.

Briggs stepped aside, allowing Keren to enter first. "Thank you. You too."

When the door closed behind them, Briggs spoke in a low voice, "Stay close. I'm not sure which room she's in." One flew ahead, stopping by a room three doors down on the right.

"I think it's that one." She pointed to where One hovered.

They walked over. Briggs pulled the chart from the door and read the name. He raised his eyebrows. "How did you know?"

She shrugged. "Just a lucky guess."

"Excuse me, may I help you?" A silver-haired man in a white lab coat approached them. He snatched the chart from Briggs.

"This is Ms. Stewart's daughter. She's here to visit." Briggs pushed Keren forward. Her skin tingled at his touch.

Sweat trickled down her back. If the doctor called security, they would arrest them both. Everything Briggs worked for would be ruined. She held her breath.

"I wondered if family could visit her." He extended his hand to Keren. "I'm Doctor Niles, your mother's physician."

Tension released from her body. She drew in a deep breath and shook his hand. "I'm Keren. Can I go in now?"

"Of course. I'll give you an update on her condition." Doctor Niles walked into Mom's room.

Briggs scanned the corridor. His rugged hand rubbed the back of his neck. "I'll wait out here." His lavender eyes met hers. She recognized the bear, just on the verge of breaking out, desperate to keep her safe no matter what the cost. His eyes softened. He leaned in and ran the back of his hand along her cheek. "Don't stay too long."

She felt her face flush under his touch. "OK." She lingered a moment, then pulled back and entered the room.

Machine wires and probes crawled across her mom's skin. Two IV bags dripped unknown concoctions into her bloodstream. One bag's liquid had a purplish hue, the other was a translucent liquid. The audible heartbeat confirmed she was alive, but her pale, drawn complexion said she clung to life.

Keren approached the bed, taking her mom's fragile hand. It felt chilled. Wide golden bands clung to each of Mom's wrists. Keren knew from watching inquisitor television shows these cuffs restricted a sorcerer's use of magic.

She frowned, scrutinizing the black spots on her palm and the charred appearance to the tips of her fingers.

"What happened?" Keren looked at Doctor Niles.

"Powerful magic struck her, and she's in critical condition. We aren't sure if she'll survive." The unsympathetic delivery slapped her in the face. She clenched her teeth, wanting to lash out at the doctor for his deplorable bedside manner.

He continued, not noticing the tension in the room, "It should have killed her." He looked at her mom's chart. "She showed the residue of an old protection spell. That's the only reason she's alive." He hesitated. "That, and she fought back." He pointed to her mom's hand.

"I don't understand."

"Magic burns humans when they use it." He stiffened. "It's not natural."

Keren's mouth went dry. The doctor had to be wrong. Mom can't use magic. "Could someone have burned her hands? To make it appear she used magic?" There had to be an explanation. Her mind raced through memories, searching for any clues to help her understand. "Or she got the burns from blocking the attack."

"It's possible." He flipped through the chart. "But these follow typical patterns for magic use."

Someone with magic could simulate the patterns. This might be a setup. But why? And who?

Doctor Niles mentioned a protection spell. Her hands trembled as bile rose in her throat. She needed to hear the truth. "Tell me about the protection spell."

"Well, we found the residue of an older protection spell."

"How do you know it was older?"

"The magic analysis report showed signs of deterioration, but it appeared strong enough to possibly be why she survived. At its full potential, it might have protected your mom from sustaining any damage at all. A pretty powerful fairy cast the spell."

Her head spun. She promised Mom she would manage the re-protect appointment, but then told Ms. Oakdove to reschedule. She was too caught up in what she wanted, not taking care of Mom. Now, because of her, she was on the brink of death.

The doctor's pager buzzed. "Excuse me, I need to address this."

"Wait, can you call me if her condition changes?"

"Yes. Write your phone number in the chart." He hurried out of the room.

She leaned close to her mom's ear. "You hang in there, you'll be fine. Just keep fighting." Tears streamed down Keren's cheeks. "I'm so, so sorry. I'll make this right." She squeezed her hand. "I promise."

Her mom stirred.

"Mom, it's me. You're going to be alright." She choked down a sob.

"Keren." Her weak voice was barely audible over the machines. "Protect...",

"Mom, yes, I'm so sorry I didn't let Ms. Oakdove re-protect the house."

"Keren," the heartbeat monitor's pulse quickened, "protect yourself."

"What, me? No, mom, I'm good. You just worry about getting better."

Her mom's eyes fluttered in their effort to open. "Dark Guild, are you safe?"

The hair lifted on the back of her neck. Could it be a coincidence Mom mentioned the Dark Guild? They have been in the news. Or maybe she's aware of the charges against her.

"Don't worry, Mom, I'll clear your name. You'll get better, and things will go back to normal." She never thought her life was normal, but compared to today, her life was downright boring.

Mom squeezed her hand. "Protect yourself, don't trust..." Mom's eyes closed. Her breathing was shallow but steady.

Even from a hospital bed, Mom thought of Keren first. "Don't trust whom?" But she didn't respond. Keren rested her forehead on the bed. "Don't trust whom, Mom?" she sobbed into the blanket.

Briggs pushed the door open. "It's time to go."

She lifted her head, wiping her tears. After placing Mom's hand back on the bed and adjusting the covers, she gave her a kiss on the cheek and followed Briggs out of the Restricted Ward.

As they approached the lobby, she heard Nadria's voice.

"Keren!" Nadria raced down the corridor, tackling her into a tight hug. "I was so worried about you. No one gave me any information."

Keren wrapped her arms around her, burying her face in the crook of Nadria's neck. She smelled like freshly fallen snow. Inhaling, the aroma soothed her frayed nerves.

The evening's events took a toll on Keren's strength. Her legs wobbled.

"You should sit." Nadria guided her to a chair. "Are you alright? Did you visit your mom?"

"I don't want to sit. I just want to leave." Keren's head swam. "I saw Mom. She's in terrible shape." Fresh tears streamed down her face.

Keren looked up at Briggs standing behind Nadria. His drawn face and glassy eyes made the dark circles even more noticeable.

"You poor thing." Nadria wrapped her arm around Keren's shoulder. "I'll stay with you tonight. You can't be alone."

Keren allowed herself to be led to the exit. "I can't go home. Our property's been seized."

"They have kicked you out of your own home?" Nadria's voice flared with anger. Her eyes shot darts at Briggs. "How can that happen?"

"It's not his fault. He helped me get in to see Mom." Keren gave Briggs a smile.

He exhaled, smiling back. "I'm heading back to the station. I have a long night ahead of me." He pulled Keren into a hug. Her body flooded with warmth, and she melted into his arms. She felt his heartbeat pounding in his chest.

"Do you want me to call my mom and ask her if you can stay over for a while?"

"She can stay with me." Nadria rubbed Keren's back.

"Alright." Briggs nuzzled her away. "Call if you need me." He kissed the top of her head and walked out of the hospital.

Keren swayed. A wave of lightheadedness washed over her.

"Whoa." Nadria caught her by the arm. "Let's get you home and in bed."

CHAPTER TEN

KEREN

Keren sat on Nadria's gray futon sofa in borrowed ninja turtle pajamas.

"Are you feeling better?" Nadria tucked a soft comforter around Keren. "Can I get you something to eat?"

Food couldn't fill the hole in Keren's stomach. Mom clung to life after a magic attack. Things would be different if only she had let Ms. Oakdove re-protect the house. Maybe it wouldn't have stopped the attack, but Mom's injuries would have been less severe. She slumped back on the couch.

"No, I'm not hungry."

"What about tea?" Nadria pushed loose strands of hair behind Keren's ear.

Keren looked at One perched on the far end of the sofa. Its wings folded in, and the unblinking ruby eyes staring at her. She looked around, spotting Two standing by the front door. She loved having her imaginary friends around. They comforted her in a way she couldn't explain. But she had to focus on figuring out how to help Mom. It was best if she got rid of the distraction.

"Tea would be nice. Do you have mine?"

"Yes, I'll make you a cup." Giving her a peck on the cheek, Nadria went to the kitchen.

One lifted off the couch and followed. The severity of the situation set in. Biting her lip, she wondered how long she could stay with Nadria until the inquisitors started suspecting her involvement. To keep Nadria safe, she'd have to find another place. Maybe a hotel where she wouldn't put any of her friends in harm's way.

"Keren, what kind of tea did you say this was?" Nadria stood in the kitchen doorway. She poked at tea leaves spread on a plate.

Keren hesitated. Had Mom ever told her about the tea ingredients? "I don't know. It's the tea Mom buys that controls my visions."

"Are you seeing them now?" Nadria looked around as if she could find them.

"Yes, Two is by the front door, and One..." she pointed over Nadria's head, "is hovering over your head."

After pushing the tea leaves around with her finger, Nadria took a couple of quick sniffs, then shook her head. "Keren, I think these herbs dampen magic. The Herbology group I attended the other night talked about this leaf. They passed around samples."

Keren frowned. "That makes no sense." She felt like she'd fallen into someone else's life. Everything she thought she knew crumbled around her - someone wanting to attack her mom, Mom asking about being safe from the Dark Guild, and now she learned her tea was an herb that dampens magic. She struggled to focus on any one thought. They swirled like a whirlpool in her mind.

Nadria brought her back to the present moment. "I know, but I'm positive these are the same. It can have some serious side effects." Nadria set the plate on the counter. Sitting on the coffee table across from Keren, she clasped her hands. "Can you do me a favor? Since the visions are calm, can you skip the tea, just for now?"

One stared at her, and Two lifted its head like they were also waiting for her answer. This seemed important to Nadria. As long as the visions didn't interfere, she wouldn't drink the tea.

She nodded, pointing to her backpack. "OK, just drop it in there."

"Thanks." Nadria dropped the tea in the backpack.

Then the floodgates opened, and everything inside Keren rushed to get out. "They charged Mom with a magic crime. They think she's a member of the Dark Guild." She put both hands on the back of her neck. "Briggs told me I'm a suspect, too, and they could arrest me at any time."

"What?" Nadria leaned back. "Thinking your mom is part of the Dark Guild is just crazy." Waving her hand in the air, she brushed the idea aside. "The charge won't stick."

"I don't know. Briggs said the trial starts next week." Keren shook her head. "That means lawyers, and I don't have the money to pay for a lawyer. She'll have to have a public defender."

With the trial coming up so soon, there's no time for a complete stranger to gather enough facts to beat the charges. This was life and death. She had to do more.

"I have to figure out who attacked Mom and why."

"Let the inquisitors do the investigating. That's their job," Nadria said.

"How do I know it wasn't one of them who framed her?"

"What do you mean *framed*?" Nadria narrowed her eyes.

"When I saw her in the hospital, her hands," Keren turned her palms up, "had black speckles. The doctor said that's a sign of humans using magic."

"We need more information." Nadria stood, walking over to the end table to retrieve her tablet. "Let's look up some facts." She plunked herself down next to Keren.

"Let's see." Nadria brought up a web browser. "We'll start broad." She typed Dark Guild in the search bar and pressed enter. A list of topics displayed. The top story headlined Keren's mom.

Keren stopped breathing. She felt like a bucket of ice water had poured over her. "Let's skip this one."

Nadria read a line further down the page. "Here's a story about some recent crimes." She clicked the link.

Keren leaned closer, reading out loud, "It says the Dark Guild's arcanum are suspects in a recent break-in at Green Thumb Gardener's Supply."

"That's owned by the Hadley's." Nadria scrolled down. "And two attacks in Winter Park. Both involved the death of shifters." She clutched the tablet. "All incidents seem to involve shifters."

Keren continued reading. "The inquisitors don't have a motive, but they suspect the Dark Guild. All the crimes have evidence of sorcerer magic."

"These types of attacks will stir up the magical races, maybe causing retaliation." Nadria shook her head. "We'll lose what little ground we've made these last few years eliminating discrimination."

Sliding the tablet into Keren's lap, she stood, pacing the room.

"We're not just magic, we're like everyone else. We work, eat, go to school, and want a happy, fulfilling life. Magic isn't evil. Any tool, like a hammer, or knife, can be a weapon. Magic is the same way. In the hands of responsible users, it's safe and useful. But this Dark Guild..." she trailed off. "It seems the inquisitors are chomping at the bit to arrest the arcanum." Nadria glanced at Keren. "Sorry, I didn't mean..."

"I know. The inquisitors sound almost blinded by their obsession to arrest the Dark Guild's arcanum and put them behind bars. That's why I don't think I can trust them to prove Mom's innocence. She's their scapegoat. If she's found guilty of this charge, they could pin all those crimes on her." Keren rubbed her hands over her face. Tipping her head back, she closed her eyes.

"You look exhausted." Nadria rubbed her arm. "You need to rest. I have the early shift tomorrow, so I'll leave before you wake up."

So many thoughts swarmed through Keren's mind. The Internet hadn't given her many leads. "I can't sleep. Would you hand me my backpack?"

"Sure." Nadria pulled the backpack from behind the couch. "Don't stay up too late. How about we meet at the Stubborn Mule for lunch? Say twelve o'clock?"

"Sounds good. I'll visit Mom in the morning. Thanks for letting me crash here."

"You're always welcome." Nadria kissed the top of her head. "Here." She put a key in Keren's hand. "This is my spare apartment key." She got up, walking to her bedroom.

"Thanks. Good night." Keren pulled her sketchbook out of the backpack. Drawing might help her settle down. She started drawing her mom, working to capture her cheerful and dynamic energy.

Scanning the room, she found both One and Two sitting by the door. She blinked her heavy eyelids. They looked clearer, more defined. She dismissed it as the light playing tricks on her tired eyes.

"Let's make a family portrait. Three, Four."

The misty figures appeared next to One and Two. Something tugged at the back of her mind. The room felt ten degrees colder. She shivered, barely able to hold on to the pencil. Something else existed in the room, and its stare burned into the back of her head. She turned, gasping at golden, glowing eyes scrutinizing her from a cloud of black mist. The mist dissipated. She'd seen those eyes twice before. Each time, she'd experienced a feeling of dread, like something horrible was going to happen.

The room's temperature returned to normal. She shook out her hands. "I'm just tired." She drew the four creatures alongside the picture of Mom.

After finishing her drawing, she snuggled under the blanket, drifting off to sleep.

CHAPTER ELEVEN

QUINLIN

Quinlin's interest peaked when he spotted the girl from yesterday outside the Restricted Ward. A neat hair bun revealed her attractive face. Based on her body language, her conversation with the guard at the door wasn't going well.

He adjusted his nametag, glancing at his blemish-free hands. They healed quickly from the attack on his father's murderer. So, magically persuading the Human Resource representative to add him to the employee database as a nurses' assistant with access to the Restricted Ward had been child's play.

He placed himself off to the side but within earshot, eavesdropping on the conversation.

"I'm her daughter. I should be able to visit her." The girl clenched her hands at her side.

The stoic expression on the guard's face made it clear he would not change his mind. "I'm sorry, Ms. Stewart, your mother can't have visitors."

So, this was that woman's daughter. He looked her up and down. Yes, he saw a slight resemblance.

She took a few steps away from the guard, then moved back to face him. She crossed her arms, scowling at him.

Apparently, the guard's unflinching posture irritated her. She threw up her hands, stalking away from him.

Quinlin tapped his chin as he watched the girl storm off. If that woman had a family who cared enough to visit, he wanted to meet them.

After he and Dan had finished constructing the control spells, he left Dan to practice for the meeting demonstration. So, he had time for a side investigation.

He followed her until he was certain she headed to the lobby. Then, after jogging around through side corridors to get ahead of her, he turned a corner in time to head her off.

She looked deep in thought and didn't notice him until they bumped shoulders.

"Oh, excuse me, miss. Are you alright?" Quinlin steadied her with his hand.

"Yeah, sorry. I didn't see you." She moved a stray strand of hair behind her ear. Her silver eyes sparkled like stars.

"I'm Quinlin." He held out his hand. "Hi."

The girl looked confused before reaching for his hand. "Hi, I'm Keren. Nice to meet you."

His thumb rubbed her silky skin as his heart skipped a beat. Reluctantly, he released her hand.

"Keren, let me buy you a coffee to make up for my clumsiness."

She stared at him for a moment, then turned to look back at the lobby, as if plotting her escape. She shrugged.

"Sure, that sounds nice. Thanks."

After taking a seat with their coffee, Keren motioned to his scrubs.

"Are you an orderly?"

"No, I'm a nurses' assistant." Quinlin sipped his coffee. Might as well throw out the bait. "I work in the Restricted Ward."

Her eyes widened. "The Restricted Ward? I have my..." she hesitated, looking up and right, "aunt in that ward." She hesitated again while she strummed her fingers on the table. "She needs protection from my uncle, who beat her up."

This girl's lying skills ranked a one on a scale of one to ten.

She continued. "I'm not allowed to visit. I realize we just met, but is there any way you can get someone into that ward?"

He admired her straightforward style, even though the lying needed improvement. "There are strict rules about bringing someone into the ward."

Keren deflated with a sigh.

He gave her a little hook. "But rules are meant to be broken." Her radiant smile made him catch his breath. It lit up the entire room. *Stay focused.*

Don't let a pretty face distract you. "Of course, I'll need to get to know you first."

"I'd like that."

Her dazzling eyes gazed into his. He couldn't tell if she was flirting because she thought him attractive or she wanted him to get her into the Restricted Ward. Regardless, he'd bought time to get better acquainted. Keren glanced at the clock on the wall.

"Oh, I have to get going." She gathered her things and stood up. "I'm meeting my friend for lunch."

"I'm just getting off my shift. Let me give you a lift." He took their cups, tossing them toward the trash can. The shot missed.

"Um, the cup sleeves are recyclable." Without hesitation, she picked up the cups. While continuing the conversation, she removed the sleeves, tossing them into the recycle bin. The cups went into the trash. "I don't want to inconvenience you. We're meeting at the Stubborn Mule."

"The place on Eola Drive? It's down the road from Lake Eola Dental." He held up his hands. "Crazy coincidence. I have a dentist appointment this afternoon. The Stubborn Mule is on the way." And there, young lady, was a lesson in expert lying.

She squinted at him. "Crazy coincidence." While cocking her head to the side, she studied him. "Alright, let's go."

He escorted her to his car, and they drove to the restaurant.

CHAPTER TWELVE

KEREN

The Stubborn Mule had a large outside seating area. Tables with umbrellas and a metal canopy that wrapped around the building protected customers from the Florida sun. Keren and Quinlin stopped on the sidewalk outside the restaurant.

Much more relaxed after their pleasant small talk in the car, Keren marveled at how at ease she felt with Quinlin. They acted like old friends. Out of the corner of her eye, she saw mist form into the shape of Two. It paced in front of the restaurant door.

Quinlin's sandy, clean-cut hair complemented his athletic physique. In another circumstance, Quinlin would be on her radar for a relationship.

It had been so long since she had a boyfriend. Her thoughts flashed to Briggs. He was the big brother she never had. She bit her lip, remembering how safe she felt in his protective embrace.

She grounded her thoughts. *Keep it together. This was not the time for romance.* Quinlin had access to the Restricted Ward, and he seemed open to helping her get in to visit Mom.

"My friend is inside. I see her car." As much as she wanted to keep Quinlin around, she couldn't have him crashing her lunch with Nadria. She didn't want him to know her mom was under arrest for a magic crime.

He hadn't asked her out on a date yet. A stipulation for helping her get in to see Mom was getting to know her better. She didn't want to resort to stalking him at the hospital, but she also didn't want to be the one asking for the first date. Was the cafeteria coffee a first date? No, she had to keep some dignity.

"OK. Well, nice to meet you, Keren." He put his hand on her arm. A warm sensation flowed up her arm. "See you around." He turned, heading back to his car.

Damn, she thought. She sighed, walking into the restaurant with Two following close behind. She looked around for Nadria. An arm waved in the air. She made her way over.

Nadria stood to meet her. "Hey, how are you?" She gave her a hug. "How's your mom doing?"

They sat at a round, high-top table near the back of the restaurant.

"I don't know. They wouldn't let me visit her." Keren stopped talking when the server came over.

They both ordered water.

After the server left the menus and hurried away, she continued. "All of this is so confusing. I'm not sure what to do." Keren rubbed her face. "I can't afford a lawyer, so they'll assign a public defender to her case."

Nadria leaned across the table. "They might surprise you. Some public defenders are skilled lawyers."

"They won't know Mom. And she's in no condition to testify for herself. Briggs said there were witnesses and evidence supporting the charge." She folded her hands on the table and lifted her chin. "I'll just have to prove her innocence." She held back telling Nadria about the protection spell. "She needs me, and I'll clear her name."

The server brought over their drinks. Keren drank half the glass of water to clear the tightness in her throat, then ordered the blackened steak flat with extra barbecue sauce and cheese. Nadria stayed with her favorite, the quinoa-avocado bowl.

Two ran between the tables. He lowered his head, charging at the back of a man's chair. The man jerked forward, spilling his drink down his shirt. Two bounded off in the other direction. Keren blinked. Did Two actually hit the chair?

Nadria's voice brought her back to their conversation. "Keren, you're not alone. I'm with you every step of the way."

"I can't let you do that. You have a life, a job." She wouldn't endanger her best friend.

"You're a big part of my life, and you can't do this alone." Nadria raised her eyebrows. "I want to help. What if you get into trouble? Who's going to know?"

She shook her head. "I don't want you getting involved because they might add you to the suspect list."

"Oh, honey." Nadria raised her hand to her chest. "I appreciate you protecting me, I really do, but we'll be there for each other, just like we always are." Nadria's eyes locked on hers. "Don't shut me out. Please, I want to help. We're a team."

Nadria's insistence chipped away at her resolve. She needed Nadria's strength. "I can't risk you getting hurt."

"I can take care of myself. I have magic. It might come in handy."

Nadria was right. The Dark Guild used magic. Her poking around to get information about the group without having magic sounded crazy and dangerous. "You're right. I need your help." She took Nadria's hand. "But, please, be careful. I'd die if anything happened to you."

Nadria's face beamed as she nodded in agreement. "We'll sort this out. What do you know so far?"

The conversation paused when their food arrived.

"I don't know much more than what Briggs told me and what we found on the Internet last night. I want to learn more about the Dark Guild, but there's limited information online."

Nadria sat straighter. "Why don't we ask Ordell?" She took a bite of her naan bread. "I'm off the rest of the day. We could ask him to meet us at my place." Nadria narrowed her eyes, challenging her to disagree. "He'll be hurt if we don't ask him to help."

A sense of calm fell over Keren. Ordell had hacker-level technical skills. This idea could work. "Alright, let's do it."

They finished lunch, paid the bill, and headed out the door. Two followed behind, pretending to attack customers in the patio area. To Keren's surprise, Quinlin trotted toward them.

"I'm glad I caught you." He smiled, showing off his dimples. "I.." he hesitated, glancing at Nadria.

"Quinlin, this is my friend Nadria. Nadria, this is Quinlin. I literally bumped into him at the hospital today." Her face flushed.

Nadria extended her hand. "Nice to meet you."

Quinlin's face turned to stone. He took her hand, gave it a quick shake, then released it. "Likewise." His words came out flat.

After turning back to Keren, Quinlin's smile returned. "I'm glad I caught you. I should have done this earlier, but can we get together later?" His eyes danced with anticipation.

This was the moment she waited for. She caught her breath. *Think straight*, she told herself. Quinlin was her one way into the Restricted Ward. There was no time for romance now. "Yes, I'd like that."

"So, how about tomorrow for lunch? Let's say one o'clock at the Osprey?" Quinlin held up his phone. "Can I get your contact information?"

"Sure." Keren touched her phone to his. "And tomorrow at the Osprey sounds good."

"Great. I'm sorry, but I have to run." He pointed to his mouth. "Dentist appointment." He locked eyes with her. "Looking forward to tomorrow." He jogged away.

"Wow." Nadria nudged her. "Isn't he adorable?"

Keren's face turned beet red. "Come on, we have research to do." They walked to Nadria's car. Two followed them.

"Why don't you call Ordell and ask if he can meet us at my house?"

"Good idea." Keren pulled out her cell phone, selecting Ordell's number.

He picked up on the first ring. Loud noises in the background made it difficult to hear. She covered her other ear.

"Keren?" Ordell's voice quivered. She barely heard him.

She shouted into the phone. "Ordell, is everything OK?"

"I'm so glad you called. Broden is missing." His voice jumbled with the background noise.

"What? Did you say something about Broden?"

"Yes, he's missing. The police are here now." He sniffled. "Can you come over?"

Keren pulled the phone from her ear. "Ordell says his brother is missing."

"What? When?" Nadria frowned. "Broden was just at the demonstration with us."

"I can't tell. There's too much noise. I think we should go over to his place."

"Of course. We should be there in twenty minutes."

"Ordell? Hang in there. Nadria and I are on our way."

"Alright, thank you." He hung up the phone.

CHAPTER THIRTEEN

KEREN

Baldwin Park's upscale neighborhood had a wide variety of home designs. Nadria pulled up in front of a light blue, two-story house. Two picturesque front windows framed each side of the front door.

A white railing surrounded the front porch, which extended the entire width of the house. White rocking chairs and a wooden double-seated swing gave the house a welcoming appeal.

Three looked out-of-place standing on the porch. Its massive body made the rocking chairs seem like playhouse toys.

Nadria knocked on the door. It only took a couple of minutes for Ordell to answer. His red-rimmed eyes revealing raw emotions.

"Thanks for coming." He stepped aside so they could enter. "The police just left. Mom and Dad are in the living room." He led them past the formal dining room into the kitchen. White cabinets with framed glass doors reached up to the nine-foot ceiling.

"I could barely understand you over the phone. Did you say Broden was missing?" Keren sat next to Nadria at the kitchen island, tossing her backpack on the floor.

He pulled a couple of waters from the refrigerator. "It's been crazy here. Right after the demonstration, Broden had planned to go to the beach with some friends for a couple of days. He was supposed to be home this morning."

He sat next to Keren, handing her the waters.

"When he didn't show up, we tried calling him. But he didn't answer his phone." He blinked several times. She noticed a tear drip down his cheek. "So, we called his friends. They said he never showed up at the beach. They figured he stayed home to study for midterms."

Nadria put her hand on her cheek. "I'm so sorry, Ordell."

His bottom lip quivered. "Mom was hysterical. We called the police. That's what you heard in the background when you called."

Keren's heart broke. "Do they have any leads?"

Ordell scrubbed his palms over his eyes. "That's the worst part, the police refused to start an investigation."

Nadria rushed to his side. She put her arm around his shoulder, hugging him close. "Why won't they search for him?"

He rested his head on Nadria's shoulder and closed his eyes. "Two years ago, Broden ran away. They ended up finding him a week later with some girl. I can't even remember her name."

Keren remembered that incident. Ordell's parents had every police division combing the city for Broden.

"Because he has a history of leaving for long periods of time and not letting anyone know where he went, they won't start an investigation. Besides, Broden's not a minor. We're supposed to call again if he doesn't show up in a couple of weeks."

Keren gasped. "A couple of weeks?" Her muscles tensed. Frayed nerves teetered on the breaking point. "That's insane."

Placing her hand on Keren's arm, Nadria spoke in a gentle tone. "We're all a little on edge right now."

Her cheeks burned. Instead of helping Ordell, she added to his stress with an emotional outbreak. She took a deep breath. "I'm sorry."

He shrugged his shoulders. "It's OK. I had the same reaction."

She changed gears, trying to redeem herself. "Can we see your parents?"

"Sure, they'd like that." Ordell hopped off the stool and led Keren and Nadria to the living room.

The couple sat huddled on the couch. Mrs. Murphy dabbed at her eyes with a handkerchief.

"Mama, Papa, Keren and Nadria are here."

Nadria rushed over to the couch. She sat down next to Mrs. Murphy, wrapping her arms around her. "I'm so sorry to hear about Broden. Is there anything we can do?"

Mrs. Murphy sat up. While patting Nadria's knee, she fought to compose herself.

"I appreciate that Nadria. All we can do now is wait." Her voice quivered.

Mr. Murphy stood, tugging his shirt down over his belly. "I don't know what good the police are if they won't help you find a missing boy." He waved his hands in the air. "Good tax money goes to supporting the police department. You'd think we'd get help when we need it."

"Take it easy, dear. Remember your blood pressure." Mrs. Murphy reached a hand out toward her husband.

Keren walked up to Mr. Murphy, catching one of his hands as it sailed by. "You're not alone, Mr. Murphy. We'll help you through this."

His bottom lip quivered. At that moment, Keren saw how much Ordell resembled his dad.

"You're a good girl, Keren." He patted her hand. "Thank you." He turned to face Nadria. "And you too Nadria. You're like daughters to us."

The lump in Keren's throat caused her breath to catch. The Murphy's had been kind to her as she grew up. They indulged her talking to and playing with imaginary friends, never making her feel stupid or silly. She'd thought of them as her second family. They didn't deserve this misfortune.

"You go along with Ordell." Mr. Murphy pulled his hand away. "We're fine."

Ordell took his dad's cue and motioned for Keren and Nadria to follow him upstairs. Nadria kissed Mrs. Murphy on the cheek before standing to follow.

At the top of the stairs, Ordell turned to face them. "I know something is wrong this time." He opened the first door on the right. The room looked neat and organized. A picture of Marilyn Monroe hung over the bed. A desk with four computer monitors sat on the far wall. He walked to the desk, picking up a laptop. "Broden would never leave this behind."

Ordell moved his hand over the laptop cover, his eyes glazing over. "Broden and I promised we'd never hack into each other's computers."

Nadria put her hand on his shoulder. "He'd understand."

"I suppose you're right." He led them down the hall to his room.

In contrast to Broden's well-kept room, organized chaos described Ordell's. Clothes covered his dresser and the unmade bed. Stacks of paper and books took up most of the floor space. Superhero figurines crowded together on a dusty bookcase, and computer components and gadgets blanketed the desk.

His cheeks blushed. "Sorry about the mess." He tossed some clothes on the floor to make room for them to sit down.

Lost in thought, Keren wandered to the bookcase. What could have happened to Broden? She noticed her favorite superhero, Aquaman, pushed to the back of the shelf. Her fingers reached out, plucking him from his prison. While brushing away the dust, she reasoned something associated with the demonstration must be connected to Broden's disappearance.

"Did Broden mention anything out of the ordinary happening before or during the demonstration?"

"He mentioned a guy at school harassing him. I can't remember why." Ordell worked on connecting Broden's laptop.

"Did he specifically say harassing him? Did he give any details?"

He stopped. "Now that you mention it, he said threatened." He rubbed his temples. "Why didn't I remember that before when the police were here?" With a sigh, he opened Broden's laptop.

"Can you get in?" Nadria stopped folding clothes and leaned over to look at the laptop screen.

Ordell smirked. "I can hack pretty much anything." He opened an application on his computer. "This is an automated process that uses well-known words and phrases to create different combinations. It will feed into Broden's laptop until something fits. I'll add some common words and phrases I think he might use. It's called a dictionary attack." He started the application, then sat back. "This might take a few minutes."

"Let's get back to the threat." Keren rolled Aquaman between her palms. "Why would someone threaten Broden?"

Ordell rubbed his face. "He said he bumped into a jerk at school bullying shifters while he was recruiting volunteers for the demonstration. He wanted to figure out a way to stop him."

"Do you know if he did? Find a way to stop him?"

"Yeah, I think so." When his computer chimed, Ordell turned back to the desk. "I'm in." After a few keystrokes, Broden's laptop came to life.

"Can you find out this guy's name?"

"Maybe. Let's see. I'll check his email first. He has a couple of addresses." Ordell flipped through several screens. "He uses this one for junk, and this one for everything else. Whoa, wait a minute."

"What?" Nadria rushed to his side.

"Broden subscribes to MAXIM." Ordell laughed.

She hit him in the back of the head. "For heaven's sake, get serious."

Keren knew joking around was Ordell's coping method. The brothers were always playing practical jokes on one another. They were only two years apart. He idolized his older brother.

She moved to the dresser, setting Aquaman in a pile of socks. Broden and this guy weren't friends. Yet he found Broden and threatened him. While moving along the dresser, she ran her fingers over the pamphlets and badges from the demonstration. She picked up a pin and turned it over in her hand.

"You said Broden met this guy, trying to recruit people for the demonstration. Do you think the guy attended the demonstration to harass Broden?" She turned to face Nadria and Ordell. "That's the connection." Keren held up the pin. "Could he have reached your brother through the website?"

Ordell's face lit up. "Yes, all the volunteers have email addresses linked to the site." He pushed Broden's laptop aside and turned to his computer. "I back everything up on the server."

Nadria smiled. "And the volunteers had personalized cards to hand out with the pamphlets. So, the guy would have Broden's name and email address."

"I found something." Ordell pointed to the screen. "This definitely sounds like a threat."

Keren and Nadria pressed close together to read the screen.

Your disrespect for the true masters of magic will be your downfall.

"I agree, its threatening and creepy. Any others?" Nadria asked.

"Yeah, here's another one." Ordell froze after reading the brief message.

Prepare to pay.

None of them spoke. The air grew heavy.

He turned off the monitor, his voice a whisper. "That's it, just those two."

Ordell slammed his hand on the desk. "We could find dantheman@internetservice.com's physical address." Pulling Broden's laptop over, his fingers pounded on the keyboard.

Keren wondered how you could make a connection between an email address and someone's physical address. Briggs might help with the inquisitor's database, but she didn't want to ask him to take any more risks for her.

"First, I'll use this online tool to find social media accounts using dantheman's email address." A list of accounts with hyperlinks showed on the screen.

Nadria peered over his shoulder. "Does that mean he has all those accounts?"

"No, the tool generates the URL as if he used the email to create the account. If you click on the link, the account will try to open." He clicked on the Facebook link.

"Bingo." Silence filled the room as they stared at the profile's cover photo. A husky man in his mid-thirties, with acne spread over his forehead and cheeks, smiled back at them. Tribal-style tattoos wound around his neck. The page displayed his timeline, friends, and photos, along with his name. Dan Mann.

"Is that him?" Nadria whispered.

With flaring his nostrils, Ordell ignored her question. "He hasn't secured his timeline. Let's hope he's sloppy with other security settings." He clicked the *About* tab, then *Contact* and *Basic Info*. "Bingo, birth date and year."

It was that simple, no special hacking required, and Ordell had Dan's personal information. Keren made a mental note to change her Facebook privacy settings.

Opening a new tab, he brought up the Voter Information Lookup site. "Now, let's hope he's registered to vote." He entered Dan's name and birth date. After checking the 'I understand and agree' and CAPTCHA boxes, he clicked the Submit button.

All three sighed when the 'no record found' message appeared.

Scratching her chin, Keren thought maybe they had the wrong information. "Does the search require the full first name? Dan might be short for something else."

Ordell changed Dan to Daniel. The same error message appeared.

Nadria rubbed Ordell's shoulders. "I guess he's not registered."

"There might be other names." Pulling out her phone, Keren searched Google for 'names Dan is short for.' "OK, I've got a list. The first one is Daniel, which we know doesn't work. The second is Danielle."

They looked at each other. Ordell shrugged his shoulders, entering Danielle in the First Name field. He got the same results.

Keren continued, "Well, we had little faith in that one, anyway. The next name is Danma, D-a-n-m-a."

Replacing the first name, Ordell's finger hung above the mouse button. "Here goes nothing." He clicked the Submit button, bringing up a full address. He smacked his hands together, then pointed at the screen. "Bingo!"

Keren chuckled. Covering her mouth with her hand, she tried to control herself. "So, his name is Danma Mann?"

Ordell and Nadria both looked at her. Their doe-eyed expression pushed her over the top. She busted out laughing.

Nadria tried to suppress her laughter but lost the battle. Ordell joined in.

Clutching her stomach, Keren leaned on the dresser for support. Tension drained from her body. It felt like a heavy weight lifted off her shoulders.

As the laughter died down, Ordell took a screenshot of Dan's address and his Facebook profile cover photo. Grabbing them off the printer, he headed to the door.

"Wait, where are you going?" Keren didn't like the look on his face.

"I'm going to pay Dan a visit." His eyes flashed with anger. "Don't try to stop me."

"Wait a minute." She stepped in front of him. "You can't just show up and ask if he knows anything about Broden."

"Why not? He's just over in Holden-Parramore."

Nadria's wide eyes showed her skepticism. "Won't that be dangerous? I mean, if he's done something to Broden, what would keep him from hurting you?"

Keren held her ground. Ordell wasn't thinking straight. "The emails came from Dan's account, but how do you know it was him? What if he's also a victim and someone is using his email?"

"We could respond to his email, see what we get," Nadria suggested.

"That would take too long. Broden needs me now." Ordell waved his hand, transforming into a black German Shepherd. His short, dense fur curled in loose waves.

As Ordell changed, Keren lunged for him, but he slipped from her grip. She fell on her hands and knees.

He sprung on the bed.

"No." Her heart raced. She had to stop him.

Two's misty body appeared in the doorway. The flames from its horns licked the top of the door frame.

Ordell prepared to leap out the door, but he let out a yip and shifted his trajectory back toward Keren. Ninety pounds of German Shepherd crashed into her. She grunted, the weight pushing her to the floor.

He changed back into his human form. "What the hell?" His ears stiffened as he scrambled away from the door. "What is that thing?"

Crawling on her hands and knees, Keren grabbed Ordell's wrist, squeezing it tight so he couldn't escape. She thought he was joking around at the café when he said he said he saw Four, but she knew he wasn't faking the panic she recognized in his eyes. "What did you see?" She had to know. Could Ordell see her imaginary friends in his animal forms?

"An enormous wolf with crazy flaming horns, right there in the doorway." A shaky finger pointed to the door.

Nadria joined them on the floor. "I don't see anything."

"That's Two." Keren put her hands on his shoulders, turning him toward her. His wide green eyes met hers. "Ordell, in the café, did you really see Four?" She shook her head. He didn't know them by name. "The monster the cats were watching?"

"Of course, I saw the monster at the café, but this one is different."

"What you saw at the café was Four." She glanced at Two standing guard in the doorway. "Two is guarding the door."

Nadria stared at the doorway. "Are you talking about your imaginary friends?"

"Yes." Keren jumped to her feet. "Wait here." She sprinted downstairs to the kitchen where she'd left her backpack, Two's opaque body vanishing as she ran through it.

Snatching her sketchbook from her bag, she ran back upstairs. Nadria and Ordell were still sitting on the floor. She shuffled through pages of drawings until she found one of Two.

"Here." She held the sketchbook out so they could see. "Is that what you just saw?"

Frowning, he leaned closer to the book. "Yes, but are you telling me I can see your imaginary friends?"

"I don't know what I'm telling you." She flipped to a drawing of Four. "And this one." She turned it so they could see. "Is this what you saw at the café today?"

Standing up, he took the sketchbook. "Yes." He flipped through the pages, then looked at her. "I don't understand."

"Neither do I." She flopped in the computer chair.

"Do you think it has something to do with the tea? How long has it been since you drank it?" Nadria stood, placing a hand on Keren's arm.

She frowned. "Well, I hadn't drunk the tea since I lost my serving job last month." Her cheeks reddened as she lowered her chin. "I didn't drink it because I think it's fun interacting with my imaginary friends. Since I was home most of the time, I didn't think it mattered. I tried to drink some at the café, but then Briggs showed up and we left for the hospital. So, I think it's been over three weeks since I had any."

"What tea?" Ordell asked.

"The tea her mom gave her to control the visions. I think it's an herb that dampens magic." Nadria tipped her head. "Why do you think Ordell can see them?"

Ordell handed the sketchbook back to Keren. "In my animal forms, I can see and hear things well outside the range of human perception. For instance, in my cat form, I have a kind of spatial perception I don't have in human form." He scratched his head. "It's hard to explain."

Keren's head spun, trying to fit the puzzle pieces together. Mom lay in the hospital, accused of using magic as a weapon. The black spots on her hands flashed in her mind. Nadria believed the tea was an herb that dampens magic. If Mom could use magic, does that mean she could, too? Briggs said it was hereditary. If that were true, why was Mom hiding it from her? Keren's heart pounded as she ran through the scenarios. Afraid of what the answers might be, she changed the topic.

"I don't know." She grabbed the printouts. "Right now, we should focus on what we're going to do about Broden. Let's think this through."

She paced the room, forcing the burning questions and doubts about Mom to the back of her mind.

"We can't be sure this is actually Dan's address. And we can't be sure he isn't a victim as well. If he is responsible for Broden's disappearance, we'll be putting ourselves in danger by just walking up and knocking on the door."

Ordell paced the room, waving his hands in the same manner his dad did downstairs. "What other choice do we have other than just knocking on the door?" His eyes pleaded for answers.

Responding to an email was the safest thing to do. But Ordell had a point. They had to find Broden before something bad happened. Her chest tightened. Unless it already has.

"Dan doesn't know we have his name and address. Since we know what he looks like, I say we wait outside this address to see if he really lives there."

"What do we do if we find him?" Nadria asked.

Compared to a full-on confrontation or passively waiting for an email exchange, Keren considered breaking and entering the middle choice. She thought about Briggs. He risked so much for her already. She'd leave him as a backup plan. "We wait until the house is empty, then look around for answers."

"You're suggesting we break into someone's house?" Nadria's hands went to her chest, her voice raising an octave. "Isn't there something else we can do?"

Ordell patted Keren's shoulder. "Now, we're getting somewhere."

Looking at Nadria, he gave her puppy dog eyes. "Please. Broden needs us."

Nadria scowled. "Fine, but I don't like it."

"Alright." Keren checked the time. It was 3:30 pm. They had plenty of time before it got dark. "Let's head over to Dan's."

CHAPTER FOURTEEN

BRIGGS

"Why don't you tell her how you feel?" asked Tabitha as she dropped money into the violin case of a street musician.

"Why don't you drop the subject?" growled Briggs. He had invited Tabitha along to check out a tip on high-human siting in a predominately magical race neighborhood. Now, he regretted his decision.

"You two have been dancing around one another for years. Just tell the girl how you feel."

"It's complicated." He hoped that answer would shut down this line of questioning.

"Not really. You're in love with Keren, and she's in love with you. What's complicated about that?"

"Plenty. First, how do you know she's in love with me? And second, I don't want to chase my best friend away by spewing romantic notions she doesn't share." Heat crawled up his neck to his cheeks. This was the first time he ever verbalized his feelings for Keren.

Tabitha's lower lip puckered out. "I'm hurt, I thought I was your best friend."

Briggs rolled his eyes.

She laughed. "Believe me, I can tell by the way she looks at you." Tabitha glanced at him. "And I can tell you already know, but won't admit it, by the way you're blushing." She poked him in the ribs.

"I'm not blushing," he snapped. "Can we drop the subject?"

"Fine." Tabitha held up her hands. "But you better say something to her before someone snatches her away from you."

Briggs pictured Keren laughing, her chestnut hair falling across her face while those dazzling silver eyes melted his heart. Ever since they met in sixth grade, he was hopelessly in love with her. He had done everything in his power to protect her through her wild high school years, and he planned to do everything in his power to protect her now.

He thought of the last time he saw her. It had torn him apart, leaving her at the hospital with Nadria. But he had a job to do, find and stop the Dark Guild. And now that job included helping to prove both Keren's and her mom's innocence.

"Here's Janson's," Tabitha's voice pulled him out of his thoughts.

When they entered the tavern, Briggs' eyes had to adjust to the dim lighting. Music from seventies blared from the jukebox as two shifter couples danced in the middle of the room. Three wolf shifters were playing a game of pool, while five others mingled at cozy circular tables. Tabitha and Briggs approached the bar.

"Janson." Briggs held out his meaty hand to the wolf shifter behind the bar whose hooked nose spoke to his years of working as a bouncer.

"Briggs." Janson took his hand, giving it a brief shake. "Glad you came."

"Anything for a friend. You playing bartender today?" Briggs gave Janson a slap on the arm before releasing his hand. "I thought the boss got to kick back and count the money."

"Well," a worried look passed over Janson's face, "with everything going on, I'm having a hard time keeping my staff. No one wants to work at a shifter-owned business after dark." His demeanor brightened as his eyes shifted to Tabitha. "And who's your partner in crime?"

"This is Tabitha. Tabitha, this is my good buddy Janson."

Tabitha smiled, nodding her head. "Pleased to meet you."

"Likewise." His eyes checked her out. "I just wish it was under different circumstances."

After giving him a wry smile, she asked, "Who reported the human activity?"

Briggs had worked with Tabitha long enough to know she let friendly flirting pass without comment. Only when guys became insistent did she start breaking bones.

Janson motioned with his head. "The guys at the pool table. I overheard them talking and thought I'd call Briggs."

"Alright." Tabitha tapped her hand twice on the bar. "I'm going over to have a chat." She left Briggs and Janson alone.

Briggs set his elbows on the bar. "Hey Janson, does your brother Shawn still work at that defense law office?"

Janson started drying glasses. "You bet. He's making pretty good money. What you did for him changed his life."

"He was a good kid in the wrong place at the wrong time."

"Yeah." Janson set the towel down and pointed at Briggs. "But you cared enough to notice and save him from a life of being shuffled in and out of prison." Tears welled in his eyes.

"Like I said, he's a good kid." Briggs leaned forward, talking in a hushed tone. "Janson, I need a favor."

"Sure, what is it?" Janson frowned, matching Brigg's tone.

"Can I have a pen and paper?"

Janson shuffled around under the bar, finding a pen but no paper, so he tore a sheet from his order pad. "Here you go."

"Would you give Shawn this information and ask him to call Keren Stewart as soon as possible? She and her mom are in serious legal trouble and are short on cash. Tell him to send any bills to me." Briggs wrote Keren's contact information, then slid the paper back to Janson. "I need any connection between Keren and me to be confidential." He stared

Janson in the eyes, knowing he would pick up on the meaning. Briggs

could lose his job, or go to jail, for trying to help someone accused of being

an arcanum.

Janson nodded. "Yeah. Sure thing." After looking at the paper, he folded

it in half then put it in his pocket. "No problem."

Before Briggs could thank him, an energy blast crashed through the front

window.

His reflexes had him sailing over the bar, tackling Janson to the ground.

Alcohol and shattered glass rained down on them.

"Stay down," Briggs ordered. While crouched, he made his way to the

end of the bar. He grabbed his radio, calling into dispatch. "I need backup

at Janson's bar on South Court Avenue. Sorcerer attack in progress."

Another blast flew into the building, exploding on the jukebox. Briggs

shielded his face from the flying metal fragments while trying to scan the

room, searching for Tabitha. He spotted her hunkered down behind the

pool table. One of the wolf shifters crouched with her. The other two lay

lifeless on the ground. The impact of the blast had torn off the arm of one

and half the face of the other.

The blasts now came in rapid succession, causing smoke and debris to

fill the room. Briggs used the army crawl to make his way over to Tabitha.

Blood flowed down the side of her face from a deep cut above her eye.

"I've called for backup," Briggs shouted over the explosions.

Tabitha nodded, then tapped on his arm, pointing to the door. Two sorcerers stepped over the rubble into the tavern. The one in back continued the rapid energy blast fire while the one in front focused on blasting the heads off any shifters they found.

A fireball shot out from behind the bar.

Briggs' heart pounded. He had told Janson to stay down. The front sorcerer threw up his hands, creating a shield right before impact. The fireball disintegrated when it struck the shield. Now, the sorcerers focused on Janson's location.

"I have to save Janson," Briggs said to Tabitha. "Cover me." He reached into his belt, pulling out two gold disks, attaching one to each palm.

She nodded, then pressed her hands onto the floor, letting out a guttural yell. Tree roots shot up from the floor like giant hands. The front sorcerer cast their shield spell, but not in time to save them both. Roots wrapped themselves around the rapid-fire sorcerer, binding his arms to his sides.

"One down, one to go," said Briggs, as he raced forward. When the sorcerer dropped his shield to shoot, Briggs leaped onto the bar, then sprung to the wall behind the bar. While using the wall as a springboard, he dive-rolled over the energy blast.

When his shoulder hit the ground, he directed roots to weave together, blocking the next blast. As the roots shattered into pieces, he jumped, clinging to the ceiling rafters over the arcanum's head. The arcanum had a confused look on his face. He clearly hadn't seen Briggs move.

With an immense push, Briggs propelled himself in a back arch from the rafters, extending his hands toward the arcanum's wrists. As Briggs' hands closed around their target, gold cuffs snapped in place, halting the arcanum's ability to wield magic. Briggs heard the arcanum's ribs crack as his full weight crashed down on him.

Sirens blared outside. With a moan, Briggs lifted himself off the arcanum. He coughed, trying to clear the smoke from his lungs. Then he remembered Janson.

"Janson," shouted Briggs. "Are you OK? Where are you?" He ran to the bar, hopping on top. He saw Janson crouched down with his hands over his head. Blood dripped from several wounds made by the broken glass. He looked up at Briggs, his face pale and eyes wide.

"Is it over?"

Briggs jumped behind the bar. "Yeah, it's over." He held out a hand, helping Janson to his feet.

"I couldn't just sit here and let them kill everyone." He reached under the bar, pulling out a beer. "You want one?" He offered the bottle to Briggs.

"No, but next time when I say stay down. Stay. Down."

"Hey," Tabitha ran up, "are you guys alright?"

"We're fine." Briggs clapped Janson on the back. Then he looked around at the bodies. His nostrils flared as he ground his teeth. More senseless deaths.

Brigg's squad flooded into the tavern. When Office Jordon spotted Briggs, he ran over.

"Captain, what happened?"

"Janson's tavern was attacked by these two arcanum." Briggs pointed at the man being held by the roots and the one in handcuffs on the floor. "At least this time we caught the assailants." This might get the Chief Inquisitor off his back for a while.

Medics came in behind the inquisitors, pulling the deceased shifters from the wreckage. A shout came from the corner by the pool table.

"I have one alive." Two medics scrambled in that direction.

Briggs looked at Tabitha. Her eye had swollen shut. "You need to get that looked at."

She nodded. "How about you drive me to the hospital? The car's only a few blocks away and you look like you need a break."

Briggs watched his squad move with practiced precision. They could handle this without him. "Deal." He turned to Officer Jordon. "Jordon, I'm leaving you in charge."

"Yes, Captain," he responded.

CHAPTER FIFTEEN

KEREN

Ordell borrowed his dad's white 1997 Ford Ranger. They squeezed into the single bench seat. Nadria sat in the middle, her legs cramped against the gearshift. A torrential downpour escorted them most of the way to Dan's house. Typical of Florida's weather, the brief afternoon shower left behind sticky, humid air.

Keren pointed out the windshield. "That's the house."

The chipped paint and unkempt hedges of the two-story beige house matched the rest of the neighborhood. One of the front downstairs windows had been boarded up. Beater cars sat in front of every third or fourth house.

She shifted in her seat. Something told her they shouldn't be here. As she reached over to push down the manual lock, Three appeared in the truck bed.

Ordell slowed down.

"Don't park in front of his house." Nadria pointed at a house across the street and a few doors down. An old-fashioned sprinkler, the type that had a metal arch that oscillated from side to side, watered the weed-infested lawn. The owner must have been oblivious to the rainstorm minutes before. "Park by that house."

Ordell drove past Dan's house, banging a U-turn at the next intersection. The truck made a grinding noise as he forced it into second gear. They all winced at the sound.

Keren looked up and down the street. The noise had caught the attention of a couple of guys standing on the street corner. Their tank tops showed off arms with muscles that only came from hours in the gym.

Her first instinct told her to have Ordell keep driving and leave the neighborhood. But given his stubborn streak, she didn't think he'd listen to her, anyway.

They weren't private detectives, and the thought of getting caught, or worse, made her heart pound. She considered calling Briggs. But what did she expect him to do? Help them break into Dan's house? She was letting her nerves get the best of her. This was their best chance to find out what happened to Broden.

Ordell set the parking brake. "Sorry."

"I don't like this." Nadria slouched in the seat. Her voice quivered. "We shouldn't be here."

Ordell reached behind the seat, pulling out a worn blanket. "Cover up with this."

They helped Nadria drape the blanket around her, leaving her worried face peering out through a small hole. He put his arm around her shivering body, pulling her close.

"You'll be alright."

Keren wasn't so sure. A shifter and a puca could turn heads in the wrong neighborhood. She hadn't thought about that. What else hadn't she thought about before masterminding this scheme?

Movement drew her attention to Dan's house. Someone stepped out the door. She grabbed Dan's picture, holding it up. He could be the same guy. It was hard to tell at this distance.

Ordell snatched the picture from her hand. His face pressed against the side window. "That's him." He reached for the door handle.

Keren lunged across the truck, grabbing his arm. "Wait! You can't let him spot you."

"I need to talk to that creep." He tugged at Keren's grip.

"Please, no," Nadria's small voice emanated from the blanket. "We're not supposed to confront him."

He relaxed his grip on the door handle. He peeked into the blanket's opening. His ears flicked back and forth. "I won't let anything happen to you."

A bold promise. Keren watched Dan turn the corner at the end of the street and disappear from view. A prickly sensation crawled in her skin. Something seemed off.

Ordell looked up and down the street. "Did you see where he went?"

"He just turned the corner." Her mouth became dry. They should leave now while they had the chance.

"Let's go." Ordell stepped out of the truck.

"Nadria can't go." Keren glared into Ordell's eyes. "Can't you tell she's scared?"

"She can stay in the truck." He looked at Nadria. His tone softened. "Lie down on the seat and lock the doors."

Something tugged at the back of Keren's mind that Nadria shouldn't stay alone in the truck. But she shouldn't let Ordell go into the house alone either. "How do you know someone else isn't inside?"

"That's what I plan to find out." He pushed the lock down and slammed the door.

Keren watched him trot across the street. The hair on the back of her neck stood up.

"You can't let him go alone. I'll be fine here." Nadria curled up on the seat.

"We'll be right back. Call if you need us." She got out of the truck, locking the door behind her.

While glancing at Three in the truck bed, she thought about earlier when Ordell saw Four at the café and then Two at his house. What if her imaginary friends were real?

Keren jumped, hearing a loud bang come from the direction of Dan's house.

She ran across the street to Dan's house, keeping her voice low. "Ordell, where are you?" More banging drew her attention to the line of trash cans against the house. Two of them were on the ground with their contents spilled. She noticed a black cat step away from the mess. "What are you doing?"

Ordell changed back into his human form. While wiping grime off his hands, he pointed to a window. "I tried to jump to that windowsill, but I slipped."

"We have to be quiet." She motioned for him to follow her around back. The backyard's overgrown shrubbery and yard clutter provided decent cover. "Let's see if we can get in the back door." She tiptoed up the creaky wooden steps.

"Stand aside." Ordell held a large rock. "I'll get us in." He pulled his arm back, preparing to throw the rock.

"No," Keren stepped in front of him, raising her hands to block the throw. "Too noisy. What if there's an alarm set?" Ordell gave her that *yeah right* face. She agreed. Odds were, no houses in this neighborhood had alarm systems.

"Then how do you propose we get in?" Ordell lowered the rock.

Keren walked up to the dilapidated door. She turned the handle and pushed. The door stuck at first, but then cracked open. While looking back at Ordell, she raised her eyebrows.

After letting out a huff, he dropped the rock. They both stepped into the kitchen, closing the door behind them. Stale pizza and tacos assaulted her nose. A pile of dirty dishes, looking long forgotten, sat in the sink. Their shoes stuck to the floor, causing suction cup noises as they walked through the room.

She turned the corner, entering the living room. Grungy carpet covered the floor. The faint light allowed through the windows by heavy curtains made hard to tell if the color was green or gray, and she didn't want to know what that large black stain was. While looking across the room, her mouth dropped open. She couldn't believe her eyes.

A banner with a black-rimmed circle containing two lightning bolts crossing over one another hung on the wall. Beneath the circle were the words 'Dark Guild - Masters of Magic.'

A knot tightened in her stomach. She couldn't believe it. Dan was an arcanum of the Dark Guild. Was he the one who attacked Mom? Her mind raced. She hadn't suspected Broden's disappearance and Mom's attack might be linked.

Her eyes wandered around the room. Newspaper clippings and pictures covered the far wall. As she walked over to get a closer look, her stomach turned. These were documented acts of violence against shifters. Some pictures were of shifters who looked unconscious - she gulped - or dead. They were lying on the ground, battered and beaten. Others kneeled on the ground with their hands behind their heads.

She jumped when Ordell put his hand on her shoulder. "This is really gross." He focused on getting some black goop off his shoe and hadn't noticed the pictures on the wall. "I'm going upstairs to search for Broden."

"No," she whispered. "There might be someone up there. The door was unlocked."

In a booming voice, Ordell shouted, "Hello, anyone here?"

"Are you crazy?" she spat out in a whisper. Her eyes darted to the stairs, waiting for an angry homeowner to stomp down, finding them snooping around. She loved Ordell, but his reckless side wasn't doing them any favors.

After a few moments of silence, Ordell shrugged. "I guess we're alone." He started up the stairs.

While taking deep breaths to calm her pounding heard, Keren turned back to the newspaper clipping wall. She scanned the articles, seeing they were about arcanum activity in the city. Bile pushed up her throat. How could anyone be this vicious toward another living being?

She froze when her eyes locked on a picture of Broden sitting at a table handing out buttons and pamphlets, a red X drawn over the picture. Her shaking hand reached for the picture. After tugging it off the wall, she headed upstairs to find Ordell. She found him sitting at a laptop in a tiny bedroom that smelled like dirty, wet socks.

He noticed her come in. "I found something, Keren. There are all kinds of emails talking about group meetings. His calendar has all the information we need to find this group."

Keren felt a prickle on her neck. This picture would break Ordell's heart. She considered hiding it until they were back at home. No, he needed to know. After walking up to him, she placed a hand on his shoulder. "I found something, too." She slipped Broden's picture onto the desk.

He stared at it for a moment, then felt his muscles tense. His head jerked up to face her, and she saw his eyes welled up with tears. "What does this mean?" His voice sounded hysterical. "What happened to Broden?"

Keren squeezed his shoulder. "I..." Before she finished, Three appeared next to her. Startled, Keren gave a little squeak, jumping back. Three met Keren's eyes, then pointed out the window. She gasped, "Nadria."

Rushing to the window, she saw the two guys from the end of the street, jumping on the truck bed and yelling at the cab. The pictures from downstairs flashed in her mind. She wouldn't let that happen to Nadria.

"Nadria's in trouble. We have to go."

Obviously torn between helping Nadria and digging further into Dan's information, Odell's eyes had a wide, frightened look. "What about the information? We have to find Broden."

They wouldn't get another opportunity for this information. Why not add theft to the list of laws they've broken? "Take the laptop." She pointed to Broden's picture. "And that."

She shot out of the room with Three close behind.

While sprinting out the front door, she shouted at the guys. "Hey! Get away from that truck." She skidded to a stop in the middle of the street.

The guys stopped jumping. They glanced at each other, then hopped out of the truck bed. The one with a baseball cap spoke, "Who's gonna make us, little girl?"

OK, not the brightest move. She choked down the lump in her throat.

Ball Cap sauntered closer. "That's what I thought." He motioned to the truck. "You can have the truck. My friend gets the shifter trash." He moved his eyes up and down Keren's body. She shivered. The scrutiny made her feel dirty. "I get you." He rushed at her.

Not good. Getting manhandled was not on her agenda today. She crouched. Memories of tag with her imaginary friends sparked to life. "Let's see what you've got."

She surprised Ball Cap by shifting out of the way. He stumbled past her. She took her opportunity, kicking him in the back. The kick, his forward momentum, and wet asphalt caused him to sprawl face down on the street.

Ball Cap's buddy pulled a knife and ran at Keren. Ducking under his arm, she elbowed him in ribs. She got two lucky shots, but she knew she couldn't hold them off for long.

"You'll pay for this." Ball Cap pulled a knife, wiping his bloody lip with his arm.

It had never occurred to her to bring a weapon. A kitchen knife or even the broom she used on One with would be better than nothing. Loud banging drew her attention to the truck. Nadria's terrified face pressed against the glass. She pointed to Ball Cap's shoes. Keren gave her a slight nod, then backed down the street. Ball Cap's buddy cracked his knuckles. His eyes were fierce, like a wild animal.

He went to move forward, but only his body moved. He dropped the knife as he tried to catch his balance. "What the hell?"

Keren looked at Nadria. Her face scrunched in concentration, staring at the guys' shoes. Looks like sticky-fingers magic is useful for many things.

"Hey, leave her alone." Ordell ran behind Ball Cap, grabbing his shoulder.

Even with his feet stuck to the road, Ball Cap sent a left hook into Ordell's cheek. He dropped like a rock.

By now, people had stepped out of their homes to watch the spectacle. Three bumbling fools who are somewhere they shouldn't be fighting two local thugs. Where's the popcorn vendor?

Both guys stalked toward Keren. Ordell being knocked to the ground must have broken Nadria's concentration. Keren knew she needed to buy time so Nadria could get him back to the truck.

"You're no match for me." Thankfully, her voice didn't betray the terror she harbored.

The men glanced at each other and smirked. Ball Cap tossed the knife from one hand to another. "I like girls with spirit."

Oh, this was getting worse. She glanced at the people standing on their porches. They didn't venture any closer. If someone was going to help her, they would have by now. Nadria had Ordell on his feet. They were almost to the truck. She had to buy more time.

"You're not my type." She hesitated, trying to think of a good comeback. "I prefer men."

Ball Cap's face turned red as a vein popped out on his forehead. Maybe that was too harsh.

"You'll pay for that." They charged at her.

She turned, bolting to the yard with the sprinkler. After making a dive roll, she snatched the hose as she stood. Turning, she swung the sprinkler at the men. It made direct contact with Ball Cap's head. He crashed into his friend. They both slipped and fell onto the wet lawn.

Exhaust fumes came from the truck. As she turned to leave, someone grabbed her foot, pulling it out from under her. She crashed to the ground, mud and wet grass splashing over her.

"I've got you now." Ball Cap grabbed her pant leg, pulling her toward him.

She kicked at his hands, but he held on with an iron grip. He raised the knife, ready to plunge it into her leg.

Time stood still. A pulse of energy ignited in her solar plexus. The pulse crawled through her chest and up her neck, ending at the back of her eyes. A flash blinded her.

When her vision cleared, Four floated over the sodden lawn. Not the misty opaque vision, but a solid, breathing creature. Water spun around its front paws. Time restarted, the knife mere inches from striking her leg. A razor-sharp stream of water knocked it away. Ball Cap screamed, then he cradled his arm. Blood flowed through his shaking fingertips.

Ball Cap's friend faced Four. "What the hell are you?"

He spun, running straight at Keren. Before she could react, a horse's hoof kicked him in the head, knocking him to the ground. Ordell stood next to her in his horse form.

The black stallion whinnied and shook his head, prancing around her. Her two assailants lay on the ground. One unconscious and one clinging to his wounded arm. Keren stepped up to Four. She put her hand on its eel's tail. It felt cool and smooth to the touch.

Its fox eyes looked down at her. After motioning with its paws, the water and mud lifted from her clothes, leaving her perfectly dry. Four turned to mist and dissipated into the air.

"Let's go." Ordell, in his human form, tugged on her arm, pulling her down the street.

Her legs threatened to buckle underneath her, but she gritted her teeth, forcing herself to keep running.

He pushed her into the truck. With gears grinding, they sped down the street. Keren's heart pounded. Had she brought Four to life?

"Oh, my god. Are you alright?" Nadria squeezed her. "I can't believe what just happened."

While taking a deep breath, Keren tried to calm herself. "You were great," she said to Nadria, "you really helped me. Why didn't you call us when those guys showed up?"

Nadria blushed. "I dropped my phone and couldn't find it under the seat. You came out just in time." She squeezed Keren's hand. "Was that one of your imaginary friends?"

Her heart skipped a beat. Four wasn't imaginary, it was real, even if just for a few moments. "I think so." She glanced over at Ordell.

He focused on the road. His cheek trickled blood, and it had already started to swell. Keren only imagined what was going through his head. She motioned her head at Ordell, hinting Nadria should turn around.

After Nadria turned, she let out a gasp. "Are you OK?" She reached her fingers to his cheek, but he jerked away.

Dan's laptop sat on the floorboard. After putting it in her lap, Keren opened it, finding the picture of Broden.

"We found this." She handed the picture to Nadria.

She put her hand to her throat. "What does this mean?"

"We don't know." Even though she feared Broden was in serious trouble, she wanted to give Ordell some hope. "But we have this laptop. We might figure out what happened to him."

Ordell's hands squeezed the steering wheel. "We'll find him." A tear dripped down his cheek.

"We will." Nadria rested her head on his shoulder.

Keren looked out the back window. Satisfied they weren't being followed, she settled into the seat, closing her eyes.

They stayed quiet all the way back to Ordell's house.

CHAPTER SIXTEEN

KEREN

The truck rumbled into the garage as the sun neared the horizon.

Ordell released the steering wheel. He peeled his white-knuckled hands off the steering wheel. "Let's go inside."

Keren followed him and Nadria into the house.

Hearing a booming voice, she couldn't help but cringe. "Is that you, Ordell? Where have you been?"

Ordell winced. "Yeah, Papa. I've been out with Keren and Nadria." He turned to them. "Stay here," he whispered and trotted off to the living room.

"Your mother's been worried sick. Can't you answer your cell phone? And what happened to your face?"

"I'm fine, Papa. It's nothing. The girls are in the kitchen."

Heavy footsteps headed their way. Keren tried to make herself presentable by running her fingers through her hair.

Ordell's dad stomped into the kitchen. He rested his fists on his muffin-top waist. "You girls don't appear in much better shape than Ordell. What have you been up to?"

His drawn face was pale. The dark circles surrounding his eyes showed the stress of dealing with a missing son and losing communication with the other. His horse ears pricked forward. She recognized this meant he was tense and on edge.

Nadria stepped in front of her. "Hi, Papa Murphy. We're fine. Just a scuffle at the café."

His face changed from anger to concern. "Well, I'm glad you're alright." He motioned around the kitchen. "Help yourself if you're hungry." Turning to Ordell, he examined the cut on his cheek. "Clean that up and get some ice on it. I'll go upstairs to let your mother know you're home." He walked out of the kitchen.

Ordell's face reddened. "Sorry about that."

After grabbing a damp towel, Nadria dabbed at his cut. "You can't blame him."

Ordell flinched when Nadria pressed the towel to his face. He dropped his chin to his chest. "I know, I wasn't thinking."

Keren rummaged through a cabinet, pulling out a box of Cheese-Its. "I haven't had these since I was a kid." She stuffed an entire handful in her mouth.

"Ew, gross. Get some manners." Nadria's nose wrinkled.

"What, I'm hungry." Cheese-It bits flew from her mouth.

Nadria shook her head. In a low voice, she asked, "What happens now?"

They found proof Broden's disappearance involved the Dark Guild. Keren shuddered, remembering the explicit pictures of violence against shifters on Dan's wall. But Broden's picture looked different. She hoped they had time to find him before he ended up like them.

The laptop they stole from Dan might help them find Broden and also give her more information to help Mom. Time was running out to find evidence to prove Mom's innocence. The trial was just days away. She picked up the laptop.

"We look at the information on Dan's computer."

"Let's go to the guest room. That'll give us some privacy." Ordell headed toward the stairs. "Let me make sure it's OK with Papa."

Nadria rummaged through the refrigerator, pulling out three water bottles. "I'll bring the food."

After picking up the laptop, Keren walked to the guest room. Polished oak hardwood floors gave the room a warm feeling. A blue daybed with Ishani weave fabric sat against the far wall. She set the laptop on the round, cushioned ottoman in front of the daybed. The faint scent of potpourri drifted in the air. Four appeared over the daybed, back in its opaque state. It flew around the perimeter of the room, settling by the far window.

Nadria brought in a plate of celery, carrots, and hummus, along with the bottled water. Keren's stomach growled. But she hated celery and healthy food.

"Papa said it was OK to use this room." After grabbing the laptop, Ordell sat on the daybed. The girls sat on either side of him.

"So, what did you find out?" Nadria crunched on a carrot.

He flipped the laptop open and within minutes had Dan's calendar open. He stopped scrolling when he reached Sunday. "Look," he opened the detail, "Masters of Magic, Initiative Update, Sunday 9 pm until midnight. No location, though."

"What's the Initiative Update?" Nadria asked, picking up a piece of celery.

Keren's stomach growled again. She picked up her cell phone. "Anyone else up for pizza?" While pulling out her credit card, she hoped the inquisitors hadn't canceled it. "I get double-meat, double-cheese, with extra thick crust."

Nadria squinted at her and chomped on the celery, chewing as loudly as possible.

Without looking up from the laptop, Ordell said, "Yeah, sounds great." He didn't notice Nadria's disapproving glare.

"I'm looking through Dan's browser settings. This guy never cleared his history or cache, and there are loads of sites here." He winced, touching his cheek. "I don't see any sites relating to the Dark Guild." His laugh came out as a snort. "But Dan sure likes his porn."

"Grow up." Nadria swatted his shoulder.

"Can I see his calendar?" Keren held out her hands.

"Sure." He passed the laptop to her. "When is the pizza going to be here? I'm starving." He cradled his face in his hand.

"Let's get you some ice and ibuprofen." Nadria stood. After taking Ordell by the hand, she led him to the kitchen.

While flipping through Dan's calendar, Keren noticed he had regular arcanum meetings on Wednesdays. This progress on the initiative was something special. A crazy idea popped into her head. They could spy on the meeting.

She rolled her eyes. Right, because they were so good at spying. While tipping her head side-to-side, she felt stiffness settling into her neck. The last thing they needed was a repeat of today's fiasco.

Ordell and Nadria came back into the room. Ordell held a mammoth-sized Ziplock bag filled with ice on his face. He sat next to Keren. "You'll have to type."

"Sure, what else are we looking for?" Her hands hovered over the keyboard.

"I found his email account. It's that icon on the right."

Keren clicked the icon. She scrolled through the list. Didn't his guy ever clean up his Inbox? Her fingers froze when she found an email from Broden. She double-clicked to open it.

"Guys, look at this." She leaned back so they could read the contents.

'I've got your number, Dan. If I see you on campus again, I'll turn your arcanum arse into the inquisitors.'

"I didn't think to check Broden's Sent emails." The ice crunched as Ordell's grip tightened on the bag.

Nadria hugged her arms around her waist. "So that's why Dan targeted Broden. He knew Dan was an arcanum."

"Do you think Broden is alive?" Ordell's eyes rimmed with tears.

Nadria grabbed his hand. "Stop. Of course, he is. We'll find him." She looked at Keren. "Won't we?"

Their hopeful eyes stared at her. Surprised, she responded, "Of course. I'm sure he's fine." But she wasn't sure he was fine.

"So, what's the plan?" They both looked over at her.

Keren swallowed the lump in her throat. She almost got them killed today. Now, they wanted her to make the next decision. Why should they trust her?

Relief flooded her body when the doorbell rang. The distraction bought her time to think. "That must be the pizza." She went to answer the door. Her mind drifted to Dan's calendar. The hair on the back of her neck tingled. That initiative update meeting was key to finding answers.

She took the two large pizzas from the delivery man and signed the credit card receipt. After grabbing a slice from one box, she took a big bite. Her idea was crazy and dangerous. But this might be their one opportunity to find Broden and get information on the Dark Guild. She walked back to the guest room, putting the pizza on the ottoman. She returned to her seat next to Ordell and pointed to the pizza.

Ordell shook his head. Apparently, he'd lost his appetite.

After eating two more slices, her stomach felt better. She wasn't able to wait any longer to let them know what she thought. "I'm guessing we need to know what's going on in Sunday's meeting."

A spark shone in Ordell's eyes.

Nadria frowned. "There's no address or information on where the meeting is."

"No." Keren braced for the explosion. "But Dan knows."

"What?" Nadria shot to her feet. "After what happened today, you want to follow Dan?"

Keren saw her eyes change from fury to fear. Nadria faced the most danger this afternoon. The pictures on Dan's wall told the story of what might have happened to her.

"I'm saying Ordell and me." Keren pursed her lips. "It's too dangerous for you, Nadria." She took another slice of pizza.

Nadria paced the floor, wringing her hands. "But I want to help."

"You will." Keren chewed and swallowed the pizza in her mouth. "You'll keep in contact by phone. If something happens, you can call for help."

Nadria chewed the inside of her cheek. "That's not a terrible idea."

Ordell chimed in. "I think it's a great idea. We'll know someone has our back." He scooted to the edge of the couch. "Once we find the location, we can bust in and search for Broden."

"No." Both Keren and Nadria said in tandem.

"Broden is in trouble. He might have something to do with this initiative update." His voice quivered. "Maybe they'll be torturing him at this meeting."

"You're letting your imagination get the better of you." Nadria sat beside him.

Keren nodded. "Us charging into a situation we don't understand will turn out like today." She pointed to his cheek. "Or worse."

He huffed but said nothing else.

"We'll follow Dan tomorrow night. We don't know where he's going, so we should show up early." The neighbors will recognize the white truck. "Nadria, can we use your car?"

Nadria had haggled a good price for her red, used Prius. She kept it clean and well-maintained. The shock on Nadria's face made her believe she'd protest. Then Nadria looked at Ordell, and her features softened.

"Sure, but only if Keren drives."

"What? I'm an excellent driver," said Ordell.

Nadria glared at him.

"Fine." He slouched back on the daybed.

Ordell was her wild card. Would he stick with the plan or act on his own again? She couldn't go alone. That was crazy.

"Don't you have your date with Quinlin tomorrow?" Nadria asked.

Crap, she had forgotten about the date. She could cancel. But he was her link to seeing Mom. You don't get a second date if you cancel the first.

"It's a lunch date. I should make it back here in plenty of time. Can I use your car in the morning too? I want to pick up some clothes at the store."

She nodded. "That's fine. I'm off tomorrow."

"When do we leave?" Ordell bounced in his seat, eager to take action.

Again, their expectant eyes stared at her. She rubbed the back of her neck. This new leadership role fit her like a too-tight pair of jeans. She picked up the laptop.

"It says here Dan has a doctor's appointment Monday at 8 am. That tells us the meeting must be local." She looked up at Ordell and Nadria. They nodded in unison. It was cute, but they offered no comments. "So, I'd say local is within a two-hour drive?" More nodding.

Alright, she had to get the timing right. Sitting in the car for too long in that neighborhood was dangerous. Dan could meet up with someone, or carpool to the location. Heck, he might spend the entire day out of town. If she got this wrong, they'd miss their opportunity. "Let's say 7 pm."

Keren blinked her eyes open. She lay tangled in a mass of blankets on the floor next to Nadria. Light peeked through the blinds. Her cell phone clock showed 8 am. They had stayed awake until after 3 am last night. At some point, they had crashed at Ordell's.

Tight muscles complained when she moved. Between yesterday's thug encounter and sleeping on the floor, she felt as though she aged ten years overnight. After finding an escape route from the blankets, she grabbed her backpack and took Nadria's car key off the chain. She tiptoed to the door.

Before sneaking out of the room, she glanced back at her best friend. Keren remembered the sleepover Nadria had hosted on Keren's twelfth birthday. Nadria had infused decorations with magic. They danced to the beat of whatever music played.

One other girl came to the party. She was interracial between shifter and human. The girl's mom was the only one, except for Keren's, who allowed their daughter to hang out with Nadria. Kids at school treated her as an outcast, something beneath them.

Through it all, Nadria held her head high and survived the racist remarks, even though Keren knew they tore her apart. Nadria grew up to be an advocate for magical races' equal rights. Yes, Nadria was cautious, but brave beyond anyone else she knew.

Light snoring came from the daybed. Ordell lay sprawled on his back. One arm and leg hung over the edge. The swelling on his face looked better. The ice bags and ibuprofen Nadria insisted on had done their job.

They had met Ordell in high school. As one of the few pucas at the school, and because of his short stature, he had endured harsh bullying. Keren had believed that was the reason he joined Nadria's equality group. But after yesterday, she realized Ordell had joined to be closer to Nadria.

As kids, Broden had stood up for Ordell on multiple occasions. Maybe that was why Broden took it upon himself to protect the other kids at school from people like Dan.

She stepped out of the room, ensuring the door didn't make a noise when she closed it behind her. While walking through the kitchen, she grabbed a piece of leftover pizza.

After getting in the car, she pulled out her phone. Maybe the hospital had an update on Mom's condition. She dialed, hoping she could get a hold of Dr. Niles.

"Orlando Regional, how may I help you?"

"I'm looking for Dr. Niles. Is he available?" She crossed her fingers.

"One moment, please." Keys clicked in the background. "I'm sorry, he's off today."

Crap, now what do I do? "I'm looking for an update on Olivia Stewart's condition."

"One moment." More clicking. "I'm sorry, I'm unable to release that information."

She sighed. "But I'm her daughter."

"I'm sorry, I can't help you with information on Ms. Stewart. Is there anything else I can do for you?"

"No, thank you." She hung up.

Keren screamed, pounding her hand on the steering wheel. Why did things have to be so hard? She opened her contacts. Her thumb hovered over Briggs' name. Would he get in trouble for talking to her? She bit her lower lip, pushing the call button.

Briggs answered in a flat, distracted tone. "Captain Briggs."

"Hey, it's me."

"Keren," his voice softened, "how are you doing? Are you alright?"

Just hearing his voice brought tears to her eyes. So much has happened over the last couple of days. She felt overwhelmed.

"I need to know how Mom's doing. The hospital won't tell me."

"Hold on a minute."

He must have put the phone on mute since she heard nothing. When he came back on the line, she heard street noises.

"I'm back. I had to step outside. But I've only got a minute. Your mom is doing better." His voice lowered. "She's more lucid."

Tears rolled down Keren's cheeks. "Really, that's great news."

"Have you thought about a lawyer?"

A chill ran down her spine. "No, I haven't had time."

"I have a friend of a friend, he'll contact you. Just keep this between us."

"But I don't have the money to hire a lawyer."

"Don't worry about it. He's paying back a favor."

She sniffed, wiping her face with her hand. "Thank you."

"OK, hang in there. We'll get through this. I've got to go. Talk to you later."

"Bye." She hung up.

After turning on the ignition, she drove to the premium outlet mall. She had to get Quinlin to help her see Mom.

CHAPTER SEVENTEEN

KEREN

As Keren pumped gas into Nadria's car, she felt relieved her credit card continued to work. She glanced in the backseat at the pile of packages. That purchase nearly put her card over the limit, but she needed to make an impression on Quinlin. Her torn jeans and T-shirt wouldn't do. She needed something with a little more punch. After checking her phone, she figured she had just enough time to change and get over to the Osprey.

At Nadria's, she took a quick shower. After styling her hair in long, loose curls, she slipped into the dress she had purchased. It was a light blue scoop-neck with plenty of visual cleavage and ruching at each side. The just-above-the-knee length made it sexy but respectable, and the cotton and spandex mix fabric flattered her figure. It had been a while since she treated herself to a pedicure, so she purchased closed-toe beige pumps. Some guys had foot fetishes, and she wasn't taking any chances.

After walking out the door, she took slow, deliberate steps toward the car. High heel walking should be an Olympic event.

She made it halfway to the car when she heard someone call out.

"Hey, cutie. You wanna take a ride?"

Keren turned, pivoting on her toes for balance. A man in flip-flops holding a frozen fountain drink walked toward her.

"I saw you take your time struttin' by me." He stopped in front of her, reaching his free hand out. "I'm all yours."

Her stomach did a back flip. She stepped back. Her foot landed on an angle, and her ankle collapsed.

The guy grabbed her arm, keeping her from hitting the asphalt. "Whoa, hey. I said you've got me." His eyes locked on her breasts. "My truck is across the street." A filthy grin spread over his face.

After regaining her balance, Keren tried pulling free. She looked around the parking lot, but no one else was around.

His fingers squeezed tighter. "You're not changin' your mind, are ya?"

Her heart pounded. These crazy shoes. She could ditch them and run. But first, she'd need to get free of this jerk. And what shoes would she wear to her date? Barefoot wasn't an option. She gritted her teeth. Guys like him thought they had a right to push women around. She'd show him how wrong he was.

While smiling, she stepped closer. She pushed her breasts up as if caught in the tractor beams of his eyes. Then, with all her strength, she drove the heel of her shoe into his foot.

The guy screamed in pain, losing his grip on her arm. After jerking his foot back, his drink hand flew forward, spilling it down the front of her dress.

Shocked from the cold and mortified he ruined her new dress, Keren stood there with her mouth hanging open.

The guy's face tightened into a snarl. He jerked forward, then paused, not sure what to do.

Not wanting to be there when he decided, she ran on her tiptoes to the car. Better to look ridiculous than risk spraining an ankle. Once in the car, she locked the doors.

The guy glared at her, throwing his empty cup on the ground. He turned and walked away. She watched him until he crossed the street.

Her eyes went back to the cup. She got out of the car, tiptoe-running to the cup. Bending to pick it up made the wet, cold fabric press tighter against her skin. On her way back to the car, she tossed the cup in the trash.

Keren checked her phone. Even if she had enough time to change and make it to the Osprey by 1 pm, which she didn't, she had nothing to change into. Nadria's wardrobe resembled hers, jeans and T-shirts. She touched the front of her dress. The frozen drink ruined it. What was worse on a first date, showing up with a frozen drink stain and a funny story, or being late and risking your date thinking you stood him up? She drove to the

restaurant.

CHAPTER EIGHTEEN

QUINLIN

Quinlin tapped on his menu. He chose a seat by the window so he had an unobstructed view when Keren arrived. The Osprey was one of his favorite restaurants. The modern design and high ceiling gave the place a homey but up-class feeling. He looked outside at his new model BMW. Witnesses who saw his car at that woman's house had forced him to discard his previous model.

He arrived early, a habit he learned from Uncle Rob. *'If you're on time, you're late.'* All Quinlin's habits and behaviors stemmed from Uncle Rob. He felt grateful he had such a powerful role model in his life.

Uncle Rob, his mom's brother, moved in with them after Father's murder. Quinlin's young age prevented him from taking over his father's role as Dark Guild leader. So, Uncle Rob acted as regent on his behalf until his eighteenth birthday.

While running the Guild with a stern hand, Uncle Rob recruited only the strongest sorcerers. Like-minded humans were taken into the lower arcanum ranks. The arcanum trained for the day Quinlin assumed his role and led the Dark Guild in completing Father's vision.

Quinlin's homeschooling comprised not only customary academic courses but intense devotion to developing his magic skills. Because of Uncle Rob's high standards, he allowed nothing short of perfection.

Personal grooming, clothing choices, and even his choice of friends required approval. Life had a plan and a schedule. Once he was of age, Quinlin's life partner would be chosen from the top ranks of the arcanum.

Growing up, he had never challenged the rules. The duty and urgency for fulfilling Father's dream of sorcerers controlling elemental magic had resonated in every lesson.

A red Prius pulled into the parking lot. Keren stepped out. Although only able to see her back, he noticed she took the time to dress for the occasion. This was a mark in her favor since most women wore jeans for everything. When she turned and started up the walk, he scowled. The front of her dress had a large red stain.

She hobbled on the high heels as if it were the first time she had worn them. Women should be seductive and intriguing, not sloppy, staggering messes.

After she entered, he waved her over to the table. He stood, moving to her chair.

"Hi, Keren."

She looked stunned as he pulled the chair out for her. What ever happened to learning proper etiquette?

"Hi." She glanced at the chair. "Thanks." She sat, and he helped her scoot to the table.

After taking his seat, he placed his napkin on his lap. Equal edges fell to each side of his legs.

"Thank you for coming." He kept eye contact. "How's your day been so far?"

She looked at her dress. "I had a run-in with a jerk and a frozen drink." After looking back into his eyes, she smiled. "I thought showing up with a stained dress was better than being late."

He gave her points for punctuality. "Don't worry about it." He smiled. "Perhaps you'll start a new trend."

She laughed. It appeared they were off to a good start. He handed her the menu.

"I recommend the lemon ricotta pancakes. We can start out with the smoked salmon board."

Keren opened the menu. She stared at one spot for a minute, then closed it again.

"That sounds great."

Maybe she was distracted by thoughts of that woman.

"So, any word about your aunt?"

She fidgeted in her seat. "They won't let me visit her. I called to get an update on her condition. They said she was conscious."

Quinlin's stomach dropped. Conscious? That was unexpected. He had hit her with a powerful magic blast that she should never have lived through, let alone be conscious.

"Wow, that's great. Have you spoken to her?"

"No, not yet." She acted nervous.

The server came over to the table. "May I take your order?" She smiled at them, then focused on Quinlin.

"We'll take two of the lemon ricotta pancakes and the smoked salmon board as a starter."

"Very good, sir." She wrote on her order pad. "Would you like something to drink other than water?"

"Water is fine for me." He looked at Keren. Not every woman appreciated the man ordering for them. He waited to see her reaction.

"Me too." She flashed a smile.

"I'll get that out to you right away." The server left their table.

He wanted to push a few of her buttons. "You know she's accused of a magic crime, right?" By the frown on her face, he guessed she was aware of the charges.

Recovering her expression, Keren became defensive. "She'd never commit a crime like that. She's a victim of a terrible attack." Then she stopped, catching her breath. "It's imperative I talk to my aunt. She might tell me who did this to her."

Yes, she might. And he couldn't allow her to tell anyone. Quinlin's face remained expressionless. Another learned behavior from Uncle Rob. When he didn't respond, she continued.

"I realize we just met, but I have to ask a favor. Can you get me in to see her?" A pleading look showed in her sparkling silver eyes.

"If you were immediate family, they might let you in to see her." He wondered how long she planned to keep up the pretense.

"Trust me, they won't," she spat the words out. Anger flashed in her eyes, then left in a moment. A less astute person wouldn't have noticed.

Given time, he'd be able to weasel the truth out of her. But time wasn't on his side, and he already knew she was that woman's daughter. At this moment, she might be talking to an inquisitor. He had no choice but to get rid of them both. That was the safest route.

"I'd lose my job." He didn't want to sound too eager to get them in the same room to deliver the final blow. Keren needed to think she convinced him to help her.

"I know we just met, but you seem to be a nice guy."

She gave him the smile that lit up a room. Warmth flooded his body.

"I need to talk to my aunt. Even for just a couple of minutes." She actually batted her eyes. "Please."

This girl needed flirting lessons. It took all his energy not to burst out laughing. He had enough. "Well, it's against my better judgment," he paused for effect, "but OK, for just a few minutes."

Her face lit up. "Thank you. When can we go?"

The sooner he took care of this problem, the better. "Let's go right now."

"Perfect." She popped out of her chair. "Let's go."

Quinlin raised a hand. "Server, we'll take our lunch to go, please."

CHAPTER NINETEEN

KEREN

Following behind Quinlin's car, Keren couldn't stop smiling. She thought convincing him to help her see Mom would be harder. Who knew batting your eyes worked? She'd keep that one in her repertoire.

The aroma coming from the to-go bag made her mouth water. Reaching into the bag, she pulled out a ricotta pancake and bit into it, enjoying the tangy taste on her tongue. She'd pass on the smoked salmon.

This seemed like a good time to check in with Nadria and Ordell. She pulled her phone out, seeing several missed calls from Nadria. Her stomach was tied in knots. She'd forgotten she put it on do not disturb during lunch.

"Where are you?" Nadria's voice was frantic. "I've been trying to reach you for over an hour."

"I'm heading to the hospital to visit Mom." Keren frowned. "What's wrong?"

"It's Ordell... No, you're not leaving. I've got her right here. He wants to go to Dan's house right now, by himself."

Keren rolled her eyes. "I thought we had a plan.' She pounded her fist on the steering wheel. "He agreed to the plan. Put him on the phone." She heard muffled voices, then Ordell's.

"Tell Nadria I'm not a prisoner."

"Ordell, wait. Stop. Take a breath. What are you doing?"

"I'm finding my brother. Dan has him, and I'm going to get him."

Keren heard Nadria's voice in the background but couldn't make out what she said. "No, Ordell. We were in the house. Your brother wasn't there. Remember, we have a plan."

"A stupid wait, watch, and do nothing plan. I need action." Ordell sounded like he was wrestling with Nadria. "Get away from the door."

"Ordell, you'll get yourself killed. Please, wait for me. I promise we'll find Broden."

The wrestling noises stopped. "We can't wait. He needs me now."

Keren took a deep breath. She understood where Ordell's feelings. Wasn't she being reckless, having almost a complete stranger sneak her into Mom's room? "I get it," she sighed, "but you're not any good to him dead or injured."

"And I'm no good to my brother hanging around here until 7 pm. Where are you, anyway?"

"I'm going to visit my mom." In reality, she was going to sneak into the Restricted Ward with an almost stranger and risk being arrested to see her mom. Minor details he didn't need to know. "I found out this morning that she's conscious."

Ordell repeated what Keren said, guessing it was for Nadria's benefit. "That good news." He sounded calmer.

"I'll be right over after I'm done. Please, wait for me." Her heart skipped a beat during the long pause. She didn't want to choose between seeing Mom and being with Ordell.

"Fine, yeah. But I'm leaving at 7 pm with or without you."

She let out a sigh of relief. "Thanks, Ordell." A tingle in her spine told her he still might strike out on his own. "Can I talk to Nadria?"

"Hey, fantastic news about your mom." Nadria sounded tired. "The inquisitors are letting you in to see her?"

She had already told Nadria about the restriction put on mom's visitations. If she told her the truth now, how would she explain the difference between her actions and Ordell's scheme to find Broden on his own?

"Yeah, they agreed to let me see her." She grimaced. Her chest tightened from the lie she told to her best friend. These last few days were filled with lies and secret plans. But what else could she do? "I'm pulling into the hospital now, so I've got to go."

"Give her my love." Nadria lowered her voice. "I'll let you know if things get bad again."

"I will and thanks." Keren hung up, taking a deep breath. Nadria would forgive her for the deception. She parked next to Quinlin. He'd selected a secluded place in the parking lot covered by overgrown trees. Stuffing the car keys into the glove box, she left everything but her phone in the car.

Before she could get out, he trotted around to her door and opened it. She could get used to this treatment. Pursing her lips, she chided herself. No, he's getting you in to see Mom. A relationship right now was impossible. She had other serious problems to focus on. Broden being one of them.

Quinlin opened the door, offering his hand. "The trees block some security cameras in this area."

Why would a new nurses' assistant know that? Sliding her hand into his, warmth radiated through her body. "Thanks." She thought it best not to ask about the cameras. She didn't want him changing his mind. One's misty body appeared, circling over Quinlin's head.

He looked up with a puzzled look on his face. "What are you looking at?"

"Nothing." Her neck felt hot. She ran her hands down her dress, smoothing it out and pulling it down since it rode up while driving.

Quinlin scrutinized her eyes as if he could read her mind. Then, giving her a quick smile, he started toward the hospital.

"This way."

CHAPTER TWENTY

QUINLIN

S omething about Keren fascinated Quinlin. He suspected under the innocent girl facade lurked something intriguing.

He stopped outside the entrance door, turning to face her. "Stay close and keep your head down." After she dropped her chin, he pulled her hair around her face, letting his hands linger on the soft tresses. A natural, almost wild scent filled his nostrils. He shook his head to clear his thoughts. "We're going to the maintenance workers' locker rooms. There's less foot traffic there."

While hurrying down the corridors, she followed his instructions. The warmth of her body enveloped him as she walked as close as possible without stumbling over him.

He opened the women's locker room door, ushering her in. "Wait here." He trotted up and down the aisles. No one else was in the room.

She stared over his head again. He followed her gaze. "What are you looking at?"

Her face reddened. "Nothing. Just thinking."

Such a distasteful habit that Uncle Rob would have never allowed. But it didn't matter. In a few minutes, Keren and her nasty habit along with that woman would no longer be a problem. A part of him lamented losing the opportunity to weasel out Keren's secrets.

"You need something to tie back your hair, scrubs, and shoes. I'm going to change, then wait for you in the corridor."

She looked around the room. "Just take someone's stuff?"

"Yes." He stared into her worried eyes.

She looked hesitant, so he waited to leave until she began opening lockers.

Five minutes later, he paced in front of the women's locker room, wondering what was taking her so long. Cracking open the door, he peeked inside the room. "Are you done?"

"Yes." She stepped into the corridor. Oversized scrubs hung off her slender frame. "The shoes are too big." After slipping a foot out, she placed it alongside the shoe to emphasize the size difference.

"You'll have to make do."

She slid her foot back into the shoe, then held out the stained blue dress. "What should I do with this?"

While pointing to the trash, he said, "Throw it away. Push it under the other trash."

She looked at the dress, rubbing her fingers along the fabric. "The stain might come out in the wash."

Someone could have seen her walking with him. He couldn't risk the dress being found in the locker room. While crossing his arms over his chest, he said, "It has to go."

She sighed, then followed his instructions.

He noticed she had her phone in her hand. "Put that away. They don't allow employees to use their phone while on duty."

She slipped the phone into her pocket. "How's my hair?"

She rotated, showing him her back. The neat bun looked like she had spent hours fussing with her hair. Her chin turned over her shoulder, allowing her to peek at him out of the corner of her eye. He caught that wild scent again and felt his heart pound in his chest.

While clearing his throat, he tugged at his scrubs' top. "Good."

He'd brought two clipboards from his locker. They had random patient papers attached. "Take this." He handed one to Keren. "Act as if you belong here."

"Do I need a badge or something?" She glanced at his badge, then again over his head. This habit annoyed him.

"I don't have an extra one. If we do this right, you won't need one."

She nodded, hugging the clipboard to her chest.

He led Keren to the maintenance elevator, pushing the up button. "Wait over there," he pointed to the side, "until I know it's clear."

When the elevator doors opened, a man with a mop bucket stood in the corner. The man pushed the squeaky bucket by the mop handle out of the elevator. "Afternoon." He nodded his head at Quinlin.

"Afternoon." He responded with a nod, shifting in front of Keren to block the maintenance man's view. She scooted into the elevator, with Quinlin following behind her.

"Is that a problem?" Her voice sounded shaky.

She must be nervous. Nervous people made stupid mistakes. "No, don't worry about it. It's not a problem." Again, she stared over his head. "And stop looking over my head."

Her eyes darted to the floor. "Sorry."

Quinlin slipped his badge into the access slot, pressing the button for the fourteenth floor. The elevator chugged in response, starting its slow ascent.

He watched the numbers climb on the elevator's digital display as he tapped a finger on his clipboard. "Your aunt's room isn't far from the elevator. It's down the corridor, then left, third door on the right."

She frowned at him.

Had she told him what room her pretend aunt was in, or what her name was? He couldn't remember. "I saw you coming out the other day."

Her eyes narrowed. She glanced over his head before focusing back on the clipboard.

Stupid mistake. He studied her. She's not only beautiful but bright. Not everyone would have noticed that slip.

After stepping out of the elevator, they walked down the corridor. He held a hand out, motioning for Keren to pause while he checked around the corner. That woman's security guard leaned against the wall.

"Use the clipboard to cover where your badge should be and stay close." Now, he had to convince the guard to let them in the room.

Quinlin walked up to the guard, with Keren close behind him. He raised his hand. "Hey, Steve, how's it going today?"

"Hey, man. Things are quiet. I thought you were off today." The guard peeled himself off the wall. "Who's this?"

He pointed a thumb back at Keren. "They called me in to do new hire training."

"Aren't you a new hire yourself?" Steve craned his neck around Quinlin to see Keren.

"Weird, huh? You know how short-staffed we are. Can't hire them fast enough." He gave Steve a friendly grin. "Can we go in the room?" He motioned his head toward the door.

Steve narrowed his eyes at Keren. "You're awful young."

Quinlin turned to face Keren. He held his breath while he waited for Keren's reply. She stood up straight, lifting her head.

"I have a Master of Science in Nursing from UCF and one year's experience at Memorial Hospital of Tampa. I assure you, I am qualified for this position."

Acceptable response. Her lying skills were improving. He looked back at Steve.

Steve held up his hands. "No offense intended." He opened the door.

Quinlin stepping aside, allowing Keren into the room first. Steve closed the door behind them. She rushed to the woman's bedside.

He positioned himself behind Keren, close enough to hear the conversation but not giving that woman a clear line of sight to him.

"Hey, it's Keren." Her voice purred as she cupped that woman's face in her hand.

"Keren?" That woman's eyes blinked.

"Yes, it's me."

"We have to stop them... information... can't let them have it..."

"Stop whom?" Keren sat on the bed. "I don't understand."

"Important... tea." That woman's voice faded.

"Don't worry about the tea." She pulled the woman's hand to her chest. "I want you to know I have a lawyer to represent you. And I have information on the Dark Guild that might help your case."

Quinlin raised an eyebrow. Alarm bells rang in his head. What information could Keren have related to the Dark Guild? He knew what had to be done. After stepping back, he raised his hands for the attack.

"*Praeminiodo*," he said, focusing on the two women. A white light circled each hand. The light spun until it formed one swirling ball. He took a deep breath, reveling in the power surging through him. Sparks shot out from the ball as it flew toward the women.

Before impact, Keren's body lit up like floodlights in a ballpark. A creature appeared between her and the magic blast. Its bat-like wings reached toward opposite walls and air pulsed in smooth, regular waves around them.

He'd seen nothing like it. Where did it come from? Was it connected somehow to Keren's light? Was that woman involved?

When the blast struck the creature, the energy ball broke in two, one piece traveling across each of the creature's wings. The right half struck the windows, causing shattered glass to rain down on them. The left half exploded on the wall, leaving a gaping hole in the corridor.

The impact's recoil tossed Quinlin backward. He slammed into the wall, knocking the breath out of him.

"*Protegioum.*"

An invisible barrier covered him, blocking the rubble ricocheting through the room. Alarms blared and screams erupted in the corridor.

From under his shield, he focused on the creature. It must use air elemental magic to generate a shield, protecting the women. He'd thought they had destroyed air elemental magic in The Dragon War, along with the dragon shifters. How was this possible? His pulse raced, thinking of the possibilities if he controlled air elemental magic.

As the debris settled, he choked dust from his lungs. While looking at Keren, he noticed she no longer glowed and was slumped over that woman. When just moments ago he wanted them dead, now he needed them alive, at least until his questions about the creature were answered.

He crawled over debris, making his way to the hospital bed. After checking both women's pulses to confirm they were alive, he realized he needed help to get them to safety. He reached down, gathering powdery smut. After rubbing it over his hands to hide the telltale black spots, he smeared some across his face.

While crawling through the hole made by the blast, he saw Steve trapped under a concrete chunk. Only his upper body was visible, at least what was left of it. His left arm had been torn off, along with half his chest. Blood drained from multiple cuts and gashes in his skin. After pressing his hands into the pool of blood, Quinlin smeared it over his scrubs and down his arms.

Just as he gained his feet, an unexpected blast of water hit him in the chest. He fell back, tripping over the rubble. A hand grabbed the front of his scrubs, yanking him to his feet.

"Who are you? What are you doing here?"

Quinlin held up both bloody palms. "I'm a nurses' aide. I was doing my rounds when the explosion happened." The eyes of a fox shifter inquisitor stared at him. Quinlin did his best to look frightened while stifling the silent scream in his head, protesting the touch of a dirty shifter. "There are two women who need help in that room."

It seemed an eternity before the inquisitor let him go. He spoke into his radio. "We have casualties here. I'm at Olivia Stewart's room."

The inquisitor pushed him aside. "Go to the nurses' station to have your wounds looked at." He crouched down and crawled into the hole.

Instead of going to the nurses' station, Quinlin followed the inquisitor back into the room. "I'm fine. Let me help."

After turning to look at Quinlin, the inquisitor snarled, "You don't look fine."

"It's not all my blood. I can help."

Before the inquisitor could answer, a bear shifter crawled into the room. She gave Quinlin a suspicious eye. "I'm here to secure the prisoner."

"We have another victim. I'm not sure who she is."

Quinlin spoke up, "She's a nurses' aide, like me. We were doing rounds together."

The fox shifter grunted. "It's odd. They don't look affected by the explosion." He did a quick inspection of the women. "I'll take the aides. You get the prisoner." Keren moaned as he lifted her off that woman.

While struggling over rubble to follow the inquisitors out of the room and down the corridor, Quinlin scrutinized the damage his attack inflicted. The half-ball blast demolished every wall in its path on its way out to the other side of the hospital floor.

Doctors, nurses, and inquisitors worked to uncover bodies buried in debris. The blank eyes of those obviously dead stared up at him, silently asking why this happened. He mentally apologized to the humans. They were unfortunate victims. But with every battle comes sacrifice. As for the dirty shifters, killing them now or killing them later was negligible.

The group fell in line with others rushing downstairs; first the bear shifter with that woman, then the fox shifter holding Keren, followed by Quinlin. He saw Keren's eyes open.

"What's happening? Where's my mom?" she murmured.

"It's alright." Quinlin stroked her head. "We'll call your mom in a few minutes."

She blinked, focusing on Quinlin. "But..." She stopped, seeing Quinlin put his finger to his lips.

Sweat dripped down his spine. If Keren said the wrong thing, this situation could turn ugly.

They climbed down all fourteen floors, emerging into a busy but organized triage area.

A nurse greeted them at the stairwell. "What have you got?" She ushered them aside so others could come through behind them.

"Olivia Stewart," the bear shifter responded.

"Our secured site is set up down the hall." She pointed to the right. "And the other two?"

"Nurses' aides. One looks to be in bad shape." The fox shifter eyed Quinlin.

Upon hearing her mom's name, Keren yelled out. "Where is she? Where's Olivia Stewart?" She struggled down from the inquisitor's hold, bolting after the bear inquisitor. Quinlin ran after her.

"Wait!" Keren's voice echoed through the corridor.

The bear shifter turned. Keren ran up to her mom, cupping her face in her hands. "Mom!"

"Who are you?" The bear shifter frowned, looking down the hall for possible assistance.

"She's delirious," Quinlin said as he caught up with Keren.

That woman's eyes fluttered open.

Keren gasped. "Are you alright?" She drew her face close to that woman's. "Please, tell me you're alright."

That woman placed her hand over Keren's. "I'm fine." She gave a weak smile.

"Back away miss." The bear shifter turned, forcing Keren's hands away. "I don't know what's going on here, but you need to step back."

Quinlin grabbed Keren's shoulders. "We're leaving."

"No, I want to stay with her." She fought against his grip.

While leaning close to Keren's ear, he whispered, "You're going to get us both arrested."

She stopped struggling.

"Your mom is alive and in custody. We have to leave." Quinlin took her hand.

After Keren let him lead her away, he let out a long breath.

"What happened?" she asked.

"There was an explosion, but you saw your mom is alright." While rushing her to the exit, he checked if anyone followed them.

"Explosion? How?" She stumbled down the corridor, then fell to her knees.

"I don't know." He yanked her up, forcing her to keep moving. They needed to get out of the hospital.

Keren's pocket buzzed. She pulled out her phone. After tugging herself free from his grip, she stopped, frowning at the screen. She looked like a drunk staggering around, trying to catch her balance.

"Oh, no."

"What's wrong." Quinlin tried to look at her phone, but she pressed it to her chest.

"I have to go." She moved with unsteady steps toward the exit. This was good, but he wondered about her sudden urgency.

"Can I help?" They walked out the same door they came in. Quinlin pressing for information.

"No, I'm late meeting up with Nadria." She opened her car door. Before she got in, Quinlin grabbed the door, blocking it from being closed.

"You're not in any shape to drive. Let me take you whereever you're going."

"No." She shook her head. "It's personal." The determined look in her eyes told him she wouldn't accept his help, no matter how much he tried to change her mind.

She glanced at her phone. "I have to go."

He decided backing off was his best bet, but he would keep close tabs on her. "OK. I'll call you tomorrow. Be careful."

She smiled, closing the car door, and driving away.

CHAPTER TWENTY-ONE

KEREN

Keren parked the Prius a block away from Dan's house, shutting off the engine. The sun hung low in the sky, its orange hues painted on the cloud-covered sky. She munched on a bag of Doritos.

"Are you going to tell me why you're wearing scrubs and shoes that are obviously too big?" Ordell poked her leg. "It's not Halloween."

She hadn't figured out what happened at the hospital. The entire event was a blur in her mind. What caused the explosion? At least she knew Mom was safe.

After wiping her hands on a napkin, she stuffed it into the McDonald's bag. The two double-cheeseburgers, fries, and a shake settled her stomach. "No, I'm not telling you."

"I'll find out, eventually." When Keren didn't respond, he changed the subject. "How do we know Dan hasn't left yet?"

She studied the house. It was hard to tell if anyone was home. Sitting here in the car put increased the risk of someone recognizing them from yesterday. The less time they spent out here, the better. Unfortunately, she wouldn't be able to talk Ordell into leaving until they knew for sure Dan wasn't home.

"We go to the house and check."

She pulled her backpack to the front seat. Ordell had let her rummage through the garage at his house. While loading her backpack with flashlights and a first aid kit, she threw in rope and duct tape. Not that she intended to kidnap anyone. They were some things she'd seen detectives use on TV.

She shifted the sketchbook to the side and pulled out a flashlight, handing it to Ordell.

"We'll get to those bushes, then cross into the backyard." She gave him a smirk. "Stay away from the trash cans."

He grabbed the flashlight from her. "Ha-ha." He turned it on and off several times.

She put her hand over the end of the flashlight. "Stop sending bat signals. We don't want to be noticed, remember?"

"Right, sorry." Ordell got out of the car.

They walked along the sidewalk toward Dan's house. When they were positive no one was around, they crawled into the bushes, maneuvering their way to his backyard.

While holding her finger to her lips, she motioned for Ordell to follow her onto the back porch. They huddled under the kitchen window. Suddenly, the backdoor flew open as Dan walked outside carrying a garbage bag.

Her heart leaped to her throat. After losing her balance, she fell off the porch. Her foot hit the railing as she tumbled to the ground. Ordell changed to his cat form as Dan turned to investigate the noise. He ran close enough to make Dan stumble, trying to draw his attention.

Keren hugged the ground on the side of the porch until Dan turned away chasing Ordell. While crawling on her hands and knees, she inched her way to the front of the house. After ensuring no one was watching, she made her way to the sidewalk and headed to the car. Dusk settled into night.

After returning to the car, she tried to calm her racing heart. If Dan had caught her, she didn't know what would have happened.

Ordell, back in his human form, got into the car. He lay his head back. "Well, he's home."

She laughed, punching his arm.

A beige Toyota Corolla pulled onto the street, stopping at Dan's house. Dan walked out and got into the car.

Keren waited to start the car until they pulled away. Her sweaty hands gripped the steering wheel. What was she getting them into?

They followed the Corolla for thirty minutes, stopping in front of Citrus Strike Bowling Alley. A sparse copse of trees lined each side of the building.

The motel to the rear of the building took up the rest of the block. She drove by the half-full parking lot, letting Dan and his friend park before she pulled in.

"They can't be bowling, can they?" Ordell pointed at the digital clock on the dashboard. It showed 8:02 pm. "They only have an hour before the meeting starts."

She had imagined following Dan to some rundown, abandoned warehouse in a secluded area. A public bowling alley didn't seem so bad. While looking around at the other cars, she wondered if they belonged to the Dark Guild arcanum.

After pulling out her phone, she Googled the bowling alley. It seemed to be a legitimate business. They had hours, rates, and pictures posted on their website. She watched Dan and his driver walked inside.

"I don't know, but at least it's a public area. Let's look around."

She grabbed her backpack and headed into the bowling alley with Ordell following close behind. They heard bowling balls rumble down waxed wooden lanes and pins crashing into the pin decks. The combined smells of disinfectant and pizza lingered in the air.

A young couple and their son laughed as his ball bounced five times off the bumpers to get him a strike. Bowlers filled half the alleys, sipping beer and chatting with friends while waiting for their turn to bowl. These people can't be arcanum.

She spotted Dan with a couple of other guys by the ball racks. While pulling Ordell to an unused lane, she nodded in Dan's direction. "Over there."

Dan and the guys moved to the back of the building, exiting through a door marked 'Employees Only.'

Keren looked at Ordell. "Ready?" He nodded.

They worked their way over to the door. While glancing around, she saw no one looked in their direction.

She took a deep breath, opened the door, and slipped inside. Ordell closed the door behind them. They found themselves in a dimly lit hallway. It took a moment for her eyes to adjust to the gloomy lighting. Window alcoves were carved out every few feet. Closed Venetian blinds acted as sentries against Florida's outdoors, while weak recessed ceiling lights glowed on the multi-pattern carpet. This must be a connecting passageway to the motel next door.

A black mouse scurried from the shadows. He waved his front paws at her. "Ordell?" Her voice came out as a harsh whisper.

He darted down the hall and was soon out of sight. After letting out a sigh, she realized Ordell had gone rogue again. She was on her own. While running her fingers through her hair, she took a deep breath. Her gut told her to leave. But she wouldn't abandon Ordell, even though he just ditched her.

She moved forward, staying close to the wall. When the door opened behind her, she pressed herself into a window alcove.

A deep-voiced man spouted orders. "Only arcanum get past this door, no exceptions. After nine, no one gets in. If you have problems, call my cell. Is that clear?"

"Yes, sir," a chorus of at least two others responded.

As footsteps approached, she stepped back, bumping into the blinds. They clattered against the window.

"Who's there?" The deep-voiced man's reddened face appeared.

She bolted from the alcove, pausing in the middle of the hallway. To her right, a red-faced man and two of his goons blocked her escape. To her left, an empty hall and double doors that must lead into what she assumed was the motel. She went left.

As she sprinted down the passageway, the men charged after her. The oversized shoes slipped on her feet, hindering her ability to run.

After bursting through the double doors, she tripped, stumbling into someone on the other side. After gaining her balance, Keren noticed she stood in the motel's lobby. There should be an exit door close by.

"Stop her!" deep-voice man bellowed. He and his goons crashed through the double doors.

Keren started running forward but let out a yell when someone grabbed her backpack, impeding her escape. Then the four of them surrounded her. Her heart pounded from the sprint and wondering how she would get away from this group. The person from the lobby, a middle-aged woman with dyed-blond hair, stepped forward.

"Who are you, and how did you get in?"

Keren's mind raced. "I want to join." The words spilled out before she could stop them. "I sneaked past the guards to attend the meeting."

The woman grabbed Keren's arm. "We allow only arcanum into our meetings."

She licked her dry lips. "I want to be an arcanum. I heard about the initiative update."

"What's going on?" A man's voice reverberated in the room. "Who is that with you?"

Keren's body trembled as she watched Dan walking toward them. He looked a decade older than his Facebook profile picture. Most of the acne had changed to facial scars.

"She knows about the initiative update." The woman squeezed Keren's arm with a vice-like grip. She tried to back up, but the woman held her in place.

Dan stepped up, standing nose-to-nose with Keren. "I don't recognize you." His rancid breath brought tears to her eyes.

Although trying to keep her voice calm, she spoke with a slight quiver. "I want to be an arcanum." This situation went from bad to worse. They outnumbered her, so she had no chance of fighting her way out. If she could get to her phone, she could call Nadria and have her send help.

While squinting, Dan grabbed her chin. "I think you are a thief." Spittle flew into her face.

"No." Keren tried to shake her head, but Dan held it in place.

"Someone stole my laptop yesterday. And now you show up to a top-level Dark Guild meeting." Dan pushed her chin away. "Bring her to the hall. I'll be there in a few minutes." He sneered. "I could use a warm-up before the main demonstration."

Jeers and snickering came from the others.

Keren's heart pounded. She jerked her arm, unsuccessfully trying to break free of the woman's grip.

"No, you don't." The woman grabbed Keren's other arm, pulling them both behind her.

She felt a muscle pull in her shoulder and let a pained wail.

Dan glared at Deep-voice. "Make sure the entrance is secure."

"You heard him." Deep-voice shoved one goon. "Back to work." They trotted out the double doors.

The woman forced her to walk further down the hall. At one time, this motel might have been a decent place to stay. But the worn carpet and stained walls said it had been years since guests walked these halls.

The woman pushed Keren toward a door marked 'Lazy Palm Hall.' Upon entering the sizable banquet area, she saw rows of folding chairs set in front of a stage. Potted plants lined the edge of the stage. The Dark Guild banner hung as a backdrop. Its crossed double lightning bolts made Keren shudder as she thought about the graphic pictures of violence on Dan's living room wall. A black curtain blocked off the far corner of the stage.

Keren gritted her teeth, hissing each time the woman tugged on her arm. She didn't like the way Dan had said *'warm-up'*. Her heart tried to pound out of her chest.

After dragging her up the stage steps, the woman took her to center stage. "You won't be needing this." She tore Keren's backpack off, tossing it to the side.

She struggled against the woman's grip, then felt a handcuff clamp over one wrist. Keren turned, looking at the metal chain tethering her to the eye hook on the stage. A piercing scream escaped from her throat. What was Dan planning to do to her? Her pulse pounded in her ears. This couldn't be happening. She tugged on the chain, but it held her in place.

While glaring at the woman, she shouted at the top of her lungs, "You can't do this. Let me go."

The woman laughed and hopped off the stage, settling into a folding chair. She put her hands behind her head and leaned back, waiting for whatever sick show Dan had planned.

Falling to her knees, a wave of dread passed over Keren. Her phone was in her backpack, so she had no way to call for help. She caught her breath, spotting movement out of the corner of her eye. A mouse crept in the shadows along the far end of the stage. Could that be Ordell? Now that the woman was alone, maybe they could overpower her. Keren pulled against the chain, the cuff cutting into her wrist. She needed to break free before Dan arrived.

Ordell sat on his haunches, waving his front paws. Keren moved her eyes to her backpack, then back to Ordell. He must have understood her message because he dropped to all fours and scrambled to the backpack. Keren let out a long breath. Hopefully, he'll get a call out to Nadria.

Keren jumped as Dan slammed the hall door open.

"Are you ready for the show?" He strutted onto the stage. "Oh, don't be upset. You asked to be part of the initiative update." He gave Keren a ghoulish grin.

She jangled the chain. "You can't do this."

"Can't? That word is no longer in the Dark Guild arcanum's vocabulary." He walked by her, stopping at the black curtain. "You see, we've mastered elemental magic."

A chill ran down her spine. Whatever waited behind that curtain made Dan's eyes gleam with excitement. With a shaky hand, she wiped sweat from her forehead.

"Let me go," she hissed after yanking again on the chain. Blood dripped from her wrist.

Dan ignored her plea, putting his hand on the curtain. "Let me introduce you to our cursed wolf." He tugged it back, revealing a cage containing a distorted creature. Its patchy fur hung in scraggly bunches over dry, cracked skin, while the lower jaw jutted to the left. Legs bent in odd directions like someone had broken them and made a mistake mending them. Its glazed-over eyes stared into space.

"You think it's locked up, with no opening to the cage. Well, you're wrong." He waved his hand over the bars.

"*Ostendoium.*"

A door seam and keyhole appeared. After pulling a key out of his pocket, he unlocked the door, pulling the cage door open.

Her eyes filled with tears. What have they done to this pitiful creature?

While knitting his eyes brows together in a mock-worried look, Dan tugged the curtain further back. "I don't suppose you know him."

Keren gasped. Broden's body lay motionless on the cage floor. Adrenaline rushed through her body. While letting out a guttural roar, she yanked at the chain, getting as close as possible to Dan. She ignored the blood dripping down her hand.

"What have you done?" Her free hand swung out at Dan.

"The same thing I'm going to do to you."

Dan held out his palms, animating the cursed wolf with words she didn't understand. It snarled, the lopsided jaw drooling spittle. He spoke again in the odd language, then his calculating eyes looked at her.

"Attack."

That word she understood.

Flames exploded around the cursed wolf's body. It crouched, ready to leap.

She pulled back, getting as far away from the creature as possible. While letting out a cry of fear and frustration, she pulled and yanked on the chain with all her strength.

Then time stood still. A familiar pulsing of energy ignited in her solar plexus. The pulse raced to the back of her eyes, exploding out like lightning bolts. Time restarted. A scent of pine filled the room as a flesh-and-blood Three appeared before her. While snarling to expose its over-sized canine teeth, Three grabbed the chain holding her to the stage, tearing the links apart as if made of paper.

The cursed wolf sprung. Three turned, blocking Keren from the attack. The wolf landed on Three's chest. Three tried pushing it off, but the cursed wolf chomped down onto its shoulder. Keren cringed at the snapping of twigs and crunching of bone. Three let out a thunderous roar. Then, grabbing the cursed wolf, Three tossed it off the stage.

Keren scrambled into the cage, kneeling next to Broden. Her heart raced at seeing the dried blood pooled on the floor. She pulled his limp body onto her lap.

"Broden!" She shook him. When he gave no response, she clutched him to her chest, rocking back and forth. His skin felt icy. She drew in a ragged breath as tears streamed down her face.

Another roar from Three drew her attention. She saw the cursed wolf had jumped at Three, its misaligned jaws snapping at its arms. Three batted the wolf away. But fire from the wolf's attack danced over Three's chest and arms.

Three's giant-sized hands peeled the flames away. While rolling the fire between its palms, it formed a lava ball. The cursed wolf regained its feet, readying for another attack. Three threw the lava ball, hitting the wolf square in the head. It staggered, stunned for a moment.

Keren heard Dan's voice. She looked over, seeing him standing next to the cage. Sweat dripped off his face. Speckles of black covered his extended palms. He chanted words she didn't understand. Somehow, he controlled the cursed wolf.

She released Broden, tenderly lowering him to the cage floor. After standing, she exited the cage to stand within inches of Dan. While swinging the arm with the shackle, she whipped the dangling chain into Dan's head. Blood sprayed from above his eye as the chain ripped across his face. His head jerked back, causing him to break the connection with the cursed wolf.

Keren turned, looking at Three. It took the now motionless cursed wolf's head in both hands and yanked it free from the body. The headless body collapsed to the ground. Three tossed the head across the room.

Pain seared through her scalp as her head snapped back. Dan held her hair in a tight fist, pulling it down and toward him. Hot, rancid breath wafted over her face.

"You'll pay for that." He held his other palm over her face.

She reached up, grasping his wrist with both hands while stomping on his foot. Dan let out a pained yell. His grip loosened enough for her to pull free. She fell back onto the stage.

Before Dan could recover, the plants lining the stage sprouted at an amazing rate. Their limbs reached like fingers, wrapping themselves around Dan.

"What's going on?" His thrashing failed to keep the limbs from binding his arms to his sides and immobilizing his feet. Wild eyes locked onto Keren. "What are you?"

The limbs wrapped themselves around Dan's mouth, leaving only his eyes and nose visible.

Keren stood, swallowing a lump in her throat. She looked back at Three, who had its hand on the stage. Apparently, it used earth magic to control the plants, saving her once again. While looking back at Dan's accusing eyes, the question rumbled through her mind. *'What are you?'* She stared at her hands, watching golden light dance over her skin. She frowned, unable to come up with an answer. Then the room blurred as a wave of dizziness passed through her.

As she scrubbed tears from her eyes with a trembling hand, she staggered back, steadying herself on the cage. Her heart felt as though it were being ripped out as she thought of Broden. It would devastate Ordell when he found out the truth. She startled. Where was the arcanum woman?

While looking around the room, she searched for the woman and Ordell. She spotted Ordell standing on a pile of folding chairs. His hair stood on end and a sleeve of his shirt had been torn off. He held a roll of duct tape in his hand.

"Ordell," Keren shouted.

He turned in her direction. While grinning, he held the duct tape over his head. When he met her eyes, his smile faded. Keren looked at Broden, then back at Ordell.

"No!" He dropped the tape, racing to the stage. After skidding to a stop in the cage, he threw himself on Broden. His body heaved with sobs as he called out for a brother that would never answer.

"Broden, come back." Ordell clenched Broden's hair, pulling his face close. "Wake up!"

Keren looked away. Her vision blurred from an onslaught of tears. If she would have left when Ordell wanted to that afternoon, maybe Broden would still be alive. Instead, she chose to go on her date with Quinlin. How would Ordell ever forgive her?

When she heard a low rumble, she looked up. Three stood in front of her. It knitted its brows together, tipping its head to the side as it held out a hand.

Keren put her hand in Three's. The prickly vines tickling her palm. After wiggling her fingers through the vines, she stroked the dark green fur underneath. A sense of calm flowed through her.

Three glanced at Dan, held captive by the plants. Then it turned back to Keren, raising its eyebrows as if asking a question.

She shook her head. "Just leave him."

They weren't safe. Deep-voice man and his goons were in the hallway. They could be on their way here right now. And the rest of the arcanum would arrive soon.

Her vision blurred and her legs trembled, forcing her to steady herself against the cage bars. While using the bars as support, she walked into the cage, placing her hand on Ordell's back.

"We have to go."

His sobs grew louder as he rocked his brother. She stepped around him, reaching down to lift Broden.

"No!" Ordell tightened his grip.

"We'll get caught if we don't leave now." She reached out again. This time, Ordell pulled away.

"I'll carry him." He stood up with Broden's limp body in his arms. Broden's head dropped back. Lifeless eyes stared into the distance. She looked away, the scene too overwhelming.

Once Keren grabbed her backpack, Three helped them off the stage. She led Ordell to the nearest exit. An alarm went off when she opened the door. Ordell didn't seem to notice. He stumbled behind her, leaning his weight on the door frame, Broden clutched in his arms.

She looked into Three's deep brown eyes. "We need to get back to the car."

Three scooped them up, Keren in one arm, Ordell with Broden in the other. It stomped through the bushes around the side of the motel and bowling alley. When it stepped into the parking lot, two women making their way back to their car screamed, running back toward the building.

Keren didn't care who saw them. All she wanted was to get far away from here. Three set them down next to Nadria's car. It turned, heading back in the direction they came from to hold off anyone in pursuit.

Her stomach clenched, forcing her to double over in pain. While leaning on the car, she guided Ordell into the backseat, Broden securely locked in his arms. She tossed her backpack in, then collapsed into the driver's seat. Her fingers wrapped around the steering wheel, clenching it until her knuckles turned white. She could have prevented this. Instead, she had sentenced the Murphy's to a life of grief after losing a beloved child and brother.

She drove out of the parking lot. Her glow faded as she pulled onto I-4, heading to Ordell's house.

CHAPTER TWENTY-TWO

BRIGGS

B riggs closed the ambulance door, leaving his hand pressed against it. A second ambulance remained, its EMT treating the other victims. A deep growl rumbled in his throat. The senseless loss of innocent lives made his blood boil.

He pulled up to the Murphy's at the same time Keren had arrived. She had called him from the car, too grief-stricken to say anything but where she was headed.

"Do you want me to go with the victim?" said Officer Jordon.

Briggs slapped twice on the door, signaling to the driver he could leave. Without turning, he said, "Yes, make sure they place the body under security. The medical examiner will perform the autopsy in the morning." He stayed professional, hiding his anguish and rage.

"Yes, sir." Briggs heard Officer Jordon's retreating footsteps. A few moments later, a car drove off.

With a sigh, Briggs turned, facing the Murphy's house. Police cars' flashing lights lit up the normally quiet neighborhood. Briggs caught movement on the outskirts of the property. Wolf shapes moved in and out of the shadows.

"What did you find at the bowling alley and motel?" Briggs asked.

Faraday stepped next to him. "I'm not sure how you do it."

Briggs grunted. Faraday had developed this odd obsession with sneaking up on him.

Once Briggs had found out both magic and the Dark Guild were involved, he called Tabitha. She had sent the warrior pack to investigate.

"Most people had left the bowling alley by the time we arrived. The report of a monster prowling the area caused quite a panic." Faraday handed Briggs a piece of paper. "We have the names of the women who reported seeing it."

Briggs nodded, taking the paper from Faraday. He'd assign one of his officers to find them. Most people didn't react well when random shifters showed up at their door. At least if they wore a uniform, there was some hope of a peaceful conversation.

Keren had described *the monster* as her imaginary friend come to life. Ordell corroborated her story. Briggs didn't know what to think.

"At the motel, we found the body of a wolf." Faraday snarled. "It looked like they had tortured it for years, ripped apart then put back together in strange ways. Its head was torn from its body."

"Did you find any arcanum?" Briggs spat out the last word.

"No, but we're prowling the area. One warrior picked up a scent. We're following that trail." He turned to face Briggs. The reproach in Faraday's eyes bore down on him. "They used earth magic on the plants. It looked like something had been contained by the plants at some point."

"Keren said the monster used earth magic." He knew Faraday thought Keren's story was a fairytale made up by a shocked mind. Although her story sounded crazy, Briggs wanted to believe Keren. He trusted her. But he couldn't overlook any suspects.

Faraday hinted at bear shifter involvement. If bear shifters were working with the Dark Guild, that made the group more dangerous than ever. "We're conducting a full investigation."

Without a word, Faraday stalked away, melting into the darkness.

Briggs wondered how the Murphy's were doing, so he made his way into the house. While passing through the kitchen, he paused. The iron cuff and chain Keren had on sat on the counter.

After he had picked the cuff's lock, he exposed the gashes in Keren's wrist. His body tensed. Whoever did this to her and Broden would pay, no matter what it took. The EMT walked in from the living room.

"Captain Wilson." The EMT paused.

Briggs nodded. "How are they doing?"

"Ordell has minor abrasions. But the gashes on Keren's wrist required stitches. She really should go to the hospital."

Briggs took a deep breath. "I know." He'd begged her to go to the hospital but, so far, she refused.

The EMT gave him a sympathetic look, then continued. "I gave Mrs. Murphy a mild sedative. It might not make her sleep, but it will calm her nerves."

"Thank you, Jeffery."

"You need me to stick around?"

"No, I appreciate the help."

Jeffery patted Briggs' arm. "Just doing my job. Take care." He walked out.

Briggs glanced again at the cuff and chain on the counter. He made a mental note to have an officer wrap them up as evidence. Then he walked into the living room.

Mrs. Murphy sat on the couch. An ice pack rested on the back of her neck. Nadria sat next to her, stroking her hand. Keren had asked for Nadria, so he had a squad car drive her over.

Off to the side, Keren stood with Mr. Murphy. Her arms draped around him. Tabitha stood behind them, resting a protective hand on Keren's shoulder. He noticed Tabitha's jaw tensed then released, her stony face struggling to contain the ferocity of her emotions. Tabitha and Keren had been friends since high school, and Keren had served as maid of honor at her wedding.

Ordell sat next to Nadria, staring across the room. His horse ears drooped to the side. Every few seconds, he twitched. Maybe the EMT should have given Ordell a sedative, too.

Mrs. Murphy's eyes met his. Her lower lip quivered.

"Have you taken my boy away?"

Briggs found it hard to swallow. His throat felt suddenly dry. "Yes, ma'am."

"We'll get him back, right? For the funeral, I mean." Tears dripped down her cheeks.

"Of course." he cleared his throat. "I'll let you know when the medical examiner clears the body."

Mrs. Murphy winced as if slapped. He berated himself. These were his friends, the people he loved. He could drop the professional jargon. He turned to Keren.

"Keren, can we talk?"

Keren gave Mr. Murphy a squeeze, then walked toward Briggs. Tabitha followed behind her.

Briggs led them into the formal dining room. "We've done all we can here for now." He brushed the back of his fingers over her face. She swayed, grabbing Briggs' arm to steady herself.

"I'm starving." She hung her head. "I know I shouldn't be, but I can't help it."

"It's a good thing." Briggs drew her into a hug. "You need to eat."

Tabitha pulled out her phone. "I'll order delivery. Any preferences?"

"Pizza's great. Thanks. Leave off the healthy stuff." Keren gave Tabitha a sly grin.

Briggs looked over as Mr. Murphy entered the room.

"Keren, the Mrs. and I would like you to stay here tonight. Nadria's already agreed."

"Thank you, Papa Murphy. I'd like that."

"Good." Mr. Murphy looked relieved. He turned to Briggs. "I'm going to take the Mrs. upstairs. Would you lock up when you go?"

"I will Mr. Murphy. You get some rest."

Mr. Murphy turned to go.

"And, Mr. Murphy?"

He turned back around. "Yes, Briggs?"

"We'll find who did this."

Tabitha patted Mr. Murphy's arm. "We promise."

Mr. Murphy nodded. "We appreciate that." He turned, walking out of the room.

Briggs knew it was time to gather his squad and head back to the station. It would be another all-nighter. He ran his hand along Keren's back. She felt small and frail. So many questions swirled in his mind related to this event. But he knew she was exhausted from the ordeal. He'd talk to her about this tomorrow after she got some time to rest.

"I checked in on your mom. She's doing great."

Keren looked up into his eyes. "She is? Can I see her?"

He shook his head. "I'm sorry. She's under protective custody." Since the magic attack on the hospital, Keren's mom had been assigned extra security. He couldn't prove it, but something told him the attack had something to do with her. His heart ached for Keren, knowing how close she was to her mom. "But I'll see what I can do. No promises."

Keren buried her face in his chest. "Thanks, Briggs."

"Sure thing. Well, I've got to get going." He gently pushed her away, lowering her into a chair. "We have a lot more to discuss. But it can wait until tomorrow."

Keren stared into his eyes. "Thank you." She looked at Tabitha. "Both."

"We're here for you." Tabitha pulled up a chair. "I'll hang out until the pizza arrives."

The last thing Briggs wanted to do was leave, but he raised a hand in farewell. "Talk to you tomorrow."

"Bye, Briggs." Keren's voice followed him out the door.

CHAPTER TWENTY-THREE

KEREN

Keren set the empty pizza box aside. She had coaxed Ordell into eating one piece. Other than that piece, she had eaten the entire pizza herself.

"I don't know how you can eat so much." Nadria sat cross-legged on the daybed.

Keren shrugged. "I don't know." This hadn't been the typical stomach growling kind of hunger. Every part of her body cried out for food. She felt like she'd just climbed Mount Everest, twice. She sighed. Her body ached, especially her wrist. She hoped the ibuprofen kicked in soon.

"A magic attack at the hospital was all over the news this afternoon. Were you there when it happened?" Nadria asked.

"What? A magic attack? I heard nothing about that." Ordell sat on the edge of the ottoman.

Keren's heart pounded. Quinlin said there was an explosion. He didn't mention a magic attack. But then, why would he? He knew no more than she did.

"Yes, I was there. It was confusing. And I don't remember much."

Nadria gasped, putting her hand to her throat. "Is your mom alright?"

"Yes, I spoke to her at the hospital after the explosion. And Briggs gave me an update tonight on her condition. He said she was doing great."

"That's good to hear." Nadria frowned. "Hey, why are you wearing scrubs?"

Keren had no other clothes to change into after taking a shower, so she put the scrubs back on. She looked at Ordell. He raised his eyebrows, pricking his horse ears forward.

"It's a long story. Can we talk about something else?" She wasn't ready to talk about Quinlin.

Ordell turned to face her. "Do you know how your imaginary friends are coming to life? We've seen Four and Three."

"I don't know. They seem to show up when I'm desperate for something." She would have been desperate to protect Mom from another attack. Did an imaginary friend come to help them? Could that be why she passed out?

"They used magic. So, that means you have magic." Nadria grabbed a pillow, fluffing it in her lap. "The tea kept that magic shrouded."

"What tea?" Ordell asked.

Keren reached for her backpack, digging down to the bottom to find the tea bin.

"Oh, no." Her fingers picked up loose tea leaves at the bottom of her backpack. All the rough treatment today must have knocked the cover off the bin. She sprinkled the leaves into Ordell's hand. Some missed, floating down to the floor and between Ordell's legs.

"Why do you think your mom would want to keep your magic subdued?" He brushed the leaves off on his pants.

A chill ran down Keren's spine. "Maybe it's dangerous." Mom thought it important. Even in her weakened state, Keren drank the tea. Her searching fingers found the tea bin. She pulled it out. The cover had popped off, and the bin had a large dent in the side.

"Oh, honey. I'm sorry. I know that was a special gift from your mom," said Nadria.

"Here," Ordell held out his hand, "let me see if I can fix it."

Keren set it in his outstretched hand.

As he turned the bin over in his hands, they heard a clinking noise.

"Wait." Keren examined the bin with him. "It looks like there are two compartments."

Ordell pried the tin open enough to reach his fingers in the smaller area. He pulled out a key, half wrapped in a pile of gauze. "What do we have here?"

Keren caught her breath as her heart leaped into her throat. She racked her brain, trying to remember exactly what Mom said at the hospital.

"Mom said we have to stop them, and then," she put her elbows on her knees, rubbing her temples, "something about information and not letting them have it." Keren gasped, sitting up. "This is why she kept insisting the tea was important. She didn't want me to drink it, she wanted me to find this key. She always said antiques hold the secrets to our souls."

Nadria took the key. "What does it open?" She looked at Keren.

"I don't know." Keren's eyes stayed glued to the key. She flipped through memories, looking for a time when Mom showed her a locked cabinet or box. Her eyebrows furrowed. She couldn't come up with anything. "It could be something at the house, or maybe at Mom's work."

More secrets and surprises about Mom. She wondered if she knew her mom at all. A tear dripped down Keren's cheek.

"It's OK." Nadria handed the key back to Keren. "You're tired. You should get some rest."

"No way I can sleep thinking about that key." Ordell stood and paced the room. "If this has something to do with stopping the Dark Guild, we have to find what it opens."

"We don't know it has anything to do with the Dark Guild," Nadria said. "Keren said her mom told her it was important. She didn't say she mentioned the Dark Guild."

"Not this time. But the first time I saw her with Briggs, she did. She told me to protect myself from the Dark Guild."

Ordell clapped his hands together. "That's it then. Whatever that key opens can bring the Dark Guild down." His eyes sparked with anger and the need for revenge.

Something inside her agreed with Ordell. This key was vital to finding the answers they needed. Both to solve Broden's murder and clear Mom's name.

"We should go to my house. Tonight."

Ordell stopped. "I thought the inquisitors had it barricaded as a crime scene."

"They do." She looked from Ordell to Nadria. "But we have to find what that key opens."

Nadria stood, holding her palms out. "Hold on here. You are talking crazy. What we should do is turn this over to Briggs. Let the inquisitors handle this."

A part of Keren clung to the idea her mom was framed, maybe by an inquisitor. She trusted Briggs but didn't want someone desperate enough to use her mom as a scapegoat getting their hands on this key. This was her responsibility.

"No, we need to do this."

Nadria threw her hands up in frustration. "Fine, I'm not letting you two out of my sight."

Keren grabbed her backpack and headed to the door. When she opened it, Mr. Murphy stood on the other side.

"Papa Murphy." Keren looked up into the man's bloodshot eyes. "We're..."

Mr. Murphy pushed his way into the room. "You're going to find what that key opens. What you're planning is dangerous." Tears brimmed in his eyes. "Do you really think there's evidence to stop the Dark Guild?"

Keren threw her arms around his waist. "I do, Papa."

Mr. Murphy held his arms out, beckoning Nadria and Ordell to join the hug. "I love you all and I don't want you to get hurt." He squeezed them. "But the Dark Guild has to be stopped." He kissed the top of their heads. "Please, be careful."

"We will Papa." Three voices chimed together.

They gave Mr. Murphy a kiss goodbye and ran out to Nadria's car.

CHAPTER TWENTY-FOUR

QUINLIN

"Dan!" shouted Quinlin as he burst into the lab. Cool air did nothing to stop the inferno burning in his chest. The first meaningful breakthrough to completing his father's dream now inhabited an inquisitor evidence room with its body beheaded. The cursed creatures were supposed to be unstoppable. It had to have been Dan's mishandling of the cursed wolf that caused its demise.

He spotted Dan sitting on the platform. His body slumped forward as he rested his elbows on his knees while his dangling feet swung back and forth. The fifteen elite standing behind him had jumped at Quinlin's voice, but Dan hadn't moved.

While storming up to the platform, Quinlin continued his rant. "I want answers. How could this have happened?" After stopping in front of Dan, he stood in a wide stance with his fists on his hips. His nostrils flared as he tensed his jaw, waiting for Dan's reply.

"Another creature appeared. It was stronger than the cursed wolf." His voice came out in a whisper.

Quinlin took a full breath, expanding his chest and holding it for a moment before responding. "That's impossible."

Dan remained slumped forward, avoiding eye contact.

While pointing to the floor, Quinlin commanded, "Stand up." He felt a throbbing in the front of his forehead.

After sliding off the platform, Dan stood in the spot indicated by Quinlin's finger, but his head remained tilted down.

When Quinlin moved to stand inches away from his lieutenant, he smelled the fear wafting around Dan's body.

Through gritted teeth, Quinlin said, "Look at me."

When Dan's eyes met his, they grew wide and dilated. He visibly forced himself to swallow. With a trembling voice, words spilled from his mouth.

"It was that girl. The creature did what she told it to do." He licked his lips. "Honest, Mr. Turner. Her creature was stronger than the cursed wolf. There wasn't anything I could do."

After Quinlin covered Dan's face with his hand, his splayed fingers pressing into the skin, the babbling stopped. He'd heard news reports about a siting of this creature Dan referred to but, so far, he'd been unable to get details. The inquisitors kept that information confidential.

But this was too much of a coincidence. He released Dan's face then turned, striding away from the arcanum who destroyed his triumph. With his hands behind his back, he paced the floor.

"What did she look like?"

"Um, well. She was a little shorter than me and had long, brown hair. Her skin glowed, and light showed in her eyes."

Quinlin stopped pacing, taking a deep breath. Keren had somehow infiltrated the Dark Guild's meeting. Questions swirled in his mind. If Dan was right and her creature had been stronger than the cursed wolf, then his plan to annihilate the shifters was threatened by this unknown force. He needed absolutes. His cursed creatures had to dominate. Without looking at Dan, he raised his arm, holding his palm toward him.

"*Potestatenum.*"

When the energy blast hit, Dan's body exploded, sending bits of him flying in every direction.

After he heard a scream from the platform, he realized he'd forgotten about the elite. His eyes snapped to the group. They cowered together, bits of Dan splattered across their skin and clothing. Then Quinlin noticed one standing away from the rest, his shoulders pulled back and his chin high. He pointed at that elite.

"You."

"Mr. Turner." The elite took a step forward.

"You're my new lieutenant."

He lifted his chin higher as a half-smile appeared on his face. "Yes, Mr. Turner."

"Follow me." Quinlin stomped over to the shifter cages stacked against the wall. His new lieutenant running to catch up. Two cages were empty, but the other eighteen held shifters kidnapped in the raids.

"Do you know the magic distribution among these shifters?"

"Four water, six earth, and eight fire."

Quinlin nodded. This elite made an acceptable lieutenant. The throbbing in his head subsided as his pulse and heart rate returned to normal. His mind shifted to the *grimoire*, mentally flipping through the pages, looking for how to make the cursed creatures stronger. Although not finding anything specific, his father had written a brief note regarding the shifter's health and the quality of the life force extracted.

While rubbing his chin, he paced in front of the cages, processing his thoughts. Then he stopped, turning to his new lieutenant.

"I want two shifters used per siphoning curse. That should make them larger and stronger than the first cursed wolf."

"That means four arcanum to cast the curse, correct?" responded the lieutenant.

"Use five to be certain of the curse's potency." Quinlin continued to ponder. Given the one-time use of the artifact, weaker arcanum would have to be brought into the elite group. "And two additional arcanum for the elemental magic curse." That should be more than enough to successfully cast the curse.

Quinlin turned back to the cages as he waved his hand in a large sweep in front of them. "Use all the shifters, create nine cursed creatures."

"Yes, Mr. Turner. Anything else?"

"Test the controlling spells. They may need multiple arcanum with the upgraded version of the cursed creatures."

He turned back to his lieutenant, placing a hand on his shoulder. "Create the cursed wolf first. Then organize a live, public demonstration of its power."

"Consider it done."

Quinlin smiled, feeling better than he had all day. He headed toward the door. Then, without turning, shouted out a command.

"Oh, and clean up this mess."

CHAPTER TWENTY-FIVE

KEREN

K eren once again crouched in the bushes with a flashlight clenched in her hands. Only this time, the bushes were outside her own house. They left Nadria's car at the gas station on the corner. The same one she paid penance at for shoplifting. She guided her friends through neighbors' yards to avoid being seen.

"Is anyone patrolling?" Nadria whispered.

While craning her neck to view the back porch, she let out a breath. "No, I don't see anything but the yellow barricade tape."

"Do you think there are magic wards to trap intruders?" Nadria asked.

She never considered that. It made sense to use wards instead of guards. "What wards might they use?"

"Well," Nadria contemplated for a minute, "there are wards that can alert someone up to one mile away if it's broken."

"The inquisitors' station is farther than one mile," Ordell said.

Nadria shifted closer to her, her voice quivering. "There's a ward that's like sticky fingers. Your feet get stuck to the ground if you step on it."

She squeezed Nadria's hand, trying to calm her nerves. "Anything else?"

"Not that I can think of," Nadria hesitated, "but I'm not experienced with that type of magic."

Ordell scooted in front of them. "I'll go to the porch and try the door."

He had been through enough. Keren wouldn't let him risk getting arrested. "No. What if you're caught?"

"Better one of us than all of us." He smirked. "Besides, you can come up with a plan to rescue me if something happens."

Keren took a deep breath, then plunked her house keys in his hand. "Text me when you're inside."

He saluted. "Yes, boss."

She frowned, shifting to a new position. Ordell hopped on the porch, disappearing around the corner.

While holding her breath, she waited for something to happen, something to snap. Her phone buzzed with a text from Ordell.

"I'm in."

They scrambled after him, entering the house.

Keren stiffened, looking around the room. Pots and pans littered the floor. Every cabinet stood open. Stunned, she continued into the living room. They tore the furniture to shreds, tables were busted, and lamp pieces lay scattered on the floor.

Emotion flooded her mind. She wasn't able to tell one from the other: anger, pain, guilt, sadness, hopelessness. They rolled in a jumbled mess.

Nadria put a hand to her chest. "They destroyed everything."

Keren gritted her teeth, fighting back tears. The Dark Guild arcanum took everything from her. Her Mom, her house, and possessions. She had to stop them.

"Let's go to Mom's office." Keren headed down the hall.

After stepping into the office, she stopped in her tracks. The room was bare. Not a piece of furniture or even a scrap of paper remained. Black scorch marks ran up the wall. This must have had been where the attack happened. She ran to the closet, throwing the doors open. Mom's jackets lay in a heap on the floor.

She bent to touch them, then realized they were shredded to pieces. After collapsing on the floor, she pulled the scraps of her mom's coat to her face. She smelled the faint scent of lilac, Mom's favorite perfume. Her shoulders heaved from the heavy sobs. Everything released. She held nothing back.

Ordell and Nadria huddled around, crying with her. They let the stress, pain, and sadness from the last two days flow out of them.

When there were no more tears to shed, Keren wiped her face. She kissed her friends on the cheek and stood. "Wait for me here."

She needed time alone, time to take in the state of her house, which mirrored the state of her emotions, broken and torn apart.

While wandering to the kitchen, she pulled the key out of her pocket.

"What do you belong to?" A misty One appeared, hovering in the doorway. His eyes locked with hers. She held up the key. "What does this open?" It did a somersault, then flew out of the kitchen.

Her heart raced as she bolted up the stairs after One. It flew into her room. She dashed in, finding it hovering over a broken pile of dressers and night tables where her bed should have been.

She sighed, dropping her shoulders. "This is my room, One." Going to her closet, she rifled through the pile on the floor. At least they didn't shred her clothes. She grabbed a pair of jeans and a T-shirt, trading out the scrubs. She turned to go. When something poked her in the back of the head.

"Ouch."

She looked back, seeing One. Did it poke her with its tail? That hurt. Flying back to the center of the room, it landed on the splintered remnants of furniture.

A tingling sensation itched the hand holding the key. This might be crazy, but it was all she had. "Guys," she yelled out the door. "I may have found something."

After Ordell and Nadria joined her, she pointed to the pile of rubble. "What we're looking for is there."

Ordell's face lit up. "Awesome. What are we looking for?"

She hesitated, considering the weight of their stare. The hopeful looks on their faces made her wish she had just ignored One.

"I'm not sure."

Nadria frowned. "What do you mean you're not sure?"

"One believes there's something here. It led me up here."

Nadria shook her head. "If your imaginary friends are part of you, they can't know something you don't know."

That made sense, in theory. But One knew the room Mom was in when Briggs took her to the Restricted Ward. Could it have a way of tracking?

"One showed Briggs and me the room Mom was in that first night." Expressionless faces gazed back at her.

Ordell moved to the pile, pulling pieces out. Keren and Nadria joined him. They cleared the pile in total silence.

With three people working, clearing the pile only took a few minutes.

"We didn't find anything." Nadria sat on the floor.

"Is there anywhere else your mom might hide something?" Ordell joined Nadria on the floor. He took her hand.

While looking at One, Keren pushed her thoughts to him. *Where is the item this key opens?*

One somersaulted over the same spot. She let out an exasperated breath, looking at the floor beneath One. A shimmer caught her eye. While thinking maybe it was the moonlight, she knelt, running her hand across the spot. Tiny ripples moved under her fingertips.

"What are you doing?" Ordell slid closer.

"I'm guessing there's a protection spell over this spot. Watch." She waved her hand over the spot again. This time, there was no doubt. Her hand caused a gentle ripple in the mirage.

"I don't see anything." Ordell moved his face closer.

"Me either." Nadria watched Keren's hand.

Keren sat on her heels, looking up at One. Was this another vision, something only she could see? While squinting at One, she pushed a thought at him. *How can I remove the spell?*

It flew over Nadria's head.

Gasping, Keren widened her eyes.

"What?" Nadria looked where Keren's eyes focused over her head. "Is something wrong?"

She grabbed Nadria's arm. "Do you know any magic that removes or inactivates protection spells?"

"Remove protection spells? No." Nadria looked into Keren's eyes. She must have seen the desperation. "Well, Granny used to be a custodian at a nursing home. She said families often came to visit the residents with memory globes purchased from fairy stores. These packaged spells left magic remnants that Granny cleaned with a wiping spell."

Ordell leaned in. "Did she teach you the spell?"

"Yes." Nadria smiled. "She'd put remnants of used magic around the house and had me wipe them. She insisted too many remnants were dangerous, and I needed to practice cleaning them up."

"I've never heard of that," Ordell said.

"Granny said magic use today was sloppy and low quality." Nadria shrugged. "She said, years ago, wielders took pride in and respected magic. Now, they mass-produce spells and potions for profit. I never questioned Granny. I enjoyed playing the wiping game."

Keren pointed to the floor. "Can you do that spell now, over this spot?"

"I can try. I'll need some water."

Ordell retrieved a glass of water from the kitchen.

"Here it goes." Nadria dipped her fingers in the glass, rubbing the water across the floor. She took a deep breath. While closing her eyes, she held her palms toward the floor. Her forearms shimmered.

The ripple turned to a vibration. "Keep going, it's working."

Ordell focused on the spot. "I still don't see anything."

Just then, the house moaned. An ear-splitting *snap* made them cover their ears. The bedroom floor cracked open.

"What's happening?" Ordell shouted.

Thick gray fingers reached through the crack. The house moaned, shaking as if caught in an earthquake. Another deafening *crack* and the gap widened enough for the creature to fit its head through. It looked to be made of clay. Expressionless eyes scanned the room.

Nadria screamed. "A golem!" She scrambled back until she slammed into the wall.

The golem worked to wiggle its way out of the crack.

"I didn't mean to." Nadria's body trembled.

Keren staggered over to her, grabbing her clammy hand. The house's shaking made it difficult to walk. "We have to get out of here."

Ordell slid over, grabbing her other hand. They used the wall as a brace to get to their feet. The house shook again. This time, the crack widened enough for the golem to slide the rest of the way out.

Sweat dampened Keren's face. She didn't know what a golem was, but she knew it wasn't friendly. Her friends were in danger again because of her. She recklessly asked Nadria to use magic on an anomaly she didn't understand.

"Let's get out of here." They stumbled downstairs.

Once in the living room, she let go of Nadria's hand. "I can't leave without whatever this key opens." She pointed to the front door. "You go, get to safety."

"No." Nadria snatched her hand back. "I'm not leaving you."

Ordell pursed his lips, then gave Keren a sharp nod.

The golem stepped up to the railing. While stressed from the monster's weight, the staircase groaned, threatening to collapse.

"What's a golem?" Keren shouted over the house's cracking and groaning. The entire place was falling apart around them.

"They create golems from earth and magic. It does the bidding of one master and won't stop until they are told to." She squeezed Keren's hand. "We don't know what its orders are."

The golem's eyes locked on Nadria. Its massive body thumped down the stairs.

Nadria screamed.

"We won't let it hurt you." Ordell picked up a broken coffee table leg. While holding it like a bat, he stood in front of Nadria.

She pushed him aside. "It will kill you to get to me. Save yourselves."

"How does its master control it?" Keren crouched low as the golem approached the bottom of the staircase.

"There's a scroll in its mouth with the master's name. Removing the scroll should make it immobile." Nadria ran to the front door. While tugging at the handle, she screamed in frustration when the door wouldn't open. "If it catches me, nothing you do will make it let go."

Ordell swung the table leg at the thick clay body. The table leg shattered. Unfazed, the golem continued its steady gait toward its victim.

Pinned in the corner, Nadria crumpled to the ground, unable to take her bulging eyes off the golem. Ordell changed to his horse form, bucking and kicking the golem. Pieces of clay sprayed around the room, but the golem kept moving.

A pulse ignited in Keren's solar plexus. She felt it explode up her neck to the back of her eyes. Two appeared between Nadria and the golem. It lowered its flaming horns and charged. Clay flew in the air as Two smashed into the golem's chest, pushing it back. Ordell continued bucking, tearing into the golem's head.

Keren took her opportunity and rushed to Nadria. She dragged her past the golem. They ducked to avoid a swipe of the monster's hand. While skidding into the kitchen, she let go of Nadria to open the back door. A scream of frustration came from Keren when it didn't budge.

She gritted her teeth, pounding on the door until her palm burned. The bandage on her wrist turned red. No matter what she tried, the door refused to open. She stepped back, her eyes sweeping the room until she spotted the broom. After snatching it from the corner, she rammed it, stick end, into a window.

Over and over, she drove the broom into the window until she stopped from pure exhaustion. Some kind of magic had them trapped inside. Her stomach clenched. She dropped the broom and doubled over in pain.

As a scream rent the air, panic gripped her when she realized Nadria wasn't in the room. Did the golem have her? The house quaked, causing her to stumble on the way to the living room. Her vision blurred while white dots danced before her eyes. After falling to her knees, she crawled to Nadria, who sat cross-legged just inside the living room. Nadria's pallor and irregular breathing frightened her. She must be in shock.

The fight with the golem shifted since their escape to the kitchen. To get to Nadria, the golem changed directions. The fight was about halfway to the kitchen; the golem gaining inches with every step. Ordell's powerful black stallion's body shimmered with sweat. His dripping mane stuck to his neck. The effort to stop the golem taking its toll.

After seeing Nadria, the golem leaned into Two's attack. Two's muscles shook, the fire on its horns less vibrant.

Keren's vision blurred. She clung to consciousness. "Ordell, the scroll." Her last bit of strength fizzled away and Two disappeared.

Falling on her side, Keren could see the golem. With the sudden disappearance of Two, it crashed face-first to the ground. A black mouse scurried under the golem's head. She took a ragged breath. Tears came to her eyes seeing Ordell's mouse form reappear, pulling a paper behind him. Ordell tore the paper to shreds, then turned back to his human form.

The golem lay motionless on the floor. Keren gathered enough strength to get to her hands and knees. She started the trek back to her room. Whatever this key opened had to be in that crack.

"What are you doing? We have to get out of here." Ordell tugged at her arm. "Can't you hear the sirens?"

She struggled to get out a complete sentence. "Something there... didn't go through this... can't leave empty-handed." She reached out to him. "Help me upstairs."

"I'll go check." Ordell changed to a raven. He flew upstairs, disappearing from Keren's sight.

The sirens grew louder.

Ordell sprinted downstairs, carrying a gray box. After grabbing Keren by the arm, he pulled her to her feet. Spots danced in her eyes. Her legs wobbled but held her upright. At least the house stopped shaking. He handed her the box. It was rectangular, and the sides smooth to the touch. There wasn't a lid or a keyhole, just a solid mass. "That's the only thing I found."

He grabbed Nadria, gently pulling her to her feet. Nadria's eyes stared straight ahead. Keren took her other hand. Her skin was clammy to the touch. Nadria allowed Ordell to guide her to the kitchen.

When Ordell reached for the door handle, Keren held her breath. As if nothing ever happened, the door swung open. The magic holding them captive must have been connected to the golem.

Boots sounded on the front porch.

Ordell dragged them through the backyard and into the neighbor's yard. Keren clutched the box to her chest. The contents of this box might have the answers she was looking for to clear Mom's name and stop the Dark Guild. They didn't stop moving until they reached the gas station and Nadria's car.

CHAPTER TWENTY-SIX

BRIGGS

Briggs walked into the inquisitor station, grateful for the blast of cool air. Although only 9 am, the humidity made eighty degrees feel closer to ninety. After perching his sunglasses on the top of his head, he approached the reception desk.

"Good morning, Mabel."

"Good morning, Captain Briggs." The elderly woman leaned forward. "When's the last time you slept?"

Briggs chuckled. "I can't remember." He pointed to the door. "Buzz me in?"

A *buzz* and *click* came from the door.

"Thanks, Mabel."

"Get some sleep, Briggs." Mabel's voice trailed off as he stepped inside and closed the door.

Normally, he would have used his access badge at the back entrance, but the Chief Inquisitor's office was located closer to the front entrance. And as tired as he was, Briggs wanted the shortest walk. He also wanted to avoid any lengthy conversations with his coworkers.

The chief had ordered him and his squad to take the day off for a much-needed break. They had worked thirty-six hours straight. First, the Green Thumb Gardener's Supply, then Ms. Stewart's attack at home and again at the hospital, followed by the motel incident, kept his team hopping.

The chief had felt generous after Faraday and the warriors had tracked down one of the arcanum from the motel. A human woman. Her hands had been duct-taped behind her back. So far, she hadn't given him any information, but the interrogation process had only started.

Briggs went over the conversation again in his mind. *I don't think Ms. Stewart is an arcanum. I think she's a target.* He needed to present facts supporting his beliefs. The problem was, there weren't any. In his heart, he believed in Ms. Stewart's innocence. He'd known her most of his life. She wasn't capable of violence. Getting someone who didn't know her to believe in her innocence would be a challenge. But he was getting ahead of himself.

Right now, he only needed to convince the chief to release her into his protective custody. Once he did that, he could work on getting evidence of her innocence. The chief might say he was too close to the Stewart family to be objective and take him off the case. That was the worst-case scenario.

Maybe he should have this conversation after he got some sleep. No, he felt Ms. Stewart's life was in jeopardy as long as her location was public knowledge. The sooner he got her out of the hospital and into a safe house, the better.

He stepped through the door marked 'Chief Inquisitor'. A young lady Briggs didn't recognize looked up from her computer, ruby red lips the most prominent feature on her face.

"May I help you, Captain?"

"Yes, I'd like to see the chief if he's not busy." Briggs shifted his weight from one foot to the other. He should have thought about making an appointment. "Tell him it's Captain Briggs."

She nodded, picking up the phone. "Sir, a Captain Briggs is here to see you." She nodded again, then hung up.

"He'll see you." Her focus moved back to the computer.

"Thank you." Briggs moved to the chief's door, putting his hand on the doorknob. This meeting was important for both Ms. Stewart's safety and Keren's peace of mind. He knew not being able to see her mom tormented her.

He stepped inside. A balding fox shifter sat behind a mahogany desk. With age, his body shape had grown thicker than most fox shifters. But he could hold his own in the annual wrestling tournament. Stacks of files sat to his right. One file lay open in front of him.

"Briggs, I gave you the day off. What in blazes are you doing at the station? Captain Samuel's squad can manage Dark Guild calls for one day."

"Yes, sir. I have every confidence in Captain Samuel and his squad. I wanted to talk to you about Ms. Stewart."

"Pull up a seat." The chief gestured to a chair. "What's on your mind?"

Briggs sat down on the edge of the chair, not wanting to get too comfortable, fearing he might drift off to sleep.

"I have a theory. Ms. Stewart is not an arcanum."

"Nonsense. We have witnesses and medical records proving she used magic."

"Yes, I'm not disputing that. But it proves she used magic, not that she attacked anyone with it."

The chief huffed. "Your splitting hairs, captain. The witnesses were traumatized. I'm confident they'll remember her attacking with magic by the trial."

"The arcanum are trying to kill her. Don't you think we should keep her alive long enough to find out why? You could release her into my custody. I could take her to a safe house."

The chief slammed his hand on the desk. "Oh, she'll be alive but in a prison paying for her crimes."

"But, sir."

"Go home Briggs. You're tired and need some shut-eye." After dismissing Briggs, the chief continued studying the file on his desk.

"Yes, sir." Briggs stood and walked to the door. No, he couldn't leave without one more try. He turned to face the chief.

"Sir, the arcanum have attacked her twice. Keeping her in a publicly known area endangers innocent citizens. I'm sure it won't take long for the press to make that connection."

Briggs watched redness creep up the chief's neck to his face. His jaw flexed.

"The bands stay on." He pointed a stubby finger at Briggs. "If you lose her, I'll have your badge."

"Yes, sir." Briggs turned. He smiled as he left the office.

CHAPTER TWENTY-SEVEN

KEREN

The morning sun streamed through the window. Its warmth promising another hot Florida day. The trio situated themselves side-by-side on the daybed.

The box sat on the ottoman next to some danishes and donuts. It was well past 1 am when they made it back to Ordell's last night. After such a harrowing day, they were exhausted. They all agreed to wait until morning to investigate the box.

"Do you know how to open it?" Ordell asked. "It looks solid."

Keren's shower-damp hair clung to the bright yellow robe she borrowed from Mrs. Murphy. Rainbow striped socks hugged her feet. She clasped her hands in her lap. The answers she needed were inside this box. As her chest tightened, she wondered what would happen if she didn't like the answers. She reached for a danish.

"That's your third one." He gestured to the box. "How can you eat when this is waiting to be opened?"

"I can't help it. I'm starving." After taking a bite of the danish, she set it aside. Her trembling hand clutched the key in the robe's pocket. The ridges cut into her skin from too tight a grip.

After releasing the key, she leaned forward, picking the box up and setting it on her lap. If mom was a sorcerer, so was she. While swallowing the lump in her throat, she held a quivering hand, palm down, over the box. She strained to remember Dan's words.

"*Ostendoium.*"

A biting pain made her pull her hand back. She looked down at the tiny black dots on her palm. A lid seam appeared on the box, along with a keyhole. After slipping her hand back into the robe pocket, she wrapped her fingers around the key.

Nadria gasped. "How did you do that?"

Keren hung her head. "If mom was a sorcerer, that would mean I was too. I guess this proves she can wield magic."

"But it doesn't mean she attacked anyone or is an arcanum." Nadria rubbed Keren's back.

"How did you know that spell?" Ordell reached over, running his fingers over the box.

"Dan used it before he let the cursed wolf out of the cage." She set the box back on the ottoman. Silence filled the room. Pictures of Broden flashed in her mind. First, the picture they stole from Dan's house. Then the lifeless body lying at the cursed wolf's feet. By the looks on their faces, Keren guessed Ordell and Nadria must also be thinking about Broden.

After a few moments, she held out the fist, palm side up, containing the key. Then she opened her hand.

She felt numb. Her life was a lie. How many more lies could she take? How many more lies would the box reveal? She had to open it. No matter what was inside, it would bring her closer to the truth. The truth about Mom, the Dark Guild, and herself. And the truth, no matter how painful, was worth the price.

After slipping the key into the lock, a chill ran down her spine. What if the key didn't open the box?

"Well, open it already. The suspense is killing me." Ordell nudged her with his elbow.

She held her breath, then turned the key, hearing a faint *click*.

As Keren looked to the side, she saw Nadria had knitted her brows together. Her breathing was shallow. Then, turning to Ordell on the other side, she saw he chewed his lower lip. His eyes focused on the box like a kid waiting to open a Christmas present.

She hesitated, her trembling hands resting on top. "Do you think another golem is inside?"

Nadria's body stiffened. She wrapped her arms around her waist. "I hope not. But if there were, it should have appeared when you cast the spell."

Keren nodded. Just open it, she told herself, like tearing off a Band-Aid. They'd deal with the consequences. She opened the lid, bracing for something to pop out and attack them.

They breathed a collective sigh of relief when they saw a pile of papers. On top was a fat envelope. She opened the envelope, pulling out a stack of fifty-dollar bills.

"Whoa! How much is that?" Ordell asked.

Keren counted the crisp bills. "Five thousand dollars." Was this an emergency bug-out kit? Mom never mentioned hidden money, but that shouldn't surprise her at this point. Mom forgot to mention a lot of things. Keren's stomach dropped. She might find Mom's guilt, not innocence, in this box.

She set the money on the table, then lifted the papers out of the box. A thumb drive fell on the floor.

"Score." Ordell snatched it. He grabbed his laptop. While looking at Keren, he held up the drive. "Do you mind?"

"No, by all means." She stood up, switching places with Ordell, allowing him to move to the middle so Nadria saw the screen. She placed the papers on her lap.

He hesitated. "Do you think there's magic protecting this drive?"

Nadria shrugged. "I'll ask around to see if anyone has heard of spells cast on thumb drives." She pulled out her phone.

"No." Keren jumped up, causing the papers to fall and scatter across the floor. "Don't get anyone else involved."

Nodding, she put the phone away.

"Here goes nothing." Ordell plugged the drive into his laptop. His fingers danced across the keyboard.

While kneeling on the floor, Keren gathered the papers. A document caught her eye. The title said, 'Certificate of Birth.' She unfolded it and frowned. This had Mom's and Dad's names, but the child's name was Katrina Louise Stewart. The birth date was the same as hers. She ran her fingers over the raised seal.

Ordell's voice broke into her thoughts. "This looks like a *Book of Shadows*."

She stuffed the birth certificate in her pocket, then sat next to Ordell.

"Only there're all kinds of notes scribbled on the sides." He zoomed in on a page.

Keren's eyes widened seeing her mother's handwriting. This information proved her mom used magic. She took a deep breath, reminding herself of what Nadria said. Just because mom used magic doesn't mean she attacked anyone.

"There are several other files." He opened a dozen. "I don't understand the writing."

"There are news articles here, too." Ordell and Nadria started reading through those.

Keren returned to the floor, picking up the scattered papers. Several pages had a strange language with scribbled translations on the side. The pages had tattered edges as if they had been torn from a book. Mom was a linguist. Translating old text was her job. Why did she have these locked in the box with a golem protecting them?

She picked up another paper. It had a Certificate of Death across the top. Her heart pounded in her chest. This must be Dad, Grandma, or Grandpa's document.

Her eyes focused on the deceased's name, Katrina Louise Stewart. This made little sense. According to this, Katrina died just over the age of three. They marked it as an accidental death. She ran her fingers over the raised seal. It appeared legitimate. Heat radiated in her body. She shifted through the rest of the papers, finding her birth certificate.

Did she have a twin sister who died at an early age? Mom never mentioned a twin. Her head pounded.

"Are you OK?" Ordell touched her shoulder. "You look pale."

She crumpled the death certificate into her pocket. She didn't want them to know. Not until she worked out the questions spinning in her head. "Yeah, I'm fine." She grabbed her half-eaten danish and took a seat next to Ordell.

"Well, there's more." He looked back to the screen. "Twenty years ago, there was a similar crime spree involving shifters. They found them beaten to death, or they had gone missing."

"Do you think it's related to the arcanum's crimes today?" asked Nadria.

"Several of these files make little sense." Ordell turned to Keren. "Too bad your mom can't help us figure this out."

Her mouth went dry. After stuffing the rest of the papers in the box, she slammed the cover down.

"Anything important in there?" Both of them stared at her.

"Just family documents." She put her hand in her pocket, running her fingers over the papers. Mom had the answers. But did she trust her to tell the truth?

She sighed. "I can't get in to visit her. I'm still restricted."

"But," Ordell said, "I thought you said you visited her yesterday."

Her heart jumped into her throat. She'd have to tell them something. Would she be violating Quinlin's trust if she told them?

She motioned for Nadria to join them on the couch. "I arrived at the hospital first thing yesterday morning. The guards refused to let me in to see her. I was desperate. I knew Quinlin had access to the Restricted Ward, so..."

Nadria gasped. "You convinced him to sneak you into the ward."

She nodded. "I dressed as a nurses' assistant, and he helped me get into her room." She hoped the flush on her face wasn't noticeable. "But then the explosion, or rather magic attack, happened."

"That's why you were wearing scrubs. You didn't have time to change back into your clothes." Ordell sounded proud that he figured out the scrubs puzzle.

She decided there was no need to tell them about the embarrassing dress meets frozen drink episode. She ruffled his hair. "Yeah, that's why."

"Don't tell me you're thinking about asking him to help you again?" Nadria rubbed her temples. "You just met the man. How can you be sure he won't turn you in to the inquisitors?"

"He won't. I trust him." She fought the giddy, girl-in-love smile and kept a stoic look on her face. "Besides, what choice do I have?" She pointed to the laptop. "We need her help to figure out what all this means."

Nadria's mouth moved, but no words came out. She furrowed her eyebrows.

"We're out of options. I need to talk to Mom." Even if Mom was a Dark Guild arcanum, Keren needed to hear her side of the story. There had to be a logical explanation. She also needed to know about Katrina.

Nadria stood, pacing the room. She picked up her car keys from the side table, putting them in Keren's hands. Tears brimmed in her eyes. "Be careful."

Standing, she pulled Nadria into a tight hug. "Thank you."

After changing her clothes, she grabbed her backpack and headed to the hospital.

CHAPTER TWENTY-EIGHT

QUINLIN

While pushing a medicine cart down the corridor, Quinlin made note of the security camera locations. Since he had destroyed the Restricted Ward, they moved that woman here, to the fourth floor, and doubled the guards outside her door. Not that they could stop him should he choose to kill her. The guards would be necessary casualties. But he didn't want to kill her, not yet. Not until he understood what happened yesterday afternoon. How and why did that magnificent creature appear? Was Keren connected to it? His vibrating phone pulled him from his thoughts.

They didn't allow hospital employees to use cell phones while working, and because he needed this cover for a while longer, he let the call go to voicemail. He stopped outside that woman's door. Since his magic attack, they had allowed no nurses' assistants into her room.

"Hey, Jack." He gave a two-finger salute to the guard. "Anything new?"

Jack glanced at the other guard, who glared at him out of the corner of his eye. "I'm sorry, I can't divulge any information." He winked at Quinlin, giving a slight tip to his head.

"Right, of course." Quinlin continued down the corridor, turning at the next corner two doors away. After a moment, he heard the approach of Jack's heavy footsteps.

In a low, husky voice, Jack spoke, knowing Quinlin would overhear him. "She's conscious and asking for her daughter. She won't talk to anyone but her." He dropped a piece of paper on the floor, turned, and went back to his post.

Jack had a crush on one of the ward nurses. But as long as Jack worked as a guard on the ward, policy restricted him from socializing with the nurses. So Quinlin offered to be the go-between to help the couple stoke their relationship fire.

He waited a few minutes before he pushed the cart back into the corridor. While stooping to pick up the paper, his stomach turned. It was bad enough to be dressed in scrubs pretending to be a nurses' assistant but delivering love messages between Jack and his nurse crush Sally was almost too degrading. But if he wanted information on that woman, he had to play the game. He pushed the cart to the nurses' station, then leaned on the counter.

"How's it going today, Sally?" He dropped the note on her desk.

She gave him a sly smile, retrieving the note. "Things are quiet today now that Mr. Blake is under heavy sedation since his outburst yesterday."

Quinlin laughed. "Seeing guards chase and tackle a naked man in the corridor was entertaining."

Sally put a hand over her mouth, stifling a giggle. After opening the note, her cheeks flushed with color. A wide grin appeared on her face. While licking her lips, she picked up a pen and paper, writing her reply. She folded the paper into a neat square. Then, checking no one was watching, she put an imprint of her lipstick on it. She slid the paper onto the counter.

Quinlin plastered a smile on his face. He took the paper, then stepped away from the counter. "Have a great day, Sally."

"You too, Quinlin."

After glancing at the wall clock, Quinlin took his lunch break. Jack would have to wait for his beloved's response. He tucked Sally's note into his pocket and pulled out his phone to check for messages. Keren had left a voicemail.

Quinlin stopped as he neared the cafeteria, seeing Keren pacing outside. After walking to the window, he tapped on the glass to get her attention.

She turned. Her face lit up when she saw him. Those sparkling eyes shimmered in the bright Florida sunshine. She motioned for him to come outside.

"I'm glad you came." Her long brown hair flowed freely. The breeze blew a few strands across her face. He fought the urge to brush them aside.

Her jeans and T-shirt hugged her skin. Normally, this style of dress put him off. But it fit Keren's personality. She fidgeted, taking a deep breath.

"I need to see my mom again."

Those glimmering eyes met his. He imagined the power that lay behind them. It had to have been her controlling the creature.

"Can you help me?"

Getting her in to see that woman was challenging the first time. Now, with heightened security, getting her in again without alerting her he could use magic seemed next to impossible. He also had the problem of being recognized by that woman. But if he got her in, maybe she would make that creature appear again. That alone was worth the risk.

"I realize you barely know me," she took his hand, "but you're my only way in."

"I feel a connection to you." His thumb rubbed the back of her hand, and his hand tingled at the touch of her soft skin. "But you're asking me to not only risk my job but risk getting arrested." He knew Keren had a sharp mind. While he had every intention of helping her, making this too easy would rouse her suspicions.

She squeezed his hand. Her stare dove straight into his soul as a warming sensation enveloped his chest.

"I think I can trust you." She looked around. "Can we go somewhere more private?"

More private. He smirked, thinking a physical encounter with Keren would be extraordinary. Unfortunately, he knew that wasn't what she meant. However, the look on his face gave away his thoughts. Her mouth fell open.

"Oh, no. I just want to talk. I mean, not that you're not hot." Her face turned crimson. "I want to tell you why I have to see to her. It's a matter of life and death."

Surprised by his disappointment, Quinlin nodded, then led her to a small courtyard with a few picnic tables. "Is this private enough?"

"Yes." She slid onto a bench at one table. He sat across from her.

"I'm sorry I lied to you about my mom being my aunt." She ran her hands across her face. "Mom was a victim of a magic attack. The inquisitors charged her with magic with the intent to kill, and they believe she's an arcanum of the Dark Guild." While leaning over the table, she folded her hands in front of her. Her face had a look of desperation while she waited for his reaction.

He had already known about the charges. But he also knew that woman had indeed, a long time ago, been a member of the Dark Guild. That's how she got close enough to murder his father. While doing an Academy Award-worthy rendition of surprise and horror, he made his body language respond to her information.

"Yeah, I know. It's a lot to take in." She reached across the table.

He took her hands. "That's terrible. But why won't they let you in to see her?"

She let out a long breath. "I'm suspected of being an arcanum of the Dark Guild, too. If they convict Mom, they'll probably arrest me and we'll both be sent to prison. But we're not guilty of the charges."

While squeezing her hand, he pressed her for more information. After all, Keren had mentioned something she found regarding the Dark Guild.

He also grappled with the fact she had infiltrated his ranks, destroying the cursed wolf. His stomach clenched. His first successful attempt at controlling elemental magic had been destroyed. It was a catastrophic loss for the mission. What was supposed to have been a celebration had turned into a public spectacle. He had taken care of the loose ends within the Dark Guild, but he didn't know the Guild's extent of exposure to the public.

"I know you love your mom, and you want to see her," he had no other way than being direct, "but why the urgency to see her now?" *Trust me*, he thought. *Tell me all your secrets.*

She sighed. "OK, please, keep this confidential. Do you promise?"

"I promise." Quinlin leaned forward, his pulse quickened.

"I've been trying to find evidence to clear my mom's name at the trial. But I'm running out of time. I've come across some information, but I need her help to understand what it means."

Alarms went off in Quinlin's head. What sort of information could Keren have that would clear that woman's charges? If it was something about the Dark Guild, the mission could be in jeopardy. Whatever it was, Keren didn't suspect him. After all, she had come here to get his help.

Without a doubt, he had to find out the details of this information and what that woman knew. He had thought he retrieved everything she stole from his father the night of the first attack. Apparently, he had overlooked something.

"This is a lot to take in." He furrowed his brow.

"I know, but please."

"I want to help, but I feel like I'm taking an enormous risk without knowing exactly why."

"Your life could be in danger if I tell you." Her voice hardened.

"My life will be in danger if you don't." He released her hands, sitting straight. "I have to know the details before I agree."

Keren's shoulders deflated as she looked down at her hands. He needed to get her to trust him. Pulling on her heart strings should do the trick.

"The Dark Guild killed my father."

Her eyes snapped to his. Good, he had her attention. Now, he needed to spin a believable story.

"He had stopped at a grocery store on his way home from work. While he was inside, the Dark Guild attacked. I'm told the place went up in flames so fast the fire department had no chance of saving it." He paused, lowering his head. "No one made it out. My mom said the police told her the Dark Guild had targeted the shifter owners. But apparently, they didn't care who was inside the store." He took a deep breath to emphasize his made-up pain and sorrow. "So, if this is about getting even with the Dark Guild, I want in."

"I'm so sorry." She scurried to his side of the table, wrapping her arm around his shoulder. "I didn't know."

"It's not something I advertise." He stiffened his body, trying to signal anger.

"When was he killed?" Her hand moved in circles on his back.

"Twenty years ago." Her hand stopped moving. Apparently, this meant something to her.

"I see."

"My mom and Uncle Rob raised me. But there's no real replacement for a father."

"No, there's not. I lost my dad in a car accident when I was young. I understand that void in your life." She rested her head on his shoulder.

"So, I want to help. Tell me what's going on."

Keren lifted her head off his shoulder. She pursed her lips, obviously torn in her decision-making. He held his breath, waiting for the response.

"There's too much speculation right now. If I can get to my mom, she should be able to help tie up the loose ends. Once I know, I'll tell you everything."

Not the response he wanted, but it would have to do. "I'm in. Let's plan how we're getting you into that hospital room."

CHAPTER TWENTY-NINE

KEREN

As she clipped on the fake ID tag, Keren wondered how Quinlin had gotten her picture on it. Only three hours had passed since they spoke this morning. She had promised to tell him everything after this, but could she keep that promise? Getting in to see Mom was worth any sacrifice, even lying to Quinlin.

"Ready?" He brushed at tiny wrinkles in his scrubs.

"Yes." She tugged at the blonde, bob-styled wig he'd brought. Something gnawed at the back of her mind. He seemed too good at this. She pushed the thought away. It didn't matter, as long as she saw Mom.

They passed the same maintenance man on the way to the elevator. Keren frowned, turning back to look at him. "Didn't we pass that guy the first time?"

"Who?" Quinlin hooked his arm in hers. "You mean John? He's harmless."

Quinlin picked up his pace, pulling her along, forcing her to pull her eyes off John. With the Restricted Ward in shambles, it made sense they had reassigned the maintenance staff in that area.

The elevator was empty when it opened. She sighed in relief.

"You have an ID now." He handed her a clipboard. "Walk and act like you belong here. This information on the clipboard is about an actual patient in the ward."

Her eyes shot to the clipboard. "My mom?"

"No. They guard those documents closely these days. It's Mr. Blake's information. He tends to, well, wander the ward." He made air quotes with his fingers. "You can pretend you're looking for him if you're caught somewhere you shouldn't be."

As the elevator neared the eighth floor, she trembled.

"Don't worry." He put his hand over hers. "Trust me. It's a believable story." He gave her a confident smile.

Warmth radiated from her hand through her body. Quinlin would keep her safe. Everything would be fine. She reached into her pocket, running her fingers along the raised seal of Katrina's death certificate. This, above everything else, was the answer she looked for.

"Remember what to do?"

"Yes." She thought the plan was vague. But with only three hours to figure it out, this had to do. "Hang back like I'm reading the notes on the clipboard. Then go into Mom's room after you distract the guards."

"Right. Let nothing sidetrack you. You'll only have one chance."

She nodded. He never elaborated on what the distraction would be. He said she'd know when it happened.

As the elevator door opened, Quinlin lifted her chin with his fingers. His radiant smile calmed her nerves. "You belong here." He tapped her nametag. "Nurses' assistant Ms. Able."

Keren's heart fluttered. She wanted to lose herself in those blue eyes. A haven from the craziness of her life. She smiled back, then followed him out into the corridor, letting him gain some distance from her. She pretended to read the file but monitored Quinlin.

"Hey, Jack." He gave one guard a two-finger salute as he walked past. He put his hand in his pocket.

"Quinlin," Jack said in a gruff tone.

The stocky guards standing outside Mom's room looked intimidating. Her stomach dropped, thinking Quinlin wouldn't be able to distract them both.

"Oh." Quinlin paused. He turned, walking back to Jack. The other guard tensed his muscles. "Have you heard? I took your advice and bought the Mustang. You were right, you only live once. She's a beauty. Thanks." He took his hand out of his pocket, extending it toward Jack. There seemed to be a piece of paper in his palm.

Jack grinned, taking Quinlin's hand. "Congratulations." The handshake lasted only a few seconds.

Turning, Quinlin headed to the nurses' station.

Jack turned to his partner. "I'm taking a quick break."

The mountain of a man gave a curt nod.

One guard down, but this other one would be tough. She didn't know how Quinlin would pull this off.

Seconds after Jack disappeared into the men's room, a shrill scream erupted from the nurses' station. Keren crouched, cringing against the wall. Jack's partner fell into a fighting stance, glancing up and down the corridor. His accusing eyes landed on her.

Sweat trickled down her spine. Was that Quinlin's signal? Or was this another attack? The clipboard shook in her hands as she struggled to remember the plan. "Where is Mr. Blake?" finally blurted out of her mouth.

Another scream came from the nurses' station. An alarm blared through the corridor. The guard at Mom's door hesitated, then ran in that direction. Jack stumbled out of the men's room. The two almost collided.

After throwing the clipboard on the floor, she crouched, scurrying to her mom's door, and slipped inside the room.

Mom looked toward the door, her face pale but eyes bright. She clenched the blankets to her chest.

"What's going on?"

After rushing to the bed, Keren tugged off the wig. "It's me."

Tears welled in her mom's eyes. "Keren."

Falling into her mom's embrace, Keren felt her mom's body heave with each sob. Tears streamed down Keren's cheeks as she pulled her mom close.

While rubbing her mom's back, Keren whispered, "We don't have much time." She pushed her gently away. "And I need answers."

"I was so worried. Are you alright? Where are you staying? I heard they seized the house."

Keren took her hands. "I'm staying with the Murphy's. I'm fine, but I need to ask you some questions."

While nodding, Mom wiped her face with the blankets. "I can't remember anything about the attack. I know I remember driving home from work then my next memory is in the ambulance being rushed to the hospital."

Keren shook her head. "Not about the attack. We found the key and the box."

Mom stiffened, grabbing Keren's arms. "The golem." Her eyes widened. "If you have the box..." She stopped mid-sentence.

"No one was hurt." The golem story had to wait for another time.

Keren reached into her pocket while her heart raced. She needed the truth about the death certificate. The problem was, she wasn't sure if she was ready to know the truth. This could just be a clerical error. If that were the case, though, why did Mom have the document locked in a golem-protected box? She pulled the death certificate from her pocket, unfolded it, then showed it to her mom.

"Who is Katrina?"

Mom gasped. "I never wanted you to find this."

Keren's pulse throbbed in her temples, not the response she hoped for. "We have a *grimoire* and a *Book of Shadows*. I think they're yours. What does this all mean?"

"I'm so sorry you had to find out like this."

"Find out what, Mom?" Keren fought to keep her voice down. "I don't understand any of this." When the alarm stopped, she glanced at the door, expecting the guard to burst into the room at any moment. "I don't have time to dance around the topic. Tell me what this means."

Mom looked away, the television drawing her attention. She frowned, snatching the remote and turning up the volume.

"This is breaking news from ABC Channel 9. A dangerous, unidentified creature has been spotted on Princeton Street in College Park. So far, it's reported one person has been killed and three injured. We're cutting to live helicopter footage."

The camera's overhead view zoomed onto Princeton Street. The area was in utter chaos. A multi-car pileup blocked the road. People ran in all directions. Keren sprung off the bed, then positioned herself in front of the television. A large dog or wolf stumbled down the street on crooked legs. Flames licked across its body but caused it no harm. Behind it walked three people. One had her palms outstretched toward the creature. The others walked on either side of her. Their palms extended outward.

Keren gasped, covering her mouth with her hand. It was another cursed wolf, only super-sized. While based on what she could tell from the television screen, it appeared to be at least double the proportions of the one at the motel. She guessed those were arcanum following behind.

Three had killed a cursed wolf back at the motel. She didn't realize there were more. Her body convulsed as memories of that night flashed through her mind. How many were there? As the arcanum group made their way down the street, fire balls flew from the cursed wolf into the surrounding buildings. A fox shifter raced out of a burning building, his entire body covered in flames. He made it halfway across the street before collapsing into a charred heap.

Then the camera panned to a dozen inquisitors positioning themselves in the street. They attacked the arcanum and cursed wolf with water jets and fire balls. But an invisible shield diverted the attacks away from the arcanum trio. The cursed wolf, who received the full blow of the attacks, kept moving as though they were only a mild nuisance. It forced the inquisitors back as the arcanum continued their procession. With a sudden jerk of its head, the cursed wolf faced the inquisitors, sending a stream of blazing fire into the group. The entire line lit up like a bonfire dowsed in gasoline.

Keren screamed at the gruesome site, stumbling backwards, and bumping into the bed.

Mom grabbed her hand. "It's started."

She whipped her head back to her mom. "What's started? What do you know about this?"

She swung her feet off the bed. "We have to go. There's not much time."

After stuffing the death certificate back in her pocket, Keren faced her mom while pointing back at the television. "What do you know about this?"

"I'll tell you everything." She grabbed Keren's shoulder to steady herself as she rose to her feet. "Right now, we have to get out of here. We have to stop them."

"Stop them? You mean the Dark Guild?" Mom had mentioned stopping the Dark Guild during her last visit. That's why they searched for the box after finding the key. But Keren didn't understand how the papers could stop the Dark Guild. "The inquisitors can't even stop them."

Who was this woman clinging to her? She looked like her mom, but the caring, warm person she remembered didn't exist. Instead, this frail person with terrible secrets expected her help to escape from the hospital. Sirens blared in the street. The entire police force must be going to fight the creature.

Keren pulled away. "No. I don't recognize who you are anymore."

Mom clenched Keren's forearm with surprising strength. "You can hate me, but think about what's happening out there. Think about what's been happening all over the city. Shifters are being persecuted." Mom pointed back at the television screen. "This," she waved at the screen, as tears flowed from her eyes, "means the Dark Guild can now annihilate them."

Nadria. Keren's heart pounded in her chest. And Briggs. The Dark Guild was targeting shifters. She had to do everything possible to save her friends.

"You'll tell me everything."

"Yes, I promise." Mom's voice sounded weak. When her legs buckled, she leaned most of her weight on Keren. Mom's eyelids fluttered. She was losing consciousness.

Keren wrapped her arm around her mom's waist, dragging her to the door. She pulled it open to peek outside. No guards in sight.

With her mom's arm draped around her shoulder, she threw the door open, hurrying toward the elevator.

"Stop right there," a voice boomed.

Keren paused, looking back to see Jack crumple to the ground. Quinlin stood behind him. "What the hell are you doing?"

"We're getting her out." Keren continued dragging Mom's limp body toward the elevator.

Quinlin let out an exasperated growl. "This is not the plan."

"The plan has changed." Keren turned the corner, pressing the elevator button.

He glanced around. "Fine." After pulling out his cell phone, he looked like he was texting someone.

They entered the empty elevator. Mom's breath was heavy, and she let out a moan.

"Is she dying?" asked Quinlin.

"No, well, I'm not sure." Keren shifted her mom's weight. "Did you see the breaking news story?" She looked over at Quinlin. He pursed his lips. But no, that couldn't have been the beginning of a repressed smile.

"Yes, I saw it."

"Then you know this is a Dark Guild attack."

"Right." He furrowed his brow.

"Mom said she can help, so I'm getting her out." Keren grunted under her mom's weight. "I could use a little help here."

As Quinlin scooped her mom into his arms, his face grimaced. Mom must have been heavier than she looked. The elevator opened. She saw John, the maintenance man, waiting with a gurney. She put a hand on Quinlin's arm, not trusting this guy. Quinlin pushed past her, stomping out of the elevator, plopping Mom down on the gurney. While keeping a suspicious eye on John, Keren pulled the blankets over her mom. She watched John as he got into the elevator. Once the elevator doors closed, she let out a sigh of relief.

Not wanting to lose another set of clothes, she raced ahead. "I'm getting my stuff. I'll meet you by the exit." She ran into the locker room, stuffing her clothes into her backpack. She grabbed another set of scrubs from a locker for Mom, then caught up with them at the exit door.

"A gurney outside will draw attention." Quinlin yanked the covers off Mom. His lip curled up. "She has to walk out."

"Here." Keren pulled the scrubs from her backpack. "Let me put these on her."

A few minutes later, they hurried from the hospital toward their cars with Mom supported between them.

After Quinlin helped her get her mom into Nadria's car, he asked her, "Where are you headed?"

She hesitated, thinking it was better if she didn't get Quinlin involved any more than he already was.

His face reddened. "I've stuck my neck out for you. The least you can do is tell me what's going on." Anger flashed in his eyes.

This was a different side of Quinlin. But given the circumstances, a quick temper wasn't unreasonable.

"I'm going to Nadria's house."

He gave a curt nod. "Give me the address in case we get separated."

Since she had gotten him into this situation, she felt she owed him a debt, so she gave him Nadria's address.

CHAPTER THIRTY

KEREN

Mom sat in Nadria's bed with pillows tucked around her for support. They had turned on the television, hoping to get an update on the cursed wolf and arcanum. While pulling the covers up around her waist, Keren noticed Mom's cold, clammy skin. The escape from the hospital must have taken a lot out of her. A breaking news alert came on the television.

The reporter stood on Princeton Street while the scene behind him showed firefighters working to put out the raging fires.

"I'm reporting from Princeton Street after the Dark Guild rampage just moments ago. They reported two people dead, twenty-four injured. This animal murdered all twelve shifters in inquisitor squad 57 in this horrific event."

Keren fought the burn of bile in her throat. So many deaths. That could have been Briggs' squad called to face the cursed wolf. It relieved her it wasn't, but her heart went out to all the friends and families of the victims.

The news reporter put his fingertips to his ear. "I'm getting a report that one of the arcanum suspects is in custody. The other two suspects and their creature are still at large. The attacks have ceased for now. Inquisitors are telling people to stay home and lock their doors."

Keren shut off the television as Nadria brought in a tray with two teacups. "I thought you might want something to drink." She set it down on the nightstand. "How are you doing?"

"I'm better." Mom's voice cracked. She smiled, reaching out toward Nadria. "Thank you for taking care of Keren."

Nadria grabbed her hand, giving it a squeeze. "Now, we're taking care of you. Ordell's here, too. If you need anything, just let us know."

Mom nodded, releasing Nadria's hand.

Nadria kissed Keren's forehead, then left the room. Mom shifted, leaning toward Keren.

"We can't stay here." She rubbed her arms. "This will be the first place they check."

"You mean the inquisitors?" Keren sat on the side of the bed.

Mom nodded. "And the arcanum."

Keren's heart shattered. Her mom just admitted she had connections to the Dark Guild. Their crime spree around the city had targeted shifters. Each attack left death and destruction in its wake. Princeton Street being their latest target. Why were they looking for her mom? She also hid the fact she was a sorcerer. And that Keren was a sorcerer, too.

But there were more family secrets that she needed to uncover. Although she knew learning about Katrina paled compared to the Dark Guild connection, she had to know the truth. She pulled the death certificate from her pocket.

"We're not going anywhere until you explain this." Tears brimmed in Keren's eyes. She clenched her jaw, trying to keep her emotions under control. When her mom reached for Keren's hand, she jerked it back.

"Tell me now or I'll call the inquisitors myself and turn you in." That came out harsher than she intended.

Mom's ashen face betrayed the pain Keren just inflicted. "You had a twin sister, Katrina Louise. That's her death certificate."

While Keren didn't want to believe it, she could tell by the look in her mom's eyes it was true. She turned away, looking down. Mom had never mentioned Katrina. Wouldn't a parent have had pictures or other items in memory of a deceased child?

"Why didn't you tell me?"

"After your dad's and grandparent's deaths, I was at my lowest point. UCF had just hired me as a linguistics teacher, but the salary wasn't enough to make ends meet. I had two preschool children to support, a massive amount of bills, and no idea how to manage it all. That's when Marcus, approached me." Mom licked her dry lips. "May I have some tea?"

The teacup rattled on the saucer as Keren handed it to her mom.

As Mom sipped the tea, she seemed to gather her thoughts. "He said I'd be contributing to a noble cause by deciphering ancient spells and offered an insane amount of money upfront. It was the miracle I was looking for." She hesitated. "At least it seemed that way at the time." She held the cup out to Keren.

She took it, setting it back on the nightstand.

Mom's eyes hardened. "Marcus gave me pages torn from an ancient *Book of Shadows* to decipher. He had told me he found them but later admitted to stealing them from the Elder's Library." She clenched her hands into tight fists. "It took some time, but I identified most of the language content. Once I completed that work, he wanted me to rearrange the wording, to twist the spell into a curse."

Keren stood. She wrapped her arms around herself as she paced the room. Nothing Mom told her so far explained Katrina's death certificate. Her chest tightened, believing Mom was stalling.

"How is this related to Katrina?"

"Marcus let me set up a nursery for you girls at the lab so I could spend every spare minute outside of teaching working on the curse." She started crying. "I never would have done it if I knew then what I know now."

Keren stopped pacing and tilted her head back, gazing upward. "And what do you know now?" Her patience was wearing thin.

"I know Marcus harbored a deep hatred of shifters. I tried to find out why, but he never told me. I know he was gathering like-minded sorcerers and humans to create his Dark Guild. I know this group committed hate crimes on shifter families. I know he planned a campaign of genocide against the shifter race." She stopped, her breath rapid and shallow. After her breathing returned to normal, she continued.

"He understood he couldn't defeat shifters with normal sorcerers' spells, so he came up with a crazy idea to harness elemental magic. He wanted to create new spells, he called them curses, that tapped into elemental magic. The innate kind shifters are born with. That's why he needed the pages translated. The spells had something to do with power transference."

"So, how does this relate to Katrina?"

Mom closed her eyes. "When I had enough of the pages deciphered to write the curses, Marcus brought animals into the lab for experimentation." Tears trailed down her cheeks.

"He wanted to summon elemental magic into the animals and then enslave them to do his bidding. With elemental magic under his control, power would tip in his favor." Her voice quavered. "It was terrible. The poor animals screamed in agony as their bodies contorted into hideous creatures. They only lived ten or fifteen minutes after being cursed."

Keren thought of the cursed wolf. It had looked like Dr. Frankenstein had sewn the body parts on wrong before bringing the creature back to life.

"Why did they die?"

"The curse wording was wrong, I guess. But we kept tweaking it, trying to find the right sequence. No matter what we tried, the animals met the same fate. Finally, I couldn't take it any longer and told him I was quitting. He offered another large bonus, enough to pay off the mortgage. Against my better judgment, I stayed. By then, I had realized how evil and crazy Marcus was, how he would do anything to achieve his dream. So, I mistranslated the more dangerous spells, the ones that required too high a price."

"Price? What does that mean?"

"All magic has a price. Since sorcerer magic flows through the hands when it's used, our hands blacken and swell." Mom opened her eyes, staring at her open palms. "The charring, if the person doesn't stop using magic to let their hands heal, can grow up their arm. A hand or arm could die and require amputation. Sometimes, the price is death." She locked eyes with Keren.

"One evening, Marcus and I were casting the curse on innocent animals. I hated it, watching those creatures writhe and scream in pain before they died."

Keren's mouth fell open. "You cast the curse?"

"That day, yes. Marcus believed the curse wasn't working because it wasn't strong enough with one sorcerer. He wanted to experiment two."

Mom took a deep breath. "He staged four sedated animals, a bat, an Alaskan Malamute, a lion cub, and an eel on the platform. It was late at night. I had put you and Katrina down hours before. I thought you were sleeping but, somehow, you got out of the nursery and wandered into the lab."

Her breathing became shallow as she pulled at the covers.

"We'd already started the curse when you crawled up on the platform. I would have stopped, but I knew Marcus wouldn't. I panicked. The only thing I could think of to save you was to change my curse so it would stop, or at least twist, the original curse."

Unable to face her mom, Keren squeezed her eyes shut. "Is that what killed Katrina?"

Mom's voice seemed far away. "I don't know. At the end, you lay unconscious on the platform. The animals and Katrina were gone." Her crying made it difficult to hear the rest. "Marcus lay on the other side of the platform, his charred body barely recognizable. I took you, Marcus's *Book of Shadows*, and all our notes. Then I set fire to the lab."

Keren opened her eyes, seeing her mom's hands covering her face. Her shoulders shook as she sobbed. Keren walked over, pulling her into an embrace. All these years, Mom lived with the guilt of this terrible secret.

Mom wrapped her arms around her. "Can you ever forgive me?"

Keren squeezed her tight, unable to find the words to express her emotions. She hated Mom for not telling her about her twin or Marcus. But she also loved her for sacrificing so much to protect her.

"Azalea cast a golem spell, hiding the box of paperwork linking me to that event. I thought you were safer not knowing. After all, I killed the Dark Guild's leader. I realized I would have to pay for that one day, and I didn't want the payment to be you."

A look of shame flashed across Mom's face.

"When you started describing your imaginary friends to me, I couldn't believe it. They were renditions of the animals used in the curse."

"That's why you wanted me to draw them."

"Yes. Deep in my heart, I hoped to see a picture of Katrina." Shifting in bed, she winced.

"Are you alright? Is there anything I can do?"

Her heart warmed seeing Mom's smile. "No, thank you. I'll be fine. Give me a few days."

"Why did you give me magic dampening tea?"

Mom froze, her eyes locked with Keren's.

"Nadria figured it out. Did you know I had magic powers, I mean other than being a sorcerer?"

"No, I had no idea." Mom looked perplexed. "I was afraid the animals might hurt you. So, I asked Azalea for the tea."

"They're real, Mom. I've seen Two, Three, and Four."

"What do you mean they're real?"

"I can summon them. They come to life. And they have elemental magic."

"I had no idea." Mom sat back. "How do you do it?"

"I'm not sure. It just happens. It takes a lot out of me. I'm starving afterwards."

Mom looked down. Wrinkles creased on her forehead. Keren thought it best to change the topic.

"Was it Marcus's *Book of Shadows* we found in the box?"

"No, that one is mine. There was a location spell over Marcus's book that wouldn't allow us to contain it with the golem spell. So, Azalea experimented with protection spells until she found one that would hide the book. She kept that spell active over the entire house to keep the book hidden from the Dark Guild. I'm not sure how, but they located it. That's why they attacked me. They wanted the book."

Keren lowered her head, clenching her jaw. That hit a raw nerve. Heat seeped into her cheeks when she realized her selfishness had caused Marcus's *Book of Shadows* to fall back into the Dark Guild's hands.

"Hey, what's wrong?" Mom leaned forward, touching her hand.

Wishing she could go back and keep the appointment with Ms. Oakdove, she shook her head, overwhelmed with shame. "It's my fault." The words croaked out. "I told Ms. Oakdove to reschedule because I wanted to go to work instead."

There, the truth was out, both hers and Mom's. Battered emotions left her vulnerable, like a vase teetering on the edge of a table.

Without speaking, Mom pulled her into her arms.

"Did you see who did it? Who attacked you?"

Mom released her. "I did, but the picture is fuzzy in my mind. I know it was a man."

"What about the other witnesses? Did they see him?"

"I don't know about any witnesses, sorry."

Keren sighed. Without a description of Mom's attacker, they couldn't pull in another suspect. Mom was still the scapegoat for the Dark Guild crimes.

"I'll go out in the living room and let everyone know we have to find another place to stay." She got up and walked out of the bedroom.

CHAPTER THIRTY-ONE

QUINLIN

Quinlin paced in Nadria's living room. This shifter's house made his skin crawl. He heard voices coming from the bedroom but couldn't make out what they were saying. As he rubbed his chin, he worked through several plans. It all depended on what that woman remembered.

Finally, he heard the door open, and Keren walked out of the room. Her bloodshot eyes and puffy face evidence she'd been crying. He wanted to get to her first, so he pushed past Nadria, practically knocking her over.

As he wrapped his arms around Keren, he purred into her ear. "It's alright, I'm here."

Nadria threw him a nasty glare.

When Keren buried her head in his chest, warmth radiated through his body. He inhaled, taking in her essence.

"We can't stay here." She struggled to talk. "The inquisitors and the Dark Guild will find us."

She was right. It would be easy enough for the inquisitors to find this place. A half-smirk appeared on his face. And the Dark Guild already has.

"Do you have another place in mind?"

She shook her head.

He wanted to keep her close, under his supervision, and he knew exactly where to take her. But he couldn't seem too obvious. The shifter might make a suggestion Keren liked, so he couldn't ask her. But the puca looked dumbfounded, standing there with his mouth hanging open. "You, Ordell, right? Do you know of anywhere we can hide?"

"Hide?" Ordell looked confused. Just the reaction he hoped for.

Quinlin kissed the top of Keren's head. "Yes, the inquisitors will figure out Keren had something to do with her mom escaping from the hospital. They know she's friends with Nadria."

Ordell shook his head. "My parents are home. We can't go there."

"We'll go to a hotel." He bent down to peer into Keren's shimmering silver eyes. "Are you OK going to a hotel?"

She nodded her head, smiling at him. He wondered if she felt the same attraction to him as he did for her.

"Pack a bag and get her mom out to the car." Quinlin started toward the door. "We'll be waiting outside."

"Wait a minute." The shifter's voice grated on his nerves. "You're new to this party. Why should we do what you say?"

"It's OK, Nadria." Keren peeked around his arm. "I think it's a good idea."

He gave an 'I told you so' look to Nadria, then stepped outside with Keren. Now that he was away from the bumbling friends, he could find out what that woman said.

"Did your mom give you any information?" He held his breath, thinking this might turn against him.

"Yes, plenty. Too much." Tears dripped down her cheeks. "I don't want to talk about it right now." She stopped, furrowing her eyebrows together.

"What's wrong?" He entwined his fingers with hers. Her soft skin melted into his.

She whispered, "I can summon creatures."

Quinlin froze. That was unexpected. But it explained what he saw at the hospital. "I don't understand."

"Well, I see them all the time. I've only started summoning them." She lifted her face toward him, then frowned, staring over his head. "And they don't seem to like you." She pulled away.

Was she saying she saw a creature now? He remembered how many times she had looked over his head or out in the distance. He needed more information, and he had to make her trust him.

"They're just jealous." He smiled.

She looked skeptical, but he gave her a goofy grin, shrugging his shoulders.

She laughed, taking his hands. "Maybe you're right. Thank you for everything. You don't have to stay with us or help. I don't want you to get into trouble."

"I'm in this now and I won't leave you. I'm as invested in finding out about this Dark Guild as you are." Not quite a lie. He needed to learn more about these summoned creatures and how she controlled them. If he was right about her, she would make a perfect partner for him.

The shifter and Ordell walked out the door with that woman supported between them. They each had a bag slung on their backs.

Ordell struggled under the weight. "A little help here."

"You get in my car. I'll help put your mom in Nadria's car." He handed her the keys.

"No, I want to ride with Mom." She clutched the keys to her chest.

As he clenched his jaw, he assured himself this was all worth it to find out Keren's secrets. Ordell stepped aside, giving him access to lift that woman. Every part of him wanted to kill her now and be done with it.

"Do I know you?" that woman asked.

"No, we've never met. I'm Quinlin. I helped Keren sneak in to visit you."

She smiled at him. "Hi Quinlin, I'm Olivia." While squinting at him she said, "You look so familiar, but I can't place you."

"I'm a nurses' assistant at Orlando Regional. I worked in the Restricted Ward." He settled her into the back seat.

"That must be it." That woman wouldn't take her eyes off him.

After closing the door, he gave a command to the others.

"Follow me. I'll take us to a hotel." He bumped into Nadria as he passed her by. *Filthy shifter*. That's the first thing to change, Keren's choice of friends.

"Where are we going?" Keren asked him when they got in the car.

"There's an out-of-the-way hotel near Daytona. I've stayed there during bike week. Since it's off-season, and should be pretty empty. Let me bring up the map."

While using the excuse to use his phone to get directions, he shot off a text to the arcanum working at the hotel saying he was on his way and that he had company. The hotel provided the perfect place to test Keren's powers and rid himself of her friends.

CHAPTER THIRTY-TWO

KEREN

Keren and Nadria helped Mom into the hotel lobby. After they settled her into a chair, Keren joined Quinlin at the hotel reception desk.

"Yes, two rooms please." He slid his credit card across the counter.

"No." Keren grabbed his arm. "I can't let you do that."

He patted her hand. "Please, I want to."

After having maxed out her credit card, buying the new dress for her date with Quinlin, and leaving the money envelope they found in the box at Ordell's house, she had little choice but to let him pay.

"OK, but I'll pay you back."

Quinlin smiled, a dimple showing on his right cheek. "No, really. It's the least I can do."

Nadria walked toward her. She jerked her head, motioning for Keren to follow.

"I'll be right back." She gave Quinlin's arm a squeeze. Nadria linked her arm around Keren's, dragging her to the far corner of the room.

"What are you doing? You hardly know this guy." Nadria's eyes flashed anger.

Keren stepped back, tugging her arm free. "He's helped me, twice."

"There's something off about him." Nadria glared in Quinlin's direction.

Keren's hands clenched, then relaxed. "You don't know him. I need him right now."

"And you need to keep a level head." Nadria pointed her finger at Keren's chest. "We are all fugitives from the law. We need a better plan than hiding at a hotel with your new boyfriend."

After walking up beside them, Quinlin looked to Keren, then Nadria. "Am I interrupting something?"

As much as it annoyed her, Nadria was right. By following her to this hotel, she and Ordell were accomplices to breaking Mom out of the hospital. Yes, they needed a plan. But she only asked for a little time to absorb everything. Couldn't Nadria give her just this one night?

"No, everything's fine." She took Quinlin's hand, leading him away from Nadria.

After unpacking and propping Mom up in one of the double beds, Ordell suggested ordering food. "I'm starving. You guys want to order pizza?"

Keren's stomach rumbled. How long had it been since she'd eaten?

Quinlin held out his credit card. "Here, use this."

Before Keren could object, Ordell took the card. "What about Ms. Stewart?"

"The pizza shop on Clyde Morris Boulevard has the best chicken noodle soup." Quinlin pulled out his phone. "Here's the number."

"OK, thanks." Ordell stepped outside to order.

After Ordell left, a strained silence fell over the room. Keren sat on the bed across from her mom, avoiding eye contact with Nadria. Quinlin wedged himself in the corner by the door. Nadria positioned herself on the far side of Mom's bed, glowering at Quinlin. Two sat at the end of the bed, his massive head resting near Mom's legs.

Ordell stepped back into the room. "Food should be here soon." He plopped down in a chair. "So, I'm at a complete loss here. Can someone please explain what's happening?"

"Did you see the news today?" asked Keren.

"No, what's going on?" Ordell leaned forward in his chair.

"Remember that cursed wolf Three killed? Well, another one attacked on Princeton Street."

Ordell's face paled, his horse ears pinning to the back of his head. "That thing killed Broden."

Keren slid off the bed, kneeling in front of Ordell. "It did." She took his hands. "And this new one has killed more people." She looked into his eyes.

"But Mom said she can help stop the Dark Guild. She needs the papers we found at my house."

Although his eyes brimmed with tears, his voice sounded angry. "I'm in. So, what do we do now?"

Keren didn't hesitate. "We stop the Dark Guild before they hurt anyone else."

"We can't do it by ourselves." Nadria stood. "We're no match for the Dark Guild."

"My creatures can beat them. Three killed a cursed wolf."

"Do you know how you did it? How you made them real?" Nadria put her hands on her hips, facing Keren.

"No, not quite, but I can learn." Keren looked at Two sitting on the floor next to her.

A knock at the door broke the tension. When Quinlin opened it, pizza aroma filled the room. Her stomach rumbled.

After signing for the food, he placed it on the bed. Keren passed the soup to her mom, then reached for a slice of pizza.

"Make one of them appear now." Nadria challenged Keren.

"Alright, I will." After taking a bite, Keren squinted her eyes, focusing on Two. *Come to life*, she thought. Two lifted its head to look at her, then laid it back down.

The room fell silent while Keren focused on Two. Then she sighed, putting her face in her hands.

"You don't know how your magic works." Nadria plopped on the bed next to Mom. Soup sloshed out of her bowl. "Oh, sorry, Ms. Stewart."

"It's OK, Nadria." Mom blotted the spilled soup with her napkins. Then her voice hardened. "Keren, look at me."

Mom waited for Keren to meet her eyes. "You said your creatures have elemental powers. You need to go to the Magic Council and ask them for help. They are the strongest of their races."

"Who are the Magic Council and how can they help me?" More secrets. Mom had never mentioned the Magic Council before today.

"They're the strongest of their races. If anyone can help you learn to control your magic, it would be them."

"How do I find them?" Keren didn't like the idea of involving anyone else. But again, Nadria had a good point. If she couldn't summon her creatures on demand, she couldn't fight the Dark Guild.

"Find Azalea, she'll help you."

Keren's face dropped. She pictured the fairy on her back, potions rolling across the porch. While scrubbing her hand through her hair, she sighed. "Where can I find her?"

"Her store, Perfect Potions, is at Church Street Station. Ask her to take you to the Magical Underground." Mom took Nadria's hand. "Nadria can go with you."

Nadria's eyes widened. "I went there once with my mom when I was a kid. It was beautiful."

Quinlin placed his hand on Keren's shoulder. "I'll go with you."

Mom shook her head. "No, Azalea's cautious. She doesn't know you."

For a moment, he tightened his grip. Keren winced at the sharp pain. After relaxing his grip, he said, "Then take my car. The inquisitors won't be looking for it."

Keren patted his hand. "Good idea. Thank you."

Nadria rolled her eyes.

While unaware of the tension in the room, Ordell stretched. "It's late. I say we continue this conversation in the morning."

"I agree." Nadria picked up her bag and headed to the bathroom.

Keren ate another slice of pizza, then cleared the food away. Talking about Broden had quelled Ordell's appetite because he shook his head when she offered him a piece. She stood, turning to face Quinlin.

"I guess this is goodbye."

He cupped her face in his hands. "For now." He leaned toward her. Her skin tingled. He brushed his lips against hers, asking for permission. She stood on her toes, pressing their lips together. Fire exploded up her spine. She melted into him. She wanted more, but he pulled away. He smiled, then left the room.

Her body still tingled as she stared at the door. She wanted to be back in his arms, where life felt safe and calm.

Ordell cleared his throat as he waggled his eyebrows at her. "So, there's more to the Quinlin story than you let on."

She swatted his arm. "You get the floor."

He shrugged, pulling the extra pillow and blanket from the closet. He fashioned a makeshift bead in the corner.

Nadria came out of the bathroom. A relieved look washed across her face when she noticed Quinlin had left. Keren didn't know why those two had so much animosity toward one another.

Nadria crawled into the other bed while Keren checked on her mom. She was already sleeping. Much to her relief, Mom's color looked better, and her breathing was smooth and regular. Sometimes parents do the wrong things for the right reasons. She tucked the covers around her, gave her a kiss on the cheek, then went to the bathroom to get ready for bed. When she finished, she crawled into the bed next to Nadria.

"Are they here, your imaginary friends?" whispered Nadria.

"Yes." Keren reached for Nadria's hand. "Just Two."

"Good, that makes me feel safer."

She leaned over, kissing Nadria's cheek. "Good night"

Long after Nadria drifted to sleep, Keren lay in bed staring at the ceiling. Thoughts about magic, her creatures, and the Dark Guild drifted through her mind. She got up. After stepping over Ordell, she knelt by Two, who lay at the foot of Mom's bed.

"Protect them." Two lifted its head as the fire enveloping his horns grew brighter. She got up, tiptoeing outside. Maybe some fresh air would clear her mind.

CHAPTER THIRTY-THREE

QUINLIN

Quinlin stood in the shadows, observing Keren as she leaned over the balcony railing, staring at the sky. She wore a long nightshirt, exposing her bare legs to the night air while the wind played with her hair. He walked over, standing close enough so their arms touched when he leaned over the rail.

"Well, hello there."

She jumped, gasping for air. When she saw it was him, she relaxed back onto the railing and laughed.

"You startled me. And hi." She smiled at him then went back to staring at the sky. "It's so peaceful at night."

As he rubbed his finger along the back of her hand, his heart raced. He breathed in her wild scent, wanting to kiss her. A mad, passionate kiss. One that claimed her as his own. But that might scare her away. He had to give her time.

"Yes, I like how this hotel sits off the road. It's hidden from the bustle of the city."

She sighed. "These last few days have been crazy."

He noticed the bags under her eyes as he brushed the hair off her face. "You need rest."

She nodded. "I know, but I can't sleep. I lay there staring at the ceiling while visions of hideous monsters, magic attacks, and the Dark Guild battle in my mind." She rested her head on his shoulder.

He took a deep breath, letting her essence envelop him. Warmth radiated through his entire body from where her head touched his skin. He rubbed her back. "You can join me in my room. We can talk until you're tired enough to sleep."

She snuggled into him as she wrapped her arms around him. "I'd like that."

After taking her hand, he led her toward his room.

She stopped, frowning. "Isn't your room next to ours?"

"No, they didn't have adjoining rooms. But we're on the same floor." He pointed at the room in the corner. "I'm the one on the end."

"What if something happens? They might need my help." She pulled away.

A chill ran down his spine. He needed her away from the room. But even more, he needed her in his arms. "No one knows we're here. If something happens, my room is just a few steps away." He ran the back of his hand over her cheek. "Please, at least rest for a short while."

She glanced at her room's door, then back at him. He had to give her a slight push. "I have feelings for you, Keren, I want to help. Please, let me into your world."

Tears brimmed in her eyes. "But I used you. You should hate me."

"No." He stepped forward, wrapping his arms around her. "You are precisely what I need in my life. I don't hate you." Without speaking again, he led her to his room. She walked with him, resting her head on his shoulder.

After he pushed the door open, he let her walk inside first. He couldn't keep his eyes off her toned legs. *Keep a level head. She's not yours yet.* "Take a seat. Anywhere is fine."

Quinlin's corner room was larger than the normal rooms. A plush couch sat across from the double dresser and a big screen TV hung on the wall. Instead of two double beds, he had one king-size bed.

"This is nice." Keren flopped on the bed. Her arms splayed out in a cross. "And your mattress is so soft."

Quinlin laughed. If she only knew he owned this hotel, and this was his room. No guests ever occupied it. The mattress was a special order from Saatva. "I lucked out I guess." He laid on his side next to her, propping his head up with his hand.

She turned to look at him. Those mesmerizing eyes drawing him in. He ran his hand over her hair, letting his fingers glide to her neck. Touching her skin sent a heat wave through his body. The quickened rise and fall of her chest told him she felt their connection. His fingers trailed across her collarbone to the center of her chest, then down to her belly button.

"So." He swirled his fingers on her stomach. "You want to talk?"

She shook her head, grabbing his shirt and pulling him toward her.

Their lips pressed together, hot and passionate. His hand trailed down the curve of her hip, running along the hemline of her nightshirt. Soft moans encouraged him to continue. He feasted on her neck, kissing every inch, feeling the blood pulsing through her veins. She entwined her fingers in his hair, arching her back.

He forced himself to pull away. "Are you OK with this?"

She swallowed hard, then nodded.

He stood up, unbuttoning his shirt, then tossing it aside. A slow smile spread across her face as she sat up, pulling off her nightshirt. They stared at one another. She reached out, touching her fingertips to his chest, sending an electrical pulse across his skin. As they leaned into one another, they locked in a fiery kiss. His head spun, drinking her in very essence.

Suddenly, Quinlin felt her convulse as a loud explosion rocked the hotel. Her body lit up, just like it did at the hospital. He shielded his eyes, temporarily blinded by the sudden flash. She tore herself away from him.

"Something's wrong. They need help!" she yelled while pulling on her nightshirt. She raced to the door, clutching her stomach as if something had struck her.

He followed close behind as she bolted out the door. By now, the others should be dead. He'd be there to console her. All of this was for the best.

As he skidded to a stop, a smile spread across his face. A massive wolf with flaming ram horns stood in the doorway of Keren's room. It repelled bursts of energy peppering Keren's room by butting them with its head. This must be the fire elemental creature. He marveled at its power.

Then Quinlin startled, realizing Keren was running straight into the line of fire. He sprinted to the railing. When he glanced down, he spotted one arcanum lying motionless on the ground. Two other arcanum discharged energy balls in rapid succession. He tried to get their attention so he could reverse the kill order, but their focus was on the battle.

A Land Rover skidded into the parking lot, its lights and siren adding to the confusion. An inquisitor leaped out of the car, releasing a powerful roar. He smashed his hand into the ground. The parking lot's asphalt groaned and cracked. Roots shot up, trying to wrap themselves around the arcanum.

They shifted their attack to the inquisitor. He bounded with incredible speed across the parking lot while using magic to direct asphalt chunks at the arcanum. Bloodied and weakened, the arcanum collapsed into the roots' grasp.

Quinlin whipped his head back to the door. The astounding creature was no longer there.

"Keren!" That woman's voice came from inside the room.

He followed Keren inside, stopping in the doorway.

"They know we're here." That woman struggled to get out of bed. He focused on her hands, searching for the telltale black spots. But that was impossible. She wore the cuffs, keeping magic from flowing to her hands. It had to have been Keren controlling the creature.

"I saw it again." The puca sat with his back pressed against the wall. His trembling hands had the covers pulled up to his chin. "It was Two. It saved us."

Keren plopped on the bed. Her eyes focused on the entrance to the bathroom. She mouthed the words, 'Thank you.' He stared into space, trying to find Keren's vision.

At that moment, the inquisitor stormed into the room, pushing Quinlin to the side. The unexpected momentum made him trip over the bags on the floor and stumble into the nightstand.

"Briggs." Keren rushed to the inquisitor, throwing her arms around his neck. Was this a boyfriend? Quinlin clenched his teeth. She spoke into his thick neck. "How did you find us?"

"You have cell phones and you're in the middle of a magic battle… again." He stressed the last word. His eyes betrayed his genuine feelings for her. "The entire precinct is going crazy trying to find you. I had convinced the chief to let me take your mom into protective custody. He almost changed his mind after this stunt. What were you thinking?" Then his eyes landed on Quinlin, and he frowned. "Who are you?"

Before Quinlin answered, Keren spoke. "That's Quinlin. He works at the hospital, and he's helping us."

The inquisitor eyed Quinlin's bare chest, then glanced back at Keren. His jaw clenched as he pursed his lips. Quinlin, wanting to stay on the good side of the inquisitor, pretended he was afraid. He gave a wave and a weak smile.

"Briggs." Keren drew the inquisitor's attention. "I have to get to Ms. Oakdove. She'll help me learn to control my magic. My imaginary friends, they're real. I can summon them."

While cocking his head, Briggs raised a single eyebrow.

"It's true, she can. And she'll need to learn how to control them," said that woman. "The arcanum have discovered how to create cursed creatures imbued with elemental magic." Nadria helped her off the bed. "Based on what that creature did on Princeton Street, they have far more power than shifters. We have to get the *Book of Shadows* back so I can locate the curse they're using. Then, with luck, we can destroy the cursed creatures before they annihilate all shifters."

Keren put her hands on Briggs' cheeks. "Please, help us."

Briggs squeezed his eyes shut, taking a deep breath. When he opened them, he gazed into Keren's eyes. "Tell me what you need me to do."

While standing on her tiptoes, she kissed him on the cheek. Quinlin let out a rumbling sigh.

"We need a place to stay tonight. Tomorrow, Nadria and I will go see Ms. Oakdove. I'd like you to keep the others safe until we get back."

Quinlin cleared his throat. The thought of being confined by this inquisitor turned his stomach but staying with this group gave the Dark Guild an advantage. "I want to help."

"Are you sure?" Keren moved to him, caressing the side of his face. The burly officer glared at him. Quinlin took her hand and placed it by her side. He edged away from her. "I'm sure."

"Alright. I'll call you when we get to Ms. Oakdove's." The hurt in her eyes stabbed his heart.

"No calling on your personal phones." He held out his hand. "I'll hold on to them." With reluctant grumbles, everyone handed Briggs their phones. Before Briggs came around to him, Quinlin opened his phone, selecting the auto-wipe security application.

A server stored backups of everything on his phone so he had no worries of losing data. It would be easy to restore it to a new phone. Once the shifter took possession of this phone, he didn't want it back.

Briggs dug in his pocket, pulling out a different phone. He handed it to Keren. "I bought this on my way to pick your mom up at the hospital. It's a burner phone. They can't trace it to you. I've programmed in another burner's number. I have that phone. This is the only way we

will communicate."

He stepped out the door. "Get dressed and packed. We're leaving for the

safe house in ten minutes."

CHAPTER THIRTY-FOUR

KEREN

A few decades ago, Church Street Station was the fourth largest tourist attraction in Florida. That was before the big amusement parks created their own night life entertainment districts. With people flocking to the new venues, the Dixieland jazz era-themed clubs offering live jazz, blues, country, and top 40 music at Church Street Station struggled and eventually closed.

That's when the magical races stepped in. They embraced the area, giving it their own twist on entertainment and shopping. Live theaters and art galleries replaced the bars and taverns. Fairies setup shops, selling magic-infused tourist paraphernalia, and shifters and pucas welcomed guests to specialty restaurants.

Keren sat in Quinlin's car in the half-full lot under the overpass. It was 10 am, the Perfect Potion's opening time. She'd just checked in with Briggs.

"You know she doesn't like me." Keren told Nadria as she grabbed her backpack and got out of the car.

"You're making a big deal out of one minor incident." Nadria started toward the shops.

Keren locked the car. "I knocked her to the ground. The look on her face told me it wasn't a minor incident to her."

They walked past Winter Wonderful Land, owned by a fox shifter. Kiddie ice slides, snowman making contests, and constant snow fall attracted customers year-round. You had to make an appointment at least six months in advance.

The sweet aromatic spices of Howlin' Moon's Barbecue had a tangy twist, making Keren's mouth water. *Focus*, she told herself. You're here to find Ms. Oakdove, not to have lunch.

Rows of rainbow pennants with tiny inlaid crystals lined the upstairs banisters. They sparkled as the pennants fluttered in the wind. You couldn't help but have your spirits lifted in such a beautiful place.

After walking upstairs and passing a few more shops, they stopped in front of Perfect Potions. The window dressing had elaborate purple velvet drapes strung across the top and sides. The door stood open, and a lilac smell drifted onto the balcony, reminding Keren of her mom.

"Are you ready?" Nadria paused, fidgeting with her shirt.

Keren fought the butterflies in her stomach. "Yes." While repeating the manta, '*I will convince her to help me,*' she followed Nadria inside the store.

Antique chairs with upholstery matching the purple velvet drapes clustered in several groups around small tables. Crystal candy dishes and fresh flowers adorned each table. Rows of potions lined the wall behind the counter.

She saw two sales associates taking care of about a dozen customers. A young male fairy approached them. "May I help you?" His curly black hair and gleaming white teeth enhanced his already handsome face.

"We're here to see Ms. Oakdove. Is she available?" asked Keren.

"She's in, but I'm not sure she's available. We're busy today, so if you'd like to take a seat, I'll be with you shortly." He gestured to some empty chairs. "We showcase most of our products behind the counter." He handed them each a pamphlet. "This has some basic pricing options." He flashed his white smile again, then scurried off.

Keren let her hand rub against the tops of the smooth velvet chairs as she walked to the indicated table.

After they sat down, Nadria flipped through the pamphlet. "Maybe we should have called first."

While tapping her finger on the table, Keren watched the sales associate as he flitted from one customer to another. Finally, he gave her a wave and headed to the back room.

"He's going to get her now." She smoothed her hair to distract herself from her quickened pulse. So much hinged on getting Ms. Oakdove to help.

A few moments later, he reappeared, signaling them with his hand to come over to the counter. He opened the gate marked 'Associates Only' and pointed to a velvet curtain covering the hallway to the back rooms.

"She's in the office at the end of the hall." He put his hand on Keren's shoulder. "Buckle up, she's in one of those moods. I'm surprised she agreed to see you." After flashing his smile, he fluttered off to assist new customers coming in the door.

Great. Keren wondered if Ms. Oakdove was already in a mood or if hearing she was here put her in one. With a sigh, she pushed through the heavy curtain.

Wall sconces lined the hallway. Each one held an electrical version of two candlesticks. A plush runner rug covered the wood floor. As they approached the closed door at the end of the hallway, Keren stopped, her nerves getting the best of her.

"Oh, for heaven's sake." Nadria reached over Keren's shoulder, rapping on the door with her knuckles. "She's not going to bite."

"Enter," said Azalea.

They walked into a room right out of the 1920s. A large, round mirror encircled with vintage light bulbs hung on the wall. Underneath stood a makeup bureau. The top tier of the bureau's shelving held two candelabras. Colored glass bottles of varying shapes and sizes lined a lower, smaller shelf.

An antique reel-to-reel film projector sat on a wooden display platform in the corner. In the center of the room stood a mannequin dressed in a ruffled skirt with a sleeveless shirt adorned with beads and sequins finishing the ensemble.

"What can I do for you?"

Azalea Oakdove sat at a round mahogany table with carved moldings on the edge. The column base had three ball-and-claw legs. Her eyes focused on a paper she held in her hands.

"I don't have all day, child." She looked up from the paper, meeting Keren's gaze.

For most of her childhood, she remembered being petrified of Ms. Oakdove. Over the years, she'd grown accustomed to her blunt, terse demeanor. Keren gritted her teeth, fighting adolescent fears holding her back from simply asking for help.

"I really like your office." Nadria walked to the mannequin. "You're a fan of the flapper era?"

"Yes." Ms. Oakdove's wings flitted. She rose high enough to fly over the table to Nadria. "The era when women gained their right to vote. It was also a time women pushed the barriers in economic and sexual freedom."

"Maybe one day, equal rights won't be something you have to fight for." A tone of sadness resonated in Nadria's voice.

Although Keren appreciated Nadria stalling for her, she had to get herself together.

"I need your help to find the Magic Council," she blurted out.

Ms. Oakdove turned to her. "And why do you need to find the Magic Council?"

"I have... powers that I don't understand. I need them to help me learn how to control them."

"Why the Magic Council? Why not seek an elder sorcerer?" So, Ms. Oakdove knew she and Mom were sorcerers.

"Because my imaginary friends, the ones I've drawn for years, are real and they have elemental magic. Mom told me the Council could help." She remembered Ms. Oakdove had provided the magic dampening tea, so she must know about the twisted curse.

"Others have witnessed these imaginary friends and their magic?"

"I have," said Nadria. "I've seen one with water magic and one with fire."

Ms. Oakdove tapped her lips with her fingertip as she circled once around Keren. After stopping in front of her, she stared into her eyes.

"You're an anomaly. You shouldn't exist."

Keren felt as though someone had slapped her. She thought of the question Ball Cap's friend asked, *'What the hell are you?'* While she couldn't answer that question today, she confirmed her determination to discover everything she could about her magic.

"I didn't ask to be like this." She folded her arms across her chest. "But I exist. And I'm here to learn how to control my magic."

Ms. Oakdove flew back, allowing herself to sit on the table. "And your thoughts on the Dark Guild? You're a sorcerer with elemental magic. Isn't that precisely what they're striving to be? They'd worship you."

"The Dark Guild arcanum are murders who need to be stopped. Shifters have the birthright to elemental magic and to live without persecution."

The fairy flew over, then hovered in front of Keren. Azalea smiled, putting her hands on Keren's shoulders. "You've grown into a strong young woman Keren Stewart."

While taken aback by Ms. Oakdove's unexpected compliment, Keren took a moment before responding. "Thank you, Ms. Oakdove."

"Azalea, you must call me Azalea."

"Alright, Azalea." Somehow, she had made it through Azalea's rite of passage to adulthood. While lifting her chin, she took a deep, satisfying breath. Once she had her magic under control, the Dark Guild's days were numbered.

"This way." Azalea flew back to the mirror. "I'll take you to the Magic Council." She tapped the mirror in the center, sending motion waves across its surface. As the waves continued, their vibrations sped up, then they disappeared. Behind the mirror's facade were two shelves containing more glass bottles.

"These are artifacts imbued with the power to unlock the door to the magic underworld." She took two off the shelf, handing one each to Keren and Nadria.

"Don't you need one?" asked Nadria.

"No." Azalea pulled a necklace from under her blouse. Its smooth glass finish sparkled in the light. "I always have one with me." After replacing her necklace and restoring the mirror's facade, she said, "follow me," then walked through the wall.

Keren held her breath, following Azalea.

CHAPTER THIRTY-FIVE

KEREN

For a moment, the world shimmered around her. Then Keren stepped into an immense cavern. As One's misty form appeared, it did a somersault, then hovered in the air.

Tiny floating lights peppered the elevated ceiling, giving the area a warm glow. Quaint homes carved into the cavern walls lined the street. Flowerpots and colorful curtains decorated their round windows. Azalea's voice drew her attention.

"Set the artifacts here." She pointed to four shelves carved into the cavern wall containing colored glass bottles of various sizes. Keren put hers down next to Nadria's.

"This way." Azalea started down the street.

As they proceeded down the street, they left behind the residential area and entered into a business district. While a produce shop's customers sniffed and squeezed the fruits and vegetables on display, children squealed, laughing and chasing one another under the stands. A restaurant's outdoor tables brimmed with shifters and fae enjoying food and the company of friends. When the trio neared, the active chatting dimmed to low murmurs as all eyes turned to them. A prickly feeling tickled Keren's neck. One circled low over her head.

"Why are they staring at us?"

"You're the first sorcerer allowed in the underground." Azalea glanced back, giving Keren a shrewd smile.

"Oh." Keren's stomach flip-flopped. Sorcerer. That title didn't seem to fit. Yet that was her heritage, a human who could wield magic. From the way the shifters glared at her, she guessed they weren't happy with her being there, and she couldn't blame them.

Nadria linked her arm in Keren's. "I've never been inside the Magic Council chambers. I've heard there are incredible ancient artworks on display." Keren figured Nadria was trying to distract her from the worrisome stares. She appreciated her efforts, but her pulse still raced. Shifters had every reason to distrust sorcerers.

"Yes. We have a few pieces on display. The most impressive being the petroglyph representing the creation of the council."

The street widened into a cloverleaf shape. Azalea turned left, then stopped, motioning with her hand at the elegant entrance before them.

"This is the Magic Council Chambers."

Stone steps led up to a half-circle platform. Evenly spaced carved columns supported a second-floor balcony. A triangular rooftop displayed carved figures of magical creatures in various poses. As they climbed the stairs, Keren saw the intricate but delicate lace patterns winding around each column.

"This is gorgeous." She let her fingers glide over a column's surface. "How was all this made?"

"With magic, of course." Nadria poked Keren's side, causing her to squeal.

Azalea chuckled. "Let me tell you a story. Long before The Dragon War, magical races segregated themselves from one another. Not out of fear or hatred, but simply because it was the way things had always been. Until one day, Aquila, a perspicacious elf, tried to convince the leaders of each race to join forces." Azalea opened the chamber door. "Come in, I'll finish the story inside."

Keren and Nadria followed her through the door. Blue-tinted glass tile adorned the main hall's stone floor. Various shades of blue mingled to imitate the look of a calm lake. Overhead, a dome colored in yellows and reds provided glimmering light. Keren wondered where the light came from. One soared up into the dome, swooping in a circle eight pattern.

"Here is the petroglyph I spoke of."

Keren turned toward Azalea, then gasped. The wall displayed carved renditions of each of the races, the tallest one being at least fifteen feet high.

"That's magnificent."

"Yes." Azalea stood for a moment, admiring the petroglyph. Then she turned to Keren. "I'll be back in a moment."

She approached a fox shifter who sat at a small desk by the door. "Zeena, please notify the council of an emergency meeting. We have," she looked back at Keren, "a situation to address." Keren felt her face redden.

"Yes, Ms. Oakdove." Zeena stood and hurried from the chamber.

Azalea walked back to Keren and Nadria, then continued her story.

"Aquila reasoned that, although each race had their own powerful magical niche, they also had weaknesses. If the races bonded together, those weaknesses could be overcome by leveraging another race's strength."

Keren frowned. "I don't recognize what race that carving represents." She pointed at a shorter carving of a figure with a crooked nose and oversized, jagged teeth.

Azalea sighed. "That's a goblin. History tells us, the only race they had bonded with were the dragons." She looked over at Keren and Nadria. "They shared a love of treasure and wealth."

"Did they disappear with the dragons?" asked Nadria.

"In a way. They sympathized with the dragons. When it became apparent the dragons were losing the war, they slipped into hiding."

"And the one next to him? She looks regal." Keren held up her hand. "Wait, she's an elf. Ordell told me elves made magic artifacts."

"Very good. Most people haven't heard of elves. After the war, they also elected to move back into seclusion. The elves believed the war could have been avoided if the races had remained apart."

"Who made this carving?" asked Keren. "The detail is amazing."

"The dragons. They made this entire underground." Keren noticed a look of sadness pass over Azalea's face. "Losing the air elemental was a monumental loss to this world."

Keren glanced up at One, still zooming around in the dome. Maybe the world hadn't lost air elemental magic.

"Aquila convinced the leaders to join together and create the Magic Council, right?" asked Nadria.

"That's right. These carvings are of the founding members." She looked at her watch. "And speaking of members, they should be here within the hour." While fluttering away from Keren and Nadria, she motioned with her hand. "Follow me to a study alcove. We should document as much as we can before the council arrives."

Azalea led them to a small room off to the side of the main hall.

After going off to gather refreshments, Azalea had left Keren and Nadria sitting at an oblong conference table.

"Do you think the council will help me?" Eventually, she knew she'd be able to learn how her magic worked. But they were out of time. The Dark Guild had figured out how to create cursed creatures. They had to be stopped before they exterminated the shifter race.

"I'm sure they will." Nadria patted her hands. "Stop worrying."

"I mean, what if they try to help me but can't?" She fidgeted in her seat. "What if I can't learn to control my creatures?" She glanced at One circling above the table.

Azalea interrupted them when she entered the room. She carried a silver tray with a teapot and three cups. Cookies lined one edge of the tray.

"Help yourselves." She pulled a book out from under her arm, then sat down. After opening the book and sliding a pen from its binder, she looked at Keren. "Where would you like to begin?"

The Magic Council members knew nothing about her imaginary friends. An introduction to them seemed a good place to start. She took her sketchbook from her backpack.

"These are the most recent drawings I've made of the creatures." She slid the sketchbook over to Azalea.

"Interesting." She opened the sketchbook, flipping through the pages.

"I've named them." Keren pointed to the book. "That one is Four. It appeared a couple of days ago. We saw it use water magic."

Azalea jotted some notes down, then flipped to another drawing. "And this one?"

"That's Three. It fought and killed a cursed wolf."

"Why were you fighting a cursed wolf?" Azalea gave Keren a disapproving look. "They could have killed you."

Keren fidgeted in her chair. "It's a long story. Let's just say Three used earth magic to save me. And that's how I know my creatures can kill the arcanum's cursed animals."

"How did it kill the cursed wolf?"

Her chest tightened thinking about that harrowing night at the motel. She touched her bandaged wrist. After taking a deep breath, she said, "It tore the wolf's head off."

Azalea's eyebrows raised, then she scribbled down more notes. "Tearing an animal's head off is not earth magic."

"Right." Keren took a cookie off the tray. "Three made a lava ball with the wolf's fire and it captured the sorcerer attacking us by making plants grow around him." She popped the cookie in her mouth. "Mmm. This good. What kind of cookie is this?"

While leaving her head tipped down, Azalea looked up at Keren. "It's a peanut butter truffle."

After glancing at Nadria's stunned face, Keren put her hands in her lap, chiding herself for allowing the distraction.

Azalea turned a few more pages in the sketchbook, then paused.

"This one is different." She rotated the sketchbook to give Keren a better look.

Golden eyes floating in a dark mist stared back at her. The room's temperature dropped a few degrees as chills ran down Keren's spine. She looked away from the picture and took a deep breath, waiting until the sensation passed.

"I'm not sure what that drawing represents. It's not one of my creatures." Keren breathed a sigh of relief when a knock at the door drew Azalea's attention. Zeena poked her head into the room.

"The Council is ready."

"Very good, thank you, Zeena." Azalea stood, turning to Keren. "Are you ready?"

With a nod, Keren followed Zeena into the main hall.

Four high-backed chairs sat in a semicircle in the middle of the hall. In three of the chairs sat a shifter from each element, water, fire, and earth. An empty chair sat to their right.

"Thank you for coming on such short notice," said Azalea.

Zeena touched Nadria's shoulder. "We can sit at my desk."

Nadria took Keren's hand. "Will you be alright? Do you want me to stay?"

While squeezing Nadria's hand, Keren's heart pounded. But she managed a convincing smile. "I'll be fine." She hadn't felt this flustered since high school speech class. While berating herself for letting her nerves get the best of her, she took slow, steady breaths through her nose to calm herself.

"OK. I'll be right over there if you need me." Nadria let Zeena lead her away.

When Keren turned to face the shifters, she saw Azalea had taken the fourth chair. Keren hadn't realized Azalea was a council member herself. A glimmer of hope sparked in Keren's chest. Maybe Azalea would help convince the others to help.

"Let me introduce the council." Azalea gestured to the fox shifter. "This is Madam Windsburrow." Red hair framed the delicate features of her face. She gave a slight nod to Keren. She returned the gesture.

"Next to her is Master Anderson." The bear shifter's salt and pepper hair gave him an air of wisdom. He adjusted his burly body in the chair.

"Nice to meet you."

"Likewise," answered Keren.

"And finally, Master Rollins." His eyes locked onto hers, sending goose bumps down her arms. She lifted her chin, returning his stare.

"Pleased to meet you," she said with a firm, confident voice.

He huffed, steepling his fingers under his chin. Azalea continued.

Then she motioned to Keren. "This is Keren Stewart. She's here to address the council. As you know, Keren is cursed."

Keren took in a sharp breath as adrenaline tingled through her body. She wanted to run and hide. They knew about the accident and Mom's twisted curse. What else did they know about her? While clenching her fists, she forced herself to remain in place.

"She has witnesses to her ability to summon creatures and these creatures have elemental magic."

Madam Windsburrow's pinched eyebrows and wide-eyed reaction told Keren the council didn't know everything about her. It also told her the council member was more appalled than pleased with the information.

Master Anderson leaned forward in his chair. "Show us these creatures."

Keren's throat tightened as her mouth went dry. All four council members waited for her to do something. She looked up, watching One flip and dart around the dome roof. *Please*, she thought. *Please come to life.* Nothing happened. Her forehead broke out in a sweat. She closed her eyes, focusing her thoughts on One. Still, nothing happened. When she heard Master Anderson clear his throat, she opened her eyes.

"I'm sorry," said Keren. "That's why I'm here. I need help learning how to summon them."

Master Anderson crossed his arms, sitting back in the chair. A look of disappointment on his face. "Then how did you summon them before?"

"They appeared when I needed them. I didn't really think about it."

The door to the hall slammed open. A tall, wild-eyed wolf shifter stormed in. A scar running down his face intensified his menacing look. Three wolf shifters marched in behind him. While glancing at their uniforms, Keren guessed they were members of the warrior pack. She remembered Briggs talking about them. They were far more intimidating than she had pictured them.

"I need to speak with Master Rollins," Faraday spoke in a grave voice.

Azalea popped up from her seat. After a quick flutter of her wings, she hovered nose-to-nose with the wolf shifter.

"Faraday, you're interrupting a council meeting." Azalea put her fists on her hips.

He snarled, leaning around Azalea and ignoring her objection. "We have a lead on the location of the Dark Guild's primary operations."

Master Rollins stood. "Let Faraday speak."

As Azalea pursed her lips, she moved to the side, letting Faraday approach Master Rollins. Keren's heart pounded. She took a few steps back to give Faraday room but stood close enough to hear the conversation.

Master Rollins put his hands behind his back. "What's the source of your information and what's the location?"

"The woman we tracked down at the bowling alley. She broke down during this morning's interrogation. She said they're at Madam Murray's Wax Museum."

He must have been talking about the woman who chained her to the stage. Her fingers wrapped around her injured wrist.

"That's an odd location. Do you have other evidence to corroborate her story?"

"The arcanum arrested in Daytona are being interrogated as we speak." Faraday's head twitched. "We're confident they'll talk by the end of the day."

Master Rollins put his hand on Faraday's shoulder. "That's promising news. Get a warrior on patrol at the location. Maybe they can also verify the woman's story."

"Already done." Faraday lifted his chest.

"Good. Check in with me in a few hours." Master Rollins returned to his seat.

Faraday turned, walking toward the front door. His warrior pack falling in line behind him.

Just as Faraday reached the door, Master Rollins called out, "and one more thing Faraday."

Faraday turned. A scowl flashed across his face. "Yes?"

"Kill this girl," said Master Rollins, pointing at Keren.

Without hesitation, Faraday and his warriors bounded toward Keren. Snarls echoed through the hall. Keren thought she heard Nadria's scream. Or was it her own? Her mind raced, trying to understand what was happening. She crouched, knowing she didn't stand a chance against four wolf shifters, but she'd go down fighting. Within seconds Faraday's body sailed through the air, yellow eyes glowing, and teeth bared in anticipation of a kill.

Then time stood still. Energy pulsed in her solar plexus, racing up her neck to her eyes. She felt her body explode with energy, then One appeared between her and Faraday. Time returned to normal and One batted Faraday away like a harmless fly. The other warriors skidded to a halt.

"Stop!" shouted Master Rollins. When Keren looked over, he had a smug half-smile on his face. "It appears you needed your creature."

Sweat glistened on Keren's arms. She drew in long, ragged breaths as her muscles quivered. Once the wolf warriors backed away, she let herself relax.

Madam Windsburrow and Master Anderson sat with their mouths hanging open, staring at One. Keren ran her hand along One's bat-like wing. It felt like soft leather. Its ruby eyes met hers as it flicked its tail over its head.

"That was uncalled for." Azalea rushed to Keren's side. "They could have killed her."

"But they didn't." Master Rollins stood, walking closer to examine One. Its sharp-tipped tail snapped out, nicking Master Rollins' cheek. A drop of blood ran down his face. After wiping his cheek, he stared at his bloodied fingertips, rubbing them together.

Keren swallowed the lump in her throat. She hadn't told One to attack him. Would Master Rollins be angry? Would he order the wolves to attack again? Her body tensed, waiting for his reaction.

His eyes snapped to hers. "Can you summon the others?"

"Right now?" So far, she'd only seen one creature at a time. "I'm not sure."

"Try." His commanding voice made her jump.

While staring at the ground, Keren focused on Two. A pulse beat in her solar plexus, then Two appeared next to her. Keren let out a laugh. She had done it; she summoned Two. Her legs wobbled as she struggled to remain on her feet.

Suddenly, something slammed into her. It was Nadria. Keren would have been knocked off her feet if Nadria's arms hadn't locked around her. "Are you alright?"

With the impact, Keren lost control of her magic. She stopped glowing while One and Two turned to mist and dissipated into the air.

"I think so." She peeled Nadria's arms away, giving her a reassuring smile, then turned to the council members.

"I say we help her." Master Anderson stood, his eyes twinkling. "Your curse has turned out to be an amazing gift." He offered a hand to Madam Windsburrow.

"I agree," she said while accepting Master Anderson's hand.

"I also agree," Azalea said as she stepped next to Master Anderson. "What is your vote, Master Rollins?"

He steepled his fingers while circling Keren. She faced forward, allowing only her eyes to follow him. He disappeared from her left peripheral vision. She could hear his steady, deliberate footsteps behind her. Then he appeared in her peripheral vision on the other side.

He placed his hands behind his back and said, "I agree." Then proceeded out of the hall.

Madam Windsburrow put her arm around Keren. "Let's work on your focus and body awareness."

Keren's stomach rumbled as it tightened into a tight knot. "Can I get something to eat first?"

CHAPTER THIRTY-SIX

KEREN

Keren focused on her breathing as she floated in a pool of water. While never having been fond of swimming, she had been skeptical when Madam Windsburrow suggested this flotation technique. But now her mind felt sharp and clear while her body totally relaxed.

"Alright, Keren. Let's try again." The water resounded with Madam Windsburrow's voice. "Draw the magic into you. You control it."

Without rushing or panicking, Keren called to the pulse. It responded, tapping at a moderate pace. She let it linger in her solar plexus, feeling how its rhythm coordinated with her heartbeat. Then she urged it on. The tapping changed to a throb, then a heavy beat. Warmth rushed up her neck to her eyes. After allowing them to flutter open, she saw the glow of her body had lit up the float tank. She smiled. This was the fourth time she'd called her magic.

"Very good. I think we can move outside the tank. Meet us in the hall."

Keren released a latch. Moments later, the lid opened. Nadria's face peered inside the pod.

"What's it like in there?" Nadria's nose wrinkled. "It smells salty."

While stepping out, Keren grabbed a towel. "It's peaceful. I felt detached yet in control of my body." She dried herself off, then slipped back into her clothes. "I summoned my magic four times." While pulling in a deep, satisfying breath, she stretched her arms out wide. She couldn't remember the last time she felt this relaxed.

"That's awesome." Nadria touched her arm. "I knew you could do it."

They walked down a short corridor leading to the Magic Council Chamber's main hall. When they entered, all the council members turned in their direction.

"You did a wonderful job." Madam Windsburrow approached Keren, draping an arm around her shoulder. "Now, let's have you try summoning your magic here." She led Keren to the center of the hall.

Keren's stomach rumbled. Azalea raised an eyebrow.

"Hungry again?"

A warmth prickled Keren's cheeks. "Using my magic seems to make me hungry. But I can continue."

Nadria laughed. "She's always had a sizable appetite."

Azalea flew over to hover in front of Keren. She examined her eyes. "Human physiology isn't meant to support elemental magic." She reached out, pulling one of Keren's eyelids up. "Look down."

Keren did as instructed. She bit her lip. Maybe summoning her creatures was hurting her physically.

"Once summoned, how long have you maintained an elemental creature?" Azalea released Keren's eyelid.

"Well," she thought back to the first time Four appeared. "Things were confusing, but I think Four was here maybe five minutes." She looked over at Nadria for confirmation.

"That sounds right." Nadria tapped her chin. "But like Keren said, things were crazy." Her face paled. "Don't forget Two and the golem. That felt like an eternity."

Keren shook her head. "I don't know how long that lasted either."

She squeezed Nadria's hand to comfort her. "Then," she continued, "Three appeared at the motel." A chill ran down her spine as visions of the cursed wolf's savage attack crept into her mind. Her chest tightened, thinking about poor Broden. "It was there maybe, ten or fifteen minutes."

"Two protected us at Daytona," Nadria added. "Again, so much was going on, but I think that was about five minutes."

"The last time was here. You saw One and Two." Keren shot a disdainful look at Master Rollins. She decided she'd have to be cautious around him. While glancing around, she didn't see any of her creatures. She wondered if that was significant.

"And how did you feel after each occurrence?" Azalea took Keren's hand, examining it with a meticulous eye.

"I felt weak and lightheaded. My legs felt like they were going to give out. Sometimes they did. But you have to remember the situations were tense with fighting and running." She thought back to the hospital magic attack. She had passed out. Could that have been because she summoned a creature?

"You may have limited capacity for maintaining the creatures." Azalea released her hand, then moved back.

Master Rollins paced the floor. "If that's the case, she's worthless in battle."

"No." Keren's heart raced. "I can learn to hold them longer."

"We're getting ahead of ourselves." Madam Windsburrow interrupted. "Let's get her to summon her magic on demand first, shall we?" She turned to Keren, taking both her hands. "Now, remember how it felt in the flotation pod."

Keren closed her eyes, trying to relax. Her breathing evened out as she felt the tension wash from her body.

"Good." Madam Windsburrow released her hands. "Now, summon your magic."

The pulse felt distant at first, out of reach. She pushed Master Rollins' comment about her being useless in battle from her mind. When the pulse drew closer, she grabbed it, pulling it to her solar plexus. It reverberated like a bass drum. Energy shot up her neck to her eyes.

"Summon a creature." Master Rollins' gruff voice broke the silence.

Keren's eyes shot open, glaring at Master Rollins. He stepped back, looking uncertain at first, then he steepled his fingers.

Thoughts of Four drifted into her mind. She focused on them. Four came to life before their eyes. Keren heard gasps but couldn't focus on anyone's face because the world spun around her. Her legs gave out, and she fell onto her knees. After she released her magic, Four disappeared.

"Bah," said Master Rollins. "She'll be useless in battle."

Keren covered her face with her hands as she leaned forward. She felt dizzy, and her limbs tingled with fatigue. *They aren't going to allow me to help.* All of this started because of her. She let the protection spell on the house grow weak enough that the Dark Guild located Marcus' *Book of Shadows.* Now, the arcanum control cursed creatures capable of elemental magic. Because of her, shifters' face a campaign of genocide.

She felt a hand touch her back. Azalea spoke in a soft tone.

"I have a potential solution."

Keren sat up, wiping tears from her face. "What is it?"

"An artifact. But be aware, they meant its magic for fae not humans. I can't guarantee what it would do to you." Azalea held out her hand. "I'll have Zeena bring a plate of fruit and yogurt."

She took Azalea's hand, grateful for the help. "Thank you. Can she bring some of those peanut butter truffles?"

Keren's strength had returned after she gobbled up all the cookies and a handful of grapes. She followed Azalea across the street to The Repository, a single-story building with four white columns supporting a flat roof.

As they walked up to the door, Azalea placed her hand on the door frame. "They entrusted fairies with the welfare of artifacts when the elves disappeared." After a faint *click*, she opened the door, ushering Keren into the building.

She wished Nadria had been allowed to come with her. After a lengthy debate, Nadria had relented to Azalea's insistence on taking only Keren.

Azalea led her across a wooden floor. On each side were four fairies seated at mahogany desks. Their eyes lifted when they walked into the room.

"Good afternoon, Ms. Oakdove," the fairies chimed simultaneously.

"Good afternoon," Azalea responded. Focusing back on Keren, she continued, "We track and record the details of each artifact, including their magical powers, if any."

While inspecting the area, Keren noticed each fairy had an object on their desk. One was a rod, another looked like a plain rock. She remembered her conversation with Ordell at the Kitty Café. Elves made the artifacts, but fairies imbued them with magic.

"How many artifacts are there?"

"In this region, we've cataloged just over twenty-three hundred. Now and again, someone brings in an object thought to be an artifact for testing. We believe there are several still at large waiting to be discovered."

"What do you do with the artifacts?"

"Sometimes we'll loan them out. A detailed request and interview is, of course, required prior to approval. We also routinely validate potency. Some magic fades with time. But mostly, we keep them secured from malicious use." Azalea stopped at the front right desk.

"Mr. Kapen, please give me the location of the Band of Endurance."

Keren raised her eyebrows. That certainly sounded like something she could use since stopping in the middle of a battle to have a snack sounded ridiculous. *Hold on a minute, bad guy, let me eat this cheeseburger.*

"Yes, ma'am." Mr. Kapen typed on his keyboard, then looked up at Azalea. "Aisle nine, bin 587. Would you like me to write that down?"

"No, I'll be fine. Thank you, Mr. Kapen."

His wings fluttered. Then he turned back to his computer.

Azalea continued walking to the far wall, where she paused. With a wave of her hand, the wall shimmered, being replaced with double doors. She opened the door, ushering Keren inside. While looking around, she saw rows of shelving lining the floor. Each shelf held several objects: vases, jewelry, rods, crystals, bottles, to name a few. They looked ordinary, something you'd find in your home.

"How would you know an object was an artifact?

While hurrying forward, Azalea spoke over her shoulder. "It's difficult. Artifacts can go undetected for years until something triggers their magic."

"What would trigger their magic?"

"A word, a touch, maybe a certain temperature. Anything really."

"Oh." Keren slipped her hands into her jean's pockets.

"Here we are." Azalea motioned her over. "This is the Band of Endurance."

To Keren, it looked like a normal bracelet. It had a red and black snake-skin pattern.

"How does it work?"

"The *Tome of Artifacts* states when this band is closed on a fae's wrist, it will merge with the recipient, giving them a prolonged ability to survive without food."

Keren crossed her arms. "Why would a fae want that ability?"

"Long ago, elves, being nomadic, traveled the world. They visited the settled fae communities, where they shared magic tales of their adventures. For efficiency, they had fairies imbue the magic of endurance to these bands."

Narrowing her eyes, Keren squinted at the artifact. "What do you mean by merge with the recipient?"

"That's what the tome states. I imagine it becomes a permanent fixture on your person. That's only my guess."

"Haven't you tested it?"

Azalea tipped her head, frowning. "No. If we had, the artifact couldn't be here."

Keren's stomach was tied in knots. While she wanted a solution to help her hold her magic, the only thing she knew about this artifact was from an ancient tome.

"You said some artifacts lose potency. Could that be true with this one?"

"We don't know. The specific potion magic used on the band has been lost."

Keren's breath quickened. She felt her heartbeat thumping in her chest. "So, you really don't know what would happen if I put the band on."

"I do not." Azalea held the band out. "It's your choice to use it or not."

With a shaking hand, Keren took the band. She turned it over, examining it. This might give her the ability to fight against the Dark Guild. Then again, fae used this magic, not humans.

"You said 'when a band is closed on a fae's wrist,' will it matter that I'm a human?"

"I don't know." Azalea moved closer. Her eyes riveted to Keren's. "It could provide the help you're looking for, or it may do nothing at all. But keep in mind, there is always the risk of it causing a serious illness or even death."

Keren gasped and her body trembled. Was it worth risking her life to be a part of the attack against the Dark Guild? She licked her lips. Her mistake had put this nightmare into motion. Without her creatures, she didn't think the shifters would survive. She had to be part of stopping the Dark Guild. She had to decide now.

"What would you do?" she whispered.

Azalea shook her head. "The choice is yours." She stepped back, giving Keren room.

Sweat trickled down her back as she stared at the band. She didn't want to die. But doing nothing while the Dark Guild annihilated the shifter race, including Briggs and Nadria, was a fate worse than death. Her muscles tightened. *You can do this*, she thought. The twisted curse had given her the power to stop the cursed creatures. She had to accept her fate. With a flick of her hand, she clamped the band on her wrist.

A scream burst from her throat as a searing pain shot through her arm. With a sizzle, the band melted into her skin. Her eyes bulged, watching it wrap itself in a spiral up her arm. She felt the burning stop at her shoulder.

While staggering back, she grasped her wrist where she placed the band. All she felt was her burning skin. The red and black colors crept along the back of her hand, then between her fingers. She flipped her hand over, seeing the colors swirl into a ball on her palm.

Azalea grabbed her other arm. "What are you feeling?" Her expression looked more inquisitive than concerned.

"It's burning my arm," Keren yelled.

"Any queasiness, lightheadedness?"

While hissing in air through her teeth, Keren nodded her head.

Azalea's firm grip kept Keren on her feet. Her arm trembled from the trauma. Finally, the burning sensation subsided. After turning away from her arm, she drew in a long, ragged breath. The artifact must have ruined her arm.

"What do you feel now?" asked Azalea.

"My arm tingles." Keren bit her lip while blinking tears from her eyes. "How bad is it?"

"It's beautiful."

Keren blinked, then turned to look at her arm. The red and black snake-skin pattern glistened on her skin. The detail of the lines made it look alive.

"Wow." While twisting her arm, she inspected the work of art. "It's like a tattoo."

She had expected a burst of energy like drinking a pack of Red Bull. But she felt normal. Other than her tingling arm, she felt no different.

"Am I supposed to have a superpower now?" She looked at Azalea.

Azalea scowled. "I told you we don't know how the magic will work with a human." She turned, heading to the door. "Let's go back to the council chambers and run some tests."

Keren pulled her chin back, furrowing her eyebrows. Azalea talked like she was a lab rat. Other than giving her a badass tattoo, it seemed the Band of Endurance did nothing for her. She hoped they would find the magical words to get the endurance to kick into action. With a sigh, she followed Azalea.

Back in the council chamber hall, Keren focused on the pulse in her solar plexus. It shot up her neck, exploding to her eyes. With a smile, she looked at the council members. Madam Windsburrow beamed at her.

Tabitha stood next to Master Rollins. She and Faraday had been there when Keren and Azalea had returned to the chamber hall. Tabitha's mouth gaped open as she saw Keren's skin light up with magic. After her initial shock, she gave Keren a warm smile.

Faraday lurked behind Master Rollins, his angular jaw clenched with tension. Did that wolf ever relax?

She focused on thoughts of One, picturing him somersaulting in the air. Within moments, he appeared before them.

Gasps came from the group. Their wide eyes converging on One. Keren lifted her chin. Yes, she summoned One. She took a deep breath, focusing her thoughts on Two. It burst into view, its flaming ram horns swaying back and forth. Sweat trickled down her face as her legs spasmed. The endurance boost could kick in anytime now.

In the same way, she summoned Three and Four. All four of her creatures surrounded her, flesh and blood, waiting for her instructions. With a gulp, she staggered. Her vision blurred as her legs threatened to give out. A hand grasped her newly tattooed arm.

"Focus on the artifact. Tap into its magic," Azalea shouted.

Keren put her fingertips on her forehead. The world spun around her, and she felt the magic fading. Then she noticed the spiral on her palm. When she concentrated on it, she felt a tingling sensation. While closing her fist, she pressed her fingers to the spiral.

Suddenly, her heart tried tearing itself from her chest. She gasped, throwing her head back. While her body convulsed, she felt another set of hands loop under her arms. She'd found the artifact's magic. Bright lights flashed in her eyes. Was this what death felt like?

"Keren." Nadria's voice sounded distant. "Keren, look at me."

She thought of each of her creatures. One, the air elemental; Two, the fire elemental; Three, the earth elemental; and, finally, Four, the water elemental.

Fingers grabbed her chin, turning her head in the voice's direction. She blinked her eyes. The flashing lights faded as Nadria's worried face came into view. She blinked again, looking past Nadria. She laughed, seeing Two's flames rising higher and burning brighter.

Tabitha's voice came from behind her. "Can you stand on your own?"

With a nod, Keren said, "Yes."

She moved away from Tabitha, then turned. There they were, all four of her magnificent creatures, alive. No, more than alive. Their colors were sharper, and she felt them pulse with energy. Somehow, she acted like a battery, feeding them energy.

Adrenaline raced through her veins while her heart pounded. All the aches and pains she'd gained over the last few days disappeared. She felt strong, invincible.

She spun around to face the council. Her eyes focused on Master Rollins. "I'm ready for battle."

His eyebrows raised. "Are you?" After placing his hands behind his back, he paced the floor, not taking his eyes off Keren. "They look impressive, and the artifact gave you the endurance to hold your magic. But how do you control them? Are you an expert in all four elemental magics?" He stopped pacing and raised his chin as if he outsmarted her, asking a question she couldn't answer.

Keren crossed her arms over her chest. "I don't use elemental magic, they do. I'm their energy source."

Master Rollins frowned. "Explain."

"I didn't tell Four to use water jets or Three to make a lava ball out of fire. They just knew."

He steepled his fingers. "So, you have no control over them. How do we know they will fight for us and not against us?"

While pursing her lips, she frowned. She hadn't thought about that. Turning, she looked at her creatures. Their eyes focused on her. While walking over to Three, she held out her palm. Three held out its palm, too, touching Keren's as she drew close. She wiggled her fingers under the branches to touch the soft, green fur beneath. Three tilted its head while wrinkling its nose.

They were connected, she and her creatures. Whereever she went and whatever side she fought on, they would be right beside her. She smiled at Three, then pulled her hand away. Turning, she addressed Master Rollins.

"They are a part of me. We fight together."

He squinted, giving her a skeptical look.

"I say she goes with the warrior pack to attack the Dark Guild," said Master Anderson.

"I second," said Madam Windsburrow.

"She's a wild card. We can't take the risk." Master Rollins went back to pacing. "If the Dark Guild survives our attack, they'll continue killing innocent shifters. Are you willing to take that responsibility?"

"If you don't take her," Azalea said, "and the Dark Guild survives, will you take that responsibility?"

Tabitha approached Master Rollins. "We need every advantage. That one cursed wolf on Princeton Street tore through twelve inquisitors' magic like paper. How many more creatures might they have?"

Master Rollins growled. "Very well. She's under your supervision."

"Yes, sir," said Tabitha. She glanced over at Keren, giving her a wink.

"You can't be serious?" Faraday spat. "She's an untrained child."

"Faraday." Tabitha's voice carried harsh authority. "The warrior pack will coordinate with Keren and Briggs' squad. Is that understood?"

Briggs? Keren's heart leaped. Of course it would be Briggs and his squad. They've been working on Dark Guild cases since they began.

Faraday snarled. "Yes, ma'am." His yellow eyes locked onto Keren's, contempt written on his face. He turned, storming out of the building.

Master Rollins waved at the creatures. "For heaven's sake, put those away."

While she looked down at her glowing arms, she realized she's forgotten about her magic. After turning to face her creatures, she said, "Get ready. We're kicking some arcanum butt." All four turned to mist and dissipated into the air after she released her magic.

CHAPTER THIRTY-SEVEN

QUINLIN

Quinlin relaxed in an overstuffed chair, staring at Keren. She sat cross-legged on the couch, wearing a short-sleeved pajama set with llamas in various silly poses. Although he preferred her in the nightshirt she wore in Daytona, her sensual features somehow muted the childish cartoons. Since she'd gotten back from the Magic Underground, she had an air of confidence about her, intensifying his attraction to her.

What he would have given to have been there when she had summoned all four creatures. With her by his side, they would rule the world. When she noticed him staring at her, she raised her eyebrows, taking a long moment to gaze into his eyes.

Ordell sat next to Keren, admiring the artifact emblazoned on her arm.

"So, this was a bracelet that burned into your skin?"

"Yes. It's called the Band of Endurance." She turned her hand over, exposing her palm with the swirl. "If I press my palm, I get an energy surge."

"That's cool. Do you think Ms. Oakdove would give me an artifact?"

"I don't know. Maybe. If you needed one."

That woman walked into the room. "I'm making tea. Anyone interested in a cup?"

"Yes, please," said Nadria. She sat on the coffee table facing Keren.

"Can you bring the bag of pretzels I saw on the counter?" Keren asked.

That woman rolled her eyes. "Sure, I'll be back in a minute." She walked back into the kitchen.

"Mom looks so much better." Keren smiled at Quinlin.

He returned the smile. "She's getting stronger every day." Although a true statement, it didn't provide Quinlin with the same happiness as Keren. That woman killed his father and yet here he was, sleeping under the same roof as her. It made his skin crawl. But even worse, he endured two shifters.

"Tell me again how you found the Magic Underground." Quinlin sat on the edge of the chair. "I found that part fascinating."

"Alright." Keren bubbled with enthusiasm. "Azalea has artifacts hidden behind a mirror in her office. To get to the Magic Underground, you need to hold on to the artifact."

"Anyone can go through?"

"I think so, as long as you have an artifact. There are several more on the other side for anyone who's leaving the underground."

Quinlin smiled, nodding his head. With this information, he'd be able to annihilate all the shifters. None of them could hide from him in the underground.

"These artifacts," he gestured to her arm, "where did they come from?"

Ordell held up his hand. "I got this."

While gritting his teeth, Quinlin kept his face neutral. He wanted to know the location of the other artifacts, not get a history lesson from a puca. A throbbing pain stabbed at the front of his head.

"Elves created the artifacts, but fairies imbued them with magic. When the elves left, the fairies took possession of the artifacts." The puca's horse ears wiggled back and forth.

That woman came out of the kitchen. She handed a cup of tea to Nadria and the bag of pretzels to Keren.

"Thanks, Ms. Stewart."

"Thanks, Mom." Keren popped a few pretzels in her mouth.

"You're welcome, girls." She sat on the other side of Keren, balancing her cup of tea on her lap.

"Are we talking five or six artifacts?" Quinlin pressed for information.

"Azalea said over twenty-three hundred are in the vault. They're categorized and labeled."

He took in a deep breath, twenty-three hundred artifacts. What an unexpected bonus. After he eliminated the shifters, he would confiscate these artifacts, claiming them for the Dark Guild.

At that moment, Briggs walked in. He'd been outside since receiving a phone call over an hour ago.

"Keren, we're leaving at 4 am sharp tomorrow."

Her hands went to her cheeks. "Is this it?"

"Yes. An arcanum broke down this evening in an interrogation. He confirmed what the woman from the motel told us."

"And what did the woman tell you?" Quinlin tried to sound casual, but his frustration with the recent sloppy work of the arcanum made his tone sharp. The inquisitor glared at him.

Keren blurted out, "They're at Madam Murray's Wax Museum."

With that bomb of information, Quinlin's heart raced. He'd been so careful. Somehow, he had to get word to the arcanum about the strike. But being cooped up here made that challenging.

Briggs never let the car keys out of his sight, and he had the only cell phone. With a seemingly unending orange orchard surrounding the house, Quinlin had no idea how close the nearest neighbor was. Every time he went outside, he saw inquisitors patrolling the grounds.

He could kill Briggs and kidnap Keren, holding her hostage while he escaped. Although that would work, Keren showed a fondness for the inquisitor. So, just like that woman, he tolerated Briggs' presence for a little while longer. At least until Keren denounced her old life and took her place by his side. He needed to come up with a different plan.

"That's at ICON Park," said Ordell. "I remember riding that giant ferris wheel that gave you a bird's-eye view of Orlando. I think it's called The Wheel. There's an aquarium and arcade there, too. I haven't been there for years."

"Right," added Nadria, "I remember a lagoon with a Bellagio-style fountain show. "

"You're not going," Briggs said in a flat tone then turned to Nadria, "and neither are you."

They both started to object but stopped when he held up his hand.

"Officer Jordon will be here tomorrow. He has strict instructions to keep Ms. Stewart safe and make sure all of you stay put." His sweeping hand movement included Quinlin. By the stern look on his face, they knew not to object.

Briggs' phone rang. He checked the caller ID, then answered.

"Captain Wilson." He put a finger to his other ear. "Yes, Tabitha and I worked out the strike details. I called my entire squad to action. No, Jordon's staying behind to..." He turned, walking outside to continue the conversation.

Quinlin leaned back, folding his hands over his stomach. A grin spread across his face as he formulated a plan.

The next day, everyone got up early to see Briggs and Keren off. Ordell and Nadria wore crestfallen faces.

"Why can't we go?" Ordell whined.

"I told you, it's dangerous. You'll be safe here with Officer Jordon." Briggs adjusted a strap on his shoulder as he clapped a hand on the officer's shoulder. "Do what he tells you. He has full authority."

Ordell looked down. "Fine."

That woman hugged Keren. "Be careful."

"I will." Keren kissed her on the cheek. Then Nadria stepped up, giving her a hug.

"I wish I could go with you."

"Me too."

When Keren finished her display of affection for the dirty shifter, she turned to Quinlin, giving him a flirtatious look as she approached.

"Take care of everyone for me?" She put her hand on his cheek.

"Anything for you." Quinlin took her hand in his, kissing it before letting her go.

A low growl came from Briggs. "Let's head out."

Keren nodded, picking up her backpack. She paused at the door, giving everyone a final farewell wave.

"Well, this really blows." Ordell plopped himself on the couch.

"Come on. I'm not that bad." Officer Jordon sat in the chair.

"It's not you." Ordell crossed his arms. "We should go too. We've been in this since the beginning." A darkness fell over his face. "I have to avenge my brother."

"Whoa." Officer Jordon held up his hands. "No avenging. Let the inquisitors handle the Dark Guild. Believe me, they won't know what hit them."

Quinlin clenched his teeth. He had to act now while he still had time to warn the arcanum.

Officer Jordon pulled out his cell phone. "Let me see what movies are available for streaming. That should pass the time."

Quinlin motioned for that woman and the female shifter to follow him into the kitchen. He wasted no time getting to the point. "Look, I want to help Keren and so do you." He looked at Nadria. "Do you have anything that would put Officer Jordon to sleep?"

She frowned. "You want to drug him?"

"Yes," that woman said, "I have to find Marcus's *Book of Shadows*. If I know what curse the arcanum used, I can reverse it."

"I don't know." Nadria frowned. "It doesn't feel right."

That woman grabbed her hand. "Please. Think of the lives we'd save if I stopped the cursed creatures." Her eyes looked desperate.

Quinlin raised his eyebrows. He hadn't expected that woman to be on his side.

Nadria let out a sigh. "Alright, I have some herbs in my bag. Let me get them." She started down the hall, then turned. "Just for the record, this is against my better judgment." She walked down the hall to her bedroom.

They heard Officer Jordon shout from the living room. "Hey, what movies do you guys like? There's a comedy and an action-adventure that look pretty good."

"Either of those two is fine," Quinlin shouted back.

That woman tipped her head, staring at him. "You look so familiar. Were you a student at UCF?"

His head throbbed. The last thing he needed was for that woman to get her memories back and recognize him as her attacker. "I was, but I graduated last year. You might remember me from when I worked in the administration office during my last semester." He scanned the hall. What was taking her so long?

"Maybe." She frowned, squinting her eyes. Finally, the shifter came back, holding a vial in her hand.

"This should make him drowsy."

"Office Jordon," said that woman in a raised voice, "would you like something to drink?"

"Yeah, a soda if you have one."

She pulled a two-liter bottle out of the refrigerator. Her hand shook as she poured the soda into a glass. The shifter sprinkled the herbs into the drink, then stirred it with a spoon.

Quinlin grabbed the glass. "You wait here. I'll send Ordell in so you can fill him in on what we're doing." He walked out before they could object.

"Hey, Ordell, Nadria needs your help in the kitchen."

Ordell frowned, giving Quinlin a confused gaze. Quinlin pursed his lips, motioning with his head toward the kitchen.

"OK." Ordell headed to the kitchen, the look of confusion remaining on his face.

Once Ordell had left, Quinlin set the drink next to Officer Jordon.

"Here you go." He moved around to stand behind the chair.

"Thanks." Officer Jordon set his phone down, then picked up the drink, taking a small sip. After setting it back down, he reached for the television remote.

Since Quinlin didn't have time to wait for the drugs to take effect, he sped things up with a jolt of energy. He placed his hand on Officer Jordon's back.

"*Parioida fulmenten,*" he whispered.

As Officer Jordon's muscles convulsed from the energy shock, Quinlin pulled him back into the chair. When his muscles stopped twitching, Quinlin wiped the drool from his face and positioned his head, leaning it off to the side. He picked up the glass, tossing its contents into a nearby planter before returning it to the table. The shifter would believe her drugs put him to sleep.

After snatching up the officer's cell phone, Quinlin paged through the messages, looking for details on the strike.

"They scheduled the strike for 6 am," he muttered to himself. Tension released from his body. He had time to get to the wax museum. After stuffing the phone in his pocket, he rifled through Officer Jordon's pockets, pulling out his car keys.

"Come in here," Quinlin shouted. "The drugs worked. He's sleeping like a baby."

The three rushed into the living room. After seeing Officer Jordon's slumped body, Nadria ran to him, putting a hand on his forehead.

"It shouldn't have worked so quickly." She checked his pulse, then frowned. "His pulse doesn't feel right. We have to get help."

With a smirk, Quinlin enjoyed watching the terror on the shifter's face, thinking she hurt the officer.

"Does he have a phone?" Ordell patted the officer's pockets.

"I found his car keys," Quinlin opened the front door, "but not a phone. Get him to a bedroom. I'll go outside to see if anyone else is around."

"Shouldn't we drive him to a hospital?" the shifter objected.

"Nadria," that woman took the shifter by the arms, "the sooner we get the book, the sooner we can get help for Officer Jordon."

The shifter pursed her lips but didn't object. He saw them struggling to lift the stocky officer as he walked outside.

When he closed the door behind him, he breathed a sigh of relief. As he had hoped, all the inquisitors that had been patrolling left with Briggs and Keren.

After pulling the phone out of his pocket, he thumbed through more messages. Only Briggs' squad and the warrior pack were assigned to the strike. He dialed his lieutenant's number.

"It's me. Yes, I'm fine. Just listen. A squad of inquisitors is planning a strike at the museum at 8 am this morning." He paced by the car, nodding his head. "Yes. The warrior pack is with them." He shook his head. "No, I don't know how many. Get as many arcanum as you can to the museum." With a nod, he glanced at the house. The others would come out any minute. "Yes, that sounds good. I'm on my way."

He hung up, then opened Google Maps. "Where are we?" he muttered. When the phone showed his location, he frowned. "Kissimmee?" After looking up the fastest route to I-4, he stuffed the phone back in his pocket.

He jumped into the police car, tossing the officer's hat to the passenger's seat, then reached under the dashboard. With a sharp pull, he yanked out the wires connecting the police radio. If anyone found out about Jordon, the place would swarm with inquisitors.

While Nadria, that woman, and Ordell raced out of the house, he stuffed the wires under the driver's seat. He sat up as Ordell hopped in the passenger front seat while the women scrambled into the back. Quinlin started the car, speeding off toward I-4.

"Did you find his phone?" Nadria asked. By the sniffling sounds, he knew she was crying.

"No."

"I'll try the radio." Ordell reached over, picking up the hand-held speaker. "I don't know how this works." He pushed several buttons, but the radio didn't respond.

Quinlin used his hand to hide a smile as he heard sobbing from the back seat.

CHAPTER THIRTY-EIGHT

BRIGGS

"Are you afraid?" Briggs asked.

Early morning sunshine streamed through the Land Rover's windshield as he turned onto International Drive. Even though the visor was down, Keren had to hold her hand up to avoid the glare. He noticed the artifact tattoo shimmering as the light hit its reflective scales.

"Yes, and no. Yes, because I've seen how ruthless the Dark Guild can be. And my magic is new. I know so little about how it works." She licked her lips and looked at him. "No, because I trust my creatures and I know you're here to protect me."

He took her hand, lacing their fingers together. "I won't let anything happen to you."

She smiled and nodded. "I know."

While wiggling his fingers between hers, he thought about confessing his feelings. Should something unfortunate happen, he'd want her to know how he felt, how much he loved her. But throwing her an emotional curve ball right before a dangerous battle wasn't the smart thing to do.

He had made up all kinds of reasons and procrastination ploys over the years to avoid exposing his feelings because he feared the possibility of Keren's rejection. That would crush his soul. Staying in the familiar best friend zone felt safer. At least it did until Quinlin entered the picture. Flashing lights up ahead distracted him from his thoughts.

As the Land Rover drew closer to the lights, he saw two police cars blocking the road. Briggs rolled down his window as an officer approached the car.

He held up his badge, addressing the officer. "Good morning, I'm Captain Wilson."

The officer stared at the badge for a moment, then waved them on.

A short ways down I-drive, Briggs pulled into the parking lot of the Citadel Hotel. Medieval-style battlements lined the rooftop with three turrets and a tower completing the hotel's castle facade. This staging area was two blocks from the strike point.

After driving to the back of the lot, Briggs parked his Land Rover next to two other SUVs. They got out, heading toward Briggs' inquisitor squad, ten shifters total, who stood off to the side. The squad wore the same uniform as him and Keren, black with body armor and a cam-fit bump helmet.

"You said these uniforms were fire-proof?" Keren asked, running her hand along the material.

Briggs knew Keren was thinking of the Princeton Street attack, where the cursed wolf had incinerated an entire squad of inquisitors. For her safety, she needed to know exactly what she was facing.

"No, they're fire-resistant." Briggs put on his bump cap. "No clothing will give you absolute protection from fire. That's why you need to be careful and stay with me."

"When someone attacked Mom in the hospital, the explosions burned and wounded several people. But not me, and not Mom. I think One protected us."

"Well then, let's hope One protects you here, too." After spotting his strike coordinator, he waved her over.

"Good morning, Office Howard. What's the status?" The fox shifter placed her hands behind her back, standing at attention.

"Roadblocks are in place, Captain, and I've stationed police officers at every hotel in the area to keep citizens off the street. Tabitha is waiting for your signal to release the warrior pack around the perimeter of the building."

He clapped her on the shoulder. "Thank you. You've done an outstanding job organizing the strike."

She nodded. "Thank you, Captain."

Briggs glanced at his watch, then addressed the squad.

"The strike begins in thirty minutes. As you know, we suspect the Dark Guild's headquarters is in Madam Murray's. Our objective is to kill the cursed wolf and to take as many prisoners as possible. However, don't hesitate to use lethal force if you, a fellow inquisitor, or a warrior pack member is in mortal danger."

Unsynchronized 'yes, sirs' rolled through the group. Then Briggs continued.

"We move in from the south, passing the aquarium and The Wheel before we arrive at Madam Murray's. By then, the warrior pack should be inside. They are the first line of attack."

Briggs could feel the tension building in the air as the squad members moved about, each performing their pre-battle rituals. One continuously adjusted their gloves while another twisted their neck from side to side.

"I want each of you to run through equipment checks and get with your assigned group leader to review your specific line of attack." As he turned back to Keren, he saw she had her arms wrapped around her waist and her body shivered. He put his arm around her. "Do you want to wait in the car?"

"No, I'm fine. Do you think the cursed wolf is there?" asked Keren.

He took a deep breath. The thought of taking Keren into battle with the Dark Guild frightened him more than anything had in his lifetime. What was the council thinking sending her on this mission? If he lost her, he'd never forgive himself.

"According to our informants, this is where they're kept. My hope is this early surprise strike will catch the arcanum off guard. Then we'll be able to capture them and destroy the cursed wolf before they organize a defense." As he put his hand on her arm, he stared into her eyes. "If they use the cursed wolf to attack, we'll need your help. Are you ready?"

She nodded, pressing her hand against his chest, sending a warm pulse through his body.

CHAPTER THIRTY-NINE

QUINLIN

Quinlin saw the flashing lights of police cars as he turned onto Universal Boulevard. He thought he would avoid roadblocks by approaching ICON Park from the back entrance. Apparently, he had been mistaken.

"Get down," he shouted while snatching Officer Jordon's hat off Ordell's head. He slowed down, clenching the steering wheel as the car rolled toward the officer who blocked his path. While scanning the area, he counted three officers. If need be, he could incapacitate them.

"Maybe we should tell them about Officer Jordon," said Nadria.

Quinlin gritted his teeth. "No. Just stay down and stay quiet." He should have killed the officer. That way he wouldn't have to put up with this incessant nagging.

When the officer waved him through, Quinlin let out a deep breath. He acknowledged the officer with a tip of his head as he drove by.

"Can we sit up now?" Ordell asked. He adjusted his body, which he somehow folded into a tight ball on the front floorboard.

"No, wait until I tell you it's safe." Quinlin pulled into ICON Park near the wax museum, parking at the rear of the building. According to the information on Jordon's phone, the strike would happen at 6 am. He looked at the dashboard clock. It was 5:30 am, plenty of time to prepare for visitors.

"Let's go." Quinlin hopped out of the car.

"Wait." The shifter stepped out of the car. "What's our plan?"

"We get in, take the *Book of Shadows*, and get out." That woman's voice grated on his nerves. But he was grateful for her persuasion over the shifter.

The shifter put her hands on her hips. "And then what? And what about Officer Jordon?"

That woman rubbed the shifter's back, speaking in a soft tone. "Then we get back in the car and find the nearest phone so we can call for help. After we have the book, I can find the curse they're using, figure out how to reverse it, and stop the cursed creatures." When the shifter didn't respond, she said, "You can stay here."

Quinlin's stomach tightened. The only way the shifter stayed was if she were dead.

Nadria shook her head. "No, I'll come with you."

"Great," said Quinlin, clapping his hands together. "Let's get moving." He jogged off toward the building.

While approaching the rear entrance of Madam Murray's, Quinlin considered the list of lies in his head to tell the others regarding how he would unlock the door.

"I got this." Ordell changed into his mouse form, squeezing into a tiny crack in the wall.

Quinlin furrowed his eyebrows. "What's he doing?"

A few minutes later, the door clicked, then opened. Ordell stood on the other side. "Alarm and cameras disconnected." His face beamed with pride.

Quinlin lifted an eyebrow. That explained a lot. He stepped inside, waving for Nadria and that woman to follow. He added a reminder to himself to look into adding pucas to the arcanum ranks.

Once the door closed behind them, it left them in total darkness. He heard Nadria's trembling whisper.

"Turn on the lights."

After allowing the women's fear to build up for a few seconds, he flicked on the overhead fluorescent lights. When the bulbs sputtered to life, he saw them huddled in the corner.

He frowned, turning in a circle. Where was the puca? After hearing a small chirping noise, he looked down. A black mouse sat on its hind legs, waving its front paws at him. It wiggled its nose, then scampered off, disappearing down the hall.

"No," Quinlin shouted. "Come back."

"Shhh, are you crazy?" That woman slapped her hand over his mouth. "They'll hear you."

After pulling her hand off, he pushed her harder than he should have. She slammed into the wall. Her eyes met his. Was that a glimmer of recognition?

While walking over, he held out his hand. "I'm sorry. I thought someone was attacking me. Are you alright?"

That woman nodded, sliding back over to the shifter. "I'm OK. Let's get what we came for and get out."

Quinlin nodded, then turned, leading them down the hall toward the lab. While clenching his teeth, he fought down anger bubbling in his gut. That woman would never again desecrate his father's *Book of Shadows*.

His eyes darted from side to side, trying to spot the black mouse. Ordell wandering around on his own could be problematic. While he had no vexation with the fae, he wouldn't hesitate to kill the puca should he get in the way.

As he walked down the hall, he jiggled the knobs of each door he passed. They were all locked, as he expected. After stopping outside the lab door, he waited for the women to catch up to him.

"We'll check in here."

"Why that room?" Nadria whispered.

Quinlin turned the knob, cracking the door open. "Because it's unlocked." He pushed it all the way open and stepped inside.

Frigid cold air washed over his body. A faint, fruity smell lingered in the air, and darkness swallowed them as they walked into the room.

"Is there a light switch?" Nadria's voice quivered.

The door gave a puny squeak as Quinlin closed it behind them.

"Keep the door open for light." The voice sounded desperate. He didn't know and didn't care which woman gave the unheeded command.

While feeling along the wall, Quinlin found the fire extinguisher. He carefully removed it, trying to remain quiet. The women's panting made it easy to pinpoint their location. He stepped close, holding the fire extinguisher to his shoulder.

"Lights!" he bellowed.

Bright overhead lights illuminated the room. Nadria's contorted and confused face became visible a few feet away. A pounding resonated in his ears as adrenaline rushed through his body. He took a giant step forward, flaring his nostrils.

"Surprise," he said, ramming the butt of the fire extinguisher into Nadria's forehead. Blood spurted in all directions from the impact. Her eyes rolled to the back of her head as she crashed to the floor. That woman screamed, her trembling hands covering her mouth. Her wide, dilated eyes glanced to Nadria's body, then back to his eyes.

"It's you!" she gasped. "You attacked me and stole the book."

Heat crawled up Quinlin's face as he gnashed his teeth. How dare she pretend to be the rightful owner of his father's *Book of Shadows*?

"You're the thief, and a murderer." Spittle flew from his mouth as he spoke. After tossing the fire extinguisher to the side, Quinlin grabbed at her, missing as she staggered back.

While letting out a guttural roar, she jumped toward him, swiping clawed fingers at his eyes. After blocking the attack with his forearm, he continued moving his arm in a circular motion, forcing her arms down. While grabbing her wrist with the blocking hand, he thrust his other hand at her throat, squeezing the soft tissue until her tongue lolled out as she gagged for air. Although her other hand pounded on him, it had little effect on his tensed muscles. That woman's face filled his vision. Everything else blurred around him. As he bared his teeth in a snarl, he watched the life seep out of her.

Then he heard a voice in the back of his mind. *This wasn't the plan.* The snarl faded from his face. *You need her to gain control over Keren.* That woman's arms dangled at her sides as her eyelids fluttered. He wanted to kill her. No, his soul demanded he kill her. Then visions of Keren and her magnificent creatures flashed in his mind. His body trembled as he cried out in frustration. With a scowl, he tossed her aside, relinquishing to his desire to have Keren as his own.

His heavy breaths pushed streams of white vapor in the air. Warm droplets of blood dripped from his arm where that woman had scratched him. The pounding in his head dulled as he reined in his emotions. His lieutenant's voice cut through the silence.

"Mr. Turner?"

Quinlin turned to face him.

The man stood straight and tall with his shoulders pulled back and down. He placed his feet shoulder-width apart and his arms hung naturally down the sides of his body. Slicked back auburn hair emphasized his prominent forehead. His pinstriped suit looked tailor-made for his slender frame. Two arcanum stood behind him.

Quinlin ran his fingers through his hair, adjusting his posture to match the lieutenant's.

"Yes." He spoke in a calm voice. "Did you bring the arcanum?"

A smile spread across the lieutenant's face. "Of course, as you requested. And may I say, it's nice to have you back."

"Thank you, lieutenant." Quinlin's pulse had returned to normal. He admired this man's professionalism. "How many are on the premises?"

"Thirty-two. I brought them over in groups from the hotel as to not draw attention. The first group crossed International Drive directly in front of the museum. They noticed shifter activity, most likely the warrior pack you mentioned."

Quinlin frowned. "Any problems?"

"No. They lurked in the peripheral shadows but didn't attempt an attack."

"They must have been scouts for the strike."

"Agreed. I split the others into two groups. One went north before crossing International Drive and one went south. Neither of these groups reported shifter activity."

Quinlin nodded. "Good." He pulled Officer Jordon's phone from his pocket, flipping through the messages. He saw one from Briggs, sent twenty minutes ago.

"*How are things going?*"

After rolling his eyes, Quinlin typed a response. "*Tough at first, but OK now. We're watching a comedy that seemed to have lightened the mood.*" Then he pressed send.

With that out of the way, he continued searching in vain for anything related to the strike. While pursing his lips, he shook his head, stuffing the phone back into his pocket. Maybe they weren't including the officer in their communications.

After hearing a groan behind him, he turned. That woman had struggled to her hands and knees. While clenching his fists, he fought the urge to strike her down and instead addressed his lieutenant.

"Take this woman into custody." Then he glanced at Nadria splayed motionless on the floor. "...and lock this shifter in the siphoning cage."

When the lieutenant tipped his head toward the women, the two arcanum scrambled to take them away.

"Mr. Turner."

"Yes, lieutenant."

"We've created one cursed crab, two cursed bears, and three cursed wolves, including the one used in the demonstration on Princeton Street. Unfortunately, some shifters were already dead when we pulled them from the cage."

"Are all the cursed creatures here?"

"Yes."

Quinlin tapped his chin, wondering how he would lure Keren into the museum before the inquisitors breached his defenses. A sly smile slid across his face as a plan formed in his mind.

"Send the cursed crab and a cursed wolf along with eighteen arcanum to the central courtyard in front of The Wheel. We'll manage frontal attacks from there. Then put six arcanum and two cursed wolves as our rear coverage."

Quinlin put his hands behind his back while he paced the floor. "Stage the wax museum's transport trucks on Universal Boulevard behind the museum. We'll be loading up the cursed creatures after I've obtained an important package."

"Consider it done," said the lieutenant.

"And, Lieutenant, this is critical. Let everyone know a woman with long brown hair and silver eyes is with the inquisitors. Under no circumstances is she to be harmed."

"Understood. I'll spread the word. Mr. Turner, may I ask where the transports are going?"

"We're going to destroy the Magic Underground at Church Street Station."

CHAPTER FORTY

KEREN

Keren let her hand linger on Briggs' chest. The steady pounding of his heart settled her rattled nerves. At the Magic Underground, she had felt invincible. Now, her trepidation had her questioning whether she would be a help or a hindrance to this strike.

She knew next to nothing about her creatures' magical powers. As she looked at the snake-skin tattoo on the back of her hand, she thought about how reckless she had been to use an artifact designed for elves. Yes, she gained power from using its potion, but at what cost? What if the potion drove her mad, and she turned on the people looking to her as their savior?

Briggs took her hand from his chest, turning it palm up.

"Take this." He dropped an earpiece into her hand. "You'll be able to communicate with me, Tabitha, and Faraday."

She put the device in her ear, then watched Briggs move several paces away. While his back was to her, he spoke into the device.

"Keren, can you hear me?"

"Yes," she answered. "Is everyone hearing this conversation?"

"We sure are." Tabitha's voice flowed from the device. "How are you holding up?"

Despite the humid air, a chill ran down Keren's spine. In a fake-confident voice, she responded, "I'm ready to do my part."

"That's my girl," Tabitha said in a calm, unwavering tone. "Remember, you're not alone. Call us if you need help."

Keren smiled, remembering the nervous wreck Tabitha had been at her wedding. Since Keren had been both the maid of honor and bridal escort, she had to practically drag Tabitha down the aisle because she had been so paralyzed with fear.

"I know, thanks."

Briggs glanced at his watch. "Tabitha, it's time for the warriors to move out. In two minutes, I'm sending out the squad then letting you take the reins."

"10-4. Warrior Pack Alpha, Bravo, and Charlie move out. See you on the other side Briggs."

Briggs monitored his watch. "One minute."

A hush fell over the squad. They looked like caged animals waiting to break free. Just as Briggs turned to signal to his squad it was time, an explosion erupted near The Wheel. On impulse, Keren ducked, covering her head. The crackle of energy blasts filled the air. When she heard the trampling of boots rush by, she looked up, seeing the squad sprinting toward The Wheel.

"Arcanum have ambushed Warrior Pack Alpha on the left." Tabitha's voice shouted through the earpiece. "We're backtracking to the front of the fountain to rendezvous with warrior pack beta."

Someone gripped Keren's arm, pulling her upright. She turned, seeing Briggs' stern face.

"We have to go," he said, urging her forward.

Her heart pounded in her chest as they ran after the inquisitor squad. When they drew nearer to the fighting, the explosions grew louder, and she felt the fireballs' heat as they whizzed by.

When she and Briggs caught up, Keren saw the arcanum had pushed Tabitha's warriors around the front of the fountain, blocking Faraday's group from advancing. The buildings on either side kept the warrior pack pressed together while the arcanum had spread out in a concave in four groups of four.

One arcanum in each group cast a shield while the others rapid-fired energy blasts into the trapped warrior pack. As the fox shifters' water jets contacted the energy blasts, they diverted them away. Then Tabitha's voice boomed in her ear.

"Warrior Pack Charlie what's your position? We need assistance breaking a blockade."

Keren knew they had assigned Warrior Pack Charlie to The Wheel side of the courtyard. They were to position themselves on the top of ICON Park's main building as snipers. Without them, the arcanum concave corralled the Alpha and Bravo Packs, giving them no space to set up a solid defense.

"Four arcanum have us pinned in position. We're trying to break free."

"Affirmative, get here as quickly as you can."

Then one energy blast slipped through the water jets' defenses. It crashed into a fox shifter. The explosion caused pieces of the shifter's body to shoot in multiple directions. Blood, bones, and flesh spewed out over the area surrounding the blast. Two other shifters lay unmoving on the ground. It hurled others standing close by into the shifters behind them.

As bits of flesh landed on her clothing, Keren put a shaky hand over her mouth, fighting the bile rising in her throat. Her chest clenched as she fought to draw in breath. As she blinked tears from her eyes, she felt an arm wrap around her.

"Keren."

She barely heard the voice over the ringing in her ears.

"Keren, come with me."

The arm pulled her back behind a line of inquisitors. When she looked up and saw Briggs, she threw her arms around him, burying her face in his neck. He squeezed her against him until she stopped trembling. Then Tabitha's voice came over the earpiece.

"Front line, to your knees. All wolf shifters open fire on left group of asssailants."

Briggs took Keren's arms, gently pushing her away to look into her eyes. "Can you go on?"

She wiped her face with the back of her hand. While giving a curt nod, she set her jaw. She had to hold it together. Then she looked back out over the battlefield.

Ten warriors at the front had dropped to their knees, allowing more of the shifters in the rear to have better vision. Over a dozen fireballs flew at the four arcanum at the far-left. All four had cast shields to block the attack.

"Bears and half the foxes, you're with me. We'll circle back and left, then come up behind the concave. Wolf shifters and half the foxes, you stay with Faraday, keeping pressure on that left side."

Briggs took Keren's hand, motioning with his head for them to follow Tabitha's group.

In a crouch, they ran behind two restaurants, then came out on a wider pedestrian walkway. While pressed against the buildings, they made a wide circle behind the fountain, which sat at the entrance to ICON Park's courtyard. The concave of arcanum stood at their front left, focused on fighting the wolf shifters, and hadn't noticed this group's approach. Tabitha barked orders to the strike team.

"We're almost in position. On my mark, wolf shifters spread your attack across the two left most groups of arcanum. My group splits; seven fox shifters and four bears are with me attacking through the main entrance. Four fox shifters and three bears cover us from a concealed position at the entrance side of the fountain. I'm heading to high ground."

Keren held her breath. It looked like the strike team out-numbered the arcanum. If Tabitha's group could break the concave, releasing the wolf shifters from their pinned position, they would have a clear path into the wax museum. She heard Briggs' voice through the earpiece.

"Keren, we'll advance with Tabitha's team, but stay in the rear and stay low."

"Got it," said Keren. Her skin tingled as her senses sharpened in anticipation of Tabitha's attack plan. Then her voice rang in Keren's ear.

"Mark!"

Tabitha and her group of shifters ran forward. Fox shifters shot jets of water into the arcanum line while the bears summoned earth magic, using roots and branches to crack the arcanum shield defense. The second group hunkered down near the fountain, providing cover for the advancing shifters.

When Keren tried to follow, she tripped, causing her to skid forward on her stomach. As she lifted her head, she saw Tabitha, in two giant leaps, throw herself onto the balcony of a restaurant behind the arcanum concave. She used the balcony plants as an aerial attack on the arcanum. Briggs stopped, running back once he saw Keren had fallen.

She scrambled to her feet as she heard a deep, dire growl from the right. Flames shot across the courtyard entrance, incinerating the shifters between the fountain and Tabitha.

Briggs sprung in front of her, spreading his arms and pushing her back to protect her from the flames. Although she could barely see over his shoulder, she caught a glimpse of the cursed wolf and its handlers. The beast stood twice the height of the one she encountered at the motel. Two arcanum held their palms toward the cursed wolf while the other held a protective shield around the trio. They must have been hiding, waiting for an opportunity to flank the strike team.

Time stood still, a throbbing pulse sprung to life in her solar plexus then shot up her neck and eyes. Light burst from her body then Three appeared as time resumed its normal pace.

With two steps, Three moved close enough to the cursed wolf to kick it under its already disjointed jaw. The crack of its neck as the head flung back sent chills down Keren's spine. With another crack, the cursed wolf pulled its chin back down then, with another low growl, turned its gaze to Three.

"Protect yourself," Keren shouted.

Three crouched as a wall of thick branches grew from its arm, creating a shield. The cursed wolf's attack sent a stream of fire into Three's shield. As the flames burned through the shield's branches, new ones grew instantaneously to replace them.

When the flame blast ended, Three swung the shield at the cursed wolf's head. The wolf ducked, letting the shield swing over its head. Quickly taking advantage of Three's exposed shoulder, the wolf locked its jaws down, causing Three release and excruciating roar.

While letting its body roll backward, Three flipped the wolf onto its back but the wolf's jaw maintained its savage grip on Three's shoulder. After the wolf twisted back up to its feet, it shook its head, tearing deeper into Three's shoulder. Three roared again, punching at the wolf's head.

While watching the two creatures wrestle on the ground, she realized the cursed wolf's strength had exponentially increased with its doubled size. She couldn't leave Three out there alone, so she summoned Two, its flaming horns lowered. It charged at the cursed wolf, ramming into its side. The impact lifted the wolf into the air, but it kept its grip on Three's shoulder. Flames from the cursed wolf enveloped Two. Keren gasped. But as the flames died down, Two stood tall, uninjured by the attack. Two leaped on the cursed wolf's back, tearing at its head with its teeth.

Sweat poured down her face as she forced herself to stand steady on wobbly legs.

Then Keren heard a splash and a high-pitched squeal. After turning toward the sound, her mouth fell open. A colossal crab had risen from the fountain. It struggled to balance itself on ten crooked legs bent in unnatural directions. Two widely spaced eye stalks protruded at different lengths from its head, turning the eyes in opposite directions. The arcanum must have hidden it under the water before the battle began. One giant pincer opened as it swooped down toward the shifter group in the back of the fountain. Keren screamed as the pincer snapped shut, severing the shifters' bodies in half.

Her vision blurred as she staggered backward into Briggs. She grabbed his arm, shouting, "Hold on to me," as she pressed her fingers to the spiral on her palm.

As if struck by an electric shock, her heart exploded in her chest. She let herself collapse into Briggs. As her body convulsed, she felt his arms wrap around her.

CHAPTER FORTY-ONE

QUINLIN

"Now, hit me," Quinlin said to his lieutenant as he pointed to his cheek. "Right here, hard enough to draw blood."

For the first time, Quinlin saw fear in the newly appointed lieutenant's eyes.

"Hit you?"

"Yes, it's part of the plan. And if you see me with a puca and I'm acting strange, play along." He held his arms wide. "I don't have all day."

The lieutenant balled his hand into a fist, then slammed it into Quinlin's face. His head jerked to the side as stars danced in front of his eyes. While moving his jaw from side to side, he touched the impact point on his cheek. After pulling his hand away, he rubbed his bloodied fingertips together.

"Nice right hook."

The lieutenant's face paled while he forced a swallow. Quinlin smirked, finishing his look by messing his hair and untucking part of his shirt.

Then he left the lab in search of Ordell. First, he ran through the exhibit halls. With just enough light from the exit signs, he wove in and out of the staged wax figures while calling out for Ordell in a hushed tone.

After the third exhibit hall with no luck, Quinlin thought the puca simply got frightened and ran away. But he still had one more place to search.

As he opened his office door, Ordell let out a yell, dropping the book he had in his hand. Heat flared in Quinlin's chest as his pulse raced. A pile of books lay in a heap at the puca's feet. He stood on them as though they were worthless trash. Before he reacted, he caught himself. Right now, the books didn't matter. Only getting Keren here mattered.

"Quinlin, thank goodness it's you." Ordell let out a long breath. "I thought you were an arcanum." His eyes drifted to Quinlin's bleeding cheek. "What happened to you?"

"Ordell, where have you been?"

"I've been going through these books. Do you know what a *Book of Shadows* looks like?" He pointed to a pile of four books on the desk. "I've set these aside thinking they could be what we're looking for."

Quinlin clenched his hands into fists, trying to add a tone of fear and panic to his voice.

"Arcanum attacked us and they captured Nadria. Ms. Stewart and I got separated. We need Keren." Quinlin's body shuddered as he watched

Ordell trample over the pile of books while running over to him. He grabbed Quinlin's arm, his face contorted with worry.

"Where's Nadria?"

"This way." Quinlin led Ordell to the lab. After entering, he pointed to the shifter cage on the platform. "There she is."

"Nadria!" he screamed, running to the platform. He pounded on the cage and pulled on the lock as tears streamed down his face. "She's bleeding!" He reached into the cage, tenderly examining her forehead where the fire extinguisher had struck.

"Ordell, get Keren. One of her creatures can open the cage."

"But I don't know where she is." He clenched Nadria's hand. "She's so cold."

"Keren's outside with the strike team. Go out and find her."

"Why me?"

"Because you can change into a tiny animal and make it through to her without being noticed."

He stood, wiping the tears from his face. "Alright, I'll go."

"This way." Quinlin led him out of the lab and down the hall to the back door, even though he actually wanted him and Keren to use the front. He knew two cursed wolves and eight arcanum guarded the rear of the building. And in a few minutes, his lieutenant would start their evacuation to the trucks waiting on Universal Boulevard.

"Let's check to see if anyone's out there." Quinlin cracked the door wide enough for Ordell to peek out. Once he heard Ordell's gasp, he shut the door.

"There are two cursed wolfs and arcanum. We can't go out there." Ordell's hands trembled.

"Then we'll use the front." Quinlin grabbed his hand, yanking him away from the door.

They ran through the exhibit halls, skidding to a stop in the lobby. The glass front door rattled from the battle raging outside.

"Find Keren and bring her back here."

"You're not coming with me?"

"No, I'll stay here and keep the arcanum away from the door."

"Where do you think she is?"

"Probably with the inquisitors." Quinlin opened the door, pushing Ordell outside. "I suggest you change into something less human."

Before his eyes, Ordell shrunk into a black cat. He ran a few steps, then looked back, his green eyes staring but not really focusing. When Quinlin motioned with his hands for Ordell to move, he snapped out of his daze, then turned and ran into the courtyard.

CHAPTER FORTY-TWO

BRIGGS

Briggs embraced Keren's convulsing body, confused by what had happened to her. When he had turned back to help her after she had tripped, those few seconds had saved both their lives. But now her creatures were gone, and he didn't know how to help. After glancing back, he saw the cursed wolf's handlers moving the creature toward the courtyard entrance. His thoughts went only to protecting Keren.

While still clinging to her, he threw himself to the ground, doing his best to cover her twitching body with his own. He held his breath, hoping the arcanum wouldn't notice the two they had left alive.

Once the wolf and arcanum had passed by, he released his breath and gained his feet. While gritting his teeth, he pulled his lips back in a snarl as the smell of charred flesh invaded his nostrils. As his pulse raced, he looked out over the devastating attack on his strike team, trying to absorb the tragic loss.

Eleven bodies, three inquisitors and eight warrior pack shifters lay in a scorched heap. While shifters' blood, three inquisitors, and five warriors the foul monster had ripped in half, seeped under his feet, his eyes darted across the carnage. He paused on Officer Howard's body. Her lifeless, accusing eyes stared at Briggs, asking why he had let this happen. While letting out a guttural roar, he swore the arcanum would pay for their crimes. Tabitha's voice broke through his bloodthirsty thoughts.

"Briggs."

His heart raced. Tabitha had survived. He whipped his head around, searching for the bear shifter.

"Up and to your left."

He looked in the direction she indicated, spotting Tabitha's waving arm. She stood on a restaurant balcony across the courtyard. Then she pointed down to the fountain.

The arcanum controlling the cursed crab had repositioned it, turning its attention to Faraday's group of wolf shifters.

"They're changing formation. Warrior Pack Bravo, there are two cursed creatures ready to attack. Retreat."

"No," snarled Faraday. "We'll climb to the roof and attack from above."

"Faraday, retreat. That's an order."

Briggs watched in horror as shifters attempted to scale the building on their right. Arcanum energy blasts picked off the first two climbers, sending a rain of blood and body parts onto the others below.

"This is Warrior Pack Charlie, the arcanum pinning us down have retreated, we're advancing."

Something about that statement bothered Briggs. The arcanum doesn't retreat. He looked at the cursed wolf. It wasn't moving toward the Bravo Pack. It moved in the opposite direction. In a few minutes, it would be out of sight.

Over the top of ICON Park's main building, Briggs saw ten shifters scaling the four-hundred-foot wheel. They positioned themselves on a half dozen of the thirty stabilized passenger capsules, sending sniping shots at the arcanum that were assaulting Warrior Pack Bravo. Tabitha's voice growled through the earpiece.

"Faraday, move your team now while Charlie has the arcanum distracted. And don't get yourself killed because I'm going to kill you myself."

Eleven shifters, including Faraday, scrambled up the side of the building, but not quickly enough to escape the cursed crab. It pulled its giant pincer back, preparing to strike down the Bravo Pack.

Then Keren jolted out of his arms and another one of her creatures appeared. This one resembled a fox in the upper body and an eel in the lower. It twirled in a circle, letting its tail whip out at the cursed crab, severing an eye stalk from its body. It stumbled, abandoning the attack on Bravo.

Keren glowed brighter as she stood with her feet wide, fists clenched at her sides. Briggs put his hand on her shoulder.

"Are you alright? What happened?"

"I super-charged myself with the artifact's potion so I could summon Four. It incapacitates me for a few minutes."

Briggs watched Four's water jet tear through one of the crab's leg joints. The crab crashed back into the fountain, causing the water to spill over the fountain's rim. Water mixed with the charred remains and blood, causing a deep maroon-colored wave to wash over their feet.

"Where's the cursed wolf?" Keren asked as she scanned the courtyard.

Briggs shook his head, then spoke to the strike team. "Charlie leader, we need eyes on the cursed wolf."

"I see three, all clustered around the back entrance of the museum. And I see ten arcanum with them. There may be more."

Three? He hadn't realized there were so many. A crash drew Briggs' attention back to the fountain. Four had severed all but one of the cursed crab's legs. As the crab shot a water jet at Four, it diverted the blast with a swipe of its tail. One more spin and Four's tail whip separated the crustacean's last eye from its stalk.

The three arcanum handlers abandoned the crab, running across the courtyard to join the other arcanum defending themselves from Warrior Pack Charlie's attack.

With a sweep of its arms, Four commanded the fountain's water to lift in the air, forming like a cloud over the cursed crab. Four spun, and the water mimicked the motion, creating a whirlpool in the air. After coming to an abrupt halt with its arms raised, Four then threw its arms down. The whirlpool crashed into the crustacean, boring an enormous hole through its body. The cursed crab let out a shriek then fell, for the last time, into the fountain's base.

As Faraday's Bravo Pack made it to the rooftop of the main building, fifteen arcanum climbed up the other side. He heard Keren's voice.

"Should I send One out to help?"

"No," Tabitha responded. "It looks like we have the arcanum outnumbered two to one, so it's only a matter of time before we finish this fight. We need you to find and destroy the rest of the cursed creatures."

"The leader of Charlie said they were behind the wax museum," added Briggs.

Then from the left came a *whooshing* sound as three fire blasts sailed from the rear of the wax museum toward The Wheel. Tabitha screamed orders over the earpiece.

"Charlie Pack, get out of there!"

The three fire blasts landed one after the other onto The Wheel. The metal supports groaned as they engulfed the entire structure in flames. None of the ten members of Warrior Pack Charlie had enough time to jump to safety.

Briggs felt a chilling cold hit his gut. As he took deep breaths through clenched teeth, he balled his hands into fists. Both arcanum and shifters on the rooftop continued their battle under the four-hundred-foot tall torch.

CHAPTER FORTY-THREE

KEREN

Keren screamed as she watched The Wheel ignite in flames, engulfing all the shifters from Warrior Pack Charlie. Her heart pounded in her ears while she struggled for breath. She turned to Four.

"Put out the fire!"

With a wave of its hand, Four commanded the fountain's blood-red water to rise. Then Four spun, and the water sailed through the air to The Wheel. When the water struck the wheel, some flames smoldered into black smoke, then quickly reignited.

"No, this can't be happening." She covered her face with her hands, turning and staggering away from the hideous scene. Those fire blasts had come from the cursed wolves. They had to be stopped.

Then an eerie calm passed through her. She took her hands from her face, revealing a savage scowl. They would pay for what they've done. Her breathing changed to loud, low breaths as she turned toward the fountain.

While looking at the dead crustacean in the dry fountain, she lifted her chin, taking a deep breath, letting her chest fully expand before exhaling. Four had defeated the cursed crab and saved Warrior Pack Bravo. Now, she would find and kill the other cursed creatures, crushing them to stop their devastating rampage. She spoke in a clear, determined voice.

"I'm going after the cursed creatures."

Briggs nodded, hearing her through the earpiece, then motioned for her to follow as he headed to the rear of the wax museum. When something moved to her left, she stopped, preparing to summon another of her creatures. Then a figure stepped into the light. Her eyes widened, staring in disbelief. When she tried to move, her body refused, remaining frozen in place. This couldn't be happening. He should have been at the safe house.

"Ordell?"

Keren released her magic, and Four disappeared. While forcing her body to respond, she dashed across the courtyard to Ordell. His wide, green eyes and twitching horse ears signaled something was seriously wrong. Her head pounded, thinking he had been out here during the battle. He could have been killed. Once she reached him, she slid to a stop, wrapping her arms around him.

"What are you doing here?"

She felt him tremble against her body. Briggs ran up beside her.

"Nadria," Ordell stammered, "she's hurt and needs your help."

Keren blinked. Had her best friend, Nadria, been injured during the battle? *No, this can't be real*, she thought. They had left her back at the safe house. The fog in her mind caused Briggs' voice to sound muffled, even though he stood next to her.

"How did you get here? Where is Officer Jordon?"

Ordell took her hand, pulling her toward the museum. "Please, help."

She squeezed her eyes shut and gave her head a slight shake to push her thoughts away and focus on helping Ordell. Keren allowed him to guide them down a path between the two buildings that led to the wax museum's front door so they had better cover. Then she stopped so she could question him.

"Where's Mom and Quinlin?"

"Quinlin said the arcanum attacked them and they got separated. He sent me to get you."

Briggs pulled out his phone, trying to call Officer Jordon. When there was no answer, he called for backup to the safe house. Then he squatted down so his eyes were level with Ordell's.

"Why did you come here?"

"Ms. Stewart thought if she could get the *Book of Shadows*, she could stop the cursed creatures. We came here to find it."

Briggs' face turned a bright shade of red. "I specifically told you to stay put."

Ordell hung his head. "We just wanted to help."

Briggs tipped his head back, forcing out a quick breath. Then he looked at Ordell, putting his hand on his shoulder, speaking in a soft tone. "Let's go find Nadria."

As they drew near the front door, she saw Quinlin had his face pressed against the glass. Blood dripped down his left swollen cheek, and his hair and clothes looked as though he'd been in a fight. He pushed the door open as they approached.

"Thank goodness you're here." He took Keren into his arms.

She wrapped her arms around him, relieved he was alive. As she pressed against him, she thought it odd that, even though they were in a life and death situation, his body felt relaxed, and his heartbeat was steady and strong. He whispered into her ear.

"They captured Nadria."

She pulled away from him, staring into his brown eyes. "Ordell told me. Where's my mom?" Keren's breathing shallowed as her stomach twisted into a knot, waiting for his response.

"I don't know, but we'll find her."

Ordell grabbed her hand, tugging her away from the door. "Come on, Nadria's hurt. We have to get her out."

Keren ran down the hall after Quinlin and Ordell, with Briggs following behind them. Quinlin shouted over his shoulder at Briggs.

"Maybe you and Ordell should search for Ms. Stewart."

"I'm staying with Keren."

Keren startled at the sharpness in his tone. He must still be angry they had escaped from the safe house. Then they stopped at the lab door.

Keren turned to Briggs. "Please. I need you to find Mom."

"I don't want to leave you." He brushed the back of his fingers across her cheek. She tenderly removed his hand from her face, its warmth soothing her icy, wet hands. She gave his hand a reassuring squeeze.

"I'll be fine with Quinlin."

A sour look passed over his face as his eyes flicked to Quinlin, then back to her.

"If that's what you want."

Ordell spoke up, "But I want to be with Nadria."

Keren put her hand on his shoulder. "We'll take care of Nadria. I need you to help find my mom. Briggs shouldn't go alone."

Ordell looked at Briggs, then back at Keren. His shoulders slumped as he let out a long breath. "Alright."

After Briggs and Ordell trotted down the hall, Quinlin took Keren's hand.

"Let's go." He led her into the lab.

When the frigid air touched her skin, a chill quaked through her body. A sickly metal smell drifted through the air. After scanning the room, she spotted a platform in the corner. Then her eyes locked on the table, noticing its covering displayed the Dark Guild's symbol. She'd seen that symbol before, both at Dan's house and the motel with the cursed wolf.

"The woman wasn't lying. This is a Dark Guild base." Her eyes drifted to the shifter cage. Then she gasped, recognizing the person inside.

"Nadria!" she yelled. After letting go of Quinlin's hand and sprinting onto the platform, she banged on the cage and tugged at the lock. "Is there a key?"

"Use one of your creatures to open it."

Of course, why hadn't she thought of that? She closed her eyes, imagining the flotation tank. While letting her body relax, she felt the pulse start in her solar plexus, then move up her neck to her eyes. As she opened her eyes, light burst from her body, and Three appeared.

Quinlin stepped closer to the platform. She heard him take in a deep breath. "Fascinating. Is this the one that killed the cursed wolf?"

"Yes." She looked at Three. "I need you to get Nadria out of the cage."

Three took the lock in its hand then twisted, snapping the padlock in half. Then she heard a commanding voice.

"Stop destroying the equipment."

Keren looked up, seeing a young arcanum with auburn hair wearing a neat pinstriped suit standing in the center of the room. He held his palm pressed to the side of her mom's head. They had her mouth gagged and her hands tied behind her back. Her red, puffy eyes showed she'd been crying. Keren gasped, putting her hands to her mouth. Ugly purple bruises lined her mom's neck. She wanted to gouge the arcanum's eyes out.

"What have you done to my mom?"

After taking a quick glance back at Three, she tried estimating how fast it could get to her mom.

"Put that creature away and release your magic. You can't reach me before I blow her brains out."

Keren looked at Quinlin. He raised his eyebrows while nodding his head. If she hadn't known better, she thought he almost looked happy.

"You had better do as he asks," he said.

She frowned as a knot tightened in her stomach. Then she released her magic. Three turned to mist, dissipating into the air.

"Very good. Now, step off the platform and join Mr. Turner."

Keren narrowed her eyes, tilting her head to the side. This arcanum knew Quinlin's name. With uncertainty, Keren did as she was told, stepping off the platform to stand next to Quinlin. He took her hand, giving it a squeeze.

"I want you to come with me. I care about you, Keren."

Keren frowned, pulling her chin back while leaning away from Quinlin. An arcanum stood in front of them threatening to kill her mom, and he decides now was the time to profess his feelings? He leaned in as if to tell her a secret.

"We'd make perfect partners."

With a broad smile, Quinlin's dimples materialized, and the edges of his eyes wrinkled. Keren shook her head, stammering with her response.

"I, I don't know what you mean."

He turned to face her, gesturing widely with his free hand. "Don't you see? This is the future of elemental magic. I want you to be part of it. You and your magnificent creatures. Don't you want to be with sorcerers like yourself?"

A wave of nausea passed over her as she tried to organize her thoughts. After yanking her hand away from Quinlin, she staggered back.

"Are you saying you're an arcanum?"

The young arcanum laughed, drawing Keren's attention. Her mom's eyes widened, and she nodded her head.

Quinlin ran to the platform, picking up the *grimoire, Book of Shadows,* and Amplification Disk, bringing them back to Keren.

"With these, I created the cursed creatures." He held up the disc, twisting its chain back and forth in his fingertips so it spun before her eyes.

"See, I have an artifact, too. This is the Amplification Disk. And soon I'll have many more. This one amplifies spells, allowing them to maintain themselves for as long as the disk exists." He twirled it while he stared at it.

"Since it's made of an unknown indestructible metal, that's just another way of saying my cursed creatures will live forever."

He slipped the chain over his head, letting the artifact dangle around his neck. "And these," he held up the books, "document my father's work."

The room spun around Keren. She frowned, stumbling back. "You attacked my mom." She shook her head. "It's been you all the time. You've been lying to me."

"Not everything was a lie." He pointed to her mom. "This woman, who had been a member of the Dark Guild, killed my father and stole his *Book of Shadows*." His voice softened. "But I'll spare her life, on the condition you become my life partner and bring your magnificent creatures to the Dark Guild."

Keren couldn't breathe, and her vision blurred. She rested her hands on her knees, trying to stay upright as the world spun around her.

Just then, Briggs and Ordell walked into the room.

"Nadria!" Ordell ran onto the platform, scooping up Nadria into his arms.

"What's going on?" Briggs took a step forward.

"Stop." Quinlin raised his arm, pointing his palm at Ordell and Nadria. "One move, and all three die."

Keren straightened, squaring her shoulders to Quinlin. Every muscle in her body tensed. She'd been a fool. Everything he'd ever said or did had been a lie. It felt like a fist tightened around her heart. She had put her friends and family in grave danger by insisting on his company. After spitting at his feet, she spoke in a scathing tone.

"You disgust me."

Quinlin let out a heavy sigh, tilting his head to the side. "I see you need more time to think." Then he spoke over his shoulder. "Lieutenant, it's time to go."

When both Keren and Briggs jerked as if to rush them, the lieutenant wrapped his fingers around the side of her mom's face.

"Don't follow us, or she dies."

Flashes of arcanum energy-blast carnage ran through her mind. Her pulse raced, thinking that might happen to her mom. Then Keren reached her hand out, catching Briggs' broad arm. She felt his muscles twitching. Since she couldn't bring herself to speak, she just looked at him as tears streamed down her face.

Quinlin and his lieutenant ran from the room, dragging Keren's mom with them.

CHAPTER FORTY-FOUR

BRIGGS

Without taking his eyes off Keren, Briggs spoke in a tired, dejected voice.

"Tabitha, there are two men exiting the wax museum. They have a prisoner. Do not engage."

"Affirmative. I see them. They're running to the last of the museum's delivery trucks."

"What's the strike team's status?"

"The arcanums' strength is running out. It's only time before the last group of four is in custody or dead. So far, all of them have fought until the casting killed them. Faraday and four pack members made it out alive." Tabitha paused, then Briggs heard her swear. "How did they know about the strike?"

Keren's sunken cheeks and pale face broke his heart. Her lips were drawn downward while the bottom one quivered. She was the strongest person he knew, but Quinlin's treachery seemed to have shattered her.

"I think we had a mole." He took a deep breath. "Come inside the museum. We're clear."

"10-4, on my way."

Briggs picked up his radio. "I need medical assistance at ICON Park, multiple wounded, multiple casualties."

Tabitha limped into the lab with a make-shift bandage around her thigh. It was soaked in blood. She stopped mid-stride after spotting Ordell and Nadria.

"Oh, my god."

She hobbled over to them, then checked Nadria's vital signs. Ordell knelt at her side, rocking back and forth.

"Is she going to be OK?"

"Her pulse is good." Tabitha poked at the forehead wound. "She's taken a nasty hit to the head. She might have a concussion." Then she pulled Nadria's eye open. "And it looks like they've drugged her."

Ordell let out a cry, flinging himself on Nadria's stomach. He sobbed into his arm.

"Please be OK. You have to be OK."

Briggs took Keren's hand from his arm. "You should sit down." She let him guide her to the platform. Tabitha helped him sit her on the platform while Keren stared out into space, not seeming to know what was going on.

"What happened to her?" asked Tabitha as she took off Keren's bump cap and ran her hand over her head.

"I don't know the entire story. I came in, and Quinlin, who turned out to be an arcanum, had kidnapped Ms. Stewart and threatened to kill her if we followed him."

"Who's Quinlin?"

Briggs clenched his teeth, thinking about Keren with Quinlin. He wondered how far that relationship had gone. Had she fallen in love with him?

"A nurses' aide at the hospital. Apparently, he'd been sneaking Keren in to see her mom. I don't think she knew he was sorcerer let alone an arcanum."

"Hey," Tabitha rubbed Keren's back, "we're tracking those delivery trucks. They can't hide from us."

Briggs paced the room. After this disastrous strike, the Dark Guild is more powerful than ever. Somehow, he had to rescue Keren's mom.

"What are we doing to stop them?"

Tabitha raised her eyebrows. "Nothing. Anyone gets near and the cursed creatures will attack. It seems the arcanum has limitless energy when it comes to controlling the creatures. We have no defense against them." She shot a look at Keren. "We're simply following them so we know where they're holding up next."

Faraday walked in. He sniffed the air, then grimaced. "I smell death."

While circling the room, he came to the cages stacked along the wall. As he let out a deep, guttural growl, he snapped his teeth. "Have you seen this?"

Tabitha and Briggs walked over to Faraday. Tabitha gasped, putting her hands to her mouth. Briggs ran his fingers through his hair as he stared at the shriveled, shrunken-skin bodies of shifters. Both of them closed their eyes, turning away from the gruesome scene.

"My god," said Tabitha, scrubbing her hands down her face. "What did they do to them?"

"They murdered them," growled Faraday. He pointed a finger at Keren. "She was supposed to kill the creatures. Instead we lost over 90% of our warriors."

Briggs stepped nose-to-nose with Faraday. "It's not Keren's fault. She did the best she could."

"Then we're all doomed." Faraday stormed out of the lab.

CHAPTER FORTY-FIVE

KEREN

While lost in her thoughts, Keren replayed her time with Quinlin. There had to be clues she had overlooked. One had never liked him. She also remembered how Quinlin and Nadria hadn't gotten along. Then when her mom had escaped from the hospital, the look on his face when he picked her up, that was disgust. The clues flashed in front of her like neon signs, but she hadn't paid attention, so her friends and family paid the price.

Her limbs felt heavy, and every inch of her body ached. If she went back to the beginning of this mess when she postponed the house re-protect, that selfish act allowed Quinlin to find the *Book of Shadows*. So, she had really murdered anyone killed by those cursed creatures. She had ruined the lives of their families. Children would grow up without a parent because of her stupid mistake.

While picturing the twirling Amplification Disk, Quinlin's words echoed in her head. *'And soon I'll have many more.'* Then it struck her, and the real world came crashing in. Nadria and Ordell were on the platform next to her. Briggs and Tabitha stood talking a few feet away. She propelled herself off the platform.

"I know where Quinlin's going."

Keren hadn't expected the weakness of her legs. As she landed, her knees buckled. Briggs and Tabitha ran over to steady her from falling.

"What are you talking about?" asked Tabitha. Her worried eyes stared into Keren's.

Keren grabbed Tabitha's arms. "The artifacts. Quinlin is going after the artifacts in the Magic Underground."

Tabitha smiled at her. "No, Keren, humans can't go to the underground, and they don't know about the artifacts."

Keren squeezed her eyes shut, shaking her head to clear her thoughts. No, she was certain that's where Quinlin planned to attack. She turned to Briggs, putting her hands on his chest.

"I was in the Magic Underground. Azalea showed me how to pass through the magic barrier. And I was in The Repository."

Briggs frowned. "But how would Quinlin know?"

Keren hung her head, her cheeks burning as her body trembled. "Because I told him."

Tabitha put her hand on Keren's shoulder. "You're sure?"

She nodded, then rested her forehead on Briggs' chest. She felt nauseous. Azalea and the council had trusted her with their secrets. Now, Quinlin and the cursed creatures were on their way to destroy them and steal the artifacts. A chill ran down her spine. With those artifacts, Quinlin would be unstoppable.

She pressed her lips together, counting each heart-beat as it pounded in her chest. She couldn't be responsible for more destruction and death. As she pushed away from Briggs, a surge of energy ran through her body. The fatigue had to be pushed aside. She had to win the war.

"Where are the delivery trucks?"

To her surprise, Faraday's voice came over the earpiece.

"They just got onto I-4 east."

"We have to warn the Magic Council." Keren scrubbed her hands over her face. It was too early for the shops to be open. Anyone else she knew that could enter the underground was here at ICON Park, and they wouldn't make it to Church Street Station before Quinlin.

Her head pounded as her mind flipped through all possibilities. Then she spun to face Briggs.

"Give me your phone." She held out her hand. Her eyes wild with desperation.

Briggs pulled his phone out of his pocket. "Who are you going to call?" He looked at her suspiciously.

She snatched it from his hand, flipping to a number she knew Briggs had saved. It rang twice. Then he answered the call.

"Hello? Papa Murphy? It's me, Keren. This is an emergency. There's something I need you to do."

CHAPTER FORTY-SIX

KEREN

Keren jumped out of Briggs' Land Rover as it screeched to a halt at Church Street Station. She breathed a sigh of relief seeing a stronghold defense set up outside of Perfect Potions. Papa Murphy had made it in time to warn the Magic Council.

Three groups of four arcanum bombarded Perfect Potions with energy blasts. Two groups were on the ground, while one group had positioned themselves on the rooftop of the building across the street. The arcanum groups maneuvered similarly to the ones at the wax museum, one or two shielding the group while the others battered the storefront with rapid-fire energy blasts.

While three fox shifters' water jets intercepted some of the energy blasts, diverting them from their target, others exploded on invisible protection spells cast by fairies. Four bear shifters used earth magic to attack the groups of arcanum, forcing more of them to shield them from the onslaught of roots and branches rather than attack. A half-dozen wolf shifters patrolled the balcony in front of Perfect Potions, strategically shooting fireballs as they identified opportunities to strike.

Keren squinted as she scanned the buildings, looking for Quinlin. He had taken her mom hostage and threatened to kill her. Briggs made a promise to save her before Quinlin followed through with his threat. If anyone could save her mom, it was Briggs.

Her eye caught a raven circling over the battle at Perfect Potions. Ordell had ridden over with her, deciding to help after he saw medics tending to Nadria. She frowned. Could that be Papa Murphy?

The snapping of disjointed limbs drew her attention. Her jaw dropped as five cursed creatures and their handlers turned onto Church Street from the railroad tracks. As they lumbered down the street, her throat tightened, realizing they were all headed toward Perfect Potions.

Briggs, Ordell, and Tabitha ran up next to her as two more police cars raced into the parking lot. Briggs gave a rundown of the situation.

"We have visuals on five cursed creatures, three fire, and two earth. Making a quick estimate, I'd say we have at least thirty arcanum. Three with each creature and visuals of three groups of four, like the setup at ICON Park."

Faraday and the four surviving warrior pack members trotted up to stand next to Tabitha. Their torn clothing exposed burned skin and bleeding gashes from the battle at ICON Park. Faraday's eyes scanned the area.

"They could be hidden in or on top of the buildings." He looked at Briggs. "We're outnumbered against the arcanum. And we're dead against the cursed creatures."

Keren winced, crossing her arms over her chest. After her performance at ICON Park, she didn't blame Faraday for discounting her magic. Her creatures were powerful enough to kill the cursed creatures, but she had failed to use them effectively. So now here they were, at Church Street Station, defending Azalea's artifact archive and the magical races that lived in the underground. Then she heard Briggs' voice.

"I'm calling in another inquisitor squad for backup against the arcanum. If we can get to the handlers, we'll stop the creatures."

"A temporary solution," replied Faraday. "Shifter magic cannot destroy the cursed creatures. It's only a matter of time before more arcanum show up."

"Buying time is the best we can do," said Tabitha. "Faraday, you and your team are helping to defend the Perfect Potion." Then she turned, winking at Keren. "While Keren takes care of the cursed creatures."

As Keren tightened her fists, she gave Tabitha a nod. Faraday and the other warriors might not have confidence in her abilities and, although their criticism stung, their opinions were irrelevant. Tabitha and Briggs believed in her, and that gave her the strength to believe in herself. This time, she wouldn't stop until she destroyed the cursed creatures. Tabitha put her hand on Keren's back.

"I'll be your cover."

After taking a deep breath, Keren looked at the procession of cursed creatures plodding down Church Street. An invisible fist clenched her gut. Three and Two had struggled with one cursed wolf. Now, she faced three wolves. And she didn't know how tough the cursed bears were. The odds were against her. She took a deep, long breath. This had only two outcomes for her. Destroy the cursed creatures and save the Magic Underground or die trying.

Briggs wrapped his arm around her, pulling her close. She let her head rest against his shoulder. "Are you ready?" he asked.

"Yes."

He scooped her off her feet. When she turned her head to look at him, their noses bumped together. She felt his warm breath on her face. He licked his lips, then swallowed. "It's easier to hold you like this."

She leaned forward, letting her lips brush against his. Then she pushed the spiral, snake-tailed tattooed on her palm.

Keren's eyes fluttered open. The adrenaline flowing through her dulled the fatigue and pain. She was ready for a fight.

"You can put me down."

But Briggs held her tighter. His lavender eyes stared into hers as he spoke. "I need you to know something."

She put her finger to his lips as her eyes welled up with tears. While leaning her forehead on his, she whispered to him.

"Please, put me down."

Without a word, he set her gently on the ground. She turned away before he could see a tear trickle from the corner of her eye. Briggs deserved better than someone responsible for the murder of hundreds of shifters. One day, she thought, he'd be happy with a wife and family and would be grateful for this moment.

With a ferocious yell, Keren summoned her magic. Light instantaneously burst from her body.

"I summon my army."

All four creatures appeared. Their colors and detail were sharp as they tensed, waiting for Keren's command.

The cursed creatures walked in formation, one wolf in front, followed by the bears, then the remaining wolves. She didn't know when they planned to join the attack on Perfect Potions, so she had to act fast. If she took out one of the cursed wolves with a surprise attack, at least the numbers would be even. She chose which wolf to focus on, then sent her creatures in for the attack.

As Three slammed its fist into the ground, roots shot up, ensnaring the legs of the cursed wolf in the rear. While Two jumped on its back, tearing at its head with its claws and teeth. Before the arcanum handlers could react, Four shot a water jet into the group, severing all their heads. Now left without handlers, the cursed wolf stopped moving. Three ran up, taking the wolf's bloodied head and, with a roar, ripped it from the body.

As a blast of fire shot toward Three, it held the severed head up, using it as a shield against the searing flames. Two lowered its horns, smashing into the side of the other rear wolf attacking Three. As Three tossed the severed wolf's head into the air, One somersaulted, batting the head with its wing like a volleyball. The head jettisoned to the ground, crashing into the second rear wolf's handlers. Once that wolf stopped moving, Three repeated the beheading process of the cursed creature.

Adrenaline flowed through Keren as she moved along the sidewalk, following her creature army. Tabitha trailed behind her, creating a living shield from the foliage to block her glow from the arcanum as much as possible while still giving her a clear view of the battle. Keren's heart pounded. They had destroyed two of the cursed creatures. She took a deep breath, enjoying the triumph. Then, while gritting her teeth, she pushed as much energy into her creatures as possible.

Both cursed bears turned toward Three, shooting a dozen crooked, leafless branches from their backs. As Keren looked closer, the branches had pointed spear-heads. Four spun, pulling the continuous snow from Winter Wonderland and blasting snow jets at the pair, freezing the bears and their handlers in place. While Two shot a fireball, burning the spears in mid-flight. As Three stomped forward, it crushed each arcanum handling team under its feet. Then, after raising its fists, it smashed them into the bears' heads. With a loud *snap*, the frozen heads cracked away from the bodies.

She pumped her fists in the air. To celebrate, she pushed more energy into her creatures. One somersaulted in the air as Four twirled in a circle. Three and Two stomped over the frozen bears' bodies. She watched as the remaining cursed wolf crashed through a storefront window, it and its handlers retreating from the scene.

"Keren."

She spun around, seeing Tabitha leaning against the wall. Her chalky face exaggerated the dark circles under her eyes. Keren glanced down, shocked by the pool of blood under Tabitha's leg. When Keren tried taking a breath, her lungs wouldn't expand, leaving her gasping for air. She couldn't lose Tabitha, too.

"This is the end of the line for me."

Keren took her arm, helping her to the ground. "You just need rest. You're going to be OK."

Tabitha patted her on the arm. "You need to finish what you started." She leaned her head back on the wall, closing her eyes. "You can do this." Then Tabitha went limp.

With shaking hands, Keren pressed her fingers to Tabitha's neck. She felt a faint pulse.

"Hang in there. This is almost over."

She stood, feeling exposed now that Tabitha's shield no longer protected her. A trickle of sweat dripped down her face as she braced against the building for support. The potion was wearing off. That last energy push for the celebration must have depleted her supply.

Since the cursed wolf had retreated, and the warrior pack and fae had a solid defense against the arcanum, she could use the artifact again, even though it would render her unconscious for a few minutes, causing her creatures to disappear.

She sat down next to Tabitha and pressed her fingers to her palm. When nothing happened, she frowned, staring at the snake-tail swirl. She pressed her fingertips to her palm again. When nothing happened, she used her other hand, driving her fingertips into the tattoo.

Her stomach churned as she beat her hand on the ground. This couldn't be happening. One cursed wolf could tear through Perfect Potion's defenses, leaving the Magic Underground vulnerable to its rampage.

She jumped when a hand appeared in front of her face. Then cringed when she heard Quinlin's voice.

"Having artifact problems?"

She batted his hand away, then glanced at Three.

"Don't even think about it. My lieutenant is watching us from that upstairs window." He motioned to the Howlin' Moon. "He'll kill your mom if anything attacks me."

Keren got to her feet. She staggered as her legs wobbled beneath her. When he reached out to help, she curled her lip, recoiling from Quinlin.

"Don't touch me."

She stumbled into the street, looking at her creatures. Their colors had faded, and the edges of their bodies blurred. As she pushed her hair out of her face, she let out a dejected sigh. She had been so close to victory. *It's not your fault*, she thought as her creatures regarded her, waiting for a command. She blinked tears away as she released them but held onto her magic. They turned to mist and dissipated into the air.

Quinlin strolled into the street with his hands behind his back.

"Let's get back to our discussion earlier before we were so rudely interrupted."

"We have nothing to discuss."

As he walked in a circle around her, the sun caught the Amplification Disk, shooting a flash of light into Keren's eyes. She blocked it with her hand.

"But we do. Decide. Are you joining me?"

"Never. I'll defend my friends and family until I die."

Her vision blurred, and the pain in her stomach was almost unbearable. With a sob, she released her magic.

CHAPTER FORTY-SEVEN

BRIGGS

As Briggs crept through the downstairs of Howlin' Moon's Barbecue, he kept his eye out for Ordell. The puca had changed into a mouse, scouting ahead for danger.

So far, they hadn't run into any arcanum. But they also weren't any closer to finding Ms. Stewart. Briggs knew it would devastate Keren if something happened to her mom. Promising to rescue her mom let Keren focus more on her magic and fighting the cursed creatures.

He grimaced, running a hand through his hair. Quinlin may have already killed Ms. Stewart. That left him to bear the terrible burden of telling Keren. No, he needed to be optimistic. He would find Ms. Stewart alive, and he would rescue her.

After what Quinlin did to Keren, lying and seducing her while all the while trying to kill her friends and family, he felt no constraints on what he would do to the sorcerer if he found him.

Then he froze, hearing Ordell's high-pitched squeaks as he came downstairs. Once Ordell's mouse form came over, he changed into his human form.

His horse ears were pinned back, and his breathing labored. "I found her. She's upstairs."

Brigg's chest tightened. This was the question he dreaded. "Is she alive?" He heard his heart beating in his ears as he waited for Ordell's answer.

"Yeah, she's sitting in a chair. They have her hands tied behind they tied her and her feet to the chair."

Briggs let out a long breath. "Is there anyone else with her?"

"Just that arcanum with the pinstriped suit. He's staring out the window."

While rubbing his hand over his chin, Briggs wondered how he would get past the arcanum. Then he looked at Ordell. He pursed his lips. Ordell's been through so much already. Could he ask him to risk his life again?

"I know that look," said Ordell as he sat on the floor. "You want me to do something dangerous."

Briggs put his hand on Ordell's slender shoulder. He had shown more bravery this past week than he'd seen from seasoned officers.

"Only if you're up to it."

The muscles in Ordell's face tightened as he sprung to his feet. "They killed Broden and hurt Nadria. What do you want me to do?"

After reaching into his pocket, Briggs pulled out a ring with two keys. He dropped it in Ordell's hand. "These are the keys to Ms. Stewart's cuffs. I need you to chew through the ropes, then unlock the cuffs." He looked around, checking to see if anyone had entered the room. When satisfied they were still alone, he continued. "Did you notice if there were any plants in the room?"

Ordell's face dropped. "No, sorry."

Briggs patted his back. "It's OK. I'll follow you upstairs. Try to be quiet."

Ordell smiled. "Quiet as a mouse." Then he changed to his mouse form. After looping his head through the ring, he bit the keys.

While nodding his head, Briggs smiled. "Smart, nothing to drag on the ground."

After Ordell squeaked, he ran upstairs with Briggs following close behind.

About halfway up the staircase, Briggs had to slow down. The wooden stairs creaked under his weight, so he needed to be careful where he stepped. He stopped a few stairs from the top, crouching down next to the wall as he took in the room.

A large wooden table with five high-back chairs filled half of the room. Pictures of various full moons decorated the walls. Sitting under the window where the arcanum stood were two books.

Ms. Stewart sat in a high-backed chair pulled to the side, her eyes locked on the arcanum at the window. Briggs couldn't see Ordell. He guessed he was working on chewing through the ropes binding Ms. Stewart's hands. When he noticed a five-foot potted cactus sitting in one corner of the room, a smile spread across Briggs' face.

The seconds ticked by as sweat dripped down Briggs' face. Depending on how thick the rope was, he could be here for a while before Ordell managed to chew through. He took slow, shallow breaths as to not alert the arcanum to his presence. Finally, he spotted Ms. Stewart's arms jerk.

Briggs held his breath as the rope dropped toward the floor. That noise would certainly alert the arcanum. His cramped muscles complained as he readied himself to pounce. Just before the rope hit the floor, Ms. Stewart grabbed it, leaving it dangling a mere inch off the ground.

She brought her hands together on her lap as Ordell started chewing the rope binding her feet. After tucking the chewed rope under her leg, she picked up the cuff's keys Ordell had dropped in her lap, then put her hands back behind the chair.

Suddenly, the arcanum turned. His eyes darting around the room until he spotted Ordell.

"Get away from her," he snarled, stomping across the floor.

As Briggs heard the clank of two gold disks drop to the floor behind Ms. Stewart's chair, she raised her palms out to the side.

"*Protegioum.*"

A shield sprung to life, surrounding her and Ordell. While skidding to a stop, the arcanum had a look of confusion on his face.

Barreling from his position, Briggs drove his shoulder into the arcanum, sending him flying over the table and into the wall across the room. Keren's mom dropped the shield long enough for Briggs to tear the ropes off her feet. Once she was free, Briggs pointed to the staircase.

"Get out of here!" he shouted.

Ordell changed to his human form as they raced to the stairs.

"*Protegioum*," she said again, raising a shield around them.

Briggs tossed the chair aside, picking up the two gold disks. He placed one in each palm.

"*Potestatenum*."

At hearing that spell, Briggs threw himself to the side. The hair on his arms stood up as the energy blast skimmed by him.

The arcanum ran forward, his palms outstretched.

Briggs catapulted to the ceiling and ricocheted off toward the arcanum. His hands reaching for his wrists. At the last minute, the arcanum twisted, elbowing Briggs in the nose. With a grunt, Briggs fell onto his back, blood pouring from his broken nose. He slammed his palms into the floor, focusing his earth magic on the cactus. A thorny limb shot out, impaling the arcanum through the chest.

As Briggs stood, he used his sleeve to wipe blood from his face. He stared at the suspended body, shaking his head. He's so young, he thought.

Thinking of Keren, he walked to the window to see how the battle was going. As he leaned forward, his hand touched the books. He looked down, recognizing one as a *Book of Shadows*, the other a grimoire. As he picked up the books, he noticed a name engraved in gold lettering, Marcus Turner.

"So, these are the coveted books," he mumbled.

"*Potestatenum.*"

In those few seconds before impact, Briggs' eyes shot to the arcanum whose shaky arms had barely enough strength to extend his palms. A wicked smile spread across his face, then his eyes closed, and his chin fell to his chest.

As the energy blast raced toward him, Keren's smiling face flashed in his mind. Her long, chestnut hair tossed free in the breeze and her silver eyes danced with a carefree life. His heart clenched, knowing he'd never see her again.

Briggs' reflexes caused him to bring the books up to block the energy blast. Upon impact, his arms collapsed, pushing the books to his chest. He felt as though a train had slammed into his chest as the power of the energy blast propelled him out the window.

CHAPTER FORTY-EIGHT

KEREN

The sound of shattering glass drew Keren's attention. She let out a scream as Briggs skyrocketed from the second-story window of the Howlin' Moon. A raven swooped in, snatching Briggs' belt. Although it frantically beat its wings, Briggs' weight was too much for the bird.

"*Parioida fulmenten.*"

A jolt of electricity zapped the raven in the breast. It spun out of control, crashing into a line of shrubbery.

When Briggs' body made impact, Keren heard the sickening sound of cracking bones. He lay motionless, face down on the pavement.

Quinlin walked up to Briggs, tapping him with his toe.

"I think you should reconsider. Let's look at the facts. Briggs being here means that he botched the rescue attempt, and my lieutenant killed your mom. And your friend Ordell is lying in the bushes."

Keren dropped to her knees. She dipped her chin while covering her face with her hands. Quinlin placed his fingers under her chin and lifted her head.

"Tell me, Keren. Who are you defending?"

She flinched as the sun's rays reflected off the Amplification Disk into her eyes. With that disk, Quinlin could continue making cursed creatures. Her artifact's power had run out. Without it, she wouldn't have enough energy to fight an army of cursed creatures.

As she looked into Quinlin's brown eyes, she knew she had to do something. Irrational thoughts of simply pummeling to death flicked through her mind.

Then her stomach churned as she heard the familiar roar of the cursed wolf. She watched as it lumbered back onto Church Street, then turn to face Perfect Potions.

An insane idea popped into her head. But she'd have to make Quinlin believe in her act.

"You're right," she said. "I'm a sorcerer and I belong with the Dark Guild."

Quinlin squinted his eyes and smirked, giving Keren a side glance. "You've never been good at lying."

She took a ragged breath. He was right. She was a terrible liar. In her mind, she blurred out Quinlin's face, replacing it with Briggs.

"Since the day we met, we've had a special bond. When I have a problem or am in trouble, you're there to help. When you wrap your arms around me, I feel safe and warm. It's like nothing else in the world matters but you and me. I can't imagine life without you."

Quinlin blinked, then smiled. "I knew you felt the same connection." He held out his hand.

Keren placed her hand in his, mindful not to cringe at his touch. When she swayed, he wrapped his arms around her. The hair stood up on the back of her neck, but she leaned her body weight into him, conserving her energy. He whispered into her ear.

"Our lives together will be extraordinary."

She put her hand on his chest, pushing away just far enough so she had room to maneuver. Her finger ran down the chain holding the Amplification Disk. Please, she thought, let me have enough energy for this one last thing.

She closed her eyes, imaging her weightless body floating in a pool of water. A calm flowed over her as she felt tapping in her solar plexus. While taking deep breaths, she let that pulse grow into a ball of energy, waiting to be set free. The pulse moved up her neck. She clutched the Amplification Disk, pulling it over Quinlin's head as she pushed him backward. The pulse moved to her eyes and a burst of light exploded around her. Then she tossed the artifact into the air.

With a roar, the cursed wolf started its assault on Perfect Potions. Its flames tore down the fairy protection spells. With the next blast, it would incinerate everyone on the balcony.

Keren dropped to her knees while clenching her fists under her chin as she used all her strength to summon her creatures. They appeared in a circle around her.

Quinlin ran under the artifact, reaching up to catch it. Just before his fingertips were within reach, Two jumped, using its horns to punt it back into the air.

Keren watched the cursed wolf inhale, getting ready to send the killing wave of fire over the Perfect Potion. Her muscles trembled as she pushed every ounce of strength she had into her creatures.

Three, as if playing basketball, tipped the Amplification Disk over to Four who used a water jet to shoot it to One. As One wrapped its wings around the artifact, Keren's strength gave out. She released her magic, falling onto her side next to Briggs. All her creatures turned to mist and dissipated into the air, along with the Amplification Disk.

Her heart broke as she watched the cursed wolf exhale. But instead of fire, it let out a pitiful noise, then fell to the ground. The arcanum handlers looked confused. While taking advantage of the moment, the warrior pack's retaliation attack overpowered the remaining arcanum.

"What have you done?" shouted Quinlin.

She felt his fingers wrap around her neck. As she struggled for air, she looked into his contorted face, her body too weak to fight back. She closed her eyes, thinking of Briggs. Even after his death, his memory had helped her win against Quinlin and his cursed creatures.

Then she heard a *click* as something tore Quinlin's hands from her throat. She gasped, trying to drag air into her lungs. When she opened her eyes, she saw Briggs standing over her, one arm bent at an odd angle and the other holding Quinlin in a choke-hold.

While staring into Briggs' lavender eyes, she tried to work out his feelings. She had never seen that look before. They showed a combination of physical pain, rage, and sadness all at the same time. Then she heard her mom's voice.

"Keren!"

She heard her mom fall to her knees next to her, then she saw her beautiful face lean over into view. Keren cried big heavy sobs that shook her entire body. Her mom lifted her to a sitting position, wrapping her arms around her.

"Are you alright?"

She couldn't answer. All the pain, fear, and anguish from the last week poured out of her. As she looked over her mom's shoulder, she saw a horse-eared figure approaching. She blinked, trying to clear her vision. Then she croaked out, "Ordell?"

His face was filthy, and his clothes were torn, but it was Ordell. Her mom released her, letting Ordell join them.

"Hey there." He looked into her eyes. "You did it." He gave her a brief hug.

"But Quinlin shot you down."

Ordell frowned, shaking his head. "No, I've been with your mom ever since Briggs helped her escape."

Then who did Quinlin shoot down? She gasped, reaching her arms out to her mom.

"Help me up."

"Are you sure, shouldn't you..."

But Keren cut her off. "Help me up now."

Barely able to hold her own weight, Keren directed her mom to the shrubbery where the raven fell. Ordell stepped forward, pushing the pushes aside. Then he let out a heart-wrenching scream. In the bushes, she saw Papa Murphy with a black hole scorched into his chest.

"Papa!" Ordell flung himself onto his father.

Keren buried her face in her mom's shoulder. Everything blurred around her and moved in slow motion. She heard sounds, but they were muffled as if underwater.

Dozens of inquisitors streamed onto Church Street. Medics fanned out behind them. Keren watched as an inquisitor tore Ordell off Papa Murphy so a medic could move the body to a gurney. The medic pulled a sheet over

Papa Murphy's head before wheeling the gurney away. Ordell broke away from the inquisitor, running after the medic and Papa Murphy.

She saw Tabitha being wheeled out on a gurney with an IV attached to her arm. Two inquisitors marched Quinlin down Church Street. As he passed, he glanced over at Keren, sending a chill down her spine. His brown eyes looked calm and calculating. She hoped they locked him up for life.

A medic ran up to her, taking her from her mom's arms and placing her on a gurney. The last thing she remembered was seeing the clear Florida sky and wondering why she was still alive.

CHAPTER FORTY-NINE

KEREN

K eren stood between Mrs. Murphy and Ordell, greeting people she didn't know. So many people had attended Papa Murphy's memorial service it ended up being standing room only. All his co-workers and friends, both magical and human races, came to pay their respects to one of the most kindhearted individuals Keren had ever known. Although her heart ached, she hadn't shed a tear. She had cried every day at first, then when the tears stopped, she existed as an empty husk going through the movements of life.

Once the crowd dwindled to a number Keren thought Ordell and Mrs. Murphy could handle, she gave them both a hug and a kiss, then walked down the street to a city park. She took a seat under a large oak tree she and Nadria had named Old Bill. After school, they would come here to do their homework and gossip about boys. But now that seemed like another person's story.

While resting her head back on the tree, she thought about all the memorial services she had attended. She'd been to the Magic Underground for the shifters murdered by the Dark Guild and the military service for the warrior pack members who had lost their lives protecting the magic community.

She had attended the inquisitors' memorial service yesterday, hoping to get a chance to talk to Briggs. Although he had attended, just like he had attended all the other services, he had avoided talking with her. Officer Jordon had attended the service. He had said after a couple of days in the hospital monitoring his heart; the doctor cleared him to return to duty. Nadria's voice pulled her out of her thoughts.

"I thought I might find you here with Old Bill."

Nadria sat down next to her, taking her hand. She had also been at Papa Murphy's memorial service. When Keren looked over, the breeze pushed Nadria's white hair off her forehead, revealing the ugly wound Quinlin had inflicted with the fire extinguisher. The doctor had said Nadria might have a permanent scar. Quinlin had left Keren with permanent internal scars.

"Are you thinking about your mom?"

Keren's relationship with her mom had been strained since the Church Street battle. So many lies had been told, and honestly, her emotions were too raw to deal with it right now.

"Yeah, she's holding up well. The lawyer Briggs recommended is doing a great job with her defense."

"I'm so glad to hear that." She shifted around so she faced Keren. "I have

exciting news." Nadria bubbled with anticipation. "Madam Windsburrow

has agreed to let me apprentice with her."

One of Nadria's dreams had been to delve into complex magic. Madam

Windsburrow made an excellent choice selecting Nadria as her apprentice.

"That's wonderful." Keren gave Nadria a hug. "You'll be impressing the

café customers with sophisticated water magic in no time."

Nadria bit her lip. "Well, I quit the café this morning. I'll be living in the

underground while I study. She said it could be a year or two."

Keren rubbed the back of her neck. "Oh, well, that's great."

"Ms. Oakdove told me she'd teach me about potions, too." Nadria's face

lit up.

Nadria's dreams were coming true. While she should be happy for her,

Keren felt only more loss and emptiness. She squeezed Nadria's hand.

"I'm so excited for you. You'll be the best apprentice Madam

Windsburrow ever had. Maybe I can visit when I go to the underground."

"That would be nice." Nadria gave her another quick hug. "Well, I

have an appointment with Madam Windsburrow's assistant to discuss

everything in more detail. So, I'll catch you later?"

"Yes, catch you later." Keren smiled and waved as Nadria walked away.

Once Nadria was out of sight, Keren stood up. A wave of nausea washed

over her, and she had to use the tree to steady herself. Ever since Church

Street, she had felt weak. Azalea had said, 'It might take time to recover from the ordeal.' She had wrapped up all the pain, bloodshed, torture, and near-death experiences into this convenient word *ordeal*.

But there hadn't been even incremental improvements. She was getting worse. No amount of food or rest dissuaded the queasiness and persistent headache throbbing in her temples.

Even her imaginary friends suffered from this mysterious illness. They would appear from time to time, but none of them showed an interest in extreme tag or any of the other games they used to play. When they showed up, they simply sat with her, not expecting anything, which she appreciated since she had nothing more to give.

She headed back to the memorial service. By now, the guests should have left and Ordell and Mrs. Murphy would be ready to head home. They had asked Keren to stay with them since the golem had destroyed her house and her mom was in jail without bond until her trial was over.

As she walked down the street, Tabitha approached from the other direction. She moved faster on crutches than most people did with two healthy legs.

When they met, Tabitha looked down to Keren's feet, then back up to her face.

"You look terrible."

"Thanks, I love you, too."

"No, really. You're wasting away, and your eyes look like they're swimming in a tar pit."

Keren sighed, shifting from foot to foot. "I'm just tired. Did you see Briggs?"

Tabitha's face softened. "Yeah, I just spoke with him." She paused, looking at the ground. Then she looked into Keren's eyes. "He's hurt. He heard what you said to Quinlin."

Keren felt her heart crack. "I lied to get close enough to take the artifact."

"I think he knows that. But it doesn't stop the words from hurting. Give him time, he'll come around."

Keren wiped her hands over her face and nodded.

"You never told me. How did you know sending the Amplifier Disk away with your creatures would destroy the cursed wolf?"

Keren shrugged. "I didn't know. I guessed, and I hoped." She sighed. "It was just some things Quinlin had said about the spell being permanent as long as the artifact existed. I thought it was worth a shot."

"Well, it was. Worth a shot, that is. No one can create cursed creatures anymore."

"What about the *Book of Shadows*?" Keren asked.

"Since the book is indestructible, as proven by Briggs when he used it to block an energy blast, we have locked it in a magic-secured evidence room."

"That's good. If you want, we can drop you off at your place. I'm sure Mrs. Murphy won't mind."

"No, thanks. My husband is meeting me for coffee. It's just a few blocks away, and I need the exercise."

"Alright, then I'll see you later."

"Alright," Tabitha moved around Keren, "and get something to eat."

As Keren watched Tabitha walk away, she smiled. It had been so long since she had smiled she had almost forgotten how.

Once back at the memorial service, she waited by the car while Mrs. Murphy and Ordell finished speaking with the guests. She was playing a game on her phone when someone spoke to her.

"Keren Stewart?"

She looked up, seeing a well-dressed, middle-aged man. Since Church Street, reporters had plagued her trying to get an interview. She had hoped they would leave her alone at Papa Murphy's memorial service.

"No interviews." She looked back down at her phone.

"I'm not a reporter."

She looked at him again. His neat clothes and perfect hair reminded her of Quinlin's lieutenant.

"If you're an arcanum and you've come to kill me, get it over with." She glared into his eyes.

"Keren, may I call you Keren?" When she didn't respond, he continued. "I'm from the Las Vegas faction of sorcerers." Then he held up his hands. "I'm not associated with the Dark Guild. You are in possession of something Quinlin Turner had stolen from us."

The only sorcerers she had ever encountered were arcanum, so in her mind, all sorcerers were evil. He was probably looking for Marcus's *Book of Shadows*.

She narrowed her eyes. "What do you think I have?"

"The Amplification Disk artifact."

Keren blinked, pulling her chin back. Why was this sorcerer interested in the Amplification Disk?

"It's gone."

She didn't have the strength or desire to summon her magic and have One bring the artifact back. Besides, she would never hand an artifact over to a sorcerer. While shaking her head, she went back to playing her game.

"It's important to control the dragons."

Keren's head snapped up. "Did you say dragons?"

If you enjoyed *Fallen Shroud*, please consider leaving a review at http://www.amazon.com/review/create-review?&asin=B09B5KYSV9 or use the QR code below. Reviews make a difference and I'm grateful for your support. Simply a line or two is all you need.

Go to **Amazon** and grab your copies of the complete *Twisted Curse Series* today!

Visit **https://www.djdalton.com** to subscribe to D. J. Dalton's newsletter and receive updates on new releases as well as other freebies. As a subscriber, you'll receive access to a free download of the novella *The Dragon War*, prequel to the *Twisted Curse Series*.

About the Author

A passionate storyteller since childhood, D. J. Dalton moves through life with enthusiasm and creative flair. Whether she's belly dancing, practicing her black belt Tae Kwon Do moves, or gliding round the roller rink (she was once crowned national roller-skating champion), she immerses herself in the artistic life wherever she can. Her writing is usually an evening pursuit, where she draws on reality and her love of video gaming to create thrilling worlds to captivate her readers. Connect with D. J. Dalton at www.djdalton.com or use the QR code above.

f   facebook.com/profile.php?id=100067778113765

a   amazon.com/~/e/B09B5PRLHD

g   goodreads.com/author/show/21681309.D_J_Dalton

BB   bookbub.com/authors/d-j-dalton

Printed in Great Britain
by Amazon

32937616R00236